WHITE WATER BROOK

Cabin of Whispers

WHITE WATER BROOK

Cabin of Whispers

by Jackson Clark

Editor

Charatie Bowen

Senior Publisher

Steven Lawrence Hill Sr.

Awarded Publishing House

ASA Publishing Company

A Publisher Trademark Title page

ASA Publishing Company
Awarded Best Publisher for Quality Books

(Wayne Commerce Park)
38640 Michigan Avenue, Wayne, Michigan 48184
www.asapublishingcompany.com

Copyrights©2009 Jackson Clark, All Rights Reserved
Book: White Water Brook "Cabin of Whispers"
Date Published: 12.09.09 /Edition 1 *Trade Paperback*
Book ASAPCID: 2380522
ISBN: 978-0-9841442-9-7
Library of Congress Cataloging-in-Publication Data

This book was published in the United States of America.
State of Michigan

A Publisher Trademark Title page

Prologue

Present

"CLEAR!!!!" Dr. Clark screamed to her team of residents and nurses, before placing the shock pads to Krista Colburn's body.

Dr. Clark delivered such a charge of electricity to Krista's torso that it jolted clear off the table, and still nothing. The only responses to the medical teams' efforts were an ever present flat line and the high pitched alarm that accompanied it. Another pointless shock was delivered moments later.

"CLEAR!!!!" The doctor yelled for a second time, once again with no vital response.

The medical team continued to work in vain to revive Krista's lifeless shell.

How did it ever come to this? Krista thought to herself as she stood outside of her former body watching in horror. *I'd always heard that when I died my entire life would flash before my eyes but all I see is what occurred in the last few weeks. It all begins with the events that led to a summer I'd never forget – for this was the summer that changed my life and led to my untimely demise.*

She walked away, unable to watch anymore, and thought about the proceeding circumstances that brought her life to such a tragic end.

----

1 Month Earlier

"Angela!! Get back in the car now! Before you get us all thrown in jail!" Krista screamed from the passenger's seat of her friend Stacy's car.

"I'm almost done Krista just give me one more second!!" Angela hollered back as she shoved the brush into the tub of black paint and sloshed the letter "E" on the silver F-150 pick-up.

"Come on Angela!! Lunch is about to start any minute now and the parking lot will be flooded with people!" Stacy bellowed from the driver's seat as Angela added the letter "R" to the truck.

She stepped back for just a moment to admire her art work. The word "NIGGER" in all capital letters laid painted sloppily across the hood of the glimmering silver pick-up. South Lyon High School's deafening bell sounded off, signifying that C-lunch was now in session. Krista glanced in the side mirror and saw a parade of students flowing from the school exits.

"Holy shit!" She screamed as she realized they were busted.

Stacy jumped out and tossed Angela in the back seat of his vehicle. He threw the 69 Firebird in gear and squalled tires out of there. They bolted across the student parking area and entered the building through an unlocked basement window. Krista looked around the noisy musty boiler room, and leaned against a pole to catch her breath.

"I'm going to the guys' locker room to rinse the paint off my hands. I'll meet you guys in the cafeteria." Stacy informed Krista and Angela.

The two girls proceeded to the ladies' bathroom on the first floor immediately after he left.

"Don't you think you may have gone a bit too far this time Angela? I knew you were a spoiled racist but this takes the cake." Krista scolded her while standing in front of the full length mirror brushing the sweat matted kinks from her honey blonde hair.

"I already told you I'm not a racist I only use the n-word in reference to the cocky arrogant jerks that think they can get away with taking my parking space. I've already warned him once." Angela replied.

Krista scanned her light colored jeans and designer top for traces of paint. Once she was satisfied she walked over to the sink to help Angela get the black stains out of her long sleeve t-shirt. Angela placed a hand on Krista's shoulder.

She glanced up at Krista with those big silver eyes of hers and said. "I was just playing a prank on him. The paint came from the pep-rally. I swear it'll wash right off. Look it didn't even stain my shirt."

Krista looked down at the spotless pink sleeve and felt a little relieved. Angela turned back to the mirror over the sink and tossed her lustrous black hair in a pony tail. They pulled themselves together, and proceeded to the packed cafeteria.

They left the lunch line with their food trays and spotted Stacy at a table all over this week's girlfriend. Stacy broke the lip lock for long enough to tell the other juniors to move aside and make room for Krista and Angela.

"So what's this one's name?" Angela asked sarcastically before digging into her veggie pizza and curly fries.

Krista elbowed her for being a bitch and properly introduced them. "Hi my name is Krista and this is my friend Angela." She stated, then put her fork aside and shook the pretty brown-haired girl's hand.

"Nice to meet you." She replied.

Angela rolled her eyes and gave an exasperated breath.

Krista changed the subject and began bragging about all the plans she had for the summer due to her parents going to Missouri. "That's right I'll have the house to myself for two whole months. No curfew! No parents! No rules!"

"Party at Krista's!" Stacy said giving her a high five.

"I already found a buyer for the keg and....." Krista stopped in the middle of her sentence when she noticed Principle Brisby weaving a staggered line through the other tables, heading in their direction.

Her heart stopped in her chest when the balding middle-aged white man stood there before them. *This is it, were screwed.* She thought to herself.

Principle Brisby cleared his throat and began to speak. "Mr. Laube how many times have I told you that this is a school not a hotel room! You've just earned yourself three days of detention."

Krista let out a sigh of relief thinking. *It sucks for Stacy to be in detention but, I'm so happy I'm not in trouble that nothing else matters.* Principle Brisby weaved his way back across the cafeteria, and Stacy and Angela laughed hysterically at her paranoia.

"You almost pissed yourself didn't you!" Stacy stated still laughing.

"Shut up!" Krista replied and hurled a grape at him.

"You've really got to lighten up Krista." Angela added.

Sixth hour rolled around. Krista balanced her seat on its two back legs and watched the clock intently. *In twelve minutes I'm off the hook. I'll bury my head in my geography book so the time will pass that much faster.* She thought feeling completely relieved.

"Krista Colburn?" She heard a rough masculine voice call down from in front of her desk.

She glanced up to see a uniformed man with a shiny gold badge that read *South Lyon Police Department.* "You're under arrest for the destruction of private property."

A single tear rolled down her cheek as she was placed in the back seat of the white police cruiser with Stacy and Angela. Angela was balling her eyes out, telling the policemen that Stacy and Krista had nothing to do with it, but they weren't hearing a word she had to say. Stacy sat back relatively unfazed by the whole ordeal, but Krista could tell he was putting on an act.

Krista was finger printed and placed in a holding cell while the police contacted her parents. The room was a bleak gray color with nothing but a bed and a ratty wool blanket.

"I would rather get the death penalty then have my mom and dad leave work early to get me out of here!" She hollered after one of the cops.

She lay back on the concrete slab they called a bed and contemplated her fait. *My parents are gonna be pissed. They're gonna kill me.*

Chapter 1

Krista sat with Stacy and Angela at a long table in front of the judge's podium. The three of them were assigned the same court date. They had all been suspended from school for the rest of the year, which luckily for them was only two weeks. Little did they know the worst was yet to come. Their parents sat on a bench behind them waiting for the judge to appear.

"All rise for the honorable judge Gorman." A voice called out.

A short portly black woman draped in black robes took a seat behind the podium. She sentenced them to 100 hours of community service beginning July 1st, which was no big deal. Krista was use to volunteering at the senior citizens home, and Angela couldn't stay away from the local animal shelters. That was one strange fact about Angela. She hated people but she loved animals.

Krista began to breathe a little easier and Judge Gorman leaned forward in her seat, stared down at them and spoke some more. "I'm not finished yet. Do to the fact that the paint was left on the truck in 90 degree weather for three hours; this usually harmless paint stripped the top coat off of Deondre Miller's F-150 pick-up. His mother has sued for 3,000 dollars in damages. That's 1,000 dollars a piece. Have a great summer."

The Judge gave them a smug grin, slammed the gavel down and began to rise from her seat.

Just then Krista heard her dad's voice echo throughout the court room. "Your honor I fully intend to pay that young man and his mother every penny, but would it be possible for us to postpone the community service until fall. My wife and I only have 30 days to go to Missouri and claim the property I've recently inherited. We were intending to leave Krista here this summer while we were away. In light of recent events there's no way in the world we're leaving our irresponsible daughter unsupervised for two months."

Judge Gorman sat back down and began to speak. "Mr. Colburn I don't feel your daughter should be getting a summer vacation after defacing private property, but I don't want to put you and your wife in a position to either lose your property or leave your kid unattended. I'll tell you what. I'll have her community service hours start September 1st but I'm adding another fifty hours. If there are no further concerns have a nice day."

Judge Gorman smacked the gavel down once more, and casually sauntered out the court room. Krista sat there afraid to turn around. *I know my parents are furious. I can feel them burning holes in the back of my head with their eyes. I may as well brace for the crash, put my head between my knees and kiss my ass goodbye.* At last she found the courage to turn and face them. *As I suspected the angry parent look painted across both their faces. Not just any angry look but that extremely cold glare that chills your very soul.*

The ride home was silent and they barely talked at dinner. Krista lay awake in her bed watching the shadows race around the walls each time a car drove passed. She tediously contemplated tomorrow's trip to Missouri, and eventually fell into an uneasy slumber.

Krista was glad to see her parents in a much better mood the next day, but still felt it was unfair for them to drag her away from her friends for the summer. *I didn't even paint the damn car.* She sat on a lower branch of the plum tree in their front yard hidden, watching her parents load the blue Dodge Ram.

"Krista! Krista! Oh there you are. Did you finish packing everything you'll need for the next two months?" Her mother called up to her.

Crap I've been spotted. Krista gave her mother a very unpleasant glare. She hopped down from the tree, and then answered her question with a question. "Mom, why are you doing this to me? My friends and I had everything planned out, and now you and Dad are making me spend the summer in some dusty old house in the middle of nowhere!"

"Honey, your dad inherited the old Colburn plantation when Grandpa passed away." Her mother replied.

Krista rolled her eyes then gave the obvious solution. "Why can't you just sell it or rent it out or something? The place is so old it doesn't even qualify as a house anymore. It's just a pile of termites standing on top of each other."

"We'd still have to make the 'pile of termites' look presentable first. Besides, we can't just leave you here alone all summer." Her mother explained.

Krista slammed the large brown suit case down in the bed of the truck and yelled. "Why not, I'm seventeen years old! I'll be graduating next spring, and I'm perfectly capable of taking care of myself."

Her mother snapped back at her. "Your father and I don't believe you're mature or responsible enough. The last time we left town for the weekend you threw a party. If we can't trust you alone for two days, how can we trust you alone for two months? And I don't even want to think about the mischief you've gotten into lately."

Krista knew her mother had an excellent point and found herself momentarily speechless. "Mom I'm sorry for what happened but, I already told you it wasn't me! Angela was messing with that guy. She borrowed the paint from the pep-rally; it was supposed to wash right off. She's my friend. What did you want me to do?" She finally stated in her own defense.

Her mother shook her head in silence. She gave her daughter a disappointed stare, and then said. "That's not the point Krista! I wanted you to be a leader and think for yourself. You're too impressionable. That's why you're coming with us."

"But Mom!" Krista protested.

"No more buts. You're coming with us and I don't want to hear another word about it."

\-

After the twenty hour train ride, Krista felt relieved when they finally pulled into the station. It was just after dark when they arrived. *It's been a very long bumpy trip. My butt is numb, my feet are tingling as if they are being stabbed with a billion tiny needles, and like all other modes of public transportation there isn't nearly enough leg room.*

Krista was 5'9" which is pretty tall for a girl. Her figure was slightly boyish, not real curvy. She got her height along with her brown eyes from her dad. She had her mother to thank for her blonde hair and full lips.

Out of the corner of her eye, she noticed her father hugging a petite, pretty young woman with wavy auburn hair and freckles on her fair skin. After a few seconds she recognized the girl.

"Jessy, oh my god! How long has it been little cuz?" Krista shouted as she ran up and hugged the girl; practically knocking her father out of the way.

Jessy then replied. "Krista, stop with all the little cousin stuff. I'm three months older than you. Not to mention, I had another growth spurt. I'll be as tall as you soon."

They both laughed, knowing that Jessy was the spitting image of her mother and would never grow past 5'2". They all grabbed luggage and headed out to the car.

"Where are your pain in the butt brothers?" Krista asked reluctantly as she loaded her bags in the trunk.

"Luckily for us, away at soccer camp." Jessy replied grinning from ear to ear.

Jessy had two younger brothers, eleven and twelve. Krista loved her male cousins, but they were at times annoying and had the tendency to be tag a longs.

"Where are Aunt Gene and Uncle Vince?" Krista asked next feeling a bit relieved that the boys would be gone the entire summer.

"They both had to work so they sent me to give you guys a lift to the old farm house." Jessy replied.

Krista smiled at her cousin thinking. *My summer could turn out great after all.*

At the end of a winding, unpaved driveway, sat an enormous multi story brick mansion. It had large marble pillars and old fashioned drapes in the windows. They opened the large white double doors and proceeded into the house. Everything inside was covered in white sheets to keep away the dust, accept for a few antique paintings of relatives Krista couldn't recognize. The largest of these paintings was of an attractive dark haired man in his late thirties sitting in a large arm chair smoking a pipe. Krista waved goodbye to her cousin Jessy and drug her luggage up to the bedroom she always stayed in on the second floor.

"Good night Krista." Her parents called after her.

I'm going to need some WD-40 for that. She thought as the door creaked loudly when she pushed it in. *Ahhh the aroma, of moth balls and dust.*

She took a good look around thinking. *It's apparent just how many summers I've spent in this room. The contents range from wooden alphabet blocks I played with when I was four, clear up to middle school math and science books. Not much from recent years though.*

I guess I can't complain too much this room is four times the size of my room back home. I always loved the floor length arched windows and the king size, four post, canopy bed. She heated a dish of peach scented potpourri and lit several candles to drive away the dust and moth ball odor. She tossed on a black camisole and climbed into bed.

Krista was jolted from her sleep moments later when she heard a far off stomping sound. She ran to the enormous arched window with her old girl scout binoculars, and peered in the direction of the slave quarters. There were five white men outside of one cabin. Three of them were holding bright flash lights. The other two were vigorously attempting to kick the door in. "Oh my God, burglars!"

She set the binoculars aside, and scrambled about the room for her cell phone. She couldn't find it anywhere. She heard another obnoxious bang and retrieved her binoculars. One of the burglars had managed to kick in the cabin door. There was already a young black man in the cabin. He was on his knees cradling a young black woman, who appeared to be hurt or unconscious. The five white men rushed into the cabin and one of them pointed a revolver at the young black man holding the unconscious girl. There was a bright flash and a blast similar to that of a firework. The sound echoed throughout the trees when the gun went off. Krista screamed in horror as the poor man's lifeless body slumped over. Then his murderer glanced straight up in her direction. She dropped the binoculars and bolted down the hall to find her parents. She pounded on their door to wake them but there was no answer. She burst into the room only to find an empty bed. Krista grabbed her father's cell phone off the night stand and dialed 911. The moment the operator picked up she let out a terrified scream as the assailant grabbed her shoulder.

Chapter 2

Krista woke up screaming, drenched in a cold sweat, and breathing heavily.

"It was only a dream Krista." Her father assured her.

She latched onto her dad for dear life, and felt better almost immediately. *I would never in a million years admit this to him, but at times it's a comfort to have the old man around.*

Once he was convinced that she was alright he returned to the garage to work on the Charger. When she got up she noticed some of the alphabet blocks had been knocked off her night stand. The letters "A" "L" "E" and "X" formed a staggered line on the floor.

She walked down stairs to the smell of pancakes, bacon, eggs and grits. Grits were a rare delicacy that she only ate when visiting her grandparents in Poplar Bluff, Missouri.

She strolled into the small dining hall and spotted her mother at the table reading the news paper, and nibbling at a bagel topped with cream cheese and strawberry jam. The articles on the front page took on the usual depressing format. *Campus dorm fire leaves one dead and thirty students homeless. Serial killer takes a third victim.*

"Do they ever print anything nice anymore?" Krista's mother questioned.

"You know nothing positive would sell." Krista replied. "Mom, since when do you cook grits?"

Her mother glanced up from her morning paper and answered the question smiling. "Actually your Aunt Gene made breakfast. She's in the garden with Jessica, and your dad is in the garage with your uncle Vince. They came over to give us a hand with the house. So eat up and start with which ever room you want."

Mom and Dad are unbelievable. It's only my second day here and I already have to do work. I guess they're intending to make me work off every penny of that $1,000. Krista thought this to herself but decided not to argue the point. *After all the sooner we get the place together, the sooner we can sell it and return to civilization.*

Krista walked over to the sink and turned on the faucet. She filled up a glass and took a big gulp before immediately spitting it back into the sink.

"That was the worst water I've ever tasted." Krista protested.

Her mother laughed and explained. "This house has well water remember. At least it doesn't have all the chlorine and other chemicals that are in city water."

"I'll take the chlorine any day. This water tastes and smells like rotten eggs. Lousy piece of crap house, built a million years ago. Even the water's old here. I can't wait until you sell this pile of termites." Krista ranted as she grabbed a glass of orange juice and fixed herself a plate.

"Krista, I'll pick you up some bottled water when I go into town later today." Her mother said, still laughing at her.

Krista sat down with her breakfast unable to shake the nightmare from her thoughts. *It all seemed so real. I can still hear the gunfire ringing in my ears. I can still see the man's body collapse on the floor. I can't help but envision the puddle of blood growing larger and larger by the second. The man from my nightmare was murdered in cabin five. I won't rest until I see for myself that no one had been out there the night before.*

After shoving down a face full of Aunt Gene's down home cooking, Krista conversed with the family for a while then scurried passed the orchard to the slave quarters. She and her cousin Jessy spent most of their previous summers camping out in the slave quarters until Krista met Stacy and Angela. There were about fifty or more small cabins scattered about the massive estate. Each one had a couple cots on the dirty carpet less floors, amongst other simple furniture. There wasn't much to them, but to a small child it was like having a multitude of club houses.

She took a deep breath and entered cabin five. *It appears as though it hasn't been disturbed in decades.* She felt silly almost immediately. *What did I expect to find, a corpse?*

She moved around the antique furniture to sweep, dust and clean the windows.

She dropped her broom as she heard a faint voice whisper in her ear. *"All you've ever known to be true is a lie."*

A cold chill swept over her body. Goosebumps began to rise on her skin.

Krista whipped around and hollered. "Hello, is anyone there? I must be losing it."

At that moment she noticed a glare coming from a hole in the ceiling. She stepped over the fallen broom and went to take a closer look. *I still can't quite make out what it is.* She reached up and took the ceiling panel down, then jumped back when she heard a loud smack. She looked down to find a black leather bound book with shiny metal accents. She could tell there was an inscription on the cover but the book was too dusty to read.

"Krista! Krista! Time for lunch!" She heard her father call.

"Just a moment Dad!" She replied as she placed the filthy old book back into the hole in the ceiling. She replaced the ceiling panel and ran to the small dining hall for lunch.

Krista and Jessy spent the rest of the afternoon at Wappapello Lake. They sat under a tree watching and listening to the waves crash on the sandy shore. It was starting to get late and most of the visitors had already left. The sun had set, and the seagulls swooped in to scour the beach for half eaten hotdogs and fallen cheese puffs.

"Jessy you're the only person I know who can managed to burn in the shade." Krista commented.

"I know. It's ridiculous." Jessy admitted. "We better head back. The beach will be closing soon."

Krista agreed and they walked back to the car.

It was dark by the time Jessy dropped her off. She jogged straight up stairs to her room and plopped down on the bed. She stared up at the canopy over her bed, unable to curb her curiosity about the book she had found. She pondered over it until she eventually fell asleep.

The next morning Krista could hardly wait to get back to the cabin. She quickly gulped down a glass of apple juice, grabbed a toaster pastry and was off. She walked briskly through the orchard. The sweet smell of wild flowers, berries, and other fruits filled the air. She stopped just short of the cabin when a puzzling thought crossed her mind. *Why would there be a book in the slave quarters when slaves couldn't read or write? Who put this book out here?*

As Krista walked through the door she heard another whisper. *"Seek and ye shall find."* She took a deep breath and removed the journal from the ceiling. She wiped off the thick layer of dust and cob webs, and then read the inscription.
"White Water Brook"

Chapter 3

April 19, 1836

16 year old Mathew Colburn crept stealthily through the long, dark corridor with only a glimmer of pale moon light to guide his path. He had planned his escape for weeks, and even with the extravagant Easter party taking place just two stories below he felt confident that the third floor of his family's mansion would remain abandoned. The stairs creaked and he dashed into an empty guest room. He gasped for air and his heart began to race as the clackity clack of foots steps drew closer to him. He stood in the dark room paralyzed peaking through the cracked door watching, waiting to be discovered. At last a young engaged couple appeared kissing passionately and embracing one another affectionately. They disappeared into a room across the hall from him and slammed the door behind them.

"They must have known this floor would be empty as well." Mathew laughed to himself and breathed a sigh of relief. *Just a few more feet.*

Mathew reached the parlor at the end of the corridor and quietly entered. The room was filled with a dim, orange, flickering light due to a tiny blaze in the fire place. There were fancy arm chairs and lounges placed about. The walls were lined with framed art work, elegant tapestries, and bronze candle holders. He dropped to his knees and pulled a rope ladder from its hiding place under a small table. He secured the ladder and glimpsed out the window. "Christ that's a long way down." Mathew said to himself, then immediately double checked the ladder making sure it was secured just perfectly. Mathew removed his dress coat and rolled the rope ladder out the window. It streamed down the side of the house like a waterfall and hit the ground with a thump.

He straddled the window pane with one foot outside and the rest of him in when he heard a voice call out from behind a tall backed chair. "Where do you think your going!"

A startled Mathew lost his balance and began falling backward. The figure rushed to the window and grabbed him by the vest, pulling him in the parlor to safety.

"Thanks I owe you one." Mathew choked out still a bit shaken from the ordeal.

He looked up to find a distinguished beau, of medium build in his late teens standing, in front of him. He had sapphire blue eyes and shoulder length brown hair tied back with a black ribbon.

"The name's Phillip, Phillip Arrington III of the Arrington estate." The gentleman stated in a British accent as he shook Mathew's hand.

"Mathew Colburn." Mathew muttered back. "Please don't tell anyone you've seen me. I was going to meet up with my friend Sarah. It's a very important night for her and I promised I'd be there." Mathew explained.

"You're going to another party aren't you?" Phillip asked excitedly. "I promise not to mention a word of your whereabouts if you take me with you. My family and I just moved to the States, and my parents have been introducing me to their stuffy old friends all night. As well as trying to match me up with several snobby, dim witted, debutantes. I ran to your third floor parlor to hide from them." Phillip explained.

Mathew looked at Phillip's clean cut appearance and answered. "I'm not sure you'll want to accompany me where I'm going."

"Anywhere away from here would be great." Phillip assured him.

Mathew agreed and he and Phillip were down the rope ladder and through the orchard in a matter of minutes.

As they drew further from the mansion the scattered conversations and smooth, elegant, classical music gradually diminished. The aroma of the magnificent feast dissipated as well.

"I'll have my driver prepare the carriage for us." Phillip

stated.

Mathew smirked and replied. "No need we won't be going that far."

"Where is this party anyway?" Phillip asked.

"Shhh. We must be cautious not to be seen or heard. We're going to the servants' Spring celebration and I'm not sure we'll be welcome there." Mathew answered whispering.

Phillip gave Mathew a puzzled look but continued to follow him. "Your friend's a slave? No wonder you had to sneak out!"

Just then a new kind of music started to fade in: very fast and rhythmic drumming accompanied by laughter, singing and an orchestra of other man made instruments. He and Phillip lay on the grass on their stomachs and watched in astonishment from a near by hill. The evening sky was illuminated by a humungous fire in the center of the slave quarters, as well as numerous strategically placed torches. Every man, woman and child was dressed in flesh baring attire with a multitude of tribal face and body paintings. Most of the people were barefoot. A few were wearing sandals. The small children were running about playing games. The older kids and adults were putting on all sorts of entertaining performances. Below stood a carnival of people; taking a break from their usually bleak existence.

Phillip climbed to his feet and dusted himself off.

"What are you doing? I told her I'd watch her match from here." Mathew cautioned.

"They seem to be having a great time. I'm going to join the festivities." Phillip replied.

Mathew gathered his nerve and headed down hill after him. To his amazement they were met with warm greetings and friendly smiles.

They came across an ellipse of spectators and walked over to investigate. In the center there was a man balancing on a large ball and juggling three apples at the same time. On the far left of him stood a woman who swallowed three twelve inch swords, one after another. On the far right of him was a teenage girl balancing on one hand on a chair while using the other hand to hold a stick close to her lips and blow flames from her mouth. The crowd cheered and applauded. An intrigued Mathew and Phillip tossed money to the performers, and moved on to the next show.

They stopped when approached by a pretty dark skinned girl holding a small wicker basket. She was wearing a brown leather top that tied around her neck and torso revealing her well shaped mid drift and the majority of her back. Her tan colored skirt was made of long blades of dried grass and it came around mid thigh baring most of her lower extremities. Her hair was braided and adorned with wooden beads and pink and white flowers.

"Happy 16th Birthday Sarah!" Mathew exclaimed as she set down the basket and ran up and hugged him. Stunned by her inappropriate action, he stood there arms frozen at his sides, for a few seconds before finally deciding to embrace her back. "Please allow me to introduce you to Phillip Arrington." Mathew continued.

Phillip greeted her then gave Mathew an impressed nod.

"Well I can see why you nearly fell from a third story window for her. She's breathtaking." Phillip commented.

"Thank you Sir." Sarah replied then flashed Mathew a concerned glare. "Promise me you'll be more careful." She scolded him.

"I had to escape somehow, and the third floor had the least amount of people." Mathew explained then enquired. "What's in the basket?"

"Just a bunch of goodies I borrowed from the Easter feast for Aaron. You know he loves to eat." Sarah explained lifting the cloth to reveal the contents.

"By the way, have you seen Seth or Aaron?" He asked next.

"They're both competing tonight. We'll have to catch up with them later. Follow me." Sarah instructed taking Mathew by the hand.

She stopped at a stand and asked two young ladies to paint Mathew and Phillip's faces. "It was so nice of you to come, Master Mathew. Who's your friend?" One of the girls inquired.

Before Mathew could open his mouth Phillip had already introduced himself.

"Hi I'm Phillip Arrington." He stated with an extended hand.

This action caused an awkward silence that seemed to span an eternity. They weren't quite sure how to react to this informality. Not many white men will reach out to shake the hand of a slave. It was obvious he wasn't from around here.

"You do shake hands in this country don't you?" Phillip asked jokingly.

"Our apologies Mr. Arrington." The girls said shaking his hand immediately.

"Just Phillip will do. Mr. Arrington is what people call my incredibly ancient father." Phillip corrected.

"I'm Mali and this is my sister Anna." Mali said.

"Do you like my artwork? It means peace and tranquility." Anna said to Mathew pulling aside her grass skirt to reveal an intricate painting on a canvas of well sculpted thigh.

"What about my tribal war symbols?" Mali questioned as she swept her braids aside to show the delicate lines weaved across an almost completely bare back.

"They're… They're both very nice." Mathew stammered, never having seen so much skin in his life. Feeling slightly embarrassed he simply pretended not to pick up on these subtle advances.

Sarah couldn't help but laugh a little. She often joked that Mathew had to have been an alter boy in a previous life because he was a devout catholic who almost never broke any rules. In fact the only time he did anything remotely wrong was under her influence. She was always getting him and herself into trouble.

"Yes those are quite lovely. Would it be possible to see the rest of you, I mean your beautiful artwork?" Phillip added, flirting shamelessly with the young ladies.

Mali and Anna giggled and whispered something to each other.

"This is a beautiful ring." Philip said, using the jewelry as an excuse to hold Mali's hand.

The ring was simple but Mali loved it: a silver band with an onyx stone in the center.

"Thank you. My father's a blacksmith. He forged it for my fifteenth birthday." Mali explained.

Mathew hadn't known Phillip long, but could already tell a couple things about the young nobleman. *Phillip is no stranger to this sort of attention. In fact he soaks it up with sponge like consistency. He's no stranger to breaking rules either.*

"And which tribe will you two be cheering for this evening?" Mali and Anna chimed in.

Mathew and Phillip gave the ladies an unknowing glance then Sarah offered them further explanation. "In Africa the people lived in tribes, sort of like the Apache and Cherokee Indians here in America. There are descendants from several African tribes on this plantation and each spring we compete against each other here at the festival. Since neither of you belong to a tribe your welcome to be a member of mine."

Mathew and Phillip both agreed.

"So it's settled they'll be cheering for the Akashi tribe." Sarah proclaimed.

Phillip and Mathew took a seat in front of the stand and Mali and Anna began deftly applying colorful paints to their faces.

"By the way, those are really beautiful." Sarah said to Anna, while Anna scribbled away on Mathew. She was referring to the peculiar pair of earrings Anna was wearing; black stones filed in the shape of arrow heads.

"Thank you. They were a gift from my mother. I'll try to hurry so you won't miss the last two events." Anna stated.

"What events might those be?" Philip enquired.

"The last two events left to judge are the arrow battles and the spear fighting competition." Sarah explained.

"So what competitions went on earlier?" Mathew asked, trying not to move too much.

"All sorts. There have been events taking place for the last two days." Sarah replied. "Boat races, foot races, dance, art, spell casting, storytelling, you name it."

"You're all set. Save us a dance." Mali and Anna said as they finished up.

"We certainly will." Phillip replied. Then he and Mathew insisted on paying the girls for their services.

"Thank you." Sarah said to the girls, then led Phillip and Mathew in the direction of the arrow battle field.

"What do you mean *we*? I don't dance." Mathew said to Phillip once Mali and Anna were out of range.

"Well tonight you do. You know I think Anna likes you." Phillip replied.

"Don't even waste your time playing match maker, Phillip. Mathew's saving himself for marriage plus he feels that any involvement with a slave would be morally reprehensible." Sarah explained in a patronizing tone.

"Oh I see, you feel you are above such a relationship." Phillip stated.

Mathew shook his head no, and explained himself. "Quite the opposite actually, I feel we are all equal in God's eyes. However as long as my parents own this plantation and every person here, this places me in a major position of authority. That fact alone won't allow for a relationship, only an abuse of power. If you're in a position to take a woman's body without consequence how could her love ever be given to you."

"I see your point, but most men wouldn't care." Phillip replied.

"There lies the difference between Mathew, the patron saint, Colburn and most men." Sarah chimed in.

"Mathew," Phillip said with a slap on the shoulder. "You should've been an alter boy."

Mathew laughed and replied. "Yeah, I get that a lot. But I'm not the angel Sarah makes me out to be. I have urges like any other man. In a moment of weakness I may act on those urges, just not with a slave."

The field had four 6ft x 4ft wooden walls, as well as tall stacks of straw placed sporadically. There were twenty males participating in this game: four teams of five. All of them were ages sixteen and up. Mathew's pal Aaron, a handsome dark skinned boy of sixteen years, was excited to be competing in the men's division. All the men were equipped with wooden bows. Their arrows had rubber tips with a tiny sack of crimson paint inside them. They each wore a bright white smock in order to recognize who was hit.

"Aaron! Aaron! Over here!" Mathew and Sarah bellowed over the multitude of spectators.

Aaron glanced back and forth searching the crowd until he spotted them. First he looked kind of shocked to see Mathew and then he gave a big grin and a wave.

"Wish me luck!" Aaron shouted from the arrow battle field.

The horn blew and the crowd roared. Each team of five gathered behind a wooden wall and discussed their strategy. When the horn blew a second time the men ran out launching arrows at one another. They ducked behind the bails of straw and the wooden stands every now and again using them for cover. Mathew and Phillip cheered Aaron on as he picked off one opponent after another. Every time an arrow collided with a player it left a large red splatter on their florescent white smock. The disappointed contender would stomp away from the field.

"Man he's really good." Mathew told Sarah.

"Yeah, he's outstanding that's why he's the youngest person to compete on this level; however, he's not a member of our tribe and he's nearly taken out our entire team." Sarah responded laughing.

Aaron only lived for four things, friends, physical activity, food, and choosing all the wrong women. He possessed strength and agility far beyond his years but he was prone to broken hearts. Though he wouldn't put it quite that dramatically. Once he took ten lashes for a girl he didn't even know. This act of chivalry along with many others gained him a reputation for being the estate's dark knight. Everyone loved him.

More marked men joined the side line and before long it was down to the last three. Aaron of the Batu tribe stood alone against two members of Sarah's tribe, the Akashi. Aaron hid behind one of the large stacks of straw eye balling one of his opponents. He aimed and drew back on his bow but it snapped rendering it unusable.

"Aaron! Aaron! Come out; come out where ever you are!" His opponents taunted him.

They were unable to see him but they were still drawing closer and closer by the second. Aaron knew he had to think fast. He sat the useless bow aside and cut open one of the bails of straw. He stuffed an abandoned smock with straw and fastened a piece of twine to it. As soon as his opponents were in position he tossed the decoy toward one of the players. The other player saw a white smock and immediately shot an arrow in the direction of it, but he hit his own team mate. Before the last boy got a chance to reload Aaron grabbed an arrow from his sack and tagged him on the back with it bringing the battle to a close. The watchers cheered and Phillip, Sarah and Mathew ran onto the field to congratulate Aaron on his victory.

Sarah hugged him and handed over the basket of goodies. Aaron immediately dug in.

"Truffles! Please marry me right now!" He shouted playfully, dropping to one knee in a mock proposal.

They moved along with the crowd as it shifted in the direction of the spear fighting ring, a grassless circle of land surrounded by fiery torches. Mathew, Aaron, and Phillip stayed to cheer on Seth, an attractive nineteen year old man, who was battling it out for the men's spear fighting title.

Seth as usual wasn't the least bit concerned about his match or much of anything for that matter. He was very pampered by Mathew's parents, and life up to this point had been a breeze for him. His unbreakable confidence along with the favor shown to him by both master and mistress won him the admiration of most ladies and the envy of all men. He was even rumored to have had affairs with white women.

Sarah jogged off to get mentally prepared for her third and final match of the evening. She didn't look like much of a fighter, but contrary to her outward appearance she had managed to win the last three consecutive years. When she entered the tent her friend Leah & 20 year old sister Marlette were waiting there to assist her.

Leah was the same age as Sarah, pretty, and petite. She was dark with large brown eyes and a beautiful smile. Sarah and Marlette loved Leah for being a loyal friend and one of the kindest people you'd ever meet. But her ability to choose all the wrong men drove Sarah crazy and infuriated Marlette. Then again, it didn't take much to anger Marlette.

"Since Aaron won the arrow battle and pushed the Batu tribe into 1st place the only way we can still win is if you manage to pull off this next match." Leah stated as Sarah took a seat to have her war paint applied.

"Hey, no pressure here," Sarah replied in a worried sarcastic tone.

"You'll do fine. You've won the last three titles in a row." Marlette assured Sarah while wrapping her hands in order to better grip the spear, minimize sting, and prevent injury.

"Yes but those were junior titles. I turned sixteen this year and now I'm in the women's division. The weapons are real now and the competition is stiff." Sarah replied as Leah finished painting the Akashi war symbols on her face, chest and arms.

"Anna was batting her lashes at Mathew again. She made him so uncomfortable his face turned bright red. It was funny. You should have seen it." Sarah informed Leah and Marlette, still chuckling.

Marlette, Sarah's older sibling, was tall and shapely, with emerald green eyes and skin the color of caramel. Marlette didn't laugh at Sarah's story or much of anything for that matter. She just appeared disgusted at Anna's shamelessness. Marlette's lack of a sense of humor, refusal to bend the rules, and no bullshit attitude earned her the title *Iron Maiden.* Marlette's biggest challenge in life was keeping her mischievous, impulsive, and defiant to the core, younger sister in line.

"What is Mathew doing here? I told you not to have him come, and I've warned you to stop being so informal with him." Marlette scolded with furrowed brows.

"Marlette can't you yell at me tomorrow? It's my birthday." Sarah whined, sticking out her bottom lip.

"Alright" Marlette said, deciding to drop the subject. "I have something for you. This spear belonged to our grandfather. I won five titles with it and now it's yours." Marlette stated as she handed Sarah the long, black, intricately carved weapon.

"I don't feel right taking this. He made it for you." Sarah replied.

"If he'd lived long enough to see you compete I'm certain he would've made you one as well, so I want you to have this one." Marlette insisted.

Sarah hugged her sister and gained a new confidence in regard to her match. She grabbed her spear and the three of them marched to the fighting ring side by side.

Sarah, Leah, and Marlette could tell by the colossal amount of celebrating going on that Seth had done well in the ring. He'd won all of his four matches that night, taking first place in the men's fighting division for his tribe, the Morisset. Sarah congratulated him on his win and took a brief look at the competition to size her up.

"Be careful. That Isabel doesn't fight fair." Leah called out.

Sarah heeded her friends warning then entered the circle and kneeled before the shaman facing her opponent. He blessed them both and the battle began. The crowd of spectators cheered almost loud enough to drown out the obnoxious clacking and banging sounds the spears made as they collided. Considering the size of the other woman Sarah was doing a decent job defending herself, but by a few minutes into the match Leah and Marlette weren't sure if that would be enough. Aaron and Mathew both cheered loudly to show support but were also concerned. Seth and Phillip watched the match intently hoping and praying that one or both of the fighters would lose an article of clothing. As Sarah wrestled herself free of her opponents grasp the men chanted obnoxiously.

"For shame on all of you!" Marlette scolded.

The Shaman stopped the fight when Sarah's spear snapped in two allowing Isabel to land a ferocious hit to her chest. Pain shot rapidly across Sarah's thorax and she fell to her knees winded.

Chapter 4

Sarah grabbed both pieces of her broken spear and climbed to her feet still covered in dirt. She walked toward the edge of the circle to grab a replacement. Isabel ignored the horn blow and took an illegal swing at Sarah, causing a superficial laceration to her left bicep. The fighters had one another by the throat before the judges ran in to pull them apart. Seth had to restrain Marlette to prevent big sis from taking matters into her own hands.

"Let me go Seth! She's not fighting fair!" Marlette shouted.

The crowd booed Isabel for taking such a cheap shot, and Sarah returned to her corner to examine her broken spear.

"I don't understand. Our grandfather carved this spear from ebony wood. That's one of the strongest types of wood there is." Sarah told Marlette.

"Do you mind if I take a look at it?" Mathew asked.

He had a gift for analyzing the makeup of things. By age 14 he could repair, design, and build almost anything.

"I already see what your problem is. Do you see how most of the surface of the break is smooth and only the very edge on this one side is jagged? It looks as if someone sawed ¾ of the way through it and placed the ribbon back around it so you wouldn't notice." Mathew explained.

"What! She ruined my grandpa's spear!" Sarah exclaimed.

"I'd be willing to bet that all your back up spears have been sabotaged as well." Mathew continued.

Sarah and Mathew snatched the ribbons off each of the spears and inspected them. Just as Mathew suspected there wasn't a single useable spear. Soon after, the judges approached and offered to disqualify Isabel because she broke several rules, and give Sarah the automatic win.

"No! Continue the fight!" Sarah insisted.

Mathew watched as the uh oh expression spread across everyone's face.

Aaron turned to him and said. "You probably shouldn't have told her that. That girl loved her grandpa and he's dead now. All she had was that spear. I don't think I've ever seen her so furious."

"This isn't going to be pretty." Seth added.

"I can't watch. Tell me when it's over." Leah stated covering her eyes.

The horn blew and Sarah threw the broken spear on the ground. She charged out to the center of the circle unarmed.

"Stop! You don't have a weapon!" Marlette cried out.

Sarah didn't even look back. She ducked out of the way of Isabel's first swing, and jumped over the second. The third time Isabel ran straight for her. Sarah moved aside and relieved Isabel of her weapon. Then Sarah used the spear she'd confiscated to deliver a combination of violent blows to her opponent. The first two relentless hits devastated Isabel's ribs and abdomen, followed by an even harsher blow to the face. Sarah swung the spear around once more and hit Isabel behind the knees, sweeping her clear off her feet in the process. Isabel's legs flew high in the air as she landed flat to her back, kicking up a humongous cloud of dirt. When the dust had settled Sarah was standing over her with one foot one her chest and the blade of the spear aimed at her throat. The Shaman blew the horn and declared Sarah the winner of the spear competition. Then immediately after the judges declared the Akashi tribe triumphant over all winners of this year's spring festival games, the crowd exploded in an uproar and surged into the fighting ring. They carried Sarah off on their shoulders, loudly chanting a song in their native tongue.

Mathew and Phillip walked to the infirmary a short while later. As they entered the cabin the scent of various dried plants, herbs, roots and fungi engulfed them. The infirmary was a rickety structure, dimly lit by candles and kerosene lanterns. It was composed of cabinets and drawers full of bandages, vials, and containers of all shapes and sizes. The walls were lined with shelves of live animals, insects, and a vast herbarium. The furniture included just two beds and a few stools. Sarah was sitting alone waiting for Leah and Marlette to return with Aunt Lizzie, the plantation nurse and mid-wife.

"Are you alright?" Mathew asked as he and Phillip approached.

"I'm sure I'll live even though it doesn't feel that way." Sarah replied laughing and rubbing the sore spot on her chest.

"This is for you." Mathew stated as he passed Sarah her birthday present.

Sarah smiled and opened the elongated black box.

"A stethoscope! Thank you!" Sarah exclaimed hugging him.

A confused Phillip opened his mouth to question why, but immediately abandoned the attempt. Shortly after Marlette and Leah entered the infirmary with Aunt Lizzie, a gray haired woman of 80 years. She was small; dark skinned, and maintained a timeless beauty. Though she'd never learned to read or write she was one of the wisest and most insightful healers in southeast Missouri and Sarah was her protégé.

"Well this shouldn't need stitches." Aunt Lizzie stated as she cleaned the small cut on Sarah's arm.

Then the old woman waddled over to the Aloe Vera plant on one of the shelves and broke a small piece off. She squeezed the jelly like contents onto Sarah's arm.

As Aunt Lizzie bandaged the cut she went on to say. "As for the hit you took to the chest today, I can see some bruising and swelling but I doubt anything is broken. Apply cold wraps whenever you can. See if Leah and Marlette will help you with your duties this week. Now I'll have to ask everyone but Sarah to leave so I can do her ankle piece." The girls agreed.

Phillip, Leah and Marlette filed outside, but Sarah grabbed Mathew's hand and insisted that Aunt Lizzie allow him to stay.

Sarah lay on her side on the bed propped up with a few pillows. Mathew pulled up a stool next to her and grasped her hand with both of his.

Meanwhile Phillip was outside watching Leah and Marlette playfully practice their spear fighting techniques.

"What's an ankle piece?" Phillip asked.

The girls stopped swinging to explain. "When you turn sixteen on this plantation you are officially an adult member of your tribe. You receive a tattoo of your tribal symbol on your right ankle as an initiation to adulthood. See, we already have ours."

Leah and Marlette showed off their meticulously drawn ankle bands. Then they went back to playing around with the spears.

"So Phillip, do you have a last name!" Leah shouted over the colliding war instruments.

"Arrington!" Phillip shouted back.

The swinging ceased abruptly and an awkward silence came over the girls. At last Marlette took the initiative to speak, "Phillip Arrington, as in the oldest son of Lord and Lady Arrington?"

"Yes, that would be me." Phillip answered candidly.

Marlette darted into the infirmary just as they were finishing Sarah's ankle piece, and Phillip and Leah followed her.

"Mathew, your friend here is royalty! What were you thinking! If he gets so much as a scratch on him you'll be fine but they'll want to see us hanged. He's got to go now! Take him back to his parents." Marlette demanded.

"Look he doesn't want to go back and neither do I." Mathew snapped.

Marlette appeared shocked at Mathew's defiance. *Sarah certainly has an influence on him and not a good one.*

"Now do you see what you've done?" Marlette scolded Sarah.

Sarah shrugged innocently and gave a coy smile.

"Where have your manners gone Marlette? That's no way

to treat a guest." Aunt Lizzie stated calmly while diligently working on Sarah's tattoo.

"Yeah that's no way to treat a guest." Phillip patronized, giving Marlette a playful wink.

"We all need a break from our lives sometimes. This doesn't seem to be the first time this young man's pulled such a stunt and it won't be the last. I'm sure he'll think of some elaborate story to tell the Lord and Lady." Aunt Lizzie explained giving Phillip a respectful nod. Phillip mouthed the words thank you.

\--

They ended the spring festival with a ceremonial dance. A panel of twenty or more African drummers set the tempo while the other instruments gradually blended in. The first dance performed was a provocative serpent routine led by Sarah, Leah, Marlette, Anna, and Mali. The crowd watched intently as the girls moved seductively with their snakes. The onlookers cheered, applauded, and tossed flowers at the end of the performance.

When the second song began everyone grabbed a partner and joined in. Mathew and Phillip both committed to the dances they'd promised Anna and Mali Earlier. Leah danced with her good friend Aaron, and Sarah danced with Seth. Marlette stood on the sideline and shot the look of death at any man who dared to look her way.

On song three Phillip shuffled to the side line and extended a hand to Marlette. She looked at the hand with cold indifference and replied. "You shouldn't be here."

Phillip knelt and picked up a broken arrow head. He stood up and said. "Allow me this one dance and I'll leave. Deny me and I'll cut my hand with this blade and tell everyone you were responsible."

"You wouldn't dare." Marlette announced with an indignant look.

Phillip placed the blade firmly against his palm. A small spot of blood emerged from beneath the arrow head.

"Okay! Okay! One dance, what are you crazy!" Marlette

shouted.

Phillip dropped the spear head and grabbed Marlette by the hand.

"You are such a rich, spoiled bastard." Marlette groaned in defeat.

"Yeah, I get that a lot." Phillip replied in triumph.

Sarah, now dancing with Mathew, stopped dead in her tracks. "Is that?" She stammered pointing at her sister and Phillip.

"Yeah, that would be the *Iron Maiden* herself dancing with Phillip. She actually appears to be having a good time too." Mathew answered.

"But how?" Sarah continued.

Mathew shrugged thinking. *I don't know how or why Phillip managed to charm Marlette, but he certainly has a way with people. The guy is impossible to dislike.*

Phillip prepared to leave after that dance as promised. He and Mathew said their goodbyes and cleaned the tribal paint off their faces.

"Do you mind if I borrow some bandages?" Phillip asked.

"For what?" Mathew replied.

"You'll see," Phillip said.

Mathew waited for Phillip to return from the infirmary, wondering what type of crazy antics he had in store. When Phillip came out with the small wad of bandages, they both began their track back to the mansion.

"Oh we're not headed back that way. By now my parents have stormed the fort looking for me." Phillip told Mathew.

"If we're not going back up the rope ladder, then just what do you suppose we do: Waltz right in the front door?" Mathew questioned.

"Yes actually", Phillip replied.

"We're guaranteed to encounter people that way, and I'm a really bad liar!" Mathew exclaimed.

"Mathew ole boy you've got to learn to relax." Phillip stated, not appearing the least bit concerned.

As they gradually approached the mansion the guests continued pouring out of the exits. Numerous horse drawn carriages lined the circular pathway to chauffeur Missouri's wealthiest and most powerful citizens. Most of them were, over fed and drunk as all hell, fighting to maintain their equilibrium. Mathew stood paralyzed when he spotted his parents conversing with the Arringtons in front of the most expensive carriage on the property. The Arringtons were surrounded by the local press. Several reporters were taking pictures and asking questions. None of it seemed to bother the Arringtons. Their only concern was their son.

"Where have you been!" All four parents shouted in unison.

Phillips parents had an even thicker British accent than Phillip. They were difficult to understand.

Mathew forced the lump down in his throat and struggled to find his words. Unable to think of any decent explanation he decided to go with the truth. *Either way I'm in a whole mess of trouble. At least this way I'm not committing a sin.*

Before Mathew could confess, Phillip chimed in. "I dropped my champagne glass this evening. I didn't want to call attention to my lack of grace and clumsiness. I tried to clean it up myself before anyone noticed, rather than call on the servants. I cut my hand in the process, and the good doctor had already had a few too many drinks this evening." Phillip explained, inconspicuously nudging his head in the direction of the intoxicated Dr. McKinley.

As everyone glanced the doctor's way, the fifty year old balding Scott fell boarding his stagecoach.

A servant rushed to help Dr. McKinley, and Phillip went on to say. "Mathew here was good enough to take me to the nurse on the plantation to be stitched up. Would you like to see?" Phillip bluffed, extending a bandaged fist.

"No that's quite alright." Lady Arrington announced holding her hand up.

Phillip knew his mother was squeamish and wouldn't want

to see the alleged wound.

"Phillip, get in the stagecoach and stop upsetting your mother." Lord Arrington ordered.

Phillip smirked at Mathew then boarded the carriage.

"Next time allow the servants to tend to such matters." Lady Arrington called after him.

"Thank you for helping our son. It was nice to meet you all." Lord and Lady Arrington stated as they boarded the stagecoach next.

Master and Mistress Colburn gave their son an approving nod then bid farewell to their other guests. Mathew watched as the Arrington's elegant black stagecoach disappeared down the gravel path.

Man that guy is good.

The fire was beginning to die down but the temperature was pleasant and summer like. The night had fallen silent, as the slaves packed up their musical instruments, bows, and spears and returned to their tiny shacks. There they rested up for another day of grueling labor in the cotton, tobacco, and sugar cane fields.

"Whew I'm tired." Mali said as she helped her sister, Anna, disassemble the paint stand.

"You can head home if you want. I'll finish up here." Anna offered.

"You can't carry the paint stand alone. Can you?" Mali asked.

"No, but I figured we can come back for it tomorrow." Anna suggested.

"Alright then I'll meet you at home. Thanks Anna, I'll be sure to light the porch lantern for you." Mali said as she jogged off.

"Good night Mali." Anna called after her.

Mali can be such an early bird sometimes. Anna thought as she stayed behind to pack up the supplies. She took her time to put away each item; dragging the task out for as long as possible. *I don't care if I'm exhausted when I report for duty tomorrow morning. It will be a year until the next festival, and I'm not ready for this night to end just yet. All I have to look forward to be another day of back breaking, inhumane work. The magic of the festival is still in the air. I must enjoy it for as long as I can.*

Anna grabbed as much as she was able to carry and set out on the ¾ mile hike to the cabin she shared with her sister. As she walked home, she thought about her life before she came to live on the Colburn plantation. *I still remember the day the Colburns had my sister and I ripped from our mother and father's arms. My sister was the mistress' chamber maid and I was her daughter's body slave. Our last owner, Master Miles, hit hard times and went to strike up a deal with the Colburns. Mali and I were devastated to find out the Colburns wanted to take our father away from us in exchange for farm equipment. We felt relieved when Master Miles informed them that our father was a talented blacksmith and far too valuable to be traded. Our relief only lasted for a brief period. The following day Master Miles decided to give my sister and me to the Colburns instead. The Colburn's decided to have Mali and I work in the cotton fields, and hire a free black man as a blacksmith. We were bought, sold, and traded like cattle for farm equipment. My life was never the same after that day.*

Anna smiled to herself as she thought. *In truth I don't even want Mathew. He's too young, and Seth is more my type. I love flirtatious, cocky, pretty boys like Seth. As far as Mathew is concerned, he's handsome enough, but I mostly get a kick out of making him sweat. I find it amusing to screw with his head and put him in awkward positions; simply because he's the heir to the estate. It's like regaining some sense of control over my life. Picking on the son of the people who dictate every aspect of my existence makes me feel the tiniest bit empowered.*

Anna's cabin was completely dark when she got home. Not even the lantern on the porch was lit. *Mali must be fast asleep. I'll try not to wake her.* Anna opened the door and felt her bare foot splash into something wet. She grabbed some matches and lit a lantern. It looked as though the house had been ransacked. The furniture was turned over and the floor was covered in blood.

"Oh my God! Mali! Mali!" Anna called as she followed the crimson trail into the tiny bedroom.

There Mali lay on her cot. She was covered in bright red blood.

"Mali!" Anna called as she ran into the room.

Mali lay on her side facing the wall, and did not respond. Anna grabbed her sister's shoulder and Mali slumped onto her back. Mali stared up at the ceiling in silence: not blinking, breathing, or moving. She was dead to the world.

Anna felt cold all over. She was faint and dizzy. The room began to spin. Her mind and body were entirely overwhelmed. She felt the urges to, cry, scream, vomit, and pass out all at the same time. Before Anna could yell for help a strong hand fastened tightly over her mouth.

Chapter 5

It was five am and the sun had not yet risen. The ringing of the gigantic bell in the slave quarters, symbolized another day of duty. Sarah yawned and climbed out of bed. *It's going to be a very long day.* She thought, still exhausted from the spring festival.

She looked around her cabin. Her entire family had already gone to work. She had to make haste. She quickly slipped on her black and white servants dress, and pulled back her thick curly hair. She walked toward the big house passing the mess hall on the way.

The more than one hundred field slaves formed two lines for morning rations. Sarah and her family worked in the house. They ate breakfast at a later time.

Sarah entered the mansion and walked directly to the small dining hall. She immediately began setting the table with fine china, crystal ware, and polished silver. The aroma drifting from the kitchen was magnificent. Mable had probably been up sense four am preparing breakfast for the Colburns.

Sarah glanced at the clock, 5:30am. *The Colburns will be up soon.* She hurried outside to pick fresh flowers for the center piece. After arranging the floral bouquet, she set out everyone's favorite breakfast sides: *strawberry syrup for Lillian's waffles, whipped cream and sliced fruit for Mistress Colburn's crapes, salt and pepper for Master Colburn's biscuits and gravy, and last but not least butter and raspberry jam for Mathew's toast.*

Mathew Colburn Sr. entered the dining room moments later.

"Good morning Sir. What can I get for you?" Sarah asked the master.

"I think I'll have......... the biscuits and gravy." Mr. Colburn told her.

Surprise, surprise, Sarah thought to herself as he took his place at the table.

"Excellent choice Sir." Sarah replied as she passed him the morning paper.

Master Colburn, a man of thirty-five years, was best described as tall dark and handsome. His dark wavy hair complemented his chestnut colored eyes and lightly tanned complexion. He was stone faced and serious, and he never ever smiled. He spoke with a heavy southern drawl and had an all work no play mentality.

The mistress, Arial Colburn, appeared just minutes later, looking radiant as always. She was petite and fair skinned, with silky blonde hair. It was barely six am and she was already so full of life. Unlike her husband she was a social creature. She found joy in hosting the most lavish parties for Missouri's rich and powerful. She came from a wealthy family in France and still spoke with an accent. She and her husband were both strong believers in order, tradition, and the separation of the classes. Appearances were everything to the Colburns.

"Good morning. I'll have the usual." Mistress Colburn called out cheerfully, her large gray eyes sparkling.

"Yes Ma'am." Sarah replied.

Master Colburn rose as the mistress entered the room, and pulled out her chair. She kissed her husband on the cheek and took a seat next to him.

Lillian came in next, still wearing her night gown. Mistress Colburn was appalled.

"Lillian you will eat properly or not at all! Go change your clothes at once." Mrs. Colburn demanded.

Lillian stomped back upstairs to her bedroom.

Lillian inherited her mother's beautiful looks, but none of the mistress' lady-like charm, grace, and sophistication. Since the moment Lillian could walk she served as a constant source of embarrassment, frustration, and disappointment for her parents.

"Where's Lillian going?" Mathew asked as he entered the

dining room.

"She was sent to her room for coming down in her sleep attire. That girl will never fetch a decent husband, behaving the way she does." Master Colburn grumbled.

"Decent husband? She's twelve." Mathew protested.

"Twelve or not, she must learn to behave like a proper lady." Mistress Colburn added.

"Good morning Master Mathew. What will it be?" Sarah asked.

"The same." Mathew announced with aggravation.

He adored his sister Lillian, and his mother and father were always so hard on her. Mathew had his father's handsome looks and quiet temperament. He was the strong silent type and usually avoided large crowds.

"I'll be right back with everyone's breakfast, should I make a plate for Lillian?" Sarah asked.

Before anyone could respond to Sarah's question, the warning bell sounded off. Everyone sprung from their seats. Master Colburn and Mathew both ran outside to a symphony of barking canines. Mathew took a look around. There were armed men with packs of hound dogs searching the property.

"We have two runaways Sir." One of the ten overseers informed Master Colburn.

"Who!" Mr. Colburn demanded.

"The two new girls, Anna and Mali, didn't report for six am field duty." The overseer explained.

"Retrieve them, and deal with them accordingly!" Master Colburn snapped.

"Father, promise me you won't hurt them!" Mathew shouted, knowing that the girls would be flogged until the brink of death.

Master Colburn placed a hand on his son's shoulder and spoke. "This is a plantation son. Runaway slaves must be punished, or else all the slaves will be taking off. You'll understand one day, when you inherit the property."

Mathew shoved his father away and yelled. "I want nothing to do with this place! It's monstrous!"

Chapter 6

In the hours that followed the disappearance of Anna and Mali, it was back to business as usual on the plantation. Sarah appeared in the doorway of Mr. Colburn's office. He waived her in from behind his massive desk.

"You wished to see me Master?" Sarah asked.

Master Colburn drawled. "Sarah, I have two issues I wish to discuss with you. The first is, my wife's sister Countess A'lice Demoniet, her husband Count Pier Demoniet, and their sixteen year old daughter Francesca Demoniet, are all arriving from France this evening. You'll need to begin preparing rooms for our guests. The count and countess will be leaving the end of this week. Their daughter Francesca will be with us the rest of the summer and she is in need of a body slave. Mable may need help in the kitchen also."

Sarah frowned at the thought of having to help Mable. Most of the house slaves felt they were superior to the field slaves, and Mable had always turned her nose up at Sarah's family because her mother Violet had married a field slave. Mable was pencil thin and black as night. She was very bossy and condescending with a personality as unattractive as her physical appearance. She had the smile of a jack-o-lantern which made her speak with a lisp.

"Master wasn't there something else you wished to talk to me about sir?" Sarah enquired.

Mr. Colburn sat back in his large arm chair then continued. "Yes actually. Aren't you fifteen years old now?"

"Sixteen sir." She informed him.

"Have you jumped the broom yet?" He questioned.

"No sir." Sarah answered.

"My first assistant, Emanuel, wishes to marry and he fancies you. Should I tell him the match is agreeable?" Master

Colburn asked.

Sarah paused for a moment and let out a long sigh. She stared wistfully up at the constellations painted on the master's ceiling. *It seems like every other week Master Colburn is coming to me and Marlette with another proposal. How many times must we inform the men on this plantation that we will have no one? Even with our descent treatment, we often fantasize about what it would be like to roam free in the distant land our father told us so many stories about. Marlette and I always felt it would be wrong to subject an innocent child to a life of servitude, and therefore made a pact to never marry. But the suitors keep coming. I can tell Master Colburn's patience is wearing thin with my inability to choose a mate. I live in dread of the day he stops asking and chooses a mate for me. It's inevitable, but I'll still put it off as long as possible.*

"Sarah, what should I tell the boy!" Mr. Colburn snapped.

Sarah hesitated a moment longer then answered. "Tell him I'm sorry but I have to decline his request."

"Very well then; send my son in. I need a word with him." Mr. Colburn ordered sounding somewhat irritated.

Sarah respectfully nodded and replied. "Yes sir, right away."

Sarah trotted down the hall to Mathew's study. He was sitting behind a desk fighting to stay awake, while a man in his late twenties stood scribbling away on a chalkboard.

Sarah waited in the doorway a few moments before politely interrupting the tutor. "I beg your pardon sir. I must call on Master Mathew. His father wishes to have a word with him."

The teacher waived his hand and ordered. "You're dismissed for the day. Read chapters eight and nine for tomorrow's lesson."

Mathew rose from his seat and joined Sarah in the hallway. "I really don't want to deal with my father right now but at least I got out of that retched, boring, medical class early today." He said with exasperation.

The only classes that interested Mathew were math, physics and art.

"Good luck with your father" Sarah said.

She forced a smile and walked down the hall in the opposite direction. Mathew could tell she was upset and immediately felt bad for his comment about school. *What a stupid thing to say. Sarah would give anything just for the opportunity to learn to read, and write and here I am taking my education for granted.*

He approached his father's door, took a deep breath, and knocked twice.

"Come in" Called the booming voice from behind the door.

"Father, you wished to see me?" Mathew asked as he made his way into the room.

Master Colburn announced. "I just wanted to tell you to watch the way you behave with the slaves this week. The count and countess will be visiting and they frown on fraternization with servants. Also, Francesca will be staying with us for the summer. Be polite to your cousin and show her around. I'll be out of town on business for a couple of days. You're in charge until I return. That'll be all."

"Yes sir." Mathew replied and left the room.

He ran down stairs and retreated outside to the barn to suffer through his frustration in seclusion. *The bible says to honor thy mother and father but there has to be some exceptions to that rule. My cousin Francesca is the most intolerable spoiled brat who ever lived. She's malevolent, vindictive, and bitter to the very core and I have no other choice but to waist my entire summer on her.* He entered the barn and started working on Dr. McKinley's stagecoach. Within minutes he was entirely engrossed.

Sarah said as she entered the barn. "I brought you some cold lemonade Master."

She was aware his father never had anything nice to say, and was rarely in a good mood. This is why she knew exactly where to find Mathew: the same spot he always went to blow off some steam.

He unburied himself from his work for a moment to smile at her and receive the glass. "Thank you Sarah. I don't mean to be cross but I hate Francesca and now I'm stuck with her the rest of the summer."

"If it makes you feel any better, I have to be her body slave so I'm stuck with her too. For what it's worth, I can't stand her either." Sarah confessed as she passed him a large bolt that was just out of his reach.

Mathew had always loved to repair, design and build things. He desired to be an architect or a structural engineer. Though he had no interest in human anatomy or the study of diseases, his parents wanted him to be a doctor anyway. They hired a teacher to come in four days a week to train him in the art of medicine. Sarah, on the other hand, wanted nothing more than to be a doctor. She spent the majority of her time assisting Aunt Lizzie in the infirmary, helping her mend broken bones, prepare herbal remedies, and many other things. She was a very bright young woman and would have most likely been a doctor had she been born a white male and given the proper schooling.

"Sarah will you do me an errand?" Mathew asked as he fastened the eight inch bolt to the stagecoach.

"Yes of course Master Mathew." Sarah replied.

Mathew fastened the nut and requested. "Will you go to the horse shed and bring me a hammer?"

Sarah made her way to the shed. When she reached the rickety old structure, the door was already open. She cautiously walked through the dim musty horse shed in search of the hammer. Just then she felt someone grab her arm. A tall light complected black man in his late twenties stood in front of her. She jerked away as she recognized the man.

He grabbed her again and announced. "Hey girl my name is…"

Sarah interrupted. "Unhand me! I know who you are! You're that free Negro the master hired as a blacksmith. You tell all the girls around here that you'll buy their freedom so they'll bed with you. My sister warned me about you."

"All lies, my dear. If you jump the broom with me I promise to buy your freedom." The man replied denying all allegations against him.

He pulled her close in a blatant effort to kiss her. Sarah broke free from his embrace and ran back to the barn with Mathew.

"Sarah what's the matter?" Mathew asked, noticing she came back out of breath and without the hammer.

Sarah took a moment longer to catch her breath then answered. "There was this man in the shed trying to paw me and kiss on me."

Mathew informed her, "That was Abraham, my father's blacksmith. I'll be sure to inform my father of his behavior. Just forget about the hammer for now and race me to the pond."

Sarah grinned at him and replied sarcastically. "Master Mathew, you know I always beat you."

Mathew thought to himself. *I love playing games with Sarah. She's one of the few slaves on my father's plantation that won't let me win at everything.*

He called out, "On your mark, get set go!"

They were off across the meadow with Sarah in the lead as usual and Mathew in a close second. He gradually passed her with the pond now in sight. He stopped just short of the pond when he heard a sharp scream.

"Sarah!! Are you alright!" Mathew shouted.

He turned around and couldn't see her anywhere. She had completely disappeared.

"Mathew!!" Sarah called.

He heard her voice but still couldn't see her.

"Where are you Sarah!" Mathew demanded.

"I'm alright. Just follow the sound of my voice! I'm down here." Sarah instructed.

At that moment he noticed a hole in the ground by the old

weeping willow tree.

"Here take my hand. I'll get you out of there." Mathew instructed.

Sarah looked around a moment then casually replied. "Actually I think you should come down here and take a look. It's a tunnel big enough to stand up in. Let's see where it leads to."

Using the tree roots as stairs, Mathew climbed down into the tunnel with Sarah. They followed the dark musty tunnel until it ended at a large cave. On the outside of the cave there sat a babbling brook. Sarah pulled up her long black dress to put her feet in the water and wash off the minor scratches she had attained from the fall. To her surprise the water was unusually warm, bath water warm, due to a natural hot spring close by that poured into it.

"What should we call this place?" Mathew said while playfully splashing around in the water.

Sarah took a moment to think then named it White Water Brook because the constant rolling of the water made it appear more white than blue.

Sarah stopped by the nursery after leaving the brook to face her mother, Violet. She knew at some point she'd have to answer to her mother for Mathew's appearance at the spring festival and she had been avoiding the encounter all day. She reached for the door knob, took a deep breath and walked in. *I may as well get this over with.*

The cabin was filled with infants, toddlers, and small children running a-muck. Violet rotated frequently, performing many tasks around the plantation but the nursery was the only place in which she found joy being. Sarah's mother was average height and slightly heavy set. She had peanut butter tanned skin and large brown eyes. She wore a black and white servant's dress and a black, cotton scarf she kept wrapped around her hair at all times.

Violet had two daughters, Sarah sixteen and Marlette twenty. Her first marriage was to Marlette's father Henry, a tall handsome millato man fifteen years her senior. He died at the young age of thirty-five when he was thrown from a wild stallion while trying to train it for the mistress. His death was hard on Violet and it took her nearly three years to remarry to Sarah's father Samson, an attractive dark skinned man of average height and muscular build. Samson hadn't been born on the plantation like most of the others. He had been captured from an Island off the coast of West Africa. He was later brought to the Colburn plantation to work in the sugar cane fields. He held a high position in his tribe back home and he was a very proud man. Although he hated his new home, he treated his family with care and compassion. Samson adopted Marlette as his own and he was very over-protective of his girls.

"You do know that you're not to talk to Mathew and Lillian this week." Violet stated while holding a whining baby in each arm.

"Yes Ma'am, we've already been warned." Sarah replied.

Violet looked at her daughter with disappointment and continued. "I saw Mathew at the festival and I know he was there because of you. I understand you and Mathew have been friends since you were very small, but he's a young man now. It's no longer appropriate for you two to spend so much time together. He's your Master. Not your playmate! I'm sorry you don't agree but this is our way of life. It's just the way things are Sarah."

Sarah mumbled under her breath. "Why am I the only one that sees a problem with the way things are."

"What did you just say?!" Violet demanded.

"Mathew says that all men are equal in God's eyes!" Sarah announced in frustration.

Violet shot back. "You will watch your tongue girl! You are not, nor will you ever be, Mathew's equal! If he can't make that distinction it's up to you to do so. From now on you will address him properly every time. No calling him by his first name ever. Do I make myself clear?"

"Yes Ma'am." Sarah answered in a hushed voice.

Violet shouted in anguish. "What did I do in my past life to deserve two insolent daughters? You do the exact opposite of everything I tell you, and Marlette's a damn shrew! Did you know people are calling your sister the Iron Maiden! That was an ancient device used for torture and killing!"

Sarah snickered a little.

"It's not funny." Violet protested, then went on to say. "I'm your mother. I'm not saying these things to hurt you. Your father has worked very hard to get his position as overseer. I have worked very hard to receive my position in the nursery. You and Marlette have both been blessed with positions in the house. The Colburn's have been very good to us, and your behavior could jeopardize everything. When will you realize that the decisions you make affect us all? You're not a child anymore Sarah."

"I'm sorry. I didn't realize the magnitude of my actions. It won't happen again." Sarah said grudgingly thinking to herself. *Growing up on a plantation teaches you one skill of survival very early in life: the ability to give a convincing apology even when you know deep down you've done nothing wrong. I'm not even mad at my mother. Unlike my father, Momma had been a house slave her entire life. The very ideas of freedom and equality are far-fetched to her.*

Violet bought the phony apology, and her mood lightened immediately.

"How is your ankle piece healing?" Violet questioned, changing the subject.

"Oh it's healing really well." Sarah answered peeling off the bandage to show her mother.

Violet examined the ankle and agreed, then went on to say. "I heard you turned down another proposal today."

Here we go again. Sarah thought to herself.

Violet placed the now sleeping infants in their bassinets and continued. "Of all the people on the plantation to turn down, why did it have to be Emanuel? He keeps track of the books, and handles all the finances on the plantation. I don't agree with what you and Marlette are doing. Life can be very cold at times and it's a blessing to have someone to share it with. Now it's your decision and I respect it. But I want you to know that I love your father dearly and I never once regretted you or your sister. Now run along I hear the mistress needs your help."

Sarah left the nursery and sped to the big house. *Why must they always inform us at the last minute?* She thought as she raced to get everything ready. It was late in the afternoon and she was extremely pressed for time. She spent the next few hours preparing all the guest quarters. She dusted and cleaned every surface. She changed all the linens and picked fresh flowers to put in each of the chambers. She took exceptional care to make sure every detail was perfect for the guests.

Darkness fell and a black and gold carriage pulled by four white horses approached the Colburn Mansion. A teenage girl with grey eyes, curly blonde locks, and fair skin was helped out of the carriage by Seth, who was the master and mistress' pride and joy, and clearly the favorite of all the slaves. They began raising him after his mother died when he was very young.

"Sarah, show my niece Francesca to her room." Mrs. Colburn urged in her French accent.

"Yes Mistress." Sarah answered as she hurried to the young ladies aid.

Francesca was dressed in an extravagant green gown with gold embroidery, and looked to be about sixteen years old. Her parents climbed out of the carriage next and the night sky lit up with camera flashes from the local press. A`lise was blonde with grey eyes and a small frame. She was the mistress' identical twin sister. Her husband Pier was of average height and build with red hair and hazel eyes. Both Pier and A`lise looked to be in their early thirties. To Sarah, their arrogance was palpable. The thought of waiting on them for only a week, was enough to make her gag.

Francesca rang for Sarah the next morning to help her

dress.

"You rang for me Miss Francesca?" Sarah asked.

Francesca stopped brushing her long blonde hair a moment and spoke in her thick French accent. "Fetch me a glass of lemonade, and this time don't put so much sugar in it. You nearly poisoned it with sugar last night. When you return lay out my pink and white summer dress. And brush my hair into a bun. Make haste! Cousin Mathew is taking me horseback riding."

When Sarah returned with the glass of lemonade, Francesca sipped it in a manner that would allow her to touch very little of the glass because servants had previously touched it.

Sarah finished up Francesca's hair and laced up her corset. After that she helped her slip on the pink and white dress and waited for further instructions.

"I suppose that will be all. You're dismissed." Francesca snapped.

Sarah left the room trying hard to hide the look of frustration on her dark pretty face. She passed Mathew in the hallway and grumbled. "She's all yours now."

On the way back to the infirmary, a girl ran passed crying.

"Lillian, what's the matter?" Sarah asked.

Lillian stopped her sniffling then answered. "Francesca won't play with me. She called me a tom-boy and said ladies of class like her don't climb trees or play horse shoes. When I asked to go riding with her and Mathew she said I was too young and I would only slow them down."

Lillian looked a lot like Francesca, minus four years and the semi permanent scowl. Unlike Francesca and her mother, Lillian's hair was straight and black. Her eyes were a simple brown. Sarah bent down to hug the girl and urged her to calm down. Francesca was always hurting Lillian's feelings and Sarah and Marlette were always there to pick up the pieces.

"I'll take you riding myself if your father says it's alright." Sarah replied.

Lillian stopped crying and flashed Sarah an angelic grin

then said "I wish you were my cousin."

Then she ran off to play with some of the slave children.

Moments after Lillian took off Sarah noticed a small red hound dog digging a hole in a flower bed. "What are you doing out of your pen?" Sarah asked as she jogged in the direction of the hound puppy. It trotted off playfully. *Oh puppy I am not in the mood to chase you.* As she drew closer to him she noticed something black dangling from the dog's mouth. *An arrow head? No an earring.*

"How did you get a hold of Anna's earring, little guy?" She questioned as she grabbed the puppy and pulled the earring from his mouth. Sarah let out a horrified scream as she saw that the earring was still attached to a petrified ear.

Chapter 7

Present

Krista slammed the book closed when her father abruptly entered the cabin.

"Krista! I've called your cell phone at least four times. You've been out here since early this morning. Your mother tells me you didn't even come in for lunch. Is something bothering you?" Her father said.

Krista's father was upset. He'd combed the property looking for her.

She took a moment to collect herself and glanced at her cell phone. The word **Searching**.... displayed on the screen.

She gathered her things and stuttered out a response. "No Dad. I'm fine. I was just doing a little reading and lost track of time. I didn't realize I wouldn't get service out here."

"What were you reading?" Her father asked.

"Just a boring romance novel. It doesn't have any hot rods, explosions, or people getting shot. Believe me Dad. You wouldn't be interested."

The concerned expression on her father's face gradually turned to a slight smile as he replied. "Yeah, you're right. I probably wouldn't be interested. I don't see how women can read that stuff. Your mother's the same way. I get temporarily divorced when she's reading a good romance."

Krista laughed and replied. "As if you're any better than Mom. I've been known to lose my father during the playoffs."

He laughed and said. "I guess you're right honey. Wash up for dinner and meet us in the small dining hall."

After her father left, she stashed the book in the usual spot. She gathered her things, and walked outside. The afternoon sky was painted in a vibrant orange, red, and lavender as the sun set behind the far off hills. Krista glanced up at the brilliant scene and couldn't believe she had been in the cabin that long. The temperature had dropped quite a bit since this morning. She walked briskly to hurry out of the cool wind.

She strolled directly to the small dining room, and helped her mother by setting the table. Even the so called, small dining room seemed quite large to Krista. The cherry wood dinette set was made to seat ten. It had large wooden arm chairs to match. The ceiling was high with a gorgeous crystal chandelier. The Victorian walls were lined with beautiful tapestries and antique bronze candle holders. Like the rest of the rooms on the main level, the floor was made of marble.

Krista sat at the dinner table in sort of a trance. *Who was responsible for the murder of those poor girls?* She wondered. *Who wrote that book, and why was it stashed in the ceiling of that creepy slave shack; that Cabin of Whispers.*

"Krista, are you going to eat your supper or knit it into a sweater?" Her mother asked jokingly.

She noticed Krista picking at her pot roast and steam vegetables with a fork. Her mother was right. Krista didn't have much of an appetite.

"I was just waiting for it to cool off." Krista explained.

"So when do your father and I get to meet the lucky young man? Usually when you lose your appetite like this it has something to do with a boy." Her mother stated.

"Mom I can assure you this has nothing to do with a guy. I'm just trying to get settled in here. I don't know anyone yet." Krista replied sounding a bit aggravated by her mother's way off base assumption.

Her father noticed her getting irritated and made a suggestion of his own. "Your cousin Jessica is dropping off her application to the University of Missouri tomorrow. The university is going to provide a tour and allow her to stay overnight in one of the campus dorms. Maybe you should go with her. It would be a great opportunity to meet new people. Jessica grabbed an extra permission slip just in case you decided to come along."

"Thanks dad, I think I will. I'm gonna get some sleep now. I'm really tired." Krista said.

She took care of her plate, and jogged up stairs.

Krista grabbed her robe and walked to the bathroom. She turned on the dial, and the water came out brown for the first 30 seconds. *Gross.* Once the shower water had adjusted to the optimal temperature and color she climbed in. *Ahhh that feels good.* She spent the first five minutes just allowing the warm water to run on her.

Krista climbed out of the shower and reached for a towel. She wrapped herself snuggly and gasped when she caught a glimpse of the mirror. A message **Help me.   A. Monroe** was traced in the steam.

Chapter 8

Jessy pulled up just after dawn in her candy apple red Sebring convertible. Krista jogged down the cement stairs with her overnight bag in one hand and the folded up permission slip in the other.

"I don't understand why we have to leave so early." Krista said as she yawned and tossed her bag in the back seat.

"Well we have to make it there in time to have breakfast with the dean at nine o'clock. The school is a half hour away." Jessy explained as she passed Krista an espresso in a Styrofoam cup with plastic lid.

"Does the name **A. Monroe** mean anything to you?" Krista asked after they pulled off.

"My brother, Alex's middle name is Monroe. Why?" Jessy stated as she made a right turn out of the drive way.

"That name was written in steam on the mirror, after I got out of the shower. It scared the crap out of me." Krista admitted feeling a little relieved.

Jessy explained. "That dork probably smudged his name on the mirror before he left for soccer camp. Human finger prints will stay on glass for an eternity unless you clean them off. My mother should've never told him the story behind his name. Now he thinks its so special he can just write it where ever he wants."

"What's so great about Alex's name?" Krista asked after taking a sip of her espresso.

Jessy merged onto the freeway, and told Krista the story. "The original Alexander Monroe was a Black British journalist. He was really famous in the 1920's and 1930's. He was known for gallivanting around the planet trying to fix all the injustices of the world, and for being a brilliant writer. Legend has it that he was lured right here to Poplar Bluff and never seen or heard from again. My mother was so obsessed with his writing she named one of my brothers after him. My mom left one of his books in the backseat." Jessy merged onto the exit and continued. "It shouldn't be much longer now. When we get there we have to remember to ask for Rachel Wilcox. She's our tour guide."

Krista took off her seatbelt, and grabbed the book from the backseat. She opened the book and flipped through the pages. There was a picture of the author on the inside cover. Krista gasped and dropped the book. She was speechless. She refused to believe what her eyes were showing her.

"Oh my god! The man from my dream!" Krista shouted.

"I know, isn't he hot?" Jessy replied.

Krista shook her head and explained. "Not the man *of* my dreams, the man *from* my dream. I saw this man murdered two nights ago."

Chapter 9

Rachel Wilcox silenced the alarm on her cell phone and climbed out of bed. She opened the blinds and allowed the sun light to brighten the room. She stepped out on the balcony of her best friend's dorm room, and filled her lungs with fresh air. *It's going to be a beautiful day.*

"Why are you awake at the butt crack of dawn? There are no classes today." Her best friend, La`Kiesha grumbled.

"You know I signed on as a tour guide. I had to pick up a second job after my dorm room burned. By the way thanks for letting me crash here." Rachel replied.

"No problem." La`Kiesha groaned, burying her head under a pillow to block the sunlight.

Rachel scolded her. "How many times have I told you not to drink tequila? You always feel rotten the next day."

Rachel walked back in the room and bounced on La`Kiesha's bed.

"Get up. You're coming with me." Rachel announced.

"I don't think so." Came the muffled groan from underneath the pillow.

Rachel pried the pillow from La`Kiesha's face and tossed it across the room.

"Alright, alright, I'm getting up." La`Kiesha moaned as she climbed out of bed.

Rachel was a short, slender black girl with caramel colored skin and large almond eyes. She wore her jet black hair in a zillion tiny braids and had a child like prettiness about her. La`Kiesha was bi-racial. Her mother was Hispanic and her father was black. She was very light skinned, with long wavy brown hair. She was small but shapely and possessed an exotic beauty. Both girls were cheerleaders, and juniors at the university. They had known one another their entire lives.

"At least I'll have impressionable high school students to corrupt." La`Kiesha announced before she downed a few aspirin, followed by a large glass of water.

"Don't even think about sinking your claws into those kids." Rachel warned.

Rachel was as straight and narrow as they come. She was a criminal justice major, and had recently applied to law school. She had a pleasant personality and got along with most people.

La`Kiesha spoke her mind and didn't take crap from anyone. She was a music major. She played a lot of instruments, but liked the violin the best.

La`Kiesha fumbled over the jewelry in her drawer and said. "Have you seen that bracelet my brother gave me? I haven't seen it since......"

Rachel interrupted. "Don't even say it. I know things have been known to come up missing when my mother visits, but the last time she was here she said she had been clean for six months."

La`Kiesha shook her head and spoke. "And you were naive enough to believe her. Every time your mother comes around she swears she's been clean for six months. Then she robs us blind. Rachel, don't take this the wrong way. I love your mother, but the woman is a crack addict."

"She promised me she quit for good this time and I believe her." Rachel protested.

"When people become addicted to drugs they're not themselves anymore. They're like zombies. They care about nothing and no one, just their own need to feed. I went through this with Shania." La`Kiesha said. She paused for a few seconds staring wistfully at a picture of her and her twin sister then continued. "The woman's an anchor. If you don't let her go she'll only drag you down with her."

Rachel finished dressing and replied. "In the sixth grade my mother's drug habit started to get out of hand. Mother's Day was approaching and I wanted to get her something special. I thought if I showed her I loved her things would change for us. I went around the neighborhood raking leaves, and doing anything I could, to earn money. Finally I was able to buy her a ring. I went home that day smiling from ear to ear. Just after I walked through the door, Child Protective Services pulled into the driveway. They pulled me, screaming and crying, from my mother's arms on Mother's Day. Before they could haul me off to foster care, I reached in my pocket, and gave the ring to my mother. No matter how strung-out she got, she never sold or pawned it. She lost everything, over the years, to her crack addiction but that ring. As long as it remains on her finger I know she's not a total zombie. There's some part of her that's still human, still my mother. That's the part I'll never give up on."

La`Kiesha gave Rachel a compassionate look and said. "I understand the significance of that ring, but did you notice if your mother was wearing it the last time she was here?"

Rachel thought quietly to herself for a moment then replied. "As a matter of fact I didn't notice."

Chapter 10

Jessy and Krista arrived at the campus around a quarter till. They entered an enormous banquet room with red carpet. There were twenty round tables topped with white table cloths and flower center pieces. Krista and Jessy grabbed a couple breakfast plates from the buffet, and sat with some students Jessy knew from her high school. There were about two hundred people at the breakfast, not including Dean Banks and the other school officials that came to speak to the local high school students about all the university had to offer.

"Dean Banks is soooo hot." One of the high school boys said as the dean stood at the podium to speak.

The breakfast lasted a little over an hour. Then the high school students were assigned tour guides.

"Hey I'm Rachael. This is my friend La`Kiesha. We'll be showing you guys around today." Rachel announced.

"What up?" La`Kiesha said with a slight hand motion.

"Hey I'm Jessy. This is my cousin Krista." Jessy stated.

Krista and Jessy spent the rest of the day hanging out with Rachel and La`Kiesha. The first place they were taken was the student recreational center. There they played pool, pin ball, and video games. Then they were given access to the gym, complete with Olympic size swimming pool, sauna, and Jacuzzi.

At the eleven pm curfew Rachel and La`Kiesha, took Krista and Jessy to the dorm room they would be staying in for the night.

"I'm exhausted." Jessy announced.

"Me too" Krista admitted.

Jessy collapsed on her bunk and fell asleep within minutes.

Krista removed her cousin's glasses and set them on the night stand. While Jessy slept Krista logged onto the computer in the dorm room. She went on the internet and searched for the name, Alexander Monroe.

Just as the information was coming up Krista heard someone knocking. She abandoned the attempt immediately and answered the door. La`Kiesha was standing there all made up dressed in clothes that were sexy but not trashy.

"Get dressed I'm taking you guys to a frat party." La`Kiesha announced as she barged into the room with a sack of fashionable clothes, make-up, and accessories.

"Hey what's going on? Where's Rachel?" Jessy asked as she awakened and reached for her glasses.

La`Kiesha explained, "Rachel's out like a light. She's my best friend but most days she's as much fun as a wet blanket. You know that dork in school that reminds the teacher about homework and quizzes? That's Rachel. I, for one, think there's more to the college experience then cramming for exams. Now get dressed."

Krista and Jessy's feelings of fatigue turned to excitement and enthusiasm. They got ready in record time and followed La`Kiesha to her car. They drove to the party in La`Kiesha's silver convertible BMW. They could hear the music blaring from clear down the block. It continued to get louder as they approached the house.

They pulled up in front of a two story blue house with yellow Greek letters. There were several students sprawled out on the lawn conversing, with red plastic cups in hand. Their three girl entourage entered the packed fraternity house and all eyes were on them. The DJ played a hip-hop tune that caught La`Kiesha's attention.

"This is my song!" She yelled over the music, and then went out on the dance floor.

She was an awesome dancer. It wasn't long before Krista and Jessy followed her.

When the song went off Krista scampered off to the kitchen to find something to drink. There were so many people and it was so hot. She opened the refrigerator and grabbed a can of Coke. *I'm already in enough trouble with my parents. The last thing I want to do is come home hung over and reeking of alcohol.*

"May I have the next dance?" She heard a British accent call out from behind her.

She turned around to find a smoking hot blonde boy in cargo shorts and a university soccer jersey that read **The Ox**. This was a fitting name because he was built like one. He had pale blue-gray eyes and lips that said kiss me. His build was large; almost imposing. He was 6'4" and as solid as they come.

"Sure." Krista told him.

"I'm Kevin Oxley. I'm a sophomore transfer student from Oxford." The guy said reaching over to shake her hand.

"Krista Colburn." She replied.

"Are you thinking about coming here?" Kevin asked.

"Actually I'm from Michigan. I'm just visiting for the summer. I've been planning on going to Michigan State since middle school, with my two best friends, Angela and Stacy." Krista explained.

"So you're a Spartan." Kevin asked wrinkling up his nose at her.

She nodded her head and replied. "Yes, I'm afraid so. Why did your teammates nickname you Ox? Is it because your last name is Oxley? Or perhaps it's because you're from Oxford. Or maybe it's just because you're a beast on the field."

Kevin grinned uncontrollably at Krista's flattery and answered. "I'm not sure, but I think all three."

The song changed, and Krista gave Kevin the next dance as promised. She was lucky. The DJ played a slow song. She rested her head on his shoulder as they swayed back and forth to the music. Krista looked to her left and laughed as she caught Kevin's frat brothers giving him nods of approval.

"Is it alright if I call you Ox, or is that privilege reserved for teammates only?" She asked flirtatiously.

He glanced down at her with those blue-gray eyes of his and said. "You can call me whatever you want, as long as you call me."

La`Kiesha made her way across the dance floor and whispered in Krista's ear. "We have to get going."

Before Krista got in the BMW to leave, she passed Ox a folded up piece of paper containing her phone number. He gave her a kiss on the cheek that set her face on fire and watched as the car pulled away.

When Krista entered the mansion the following morning she found a letter from her parents on the refrigerator.

Krista,
Your father and I have an important business meeting to attend in regards to the house. We'll be back later this afternoon. If you need anything call our cell phones. We prepared a lunch for you and left it in the refrigerator.
P.S.
We hope you and Jessica had a great time at the University.
Love Always,
Mom & Dad

Krista strolled out to the slave quarters. She cautiously entered the Cabin of Whispers and retrieved the journal from the ceiling. *I'll bring the book in the house with me since no one else is home.*

She returned to the mansion and grabbed her lunch. Then she searched the eighteen rooms on the third floor for a comfortable place to read. At last she found a room at the end of the long corridor. *This must've been the master's chambers. There's very little modern advancement; just a computer, and the pile of goose down pillows next to the fireplace. Other then that this chamber is like stepping back into the 1800's.*

The large room was filled from wall to wall with shelves of books. There was an antique ebony wood desk and chair that sat in front of two wall size maps. The maps were eloquently drawn. Krista studied the charts a moment longer then cuddled up in the pile of goose down pillows next to the fireplace. She opened the book to the page she left marked with a black ribbon and began to read.

Chapter 11

April 21, 1836

Sarah wrapped the severed ear in a white cloth and ran into the mansion. She sped up the stairs to the third floor, and pounded on the master's door.

"Master Colburn!" She shouted.

When she heard no response she continued to beat on the door and shout. "Master Colburn!"

Emanuel emerged from his office across the hall. No one knew why he was even considered a slave. He possessed the appearance and proper speech patterns of any other white man, and he ran the entire plantation. He was average height with light brown hair. He wore thin rimmed spectacles over pale blue eyes. He was 18-years-old, very well kept, and dressed in the finest clothing. Emanuel was a good looking man, with a lot going for him. There was no wonder Violet was upset over Sarah's refusal to except his proposal.

"What's the problem, Sarah!" He shouted, grabbing her shoulders to calm her.

"This is the problem! Something terrible happened to those girls!" Sarah exclaimed as she shoved the wad of cloth at Emanuel.

"What's this?" He asked with a confused look on his face.

"Someone came to this plantation, and killed Anna. This is her ear. I recognized the earring. Something's telling me Mali didn't make it either." Sarah explained as a wave of nausea swept over her.

Emanuel's handsome face went pale white. He removed his glasses and rubbed his eyes in disbelief.

"Dear God in Heaven. Please step into my office. Severed body parts aren't really my thing. So I'll just take your word for it." He said as he sat the bundled up ear on his desk without looking at it.

Sarah followed Emanuel into his office. She continued to fight down the sick feeling that was rising up in her stomach.

Emanuel passed her his handkerchief, and tried to explain. "Sarah it's truly regrettable what happened to Anna, but this estate is surrounded by woods. Coyotes and wolves live in these parts. Wild cats live in the nearby mountains. Anna could've easily been attacked when she and her sister ran off; and how do you know Mali didn't get away safely?"

Sarah shook her head in disbelief. She was breathing heavily, and tears were streaming down her face.

She pointed to the ear and said. "If there's one thing I've learned from spending so much time in the infirmary, it's the appearance of human flesh. The surface is smooth and straight at the point of separation. Her ear wasn't ripped or chewed off by an animal. A precision cut was performed. Someone sliced Anna's ear clean off. If you'll just look right here…" Sarah explained, reaching for the cloth containing the ear.

Emanuel put his hand up to stop her then said. "Once again I'll take your word for it. Master Colburn left town an hour ago. He won't be home for a couple of days. Master Mathew should be back from his ride with Francesca soon. I'll round up the seven overseers and the blacksmith that are working today, and speak with the other three employees tomorrow. Master Mathew and I will hold a meeting in order to decide the best course of action. Wait here. We'll need to know where and when you found this, as well as any other helpful information you may have. When I return, tell Master Mathew and the overseers everything you told me." Emanuel instructed.

"Thank you." Sarah said.

Emanuel's pale blue eyes filled with compassion. He put a comforting hand on her arm and said. "It's going to be alright Sarah. We'll catch the man who did this."

Sarah walked out of the room and watched the dashing figure disappear down the hall. Her heart was pounding, and her head was spinning. She leaned against a wall in the hallway and slid down to the floor. There she waited for Mathew, Emanuel, Abraham and the seven overseers to return.

"Sarah, what's going on?" She heard a man's voice call from above her.

Sarah looked up from her seat on the floor to find Frank Welch. He was the first to return. Ole Frank, as the slaves called him, had dusty gray hair and squinty brown eyes. He was short and plump. He had a large belly that hung over his belt, and he usually appeared to be sunburned. Ole Frank was forty years old but looked around fifty. He and his son were the only two overseers that didn't live exclusively on the estate. They stayed four days a week in a cabin on the plantation, and the other three days at a lake house in town.

"Someone attacked one of the girls, so Emanuel called this meeting." Sarah explained.

"That's terrible." Frank said.

He walked in the office and waited for the others.

Abraham gave Sarah a lustful glare and a wink as he entered the office moments after Frank. He was 14 years her senior and still incredibly good looking. He was the largest man on the plantation at 6'6" 265 pounds of pure muscle. Sarah rolled her eyes and thought to herself. *What a smug womanizing jerk.*

Robert Welch, Frank's son journeyed up the corridor next. Robert passed Sarah without acknowledging her existence and sat in Emanuel's office next to his father. Robert was a younger more attractive version of his father. He was 19, with straw colored hair and a short stocky frame. Robert, like most of the other overseers, was arrogant, cruel, and used the whip far too often. He was nothing like his father Frank.

"Poppa." Sarah called as she saw her father, Samson, come up the stairs next.

She climbed to her feet and hugged him.

"I heard what happened. I'm sorry. Are you alright?" Samson asked.

Sarah nodded her head, and he entered the room with the others. Samson was a handsome man, with the statuesque build that came from more than a decade of field service. His skin was midnight black and his eyes were a mystic gray. Even after two decades of being in the US, he still possessed faint traces of a West African accent. Samson and Frank were the only two overseers the slaves did not despise. They were both decent men.

"Shall we wait for the others?" Emanuel asked Mathew as they made their way up the hall.

Mathew stepped into the office and said. "Show it to me right now."

Emanuel grabbed the wad of cloth from the desk and passed it to Mathew. Mathew took a deep breath and carefully unwrapped the disturbing package. All the color drained from his face. His brown eyes flared.

He turned to Emanuel and yelled. "This handkerchief is empty!"

Chapter 12

"Will someone please tell me what the hell is going on?!" Mathew said as he threw the empty handkerchief on the desk.

Sarah stood frozen in shock.

Robert Welch stood up from his seat and asked. "Emanuel did you actually see the ear?"

Emanuel put his head down and answered. "No but….."

Robert scoffed and interrupted. "I'll tell you exactly what's going on! These lazy, spoiled, house niggers have far too much time on their hands. She made up this fictitious claim. She wants us to believe those girls are dead so that we'll no longer pursue her friends."

"Are you calling my daughter a liar?" Samson asked in his booming voice; his gray eyes narrowed with anger.

Frank Welch stood up and said. "Quiet son."

Frank turned to Sarah and asked? "When was the last time you actually saw the ear?"

"In… In the yard before I wrapped it up, and ran inside." Sarah stuttered.

"So you haven't un-wrapped it since you've been in the house?" Samson asked.

"No Sir." Sarah replied.

The last four overseers appeared in the doorway then crowded into the room. One was a free black man and the other three were white.

"Is it possible that the ear may have slipped out when you ran in the house?" Mathew asked.

Robert threw his hands up in the air and interrupted. "This is ridiculous! This girl is obviously lying! The night those two girls ran off their paint stand was left in the middle of the slave quarters. They didn't bother to take it home because they knew they wouldn't be staying any longer. It would've been impossible for them to run with such a heavy item, so they just left it. Banish Sarah to the tobacco field for two weeks! I promise you. I'll straiten her out."

Robert stomped across the room and grabbed Sarah by the arm. "I shall see her beaten for her lies, and no food rations for three days!"

"You will not touch my daughter!" Samson yelled as he grabbed Robert by the shirt and slammed him onto the desk.

"Poppa no!" Sarah screamed.

Frank and the other four overseers pulled Samson off of Robert and restrained him. Robert climbed to his feet with a dazed expression on his face. As if his brain hadn't yet registered, what had happened to him.

Sarah looked on in terror thinking. *My father has already been lashed once before over my mother. Poppa threatened Master Colburn's brother, Pete for trying to force Momma into his bed. When Poppa was informed that he would be flogged for the threat, he smiled and replied. "I guess we'll both be taking a beating today." Poppa battered Pete Colburn so badly that he never came back to visit. Now he's about to be punished again for protecting me, his own daughter. Only this time his position as overseer is at stake as well.*

"We'll bind him to the whipping post, Sir." One of the overseers informed Mathew as they drug Samson into the hallway.

"Release him." Mathew said.

The overseers glanced at Mathew in silence; bewildered expressions covered each of their faces.

"I said release him!" Mathew demanded.

The gang of overseers complied right away.

Robert's face turned red with anger. His nostrils flared. His yellow hair matted to his forehead with perspiration.

He turned to Mathew and said. "If you expect to run a successful plantation one day, you would do well to train your slaves how to behave in the presence of white men."

Mathew's brown eyes narrowed with aggravation.

He got right in Robert's face and replied. "If you value your employment here you would do well not to tell me how to train my servants. If any of you have a problem with the way I do things, there's the door."

Mathew turned to the last four overseers that came upstairs and said. "I want you four to search the premises. Sarah may have been so scared, she didn't notice it fall."

The men nodded and proceeded outside. Samson, Frank, Abraham and Robert remained.

Mathew turned to Emanuel and said. "I know you didn't actually un-wrap the cloth and look in it, but when Sarah passed it to you, did it feel as if there was anything at all in it."

Emanuel said. "Yes, there was definitely something in it."

Mathew turned to the three overseers and the blacksmith and said, "I'm sorry but you four were the first ones in the office. Help me search them, Emanuel."

"I understand." Samson replied as they searched him.

"Whatever it takes to get to the bottom of this," Frank said while being patted down.

Abraham announced in his usual smartass manner. "If you're gonna play with my balls the least you can do is buy me a drink first."

Emanuel finished searching Abraham and replied with a smirk. "That's exactly what I told your mother."

"This is insulting. I won't have it." Robert announced as Mathew walked in his direction.

"Either you'll submit to the search or resign." Mathew informed him.

Robert threw his hands up and Mathew proceeded to search his person.

Mathew glanced over at Sarah and said. "He's clean."

"May I go back to work now?" Robert asked sarcastically.

Mathew gave a silent wave and Robert, Frank, Abraham and Samson left the office.

Sarah walked over to Mathew and said. "Thank you for saving my father."

Mathew assured her. "No man should be beaten for showing the most basic of human instincts, the need to protect his own child."

Sarah helped Emanuel pick up the mess that her father caused. Several items went crashing to the floor when Samson threw Robert on the desk.

"I'm sorry about your things. My father earns a small pension. I know he'll replace everything." Sarah informed him.

"That won't be necessary. I actually thought that was amazing, the way your father stood up for you. He's a brave man." Emanuel said with a slight smile.

"I swear I'm not going crazy. I know what I saw." Sarah insisted.

"I believe you." Mathew assured her.

Emanuel placed the last item back, on his desk and made a suggestion. "You should go to their cabin. If Anna and Mali were kidnapped, there should be signs of a struggle."

Chapter 13

Mathew and Sarah stood in front of Anna and Mali's cabin. They glanced at one another. Both of them feared the ghastly display that most likely lay on the other side of the door. Sarah gathered her nerve and took a step forward. Mathew put up an arm to block her.

"I'll go first to make sure it's safe." He instructed.

Sarah agreed and waited outside. Mathew pushed in the creaky splintering door, and cautiously entered the cabin. He exited moments later with a shocked look on his face.

"What's wrong Mathew?" Sarah demanded.

His troubled expression remained, and he said nothing. Sarah pushed past him and barged into the cabin.

She walked from room to room and said. "The place is spotless. The furniture is upright. There's no blood; no broken artifacts. There's no sign of a struggle what so ever. I was mistaken. They must've run away."

Mathew walked back in the cabin and said. "That's what concerns me. The place is too clean. I've been out here once to fix the door, and twice more to fix the leaky roof. Anna and Mali were not meticulous tenants. On all three of my visits the place looked as if a tornado came through. So why would they wait until the night they run away to tidy up the place?"

Sarah looked at him in shock and replied. "Now that you mention it, they were poor housekeepers."

The bell rang in the slave quarters, signifying break time. The slaves worked from 6am-6pm. They had a break from 12-2pm every day.

"We should probably get going. Seth, Aaron, and Leah are meeting us at White Water Brook for break. If we don't show they'll know something's wrong. I don't want to alert anyone else until I figure out exactly what's going on." Mathew stated as he left the cabin, and walked toward the tunnel entrance.

Sarah left with him, and Mathew went on to say. "If the cabin was messy I would've assumed that maybe they had run away, and were later attacked by animals. If there had been signs of a struggle I would've thought Anna and Mali were abducted by a novice who acted on impulse. Such a criminal would be easy to apprehend. Whoever committed this atrocity knew exactly what he was doing. This whole thing was planned."

Sarah came to a sickening realization as she strolled alongside Mathew.

She turned to Mathew and said. "Whoever did this was no stranger to this plantation. I find it convenient that the two girls attacked just happened to live all alone. Anna and Mali had no father or brothers here to protect them. The killer knew that."

Mathew glanced back at her and added. "The killer also knew that, with these girls having no other relatives on this plantation, no one would notice them missing until they failed to report for 6am duty. He was well aware that he'd have plenty of time to clean up."

Sarah added. "Anna and Mali lived in the cabin furthest away from the others. They were attacked just after the Spring Festival, which just happens to be the busiest night of the year. The festival created the perfect diversion."

Mathew sighed and said. "Not only did the attacker know exactly what he was doing, he was familiar with every aspect of this plantation. The killer works here, and if I don't stop him he'll kill again."

They reached the tunnel entrance and Mathew climbed in.

"I'm going to get you and Seth's lunch from the kitchen, and meet you there." Sarah called down to him.

"Bring enough for everyone." Mathew called up to her.

"If Mabel let's me. The only two slaves allowed to eat when you eat are Seth and Emanuel. The rest of us eat twice a day, only." Sarah explained.

"Well tell Mabel I said you could have the food." Mathew replied.

Sarah nodded and jogged to the mansion.

She entered the kitchen and Mabel was nowhere to be seen. *Whew, I'll stuff this picnic basket before she returns.* Sarah thought as she packed the basket to the brim.

"What is this!" She heard a voice call out from behind her.

Sarah turned around surprised to see Francesca standing in the kitchen.

"Are you stupid? I asked specifically for crimson gerberas!" Francesca yelled.

"What's that, Miss?" Sarah asked.

"It's a red daisy. You put white daisies in my room." Francesca explained in aggravation, violently waiving a handful of white flowers.

Sarah fought to maintain her composure and explained. "The red daisies only grow in Blue Valley. I'm not allowed to travel that far without a pass. The overseers will assume I'm running away. That's why I picked the white daisies from the orchard."

The Mistress staggered into the kitchen with a glass of wine in hand. Red drops splashed on the floor with each clumsy step. It was barely noon and she was already boozed up.

"What's all the commotion about?" Mistress Colburn slurred.

"This idiot got me the wrong flowers. I asked for red daisies." Francesca explained.

The mistress dipped the pen in ink and scribbled a few lines on a sheet of paper.

"Here's a pass. Show this to any overseer who questions you. You'll be needed here all day, so wait until later on tonight to go. Take your sister with you so you won't get lost." Mistress Colburn instructed.

"Yes Ma'am" Sarah replied.

Francesca slammed the flowers in Sarah's chest and said. "Get it right this time." Then she left the kitchen with the mistress.

Sarah looked thoughtfully at the white flowers for a few seconds before throwing them away. *Christ, all that over a bouquet of flowers.*

The kitchen door swung open once more. Sarah turned to find Till, Anna and Mali's mother. Till was very dark and thin, with short black hair. She was a beautiful African woman, in her mid 30's, who spoke with a deep accent. She walked with a slight limp, and wore an ankle brace to support the fallen arch in her right foot. She came periodically from her plantation to deliver milk and other dairy products.

"Where should I put these?" Till asked, referring to the two large containers of milk she was holding.

"I....I'll take those." Sarah stammered.

Till was smiling so brightly, every ivory tooth displayed.

She passed the milk to Sarah and said. "Today's the day I get my daughters back. Master Miles went into debt a short while ago, and had to sell the girls. My husband almost worked himself to death to help Master Miles buy them back. We had the money by Easter, but the Master said it would be the proper thing to wait until after the holiday. He's in the next room negotiating Anna and Mali's return now."

Sarah froze. She didn't know what to say. Her eyes filled up with tears as she thought to herself. *Dear God she doesn't know.*

Chapter 14

Later that night Sarah and Marlette reached Blue Valley and climbed down from their horses.

"I can't believe Till came for Anna and Mali today. That's so screwed up. She only missed them by a couple of days." Marlette said, as she picked a handful of red daisies and added them to her basket.

Sarah packed her basket with flowers and replied. "I didn't have the heart to tell her the truth. What was I supposed to say? Your daughters are missing and most likely dead! Till and her husband raised enough profits for Master Miles to get the girls back by Easter. If he'd gotten off his ass and come as soon as he had the money, Anna and Mali would be alive right now!" Sarah shouted in anguish.

"So what did you tell her?" Marlette asked.

"I told Till they ran away." Sarah replied.

"How did she take it?" Marlette questioned.

"She expressed sorrow because she'd probably never see them again. She was relieved because all she could offer Anna and Mali was a life of slavery. It was the strangest thing." Sarah explained.

Marlette shuddered when she heard a noise in the distance. She grabbed her lantern and whipped around; glaring in all directions.

"Sarah, did you hear that?" Marlette asked.

"Hear what?" Sarah replied.

"I could've sworn I heard footsteps." Marlette explained.

A cold sensation trickled down Sarah's spine.

"They would wait until the week some crazy person is dismembering slave girls, to send us out in the middle of the night." Sarah complained.

"Shhh, I can see a light coming from behind that rock. It's probably just runaways from a nearby plantation. We should see if they need help." Marlette said as she held the lantern out in front of her and walked in the direction of the noise.

Sarah grabbed a second lantern and followed close behind her. As they approached the footsteps grew louder. They began to hear muffled conversations. They worked together to push aside the big boulder, which covered the entrance to a large cave.

"What are ya'll doing out here!" Marlette demanded.

The cave held seventeen of the field slaves from the Colburn plantation and ten of the area's white kids.

There were torches along the walls to light the place. The young women and men were dancing and playing harmonicas, banjos, fiddles, drums, and other instruments. Their ages ranged from mid teens to mid twenties. Most of the young white people were poor, but there were a few from wealthy families that didn't hesitate to sneak enough of their father's whiskey, brandy, and wine to go around.

Sarah and Marlette looked around in awe. There was something so incredibly strange about this scene. No one was giving or receiving orders. Everyone was speaking to one another casually. All formalities had been dropped at the entrance. In this place there was no master and servant, black and white, or rich and poor. There was just a bunch of young people having a great time.

The girls paused when approached by a striking young man with brown hair, a chiseled frame, and eyes like sparkling diamonds. He kissed Marlette's hand and then Sarah's.

"So we meet again, Lord Arrington." Marlette said over the music.

"We urge you lovely ladies to stay and have a glass of wine with us. The titles aren't necessary. Just plain Phillip will do." Phillip requested.

"We would love to Lord Arrington but we really must be going." Marlette replied in a snide tone.

She was certain to emphasize Phillip's title. She could tell that he hated it.

"Perhaps another night then?" Phillip asked.

Sarah stood back and watched. She found this constant face off between Phillip and her sister to be amusing.

"We'd love to come back another night, Phillip." Sarah blurted out, to make things more interesting.

Marlette elbowed Sarah for making such a bold statement, and pulled her out of the cave.

"I'll be looking forward to seeing you again!" Phillip hollered after them as they made their way back to the horses.

"What have you got against Phillip? He really seems like a nice man." Sarah asked as she adjusted her horse's saddle, threw one foot in the stirrup, and climbed on.

Marlette boarded her mare and scolded Sarah. "Lord Arrington is a spoiled ass, who takes the privileged life he was born into for granted. I loathe the very sight of that man. Why would you tell him we'll be back? You know Poppa would kill us both."

"What Poppa doesn't know won't hurt him. For the same reason he won't hurt us. Race you to the stables!" Sarah yelled back to Marlette as she took off on her spotted Mustang.

It was a quarter till noon, and Sarah couldn't wait to fill Mathew in about the previous night's events. She glanced out of the kitchen window and saw him outside chopping wood with Seth and Aaron. She briefly prepared a basket of sandwiches and fresh fruit. She grabbed the basket of food in her left hand. On her right hand, she balanced glasses of lemonade, tea, and water. She carefully backed out of the door, and made her way to the lumber yard.

Sarah's friend Leah met her half way to the lumber yard. Leah relieved Sarah of the sterling silver tray that held the drinks.

"Thanks. How'd you manage to leave the field so early today?" Sarah questioned.

"I was sick as a dog, but I'm feeling better now. Your dad sent me to the infirmary to see Aunt Lizzie." Leah explained as they continued forward.

The crack of the splitting wood grew louder as Leah and Sarah approached. Mathew, Seth, and Aaron continued to work without noticing the girls. Seth had grown to be 6'3'' with smoky gray eyes and caramel brown skin. He was the most well dressed, well educated, and well spoken slave on the plantation. He had a tiny trail of freckles across a perfect nose and a rock solid physique. Aaron had dark seductive eyes, and skin the color of milk chocolate. He had full sensuous lips, wash board abs and a smile that captivated.

There certainly wasn't a single ugly duckling in the bunch since Mathew had grown up to be quite the looker as well. His jet black hair was wet with perspiration. It was an April day in Missouri, and the sun was unusually harsh. Most men of class dressed in layers of fancy clothing, and delegated any task having to do with manual labor to their slaves. Mathew, on the other hand, didn't mind doing hard work. He often wore plain black breeches that were usually covered in saw dust and wood chips and a thin white shirt with the sleeves rolled up to his elbows.

Sarah walked slowly; watching Mathew's muscles flex with every swing of the axe. He had evolved into a striking young man and it was hard for her not to notice sometimes. *Why couldn't we be born the same color? Why does color have to matter anyway?* She thought to herself.

She snapped out of her day dream when she heard Leah asking her questions. "Is it true that Seth has a bedroom in the big house?"

Sarah replied whispering. "Yeah, Seth has a master suite in the mansion. He's always been the favorite, with Emanuel ranking a close second. Emanuel is Master Colburn's right hand man and he sleeps in a shack at night like the rest of us. Both of them have to beat the girls off with a stick."

As Sarah drew closer Mathew put down his axe and relived her of the basket. He thanked her with the same charming smile he'd given her as a boy. Being this close to him allowed her to see the flecks of gold in his chestnut colored eyes and beads of sweat glistening on his perfectly tanned well sculpted body. Sarah thought to herself. *It would be so much easier for me if you were only good looking. Why do you have to be intelligent, generous, and kind hearted as well? Why do you have to be so wonderful?*

"We should all eat lunch at the brook again." Mathew suggested.

Everyone agreed, and the five of them walked toward the tunnel entrance.

"You wouldn't believe who I saw drinking and fraternizing with slaves." Sarah announced, trying to shake the impure thoughts of Mathew from her head.

"Who?" Mathew questioned.

"Phillip Arrington was partying in a cave in Blue Valley." Sarah answered.

Mathew laughed and said. "Why am I not surprised?"

"A lot of noble women and men do more than fraternize with the slaves at night, but during the day they wear masks." Seth added.

"Phillip just doesn't give a damn though. He talks to whoever he wants whenever he wants. It drives his parents nuts." Mathew replied.

They stopped at the tunnel entrance and climbed in, one after another. Aaron held up a lantern and guided the way through the dusky tunnel.

"I have to ride into Blue Valley tonight to get Francesca's stupid red daisies. I can show you where the cave is." Sarah offered as they reached White Water Brook.

Mathew nodded and said. "I'll meet you in the infirmary at eleven pm."

It was half passed eleven. The blistering sunny afternoon, had transformed into a cool pleasant evening. Sarah and Leah stood back as Mathew, Seth, and Aaron forced open the entrance to the cave at Blue Valley. Music and light blared from the opening in the cave wall; disturbing the calm silent night.

Phillip appeared at the entrance and invited everyone in. The gathering was even bigger than it had been before. It was packed with young women and men, conversing, laughing, dancing, and playing instruments.

"I'm glad all of you could make it out tonight. Have a drink. Make yourselves at home." Philip said pointing to the infinite supply of booze.

Aaron and Seth walked over to pour themselves a glass of scotch. They were snatched up almost immediately to go dance.

Sarah and Leah helped themselves to a glass of red wine.

Mathew didn't have anything to drink. It was against his morals. He found himself being eye-balled by two beautiful young women, one white and the other black. They conversed amongst each other until one gained the courage to step forward. A pretty girl with fair skin, auburn hair, and green eyes, asked him to dance. He extended a hand to the girl and promptly accepted.

Sarah felt a hint of jealousy when she noticed Mathew disappear for a while. *What am I thinking? I should be happy for him.* She scolded herself as she poured another glass of wine.

"I need some fresh air. I don't feel so good." Leah announced as she made her way to the exit.

Sarah followed her outside and said. "You only had half a glass of wine."

Leah felt better as soon as the night air hit her.

She turned to Sarah and confessed. "It's not the wine. I'm pregnant."

"Congratulations. When will you tell the father?" Sarah asked, excited for her friend.

"He already knows. He doesn't want anything to do with me or the baby. Now he's messing with some twelve-year-old girl named May; lousy pervert." Leah explained.

She then buried her face in her hands and sobbingly confessed the father to be Abraham.

Sarah hugged her and said. "It'll be alright. I'll see if the mistress has some work around the house for you. You can't labor in the field all day long anymore. You could lose your baby like that. I see it happen a lot."

"Is everything alright?" Mathew asked as he wandered out of the cave.

Leah quickly wiped away her tears and straitened herself up.

"Everything's fine." She replied.

"How are things going with your friend?" Sarah asked Mathew, changing the subject.

Mathew laughed and replied. "That was Katherine McKinley, Dr. McKinley's daughter. It was going well at first. She kissed me a few times, and gave me an invitation to her sixteenth birthday party. Then Phillip informed me that she's already betrothed to my uncle, Pete Colburn. She had too many glasses of brandy that's all."

They all had a good laugh at Mathew's misfortune and returned to the party.

Sarah wouldn't have laughed quite so free heartedly if she knew the killer was with her that night. In fact she had been trailed, stalked, and watched from afar for years. At that very moment the eyes of her greatest admirer were fixed on her, as she filled her glass and chatted with Leah.

I've been patiently waiting for you, Sarah. The killer thought as he blended into the crowd and peered at her from a distance. *I orchestrated an attack on two girls just to tide myself over. Mali and Anna couldn't pacify my urges for long. Nothing seems to quench my hunger for you. I have an insatiable lust that only you can gratify. Each passing day I yearn for the touch of your skin and the warmth that follows. Now the time has come to take another in your place, and pleasure myself to thoughts of you. This substitution will suffice for now; but Sarah, my sweet Sarah, I will have you soon enough.*

Chapter 15

It was nearly noon and Mathew had been missing since breakfast. Sarah could only think of one place he would be. *I'll take his lunch out to the barn. Something's obviously bothering him. It's Master Colburn's first day back and he's already managed to upset Mathew.* She thought as she arranged the food and drink on a silver platter.

She walked outside to find a blanket of gray clouds stretched across the sky. The humidity was unbearable, yet it refused to rain. She balanced the tray on one hand and pushed open the barn door with the other. There he was at his work bench, just as she suspected.

"I brought you a bite to eat Master Mathew." Sarah said as she walked into the barn.

"Just sit the tray over there. I wish to be alone right now." Mathew said sternly as he snatched a gray tarp down over what he was working on.

"What has your father done now?" Sarah asked with a concerned expression, as she sat the tray of food aside.

"My father isn't the problem. It's you!" Mathew replied vehemently.

"What did I do?!" Sarah demanded.

Mathew gave Sarah an unforgiving scowl and said. "Why didn't you tell me you were engaged to be married?"

Her concerned expression abruptly changed to one of confusion.

"I don't know what you're talking about!" She shouted, waiving her hands in frustration.

She bumped the glass of orange juice by accident. It went tumbling to the ground, spilling all of its contents.

Mathew snapped. "I overheard your mother and my father discussing it early this morning. He's going to buy your freedom. The wedding is in two weeks."

"Who, Mathew? Who am I marrying?!" Sarah demanded.

"Abraham, my father's blacksmith!" Mathew answered impatiently.

He turned his back to her and stormed off in the direction of the big house.

Sarah walked quickly behind him, almost having to run to keep up, and pleaded. "Please come to Blue Valley tonight. We won't have another chance to talk unless you do. I need to know what's going on."

Her cries fell on deaf ears as Mathew continued trudging toward the mansion.

Sarah walked back into the barn to clean up the broken glass. A strong wind blew, and the tarp flapped momentarily before sliding off the work bench. She felt that much worse when she caught a glimpse of Mathew's project. *My grandpa's spear, Mathew fixed it. This is what he's been out here working on.*

Sarah stormed out to the nursery and weaved through the mass of noisy children. She stood before her mother speechless. Violet was beaming. Sarah had never seen her so happy.

"Sarah! I have great news." Violet said as she reached over and hugged her. "Abraham's willing to buy your freedom. It's official; the wedding's in two weeks."

"Momma how could you!" Sarah demanded.

Violet looked up with surprise and said. "Abraham told me you two were in love. He informed me you were too embarrassed to tell me yourself, so you asked him to do it. I figured you wouldn't pass up a catch like Emanuel unless there was a better offer on the table."

"I hold nothing but contempt for that man. Everyone and everything I know and love is here. He's going to take me away to his house in the city." Sarah replied solemnly.

"You'll be free. Your babies will be free. Isn't that what you wanted?" Violet asked with a confused expression.

Sarah shook her head in anger and disbelief and replied. "I don't consider being bound for life to a man I loathe the same as freedom. What's the difference between being a slave to the Colburns and a slave to Abraham? My slave status will remain the same. The only thing that will change is the owner."

"What have I done?" Violet said as she sat down in a rocking chair.

Her eyes filled with tears. She began to sob uncontrollably.

"Why does it look like a funeral in here?" Marlette asked as she walked into the nursery.

"Actually it's a wedding Momma's crying over, my wedding to be exact." Sarah explained.

"I thought you wanted Sarah to marry Emanuel. He's a nice man. I don't understand why you're sad Momma." Marlette said as she walked over to console her mother.

Violet explained between heaving sobs. "It's not Emanuel she's betrothed to. Abraham told me they were in love. So I petitioned a marriage from Master Colburn this morning. Abraham put such a hefty offer on the table for Sarah's freedom, that their union became a business deal. It's no longer up to me and your father, what happens. Either Abraham or Master Colburn will have to call off the wedding."

Marlette glanced out the window and darted outside without saying a word. She saw Abraham on his way to the smithy and walked briskly over to him.

"Congratulations. I hear you're marrying my little sister." Marlette said with her arms outstretched for a hug.

Abraham smiled and embraced her. Marlette delivered a swift knee to his groin, and he fell to the ground in the fetal position.

Marlette shouted at him. "You lying bastard! My sister despises you! My mother is inconsolable! You just wait until I tell my father! He'll have your head on a spit for this!"

Sarah pulled Marlette away and said. "Beating the crap out of him won't change anything! Poppa can't know what Abraham's done. We must allow Poppa to think this is what I wanted. Abraham isn't a slave. He works for the Colburn's. Poppa will lose his job and be strapped to the whipping post for confronting Abraham."

"Then what do you think we should do?" Marlette asked.

Abraham climbed to his feet and dusted himself off.

He threw back his head and laughed. "There's nothing you can do about it."

Chapter 16

The humidity had grown so heavy by nightfall that it felt as if Sarah was breathing under water. The clouds over head were so dense that not a single star was visible. It had been a sticky, miserable, day and by evening it still hadn't rained. She tied up her horse and entered the cave at Blue Valley. She scanned the faces looking for Mathew. He didn't have lunch at White Water Brook with her and the rest of the crew. He'd spent the majority of the afternoon avoiding her at all costs.

She caught a glimpse of Katherine McKinley, the pretty girl with the reddish-brown hair Mathew was dancing with the night before. Katherine was conversing and having a glass of wine with a beautiful young black girl named Sally. Sally was Katherine's ladies maid. The two were inseparable.

"Miss McKinley, have you seen Mathew Colburn?" Sarah called out to her over the music.

"You must be Sarah. He's been blathering on and on about you all night. I'll take you to him." Katherine said with a roll of her eyes.

"Sally, can you tell Clyde to prepare the carriage. We really must be going soon." Katherine requested.

Sally nodded and left the cave. Katherine took Sarah by the hand and led her through the crowd. They found Mathew huddled in a corner with a glass of whiskey in hand.

Sarah gasped and said. "Mathew, oh my goodness! You're drunk!"

Mathew took another gulp from his glass and slurred. "It was lovely to find out that you're in love with this guy and you've been courting him in secret for two months! You told me you hated Abraham."

"I do hate him! And even if I love him, what the hell does it matter to you?" Sarah demanded.

"I love you Sarah. It just didn't dawn on me until I was faced with losing you forever." Mathew admitted.

He lost consciousness moments later. Sarah took the glass of whiskey out of his hand. With Katherine's help she pulled him to his feet.

"I'll help you get him outside." Katherine offered.

She put Mathew's arm over her shoulders and Sarah did the same.

"Thank you." Sarah said as they dragged him out of the cave.

Sarah and Katherine laid him sideways over the mustang.

"You're a lucky girl. He really does love you." Katherine said with a slight grin.

"He's drunk. He would never say anything like that otherwise." Sarah replied as she untied the horse.

She rubbed the mustang's spotted face and it whinnied.

"My mother always said a drunk tongue tells the sober truth. It seems we have something in common. We're both engaged to complete scoundrels." Katherine said.

Sarah laughed and led the horse away by the reigns.

She glanced over her shoulder and called back to Katherine. "Thanks for everything."

Katherine gave a slight wave and walked in the opposite direction to her carriage. Her driver, Clyde tipped his hat to her and climbed behind the reigns. Sally adjusted the luggage strapped to the back of the carriage.

"Everything's packed, Miss Katherine." Sally said with a slap on the large black trunk. "You can still go home and get married tomorrow, if you've changed your mind about leaving." Sally continued.

"Not a chance in hell." Katherine replied vehemently.

Katherine boarded the stagecoach with Sally. There was a small window in the front of the carriage they could see Clyde through. Katherine gave a knock on the window to tell Clyde they were ready. He cracked the whip and the horses began to gallop.

"There's still time to drop you off in case you've changed your mind." Katherine said to Sally.

"I belong where ever you are Miss Katherine." Sally assured her.

"You really must stop calling me Miss. We're going to Canada where we can all be free." Katherine instructed her then went on to say. "We just have one last stop to make. I want to visit my mother's grave for the last time."

Sally pulled out a bottle of champagne. The cork flew across the carriage with a loud pop. Champagne foamed out of the top of the bottle, and she filled two flutes.

Sally raised her glass high and said. "I would like to propose a toast to my best friend Katherine and our freedom."

"To Freedom!" The girls shouted, clinked glasses, and drank.

Katherine set aside her champagne flute when she noticed the stagecoach speed past the grave yard.

"Clyde! You passed the cemetery!" Katherine shouted and knocked on the window.

Clyde cracked the whip and the horses took off even faster.

"Clyde! Stop this carriage at once!" Sally screamed and beat on the window.

Clyde cracked the whip again. The horses were galloping at lighting speed. Sally and Katherine grabbed hold of each other to prevent being tossed all over.

"Stop this carriage at once!" They bellowed.

The carriage was traveling so fast Clyde's suit jacket flapped in the wind like a flag. His hat went flying off of his head and he turned and gave the girls a sinister grin. Sally and Katherine screamed in horror when they realized it wasn't Clyde driving at all. They hit a bump and the girls tumbled onto the floor. Katherine stared up at the large black trunk through the back window of the stagecoach. Blood was beginning to seep from its' seams and hinges. Katherine clung to Sally and wailed in terror as she realized where the real Clyde was.

Chapter 17

Like the other master suites in the big house, Mathew had a bedroom fit for a king: spacious quarters, with a private bath tub, high ceiling, and large arched windows. His bed was enormous; covered with only the finest linens, pillows, and comforters.

Mathew hurt all over when he woke up the next morning. He had a massive headache, a rancid taste in his mouth, and almost no recollection of the night before. He sat up in his bed with a groan, and fought down the wave of nausea that washed over him. He glanced at the clock on the wall. *How did I manage to sleep until 11:15am? I missed Katherine and Uncle Pete's wedding. Why on earth am I naked?* He thought as he scanned his massive bedroom for fallen clothing. He wrapped a sheet around his waist and shuffled over to the window. He peered across the lawn, and spotted last night's clothes hanging on the line to dry. *How did I get home last night?*

Mathew cleaned himself up and threw on a fresh pair of pants and shirt. He was lathering up his face for a shave when he heard a knock on his bedroom door.

"It's Seth!" Called the voice from the other side of the door.

"Come In!" Mathew shouted. "Just leave the door open and let the breeze blow through. It seems to have finally cooled off." Mathew instructed as Seth entered the room.

Seth walked over and said. "That's because it finally rained. In fact there was a really nasty storm last night. There are fallen trees all over town."

"I must've slept right through it." Mathew said in disbelief.

"It's good to see you in the land of the living again. Sir, you look like eight miles of rough road." Seth joked as Mathew swiped his straight razor up and down a leather belt to sharpen it.

"I feel like eight miles of rough road." Mathew admitted in a gruff voice.

He ran the razor over his jaw, taking off a stripe of soap and stubble. He rinsed the razor in a bowl of water, flung off the excess liquid, and repeated the process.

Mabel peered in at Seth through Mathew's doorway. *Now's my opportunity to wipe that smug little grin off of his face.* She thought.

Seth straightened his collar in the mirror and said. "I'm proposing to Leah today. She's obviously not with what's-his-name anymore so... "

"Seth there's something you should know." Mabel interrupted from Mathew's doorway.

"Was anyone talking to her? I sure as hell wasn't. Were you?" Seth asked Mathew sarcastically.

Mathew laughed and shook his head no.

"What is it Mabel?" Seth asked with utter exasperation.

Mabel sauntered into the room and said. "I just thought you'd like to know that your precious Leah sleeps around. The only reason that girl was moved into the kitchen from the field is because she's big-bellied."

Seth turned red with aggravation and yelled. "I know she's pregnant Mabel! I made her that way! Now fix my God damned lunch, and stop wasting my time!"

She looked dumbfounded for a few moments then stammered. "My apologies Seth, I was just looking out for you. I didn't know you were the one..."

Mabel was entirely defeated. She bolted out the door and retreated to the kitchen like a dog that had been kicked in the backside.

"I hate that nosey old bitch!" Seth said as he stomped over to the door and slammed it so hard it nearly came unhinged.

Mathew wiped off his face with a towel and said. "Congratulations Seth. I didn't know you and Leah were...."

"We're not." Seth interrupted.

He slumped onto the bed and fell silent.

"I'm sorry." Mathew replied and patted Seth on the shoulder.

Seth stood up and said. "You know what, I don't care. I love her and I'm asking her to marry me."

"Good Luck." Mathew said with a nod.

Seth stopped short of the door and replied. "I don't need luck I'm Seth."

He ran into Mathew's parents in the hallway and asked. "How was the wedding?"

"The wedding was uneventful." Mistress Colburn told Seth.

"Ahhh, your typical boring nuptial." Seth replied.

Master Colburn went on to explain. "No. Uneventful as in there was no event. Katherine McKinley left my oldest brother standing at the altar in front of all our family and friends. Apparently she packed all her belongings and ran off with Dr. McKinley's money, his stagecoach, four of his horses, and two of his servants."

"I'm sorry to hear that." Seth replied.

Mr. Colburn grumbled. "I warned Pete not to choose a 15-year-old girl for a bride. The man's pushing fifty. He's so humiliated he's actually considering moving back to New Orleans."

"I almost forgot. Today is the day isn't it?" Mistress Colburn said, with a smile.

Seth nodded and replied. "Mabel tried her very best to ruin things. I can't deal with her anymore. She went too far this time."

Mrs. Colburn hugged Seth and said. "I wish you and Leah the best. Don't allow Mabel to drive a wedge between you."

Mr. Colburn gave Seth an approving slap on the shoulder and said. "Go get her."

Seth found Leah leaned over the kitchen sink, up to her elbows in soap suds. She looked even more beautiful than the last time he saw her. She was dressed in a black house servant's gown, which was far more flattering than the baggy tan summer dress she formerly wore in the field. The bell rang for noon break and she dried her hands on her apron. She turned to grab the picnic basket when she noticed Seth standing there.

"Where's Mabel?" Seth asked.

"She went to snitch on a field servant for sneaking a ham from the smokehouse." Leah answered.

"That woman thrives on the misery of others. Leave the basket and come with me." Seth instructed.

Leah followed Seth outside. They carefully stepped around the fallen branches until they reached the pond near the infirmary. They walked out on the dock which had a small boat tied to it. The entire inside was covered in rose petals. Seth helped Leah into the tiny vessel. He untied the boat, and then rowed out on the shimmering water. He stopped under a large willow tree, which grew over the pond. Its hair-like branches hung clear down to the water and hid them from the entire plantation.

"Seth there's something you need to know." Leah said nervously.

Seth interrupted and said. "Please allow me just five minutes. I know Mabel has probably told you all sorts of horrible things about me. Today I'm going to separate fact from fiction. No, I haven't had numerous affairs with white women. Yes, I slept with one once at a Christmas party. It was a long time ago and I was drunk as all hell." Leah chuckled and Seth continued. "Yes, the Colburn's legally adopted me. No, I'm not a slave. I can leave whenever I want. Yes, I am privileged, cocky, even borderline arrogant. I admit to being all these things, but I'm not the whore Mabel made me out to be and neither are you. I already know you're pregnant and I don't care. I didn't bring you out here to pry into your past. It's irrelevant. I only have one important question for you."

"And that is?" Leah asked.

Seth took both of Leah's hands in his. He locked his beautiful gray eyes on hers and asked. "Do you love me? Because if you do nothing else matters."

Leah's eyes filled with tears as she replied. "More than anything in this world."

"Then marry me." Seth said with a passionate kiss.

Sarah spent much of her day in the infirmary. She knew Mathew would be at the brook, and she'd been avoiding him all day. Aunt Lizzie was away delivering a baby on a nearby plantation and there were no patients at the moment. She sat on one of the beds confessing her sins to Marlette in hope of receiving useful advice. Marlette had become a mastermind at cleaning up the messes Sarah made for herself. Marlette paced back and forth in front of her. Sarah knew that was a sign her sister was really mad.

"I can't believe you went back to that place!" Marlette scolded her, referring to the Blue Valley cave. Sarah looked away and Marlette continued. "I warned you not to spend so much time with Mathew, but you didn't listen to me. You never listen to me! Mathew's not the type to take you against your will, but you have to end this. It's already gotten out of hand."

"And how do you suppose I go about ending it?" Sarah asked.

"What have you done so far?" Marlette questioned.

"So far all I've done is avoid him. I didn't know what else to do." Sarah admitted.

"Good that's a start. Now just let him know you don't feel the same way. Tell him you don't love him." Marlette instructed.

Sarah shook her head no and said. "I can't."

"Why not?" Marlette demanded.

"Because it's cruel, and a lie!" Sarah shouted.

Marlette's eyes narrowed with agitation as she replied. "Then lie to him. You've gotten good at doing it to me."

Sarah's eyes filled with tears as she spoke. "I'm sorry for lying to you. I promise to never do it again."

Marlette sat down on the bed and hugged her as she cried.

She passed Sarah a tissue and said. "I know you care for Mathew, but the decisions you make affect us all. If the Master and Mistress suspect you of corrupting their son, they could banish our entire family to the field. Momma and Poppa would lose everything they worked for. The Colburns could have you sent to another plantation far away. We might never see you again. Or even worse, they might have you hanged. If they did that they wouldn't have any other choice but to kill me, because I would take them out." Sarah smiled through her tears and Marlette continued. "Now I'm sorry you think you love him, but this has to stop."

"I understand." Sarah agreed.

Marlette rose from her seat and said. "Now I just have to figure out which one of these venomous reptiles or insects to slip into Abraham's bunk."

Sarah's eyes widened with surprise.

She pulled her sister away from the wall of slithering, poisonous animals and shouted. "Marlette, you can't kill him!"

"Well I can't think of anything else to stop the wedding." Marlette protested.

Someone knocked on the infirmary door.

"It looks like you have a patient. I should probably go." Marlette said.

As she walked out a five year old slave boy entered the infirmary. He was covered from head to toe in bumps. Sarah sat the boy on a stool and examined him. She took a bottle from the cabinet and began rubbing the thick pink liquid on the affected areas. She looked up and noticed Mathew standing in the doorway. She shot him a dirty look and focused her attention back on the boy.

Sarah finished administering the medicine and instructed the child. "Tell your momma to put this lotion on you once in the morning and once at night. Remember not to scratch. If it doesn't clear up in a week or so, come back and see me."

"Yes, Miss Sarah." The child replied and went about his way.

"What's wrong with him?" Mathew asked as he walked into the infirmary and took a seat.

"He's got the pox." Sarah answered.

"My goodness, the small pox?" Mathew questioned.

Sarah removed the scowl from her face and laughed a little. "No Sir, Just the chicken pox. What do you do with all those medical books? You obviously don't read them."

"The rare occasion I'm awake in class I doodle on the pages. You can have them if you want. I'll teach you how to read them." Mathew offered.

"You know that's illegal. Your father would kill you." Sarah warned then went on to say. "I'm sorry I had to remove your clothes. You puked bourbon all over yourself and me. I had to wash away the evidence before the Master and Mistress woke up."

Mathew's handsome face turned bright red with embarrassment.

"I actually came out here to apologize for last night." Mathew explained.

Sarah smirked and replied sarcastically. "Exactly what are you sorry for? Are you referring to the three times you called me a liar or the two times you told me to go to hell? Maybe you're just sorry for painting my wardrobe with your dinner."

"You're not going to make this easy for me are you?" Mathew asked with a grin.

Sarah scoffed and replied. "Not a chance, but if you assist me today all is forgiven."

Mathew let out a long exasperated breath thinking. *I possess neither the interest nor the stomach for working in such a place, but there's no way I can admit it. If assisting Sarah for a few hours will earn her forgiveness, it has to be done.* At last he grudgingly agreed.

At that moment a frantic slave woman appeared with her eight year old son in her arms. The woman was horrified, and the child was crying and sniffling. Mathew took the child from her and laid him on one of the beds for Sarah to examine. His right foot was completely dislocated and faced inward.

"How did this happen?" Sarah asked.

The woman grew hysterical and babbled the response in French. The only words Sarah understood were *Robert Welch*.

Chapter 18

Sarah turned to Mathew and said. "She must be Creole. Can you understand her?"

"Her dialect is very different from my mother's, but I believe she said Robert Welch struck her son for not working fast enough, and the boy tripped over a fallen tree limb." Mathew interpreted then went on to say. "What kind of despicable, pathetic excuse for a man would do this to a child?"

Sarah searched through a cabinet of medicine and said. "Over half the injuries that come through these doors are caused by overseers. It's not just Robert."

She grabbed a vile of ether and a piece of cloth and returned to the boy.

"Tell the mother I'll need to sedate him while we set the broken ankle. The pain will be excruciating if I don't." She informed Mathew.

Mathew stopped in the middle of his translation and said. "What do you mean, we?"

I want no part of this. He thought, peering at the boys grotesquely distorted leg.

"You agreed to assist me." Sarah reminded him.

She splashed the chemical on the cloth then covered the boy's nose and mouth. The child struggled momentarily, but lost consciousness in a matter of seconds. Then she placed Mathew's hands on the boy's lower calf, and grabbed hold of the dislocated foot.

She looked at Mathew from the end of the bed and instructed. "On the count of three, yank back as hard as you can. One, two, three…"

There was a grinding noise and a loud nauseating pop as Sarah forced the bones and joints back into place.

Sarah gave Mathew an approving nod and a smile then said. "You did a great job. See that wasn't so bad. Now all we have to do is splint and wrap it."

That was the sickest most horrific thing I've ever witnessed. Mathew thought as he battled with his gag reflex.

He forced a smile for Sarah and lied. "No, it wasn't that bad at all."

Where is Francesca when you need her? The mistress thought as she sat in the elegant parlor with Phillip Arrington and his 15-year-old brother Maxwell. *My niece Francesca is well versed in literature, world history and the arts. She displays all the proper etiquette of a lady of the French court. She's just who I need at the moment to entertain our young royal guests.*

The Demoniets were enjoying an afternoon ride and Master Colburn left briefly on business. This left only Mistress Colburn and her wayward daughter Lillian to entertain the Arrington brothers.

Maxwell Arrington was a dashing beau with hazel eyes and hair the color of fire. He took after their mother, and Phillip looked more like their father.

Phillip took a sip from his glass and laid out his proposition. "My father has fallen deathly ill and is not expected to recover. He relinquished his Lordship to me for this reason. My mother planned a gathering for tonight to announce the passing of this title. Royalty from all over Europe are expected to show up in a matter of hours. Thanks to last night's storm, there is an enormous oak tree lying in our grand ballroom. This damage will take weeks to repair. You have a reputation for putting together this town's most lavish parties. I thought it would be a smashing idea if you would do me the honor of hosting this evening's event."

The mistress' gray eyes lit up like stars. *This would be the grandest event the state of Missouri's ever seen.*

"We'll do it." Mistress Colburn announced barely able to maintain her composure.

Phillip passed Mrs. Colburn the guest list and seating arrangement and said. "Thank you for extending a hand in our greatest time of need. You will be greatly compensated."

"I'll just pass these on to my head chef." The Mistress said delighted.

Mabel sauntered over. She gave Leah a smug grin and casually accepted the guest list.

Mistress Colburn smiled politely at Mabel and said. "Would you mind taking these to Leah? She's our new head cook now. You've been sold to the Arringtons. Pack your belongings. You're leaving after the ball."

Mabel's eyes grew as big as saucers. She stood in the parlor with her mouth wide open and her brows furrowed.

The mistress stood up and whispered in Mabel's ear. "You've given us many years of service. This is the only reason you're not bound to a whipping post right now. Nobody messes with my children this includes Seth."

Leah, who was serving refreshments to the guests, almost fainted. *I just started working in the kitchen. I don't know how to coordinate such an event.* She thought as Mabel picked her jaw up off the floor, and grudgingly forked over the guest list and seating arrangement.

"Welcome to the house." The mistress said to Leah.

"Bullox!" Maxwell shouted and stormed out of the room.

Phillip walked out after him and said. "Maxwell, you're being rude."

"Our father is dying! I'm sorry I don't feel that's a cause for a bloody celebration." Maxwell said with aggravation.

Phillip gave his brother a supportive hand on the shoulder and said. "I don't like it anymore than you do. I feel this whole idea is rubbish, but its tradition. You know Mother won't allow this to rest. Let's just get it over with."

"You're right." Maxwell said with a deep breath, and then walked back into the parlor.

"Is everything alright?" The Mistress asked.

"Our father's dying. It's been a long week for him." Phillip answered, knowing that it had been a long week for both of them.

Phillip had the ability to be charming and charismatic under any circumstances. This rare capability was a gift because no one ever knew when he was suffering, but it was also a curse for the same reason.

"How about, you add an item to the menu. It can be anything you desire." The Mistress offered.

Maxwell pondered for a while then said. "Deer, my father loved deer. I haven't eaten it in ages."

The Mistress smiled and replied. "I'll send my servant Aaron. He's an accomplished marksmen the best hunter I've ever seen."

Phillip thought for a moment then told Maxwell. "You should accompany him. You always enjoyed hunting with father. It may help take your mind off of things."

Maxwell agreed and the mistress said. "Lillian, please show young Mr. Arrington to the hunting lodge."

Lillian felt uncomfortable and out of place. She was actually clean for once, and the mistress forced her into one of Francesca's elegant purple gowns. Lillian had no nice gowns of her own. She was hard on dresses and her father refused to continue wasting money on designer gowns for her to destroy.

"Right this way" Lillian said and led Maxwell up the corridor and down the cement steps.

She walked through the lumber yard and called out. "Aaron! You've been summoned for a hunt!"

Aaron dropped his axe and jogged over to Lillian and Maxwell.

"What game are we hunting?" Aaron asked as they headed toward the lodge.

"Wild bucks, we'll need two of them to serve the guests this evening." Maxwell answered.

The hunting lodge was a spacious log cabin, built in the shape of a pyramid. The inside walls were line with the heads of moose, and bucks. A bearskin rug lay stretched out in front of an elegant stone fire place. Various animal hides decorated the backs of the chairs and couches. There was a table designed especially for skinning and filleting. More than thirty rifles stood on display.

"This place is a hunters dream." Maxwell said as he stepped in and marveled at the structure.

"My brother Mathew designed and constructed it himself as a gift for our father's birthday. Aaron made most of these kills." Lillian told him.

"You can change in the room over there." Aaron instructed.

Maxwell threw on a green safari shirt with short sleeves and numerous pockets, His tan colored breeches were the usual hunting style: loose at the thighs and fitting around the ankles. He wore tall black boots that came clear up to his calves and a safari hat with a brim at the front and back. Maxwell walked out of the room in shock to see Lillian dressed in the same attire he was. She had discarded the beautiful purple dress she was wearing, and glanced over the gun rack for the rifle of her choice.

"You couldn't possibly be coming with us." Maxwell announced.

Lillian grinned and replied. "You know when I said that Aaron made the majority of these kills. Well I made a few of them as well."

Maxwell scoffed and said. "There's no way I'm taking a woman hunting."

Lillian took offence and replied. "I'll bet you two weeks allowance that I take down a bigger deer then you do."

"Since only two kills are needed I'll serve as your guide this afternoon." Aaron said with a respectful nod and led them to the woods.

"How old are you?" Maxwell asked still a little bewildered.

"I'll be thirteen tomorrow." Lillian chimed in as she tracked through the woods with the rifle on her shoulder.

"Why is it that I didn't merit an invitation to your coming out party?" Maxwell asked.

Lillian laughed and said. "I'm not having one."

Maxwell glared at her with a confused look and asked. "How else will you be introduced into society? How will you meet suitors? How will you marry? How will you settle?"

Lillian grinned and replied. "I never planned upon settling. I want to travel and see the world. I want to hunt the biggest most dangerous game on every continent. You can't find ammunition around these parts for the kind of beasts I'm going to hunt. I intend to have a life of adventure."

Sarah had just finished wrapping a splint around the child's foot. The mother sat on a stool at the head of the bed. She blotted her son's forehead with a cool towel, and hummed to him as he came to. The child whined and sluggishly moved his head to and fro before opening his eyes.

Mathew and Sarah stepped outside for fresh air, and gave the mother a moment alone with her child. The sun was beginning to shine again which made the nearby pond shimmer.

Mathew looked over at Sarah and said. "You have a gift for healing. I was serious when I said that I'll teach you to read and write."

"What if your father finds out?" Sarah questioned.

Mathew bent down, picked up a stone, and skipped it across the pond.

Then he turned to Sarah and spoke. "Don't worry about my father. That hypocrite taught Seth and Emanuel to read and write. Seth and Emanuel use to go to class four days a week, same as I. When my mother was sent to Missouri to marry my father she couldn't speak a word of English. Seth's mother was a free Creole woman named Lillian who spoke both English and French fluently. She showed my mother kindness. She helped my mother adjust to life in America. She even posed as an interpreter until my mother picked up the language. They were friends up until the woman's untimely death of yellow fever. My mother swore to Lillian on her death bed she would adopt Seth and raise him like her own child. My parents later named my sister after her."

Mathew and Sarah paused when they saw Maxwell Arrington running at full speed toward them.

Maxwell heaved to catch his breath, and shouted in a panic. "There's been an accident! Lillian's hurt!"

The three of them ran as fast as their feet would carry them. They found Aaron in the woods kneeling over Lillian's unconscious body. Aaron scrambled frantically to stop the blood from pouring from her head.

Chapter 19

Lillian regained consciousness hours later. She opened her eyes and glanced around her bedroom. Dr. McKinley examined her while Mathew and Maxwell stood watch. They were all dressed in tuxedos and she was still wearing her hunting clothes. Phillip's party had just begun. She could smell the feast and hear the elegant string instruments all the way up stairs.

Dr. McKinley put on his glasses and inspected the stitches on her forehead.

He turned and spoke to Mathew in his gruff Scottish voice. "Your medical studies are paying off. These sutures are perfect. There should be very little scarring."

"Actually my servant, Sarah, stitched her up." Mathew replied.

"Well she's very talented." Dr. McKinley said as he continued his examination.

"One pupil is clearly dilated more than the other. She has a minor concussion but she'll be fine in a short while." The Doctor informed Mathew, and then placed his instruments back into their bag.

"But there was so much blood." Mathew replied.

"Head wounds have the tendency to bleed profusely. She should be back on her feet in a matter of days." Dr. McKinley explained as he rose and walked toward the door.

"Thanks for everything." Mathew said to him.

"Thanks for working on my stagecoach." Dr. McKinley replied as he left the room.

Lillian sat up in her bed and groaned. "What happened?"

Maxwell came over to explain. "You forgot to anchor the butt of the rifle in your shoulder to absorb the recoil. When you aimed and fired, the gun flew up and bonked you on the forehead."

Lillian laughed and asked. "Well did I at least get the deer?"

"You gave yourself a concussion and all you're concerned about is whether or not you got the deer." Mathew scolded playfully, then flexed his bicep and said. "Who's my big strong girl?"

Lillian answered with a flex of her arms.

Maxwell replied excitedly. "You got it clean through the heart. It had to have been the largest buck I've ever seen. It must've had 16 points on its antlers."

"Did you get your kill?" Lillian inquired ecstatically.

"Yes, however it wasn't nearly as grand as yours." Maxwell answered.

Mistress Colburn stormed into the bedroom and said. "Lillian what have you to say for yourself?"

Lillian grinned and replied. "Venison anyone?"

Mathew and Maxwell laughed hysterically, but the mistress didn't find Lillian's remark the least bit amusing.

Mathew pulled Maxwell away and said. "Believe me. You don't want to be present for this."

The men returned to the party while Mistress Colburn berated Lillian. "You put on a ghastly display today: running about the forest and making a spectacle of yourself. And what in the world are you doing wearing trousers! This is highly inappropriate. You can see the entire form of your legs and hips! Ladies are not to wear pants!"

Lillian snapped back at her mother. "Would you rather I had gone hunting in a dress, which may have been easily snagged? If the beast had charged me, I may not have gotten away in a big fancy gown."

"We would've rather you not gone hunting at all!" Her father shouted as he entered the room. "You are a girl Lillian! A girl! How many times must I tell you you're a girl!" Master Colburn yelled out in frustration.

As the end of the night approached, Mistress Colburn and Francesca escorted the Arrington's outside. The gravel plot in front of the mansion was covered in horse drawn carriages, only this time the passengers climbing aboard were European royalty. They stopped in front of the Arrington's stagecoach. Lady Arrington was a hefty woman with red curly hair and fair skin.

Her paper thin lips parted in a smile as she said. "Your niece is a lovely young woman Mrs. Colburn, and as always we had a splendid time. It was truly remarkable the way you pulled the whole thing together on such short notice. I hope it wasn't too much trouble."

Mrs. Colburn beamed and replied. "It was no trouble at all. It's been an honor to host your party."

"Thank you once again Mrs. Colburn. I'm certain you'll find the payment agreeable." Phillip said as he passed the mistress a small black velvet sack. Then he boarded the stagecoach.

Lady Arrington turned to Francesca and said. "I appreciate the manor in which you kept my youngest son company, the entire evening. I haven't seen Maxwell smile like that since before his father fell ill."

Francesca gave Lady Arrington a charming smile and replied. "The pleasure was all mine, I rather enjoyed his company."

Lady Arrington smiled once more at Francesca before boarding the stagecoach.

Maxwell kissed Francesca's hand and said. "I had a lovely time. Thank you."

He turned to Mrs. Colburn and asked. "May I trouble you to return tomorrow afternoon?"

Mistress Colburn smiled and replied. "It would be no trouble at all. You're always welcome in our home."

Maxwell climbed into the stagecoach and it pulled away. Francesca watched the carriage disappear thinking. *I never cease to amaze myself. I managed to snag an Arrington. I could've probably taken the oldest had he not already been betrothed.*

The next day on twelve pm break Sarah walked through the dim musty tunnel that led to White Water Brook. She was informed that Mathew wouldn't be there so she figured it would be alright to go. *Marlette is right. We've spent entirely too much time together. The decisions I make effect more than just me. It hurt so bad to deny myself those reading lessons, but it had to be done. If Mathew teaches me to read not only will we be spending a lot more time together, we'll be spending the majority of that time alone. I don't know if I could handle that.*

She reached the cave and carefully weaved her way through it. She could already hear the waterfall rushing. She was beginning to smell the sweet spring flowers. She could hear the song of the birds and the scurrying of the squirrels and chipmunks. The brook was a beautiful place she never tired of visiting. She reached the opening to the brook and climbed out. On a large blanket sat Aaron, Seth, Leah, and much to her surprise, Mathew. Sarah and Mathew looked surprised to see one another then cast an evil eye on Aaron.

As she joined everyone Aaron said to her. "Yes I lied to you, and no I'm not sorry. This has gone on long enough. Mathew's avoiding you. Then you're avoiding Mathew. This is childish. We're all supposed to be friends."

Seth added with irritation. "Leah and I got engaged the other day and instead of celebrating with us, you were too busy avoiding each other. I don't know what happened the other night at Blue Valley nor do I care. All I know is this awkwardness is ending here today."

Leah spoke in a frustrated tone. "We think you two should just kiss and get it over with. The lack of knowing whether or not there's chemistry is driving you both insane. And you are driving your friends insane."

Sarah laughed and replied. "I don't feel that way about Mathew. We've been close since we were in swaddling clothes."

Mathew turned to them and said. "That won't be necessary. Sarah and I have been pals for a long time, nothing more. I was afraid of losing her as a friend that's all."

Aaron replied sarcastically. "If you have no romantic feelings for her then it should be that much easier to kiss her. You've both gotten on my nerves so bad that neither of you are leaving this place today until you do."

Sarah rolled her eyes and said. "Well I hope you brought an extra blanket because we're spending the night."

Leah announced. "Well there you have it. They obviously like each other or they wouldn't have made such a big deal out of a kiss."

Mathew grew irritated and asked. "If I kiss Sarah will you leave us alone?"

"You'll never hear another word about it." Leah said making an X over her heart with her finger.

"Fine." Mathew said.

Sarah closed her eyes and took a deep breath. Then she waited; waited for the inevitable engagement of their mouths. Mathew's hands slid gently over her back as he wrapped his arms around her. He held her body close to his and at last the moment came. His lips felt like two satin pillows against hers: smooth and soft to the touch. He danced gracefully within her mouth, tempting her, causing her to become even more enamored. In Mathew's arms nothing else mattered; not her life as a slave nor her engagement to Abraham. For the first time in her life she was free.

As Mathew released her Seth asked. "Don't you feel better now that you got it out of your system?"

Mathew didn't answer. He was lost in his own thoughts. *Why was I stupid enough to kiss Sarah? It only made me want her more. If there wasn't an audience I could tear off her clothes, and take her; here and now. What the hell am I saying? I can't have my way with a girl who's under my authority. That's rape not passion. The very thought of it may condemn me to hell. I need to see the priest, confess my sins, and pray for forgiveness.*

"Mathew" Seth called.

Mathew finally cleared his head and lied. "You were right. I feel much better now."

After brake Seth returned to the lumber yard. He was alone stacking wood when Abraham approached him.

Seth noticed the angry expression on Abraham's face and asked. "Is there a problem?"

Abraham got in Seth's face and said. "Mabel told me you're trying to steal my woman!"

"I think you have me mistaken for someone else. I'm engaged to be married to Leah." Seth explained.

Abraham gave Seth a forceful shove and shouted. "That's who I'm talking about pretty boy!"

Seth grew impatient and shoved Abraham back. "Last time I checked you were betrothed to Sarah! What Leah and I do is none of your damned business!"

Leah could see the argument heating up and ran outside to help resolve the confrontation.

"Go back in the house Leah!" Seth demanded.

Leah ignored the warning and yelled. "It's over Abraham! Please just leave us alone."

Abraham narrowed his eyes at Seth and replied. "You're nothing but a proper talking, proper dressing, Uncle Tom. You're the master and mistress' bitch. I won't have a spoiled, weak, pussy like you raising my kid."

Seth scoffed, gave Abraham a smirk, and said. "Your kid huh? You sure about that?"

Abraham's eyes filled with rage and his nostrils flared. He brought his right fist across the left side of Seth's face sending him hurdling to the ground.

Chapter 20

Leah screamed and ran to Seth's aide.

Abraham grabbed her by the arm and yelled. "You played me for a fool! How long have you been screwing him! I won't have another man touch you!"

Seth tackled Abraham to the ground and they rolled and tussled about the lumber yard. They sent fearsome blows to one another's face and torso. Aaron and Mathew came running to the scene. By the time they got there Seth had nearly choked Abraham unconscious. Abraham's face grew ashen. His lips were beginning to turn blue. Seth was a lot stronger than Abraham had anticipated. He struggled desperately pulling at Seth's arms. Mathew and Aaron pried Seth's hands away from Abraham's throat. A badly beaten Abraham rolled onto his side coughing and heaving to catch his breath. Mathew and Aaron grabbed Seth by the arms and dragged him away from the scene of the fight.

Seth hollered out to Abraham. "If you ever come near me, Leah, or our child again, I swear to God you'll never see another day forth!"

An hour after Seth's fight with Abraham, Mathew sat at his cluttered drafting table. Protractors, rulers, and calipers lay in disarray to the left of him. Various instruments for drawing, measuring, and gauging lay scattered to his right. In front of him sat a roll of blueprints.

His father had given Seth an advance on a few acres of land. Mathew had been entrusted to design the house, which would be constructed on it. Mathew smiled as he unrolled the blueprints because Seth and Leah granted him total reign of creativity. He jotted down a few calculations and dimensions, then added a couple more lines to the blueprints.

Aaron burst through the door and yelled. "Come quick! Robert Welch has your sister!"

Mathew sped downstairs and out the front door after Aaron. Robert trudged toward the horse drawn carriage with Lillian tossed over his shoulder.

Lillian screamed and pounded on Robert's back with her fists. "Nooo!! I won't do it. No!"

"Drop my sister this instant!" Mathew demanded.

Robert ignored him and kept walking. Mathew ran down the front steps and punched Robert in the face.

Robert released Lillian and shouted. "Hey I'm just following orders!"

"Who's orders?!" Mathew demanded.

Robert wiped the spot of blood from the corner of his mouth and said, "Your parents'."

At that moment Master and Mistress Colburn appeared on the porch.

Lillian stood before Mathew and pleaded through choked sobs. "Please don't allow them to send me away Mathew."

Master Colburn walked over and boomed in his baritone. "She's going to France with the Count and Countess. She'll learn proper etiquette, and receive an exceptional education."

His mother called from the porch. "We're only trying to do what's best for her. I only pray my sister and brother-in-law will succeed where we have failed. Whether you like it or not she's going to France!"

Mathew pushed Lillian behind him and replied, "Over my cold rotting corpse! I can't believe you would ship off your only daughter like a crate of cargo, and on her birthday no less. For what? To transform her into another Francesca."

Master Colburn replied. "You won't always be around. The moment you lose sight of her, she's going. She'll have a safer trip with her aunt and uncle."

Lillian realized her father was right. She was only postponing the inevitable.

She wiped the tears from her face, and stepped out from behind her brother.

Lillian hugged Mathew and boarded the stagecoach with the Demoniets. Aaron climbed into the chauffeur's seat and cracked the whip in the air. The horses broke into a trot. As the carriage pulled away Lillian watched her brother through the window. She forced a smile for him and flexed her muscles. Mathew raised an arm and flexed his back.

The carriage disappeared and Mathew sat down on the cement stairs.

Master Colburn sat down next to him and said. "You must think we're terrible people."

Mathew didn't respond.

They both rose when they saw the Arrington stagecoach coming toward the mansion. It pulled up in front of the steps and Maxwell Arrington climbed out with a white box.

Mrs. Colburn sauntered down the steps smiling cheerfully and said. "My niece, Francesca, will be delighted to know you're here."

The mistress turned to send one of the servants for Francesca but she was already standing in the doorway.

Francesca walked gracefully down the front steps and said. "I've been looking forward to your visit."

Maxwell cast a confused glare and replied. "I came here today to call on Lillian."

Dumbfounded expressions covered the faces of Mathew's parents and Francesca.

Mathew led Maxwell to the horse stable and said. "You just missed her. If you take the Indian trail through the woods you may be able to cross her path before they reach the train station." Mathew quickly saddled a black horse and continued. "Your stagecoach is too large for the trail. You'll have to make the journey horseback."

Maxwell threw his foot in the stirrup and flung himself onto the saddle.

He glanced down at Mathew from atop the horse, gave a nod, and said. "Thank you."

Maxwell took off through the slave quarters and reached the forest. He found the trail Mathew mentioned and raced down it. The horse galloped through the forest until the trail ended. Maxwell stopped in the middle of a road. His horse reared up on its hind legs and neighed loudly as Lillian's carriage came barreling down the street. Aaron looked up with surprise and brought the carriage to a screeching halt.

The Demoniets and Lillian climbed out of the carriage, and Maxwell climbed down from his horse.

The Count Demoniet scolded Maxwell, "You stupid boy! You might have gotten yourself killed just now. What have you to say for yourself?"

Maxwell grinned at Lillian, passed her the white box and said, "Happy Birthday."

Lillian's face lit up with a smile as she threw her arms around him.

"Promise me you'll write." Maxwell said.

"Everyday" Lillian replied as she climbed back into the carriage. Maxwell climbed back on his horse and the stagecoach pulled away once more.

Lillian waved goodbye through the window as her uncle continued to rant. "That boy could've been trampled, and for what, to give you a box of chocolates. You don't even like flowers or chocolates."

Lillian blocked out her uncle's complaints and opened the white box. A small note sat on top of the contents.

Dear Lillian,
You're the most remarkable girl I've ever met. I searched eight cities for a gift I thought you would enjoy. I hope you find it to your liking. Happy 13th Birthday.
*   Yours truly,*

Maxwell Arrington

Lillian set aside the letter and laughed when she saw the contents of the box. *Large game ammunition. Maxwell I think I love you.*

Sarah stood in the infirmary helping Aunt Lizzie gather her medical supplies. Seth had gotten into a fight with Abraham earlier, and Aunt Lizzie was going to the mansion to examine him.

Sarah closed the bag of supplies and asked. "Are you sure you don't need me to assist you?"

Aunt Lizzie gave Sarah a pleasant smile and said. "I need you to be here in case someone needs help. I should only be gone for a short while."

Sarah handed her the bag and Aunt Lizzie hobbled out the door. Though Sarah tried to pretend as though nothing had happened between Mathew and her, she still found herself alone in the infirmary thinking about the time she saw him naked and the kiss they had shared by White Water Brook. That passionate kiss that set her lips aflame was still haunting her hours later.

The door of the infirmary creaked and her betrothed walked in. Abraham held up a tiny gold band and said. "I think you should be wearing this."

Sarah snatched it from him and slapped it on her finger.

She rolled her eyes and replied. "You didn't have to go through the trouble to buy me a new ring. I could've very easily borrowed the one you gave Leah a few months ago. If that one didn't fit I could've certainly used the one you gave May almost immediately after you got my friend, Leah, pregnant and left her."

Abraham replied smugly. "Ouch, Love. Why do you play these games, like you don't want to be with me when you know that you do? You were probably sitting here thinking about what you're going to wear to our wedding next week, and fantasizing about the way I'm going to deflower you on that sacred night."

He rubbed her arm and moved in to kiss her. Sarah turned away and Abraham settled for a kiss on the cheek as a consolation.

"Could you at least try to be a little less disgusting?" Sarah snapped then went on to say "I don't know what I'm wearing to that god forsaken event but it damn sure won't be white. Please believe someone's already picked this flower, and in the event that you take my body I'll be certain to call you by his name."

Abraham stormed out of the infirmary shocked and disgusted.

Leah walked in after he left and closed the door behind her.

She glanced at Sarah's hand and said. "Ah, gold this time, instead of silver. At least he's trying to be somewhat original. What did that lousy sack of swine want?"

Sarah sighed and answered. "He just wanted to torment me. I told him I wasn't a virgin and he got furious and left."

Leah laughed and added. "Abraham's really possessive. He can't stand to hear things like that. Earlier today Seth implied that we were having sex while Abraham and I were together."

"How did he take it?" Sarah asked; her mood lightening momentarily.

Leah replied. "They got in a fight remember."

"Is Seth alright?" Sarah asked.

"Seth is fine. I'm the one that's not alright." Leah answered.

Sarah looked down and noticed the cloth wrapped around Leah's hand. It was saturated with blood.

Leah went on to say. "I cut my hand on a kitchen knife."

Sarah un-wrapped Leah's hand and said. "This is pretty nasty you'll need five or six stitches."

Sarah cleaned Leah's laceration, and numbed it with a pain remedy derived from cocaine.

Sarah began to suture Leah's cut and said. "You've been sleeping with Seth all this time."

Leah laughed and replied. "No, but I'm going to allow Abraham to think that. Seth and I made love just once before I ever got with Abraham."

Sarah tied a stitch and began another, then asked. "How was it?"

Leah gazed up wistfully and answered. "The man's a magician." Sarah laughed and Leah went on to say. "I wish I could've seen the look on Abraham's face when you told him you weren't a virgin."

Sarah sighed and solemnly replied. "The only problem is that I was lying. I've never been with a man. I only told Abraham that to get rid of him. I had hoped he might be so disturbed by it, that he'd call off the wedding. Of course he didn't, stubborn jerk. I've never felt such a lack of control over my life until now. I do not want to give that horrible man my virginity."

Sarah finished the last stitch and wrapped Leah's hand with gauze.

Leah headed for the door and said. "You know Sarah there's still one thing you have control over. You don't have to allow Abraham to take your virginity."

Mathew lay awake in bed unable to rest. *It's been an awful day. Seth was attacked by Abraham. My parents sent Lillian to France. And I'm in love with a woman I'd be condemned to hell for touching. Who am I kidding? Sarah's marrying another man in less than a week. I'm already in hell.* His thoughts were interrupted by tapping on his bedroom window. He climbed out of bed and opened the window.

"Sarah? Is everything alright?" Mathew asked as he helped her climb inside.

"I'm sorry. I couldn't sleep." Sarah explained.

Mathew pulled a pillow and a blanket off his bed and made a pallet on the floor.

"Well you're welcome to lay down in here. Take the bed." He insisted, and then laid down on the floor.

Sarah unlaced the bodice of her servants dress and slipped out of it. She let her hair down and climbed into the enormous bed. She lay down on her side and stared out the window at the silver moon and twinkling stars.

"Please lay with me." Sarah implored him.

Mathew silently prayed. *God give me the strength to just lie next to her.* He climbed into bed behind Sarah and placed his arm around her waist. She smelled like the sweet oils and fruit extracts she softened her skin and hair with daily. As Mathew lay embracing Sarah between the sheets he fantasized. *She's wearing next to nothing and her practically bare body feels soft and warm pressed against mine. I'll scoot back a bit so she won't notice how much I truly appreciate this moment.*

Mathew cleared his thoughts and said. "I have to ask. What has you up in the middle of the night?"

Sarah pulled him back close to her then answered his question. "All I keep thinking about is what Abraham said about deflowering me. Next week I'm going to have my maidenhood stolen by a pompous, arrogant, jackass. The very thought of this disturbs me so much I can't sleep at night." Sarah turned to face him and asked. "Mathew will you do something for me?"

Mathew kissed her forehead and answered. "You know I'll do anything you ask of me. Just name it."

Sarah looked him in the eyes, kissed his lips, and whispered. "Make love to me."

Find strength Mathew. Find strength. He scolded himself then replied nervously. "Sarah, I've loved you my entire life. I find you irresistible and it feels as though I've waited an eternity to hear you say those words but I can't take advantage of you."

Mathew watched Sarah slip off her only garment, and his longing for her grew even stronger. She tenderly kissed his chest, and massaged his neck with her lips. He fought to control his desire for her. *It's impossible to resist with her naked chest pressed against mine. She's so beautiful, so tempting, and her lips feel so soft on my neck. How can this be wrong when it feels so good; so right?* He caressed her naked body, and braced her with a long passionate kiss.

At last he pulled away and said. "Sarah you don't know how bad I yearn to be inside of you right now. But I...I can't."

She placed his hand on her bare supple breasts and said. "I want this to happen with someone I love."

"You love me?" Mathew asked.

Sarah shook her head yes, kissed his lips once more and replied, "With every fiber of my being."

Mathew found himself desperately overwhelmed by passion. He pulled Sarah onto her back and placed his masculine frame upon hers.

She trembled at his touch and he asked. "You're not afraid are you?"

"A little." She admitted.

Mathew kissed her and assured. "Sarah, I would never hurt you."

His lips moved softly about her lips, neck and collar bone. He moved south to her breast and placed the tender mass into his mouth. She moaned with pleasure as he delicately teased them. He ran his hand up her silky smooth thigh until he reached her center. *Perfectly moist and mine for the taking.* He thrust himself deep inside of her and she winced slightly in pain.

Mathew whispered in her ear. "I'm sorry. Do you want me to stop?"

Sarah implored him. "Please continue."

She held him close and gently clawed his back, as he moved back and forth on top of her repeating the words. "I love you, Sarah."

Mathew was awakened the following morning by a loud tapping at his bedroom door. He immediately rolled over to wake Sarah.

"Sarah, get up. We must have over slept." Mathew whispered as he gently shook her shoulder.

The knocking started again and Mrs. Colburn shouted from the other side of the door. "Mathew Dear, are you feeling well!"

"Just a moment Mother!" Mathew replied.

Sarah heard the mistress' voice and sprung out of bed.

Mistress Colburn went on to say. "I shall fetch Sarah to bring you some warm chicken broth!"

"Mother I can assure you that won't be necessary!" Mathew said as he and Sarah clumsily scrambled around the room for their clothes. Sarah began lacing up her bodice. Fear overwhelmed her. Her heart raced as the door knob began to turn.

Chapter 21

Mathew, realizing he couldn't get dressed in time, leaped back into bed and pulled the covers up to his chin.

At that very moment the mistress walked through the door and said. "Sarah, there you are. I sent for you a moment ago, but as I can see you're already looking after my boy. We're all blessed to have such a dedicated nurse."

Sarah smiled and said. "Thank you Mistress."

Mathew's mother sat on the bed next to him. Her face filled with concern.

She put a hand on his forehead to check for a fever and said. "This is the second time this week you've been sick. I do hope it isn't anything serious."

Sarah assured her. "He'll be fine Ma'am. It's just the change in weather."

The mistress' concerned expression faded.

She rose up and said to Mathew. "As soon as you're feeling better your father would like a word with you. Don't forget about Seth's wedding today."

"Yes Mother." Mathew replied.

After the mistress left Sarah and Mathew looked at each other and let out a sigh of relief.

"I promise to see you soon." Mathew said as he kissed Sarah on the forehead and walked briskly to his father's chambers.

An hour after the chat with his father, Mathew sat in the confessional at the Catholic Church. The priest, Father Murphy, waited on the other side of a divider to hear Mathew's sins. As a Roman Catholic, confession was a common routine for Mathew, but he still never stopped dreading it. *Pouring out my sins before this man of god: how embarrassing.* Mathew thought to himself. *At least the old grumpy priest was promoted to bishop and replaced by a younger more relatable man. Father Murphy tries to make this as painless as possible.*

Mathew fumbled with his rosary, cleared his throat and spoke. "Forgive me Father, for I have sinned. It has been one week since my last confession."

Father Murphy replied. "How have you sinned my child?"

Mathew took a deep breath and rolled out the list. "I've been an insubordinate son, lied three times, gotten drunk; I've punched a man in the face, and… committed fornication.

Father Murphy replied in a jovial manner. "Mathew, you're one of my most pious and devout followers. You're usually only here to confess to saying unseemly things about your cousin. It seems this has been a rather busy week for you." Mathew laughed and the priest continued. "What is going on in your life that has you lying, fighting, getting intoxicated, and having premarital sex?"

Mathew went on to admit. "I'm in love with a girl who's betrothed to a horrible man. She loves me and asked that I take her virginity to prevent him from doing so."

Father Murphy asked. "If you love her then why don't you marry her.?"

Mathew went on to explain, "Because she's black Father Murphy. If we were to marry and have children the law would see our union as illegitimate. If something were to happen to me my white relatives would inherit everything and leave Sarah and our offspring penniless. Our marriage would make no difference in the eyes of the law."

Father Murphy replied. "It makes a difference in the eyes of god."

At sunset Seth and Leah publicly proclaimed their love for one another in the most elaborate wedding anyone had ever witnessed for two blacks. The master and mistress even attended and gave all the field hands the day off. Mathew and Sarah served as the best man and maid of honor. The wedding was held in the orchard with a multitude of flowers and decorations. The Colburn's also provided an abundance of gourmet food and champagne; enough to serve over 100 guests.

As the reception continued well into the night Seth danced with Leah under the stars. Sarah gazed at Mathew from across the orchard. He was having a toast with Aaron. She thought wistfully to herself. *It's so difficult for me, not to show him affection in front of his parents; especially after all that's happened. It doesn't seem to bother Mathew at all.*

The mistress drunkenly stumbled over to Sarah and giggled. "I need you to grab another case of wine from the cellar."

"Yes Ma'am." Sarah replied, taking the keys.

Sarah tracked across the orchard to the cellar and unlocked it. She swung open the heavy iron double doors and descended the stairs. It was so dark she could barely see her hand in front of her face. She made her way through the darkness in search of a lantern. She shivered at the sound of footsteps behind her. *Get a grip Sarah. You're imagining things.* She scolded herself as her heart began to race. The footsteps continued. She screamed as the cellar doors slammed closed.

A hand briefly covered her mouth and a voice called into her ear. "Sarah It's just me, Mathew."

"Jesus Christ Mathew! You nearly gave me a heart attack!" Sarah exclaimed as Mathew lit the lanterns on the walls.

The lanterns cast the cellar in a soft yellow glow, illuminating the racks, barrels, and crates of expensive wine. The room was cool and possessed the pleasant scent of vine ripened grapes.

She hugged Mathew and said. "You looked so handsome tonight."

Mathew modestly shook his head no, and then replied. "It was you who looked radiant, as always."

Mathew took Sarah's hand in his and said. "I've been waiting all night to do this. You know this morning when my father wanted to speak with me?" Sarah nodded her head yes and Mathew continued. "It was to give me this."

Mathew pulled a small black case from his pocket. It contained a silver necklace, with a large red ruby in the center of an oval charm.

Sarah said with a puzzled look. "That's your mother's necklace."

Mathew went on to further explain. "My mother and paternal grandmother have necklaces identical to this one. The Colburn family crest is inscribed on the back of the charm. My father had this necklace special made for me to give to the woman I love and intend to marry."

Mathew got down on one knee and removed the necklace from its case.

Sarah's eyes filled with tears and for a brief moment she found herself unable to breath.

Mathew gazed up at Sarah and said. "When I woke up next to you this morning I knew beyond a shadow of a doubt that god favors me. He sent me his most beautiful angel. Marry me Sarah. Even if we have to runaway together, marry me."

Unable to speak, Sarah nodded her head in agreement. Mathew wrapped the silver ruby necklace around her wrist and kissed her long and deep.

When he released her he asked playfully. "Why are you in the cellar?"

Sarah grinned and replied. "Your mother sent me after a case of wine. But either she didn't mention what kind or I forgot. Mathew what's your mother's favorite bottle of wine?"

Mathew laughed and replied, "An open one."

"That's not funny." Sarah scolded him playfully.

Mathew grabbed a random case of wine and walked Sarah back to the reception.

As they approached the party Mathew said. "We'll need two witnesses. There are only two men, other than Abraham and the overseers, who can leave the plantation at will. There's Seth, who's already agreed to do it, and Emanuel. I haven't talked to Emanuel yet but this whole elopement is riding on his decision."

Sarah replied in shock. "Our marriage is riding on a man who loves me. Emanuel will never agree to this. He proposed to me not very long ago and he's your father's right hand man. How do you know he can be trusted?"

Mathew calmed Sarah and said. "Because he's a good man; if he truly cares for you he'll wish for nothing more then your happiness. Besides, I don't think Emanuel's hurting for female companionship."

Mathew gave a nod in Emanuel's direction. As usual Emanuel had been swarmed by a flock of beautiful girls. He and Seth had always been the plantations most sought after bachelors. Now that Seth was taken Emanuel had to beat girls away with a pointy stick.

Sarah smiled and replied. "You're right." Then she left to join Leah and Marlette.

Mathew sat down the case of wine and walked over to Emanuel.

Mathew waded through the crowd of women that surrounded Emanuel and said. "May I have a word with you in private?"

Mathew led Emanuel away and the girls sighed with disappointment.

"Is everything alright?" Emanuel asked.

Mathew took a deep breath and confessed. "I'm in love with Sarah. We're planning to elope. I know that you have feelings for her because you proposed. I didn't want to ask you to do this but we're one witness short."

Emanuel smiled and replied in a jovial manor. "That proposal was your father's idea, not mine. He wanted me to breed him free labor that's all. The woman I desire lies out of my reach. Her name is Marie. The 1/16 black blood which flows through my veins, prohibits me by law from marrying her. Your father was against a union between Marie and me because the slave status of children depends on that of the mother. If I had children with Marie he would have no rights to them. This is why he tried to fix me up with Sarah instead."

Mathew breathed a sigh of relief and asked. "Does this mean you'll help us get married?"

Emanuel's face grew heavy with concern as he replied. "I'll only do it under the condition that you don't run away. I understand how you feel, but you don't know the cruel and inhumane punishments inflicted on runaways. Some of the runaway slaves who are captured have both ankles crushed with a large hammer. Others are stripped naked and flogged until near death. All of them are branded with the letter "**R**" by a red hot poker iron. Not much would be done to you, but for Sarah to run away with the master's own son would earn her a punishment far worse than all the others. They could take her life for such an offense. Even if you got away you would be forced to live as fugitives. You would never know when someone would come to capture you and your children. You would never have a moment's peace. Wait until you've saved enough money to buy her freedom, or at least enough to live off of for a while."

Mathew explained. "If we stay here my father is going to sell her to Abraham."

Emanuel smirked and said. "You concern yourself with picking out the right tuxedo. I'll handle your father."

"Thank you for everything." Mathew said, and then walked away.

"And Mathew!" Emanuel called out. Mathew turned around and Emanuel said. "Congratulations!"

Mathew gave an appreciative nod and returned to the reception.

The following evening Sarah sat in a room in the east wing of the Cathedral putting the finishing touches on her hair and make up. She borrowed a satin, cranberry colored gown from Francesca, with a low neck line and a rhinestone embroidered bodice. It was an exact match to the vest under Mathew's Tuxedo. She wore her lustrous, black hair down, straightened with very slight curls at the end.

"Are you ready?" Emanuel called from the other side of the door.

Sarah took Emanuel's arm, and he said. "You look stunning. I'm sorry your father couldn't be here."

She whispered to him as he escorted her to the sanctuary. "Thank you for giving me away."

Mathew waited at the front of the church with Seth. He anticipated the moment that Sarah would saunter down the aisle. At last she appeared arm in arm with Emanuel. *She's breathtaking; an astonishing vision of a goddess in dark red satin.* Mathew gave silent reverence to God and beheld his bride.

Sarah and Mathew bathed together under the stars at White Water Brook. The waterfall even looked magnificent at this time of night. Sarah realized how late it was getting and got out of the water.

"It's our wedding night. Stay a little longer." Mathew implored her.

Sarah dressed herself and solemnly replied. "We can't afford to oversleep again. We may not be so lucky next time."

He realized she was right and grudgingly climbed out of the water. He clothed himself and they ventured back through the cave. They had just reached the surface when they began to smell smoke.

Mathew emerged from the tunnel entrance and saw the midnight sky lit up with bright orange flames. The infirmary was completely engulfed and Sarah was running at full speed toward it.

"Sarah, wait!" Mathew hollered as he grabbed her and pulled her away from the burning structure.

"Mathew, Aunt Lizzie's in there!" Sarah shouted.

"Ok, I'll go in and look for her! You go get help!" Mathew yelled, pointing her in the direction of another cabin.

Sarah ran from cabin to cabin beating on each door. The slaves and overseers came pouring out of their homes fetching buckets of water from the pond and dousing the harsh untamable flames.

Emanuel and Aaron came running from their cabins and shouted. "Sarah where's Mathew!"

Sarah pointed at the burning building with a trembling hand. Just then they heard the thunderous crash of the roof collapsing and the crowd broke into a panic.

"MATHEW!!!" Sarah screamed and darted toward the fire but Aaron restrained her.

She stood there fighting to free herself and watching in horror as the infirmary burned with the love of her life and her mentor both trapped within its walls.

The terrified crowd broke into a cheer as Mathew emerged from the fire with Aunt Lizzie in his arms. Sarah ran over to check them both out. Mathew was fine except for a few minor burns, but Aunt Lizzie was completely unconscious. She didn't appear to be badly burned but she had succumbed to the blistering hot smoke. In spite of all Sarah's efforts to save her she didn't make it.

Sarah grew hysterical and Mathew pulled her away.

"She's gone Sarah! There's nothing more you can do for her." Mathew stated.

Sarah broke down and sobbed in Mathew's arms.

Chapter 22

Mathew found Sarah the following morning picking through the charred remains of the infirmary. She gave her best effort to salvage what she could. She thought sadly to herself. *Half of my heart aches for the beloved teacher I've lost, and the other half aches from the site of my favorite place being reduced to a smoldering pile of rubble.*

It took almost the entire night to extinguish the blaze. Cabins were rickety wooden structures lit by candles and kerosene lanterns. It was a common occurrence for them to catch fire. Sarah looked up at Mathew with red watery eyes.

She wiped the tears from her cheeks and said. "I don't believe I ever thanked you for trying to save Aunt Lizzie."

Mathew wrapped her in a warm embrace then replied. "I only wish I could've gotten to her in time. I know there's nothing I can do to bring her back but I promise not to rest until I've built you a new infirmary."

Mathew caught a glimpse of a strange eight inch long bolt.

He reached down to retrieve it then turned to Sarah and said. "I'm going to take this bolt to remember this place by, and we're going to start over. Aunt Lizzie would want us to move on."

They began to hear the tune of *Swing Low Sweet Chariot* coming from the direction of the slave cemetery.

Sarah took a deep breath and said. "It looks like the funeral is starting. I better get a move on."

Emanuel went to the master's chambers later that afternoon.

Master Colburn was in his office with his older brother Pete. Pete Colburn was an older flabby version of Master Colburn. It wasn't difficult to tell at some point he'd been a very handsome man, but decades of inactivity, booze, and deep fried southern foods had taken their toll. He was well dressed and spoke with the deepest of southern drawls.

Emanuel cleared his throat and said. "As your financial advisor, I would recommend you not sell Sarah. With all due respect Sir, if you sell Sarah you'll lose a valuable asset to the plantation. She's a talented nurse, mid-wife and chamber maid."

Master Colburn sat back in his chair and replied. "I can't just pass up a good offer for Sarah because you want to keep her around for yourself."

Emanuel replied sarcastically. "Yeah, you got me." Then he went onto say. "In light of the recent tragedy, we've lost the plantation nurse. No one else is qualified to run the infirmary but Sarah. Have Sarah replace Aunt Lizzie as plantation nurse and mid-wife. If you sell her, you will only have to purchase another nurse."

Master Colburn replied. "Our recent loss does pose a bit of a problem; however, Sarah is getting married in a few days. I already gave her mother and fiancé my word. Besides, how do you know Sarah doesn't want to be married and receive her freedom?"

Emanuel replied with sarcasm. "Somehow I don't believe she'll mind staying. And there's something you should know about Sarah's fiancé, Abraham."

Master Colburn walked toward the smithy briefly after his chat with Emanuel. Sparks flew as Abraham pounded a red hot horseshoe against an anvil.

Abraham sat aside his hammer when he noticed the master enter the smithy.

"Afternoon Sir." Abraham said with a tip of his hat.

Without saying a word Master Colburn walked over and socked Abraham in the gut. Abraham folded over and grabbed his abdomen.

As Abraham coughed for air Master Colburn said. "No one attacks my children. This includes Seth. You're fired."

Master Colburn then turned to the overseers and said. "Escort this man off the premises."

Abraham tried vigorously to explain himself as the overseer's hauled him away.

Mathew sat at his drafting desk twirling the eight inch bolt between his fingers.

Emanuel walked in and announced. "It's official. Sarah's staying."

Mathew didn't show nearly the amount of joy Emanuel had expected.

"Is everything alright?" Emanuel asked.

Mathew snapped out of his trance and said. "That fire was no accident. Aunt Lizzie was murdered. I just didn't have the heart to tell Sarah yet. She's already devastated. She and Aunt Lizzie were very close."

Emanuel's face went ghost white as he replied. "How do you know this? Those cabins often burn down."

Mathew held up the long black bolt and explained. "Because of this; these particular bolts are only used to build the frames of expensive Scottish stagecoaches. American carriages are made of entirely different materials. There were only two stagecoaches in town imported from Scotland. They both belonged to Dr. McKinley. His daughter Katherine disappeared with one of them. A plantation nurse would have no need for such an item, yet it was found in the burned remains of the infirmary."

Emanuel listened in horror intrigued by Mathew's intuitiveness.

He looked at Mathew and questioned. "What exactly are you trying to say?"

Mathew set the bolt aside and continued. "Katherine McKinley never made it to Canada. She never made it out of the city. Someone knew she was planning to run away. He knew that no one would expect foul play for this reason. The scariest part about it all is that this person is stalking Sarah. What did he have to gain by killing a harmless old woman, other than to keep Sarah here? He torched the infirmary and used the fire as an opportunity to get rid of Katherine's stagecoach."

Emanuel replied with a horrified expression. "Your last teacher was right when he said you were a genius."

Mathew gripped the bolt in anger and spoke scornfully. "Someone murdered all these people, and is stalking my wife. I won't rest until I drive this very bolt through his heart."

Chapter 23

Mathew and Emanuel stood in the slave cemetery over the body of Aunt Lizzie.

Emanuel raised a scalpel with a trembling hand and questioned. "Are you sure you don't want Dr. McKinley to do this?"

Mathew replied. "My father isn't going to pay the doctor for an examination of any slave; especially a dead one. I won't have Sarah do it because she was close to the woman, and I never paid attention in medical class. I'm sorry Emanuel but you're the only other person here with any medical experience what so ever."

Emanuel looked at Aunt Lizzie's Corpse with disgust and said. "Did it ever occur to you that I didn't go into medicine because I'm not fond of cutting into people; especially dead ones."

Mathew pleaded. "Emanuel please, I just need you to examine her and find out whether or not she died in the fire."

Emanuel nodded and began the examination.

He lifted the dead woman's lips with a pair of tweezers and said. "There are bruises and scrapes on the inside of the upper and lower lips; indicative of pressure being applied to the mouth." Emanuel lifted the eyelids of the corpse and continued. "The right and left eye both display petechia hemorrhaging; a trait common with asphyxiation. Now for the part I really hate." Emanuel said as he made an incision into the chest of Aunt Lizzie's dead body."

Mathew walked away and said. "I'll excuse myself for this part."

After 20 minutes or so, Emanuel walked over to Mathew wiping the blood from his hands.

Emanuel glanced up at Mathew and said. "The lungs were pink and expressed no signs of smoke inhalation. My opinion is that she was deceased before the fire ever started. The most likely cause of death appears to be smothering; either with an object such as a pillow or even a hand."

Mathew replied. "Thank you, Emanuel. You truly are brilliant."

Emanuel said nothing. His eyes rolled back.

"Are you alright?" Mathew called out as Emanuel fainted.

Later that afternoon Dr. McKinley confirmed Emanuel's findings. Master Colburn launched a full scale investigation. The plantation was crawling with the sheriff, his deputies, and their blood hounds. Sheriff Briggs was a short gray haired man with steel rimmed spectacles and a scruffy mustache.

He had already searched the cabins of Abraham and eight of the overseers, including Sarah's father. Mathew, Sheriff Briggs, and the gang of deputies approached the cabin of Frank and Robert Welch. As soon as they opened the door the blood hounds went mad. The dogs barked hysterically and clawed at the floorboards. Frank Welch watched with a puzzled look on his face as the sheriff's men pried up the wooden planks.

"What do we have here?" One of the deputies asked as he pulled out a metal, bait and tackle box.

The deputy banged the lock on the box with the butt of his gun until it came loose.

He opened the box and ghastly expressions covered the faces of everyone watching. Inside laid a tossed salad of dismembered body parts; ears, toes, fingers, even noses. Mathew grew sick as he recognized the ring on one of the fingers belonging to Mali.

Frank Welch's expression changed from disgusted to hurt and disappointed.

He backhanded Robert and said. "You were in the office the day the ear came up missing!"

As the deputies seized Robert Welch he called out. "Father I didn't do this! Have I ever shown a propensity toward slave women?!"

At that moment Emanuel walked up with the Creole woman whose son Robert injured. She was a tad calmer this time and was able to concentrate well enough to speak English.

Emanuel looked at the sheriff and said. "This is Saphirra. She has information you need to know. Go ahead and tell them what you told me Saphirra."

Tears streamed down Saphirra's face as she spoke. "Robert Welch raped me and at least three other women. The real reason Robert hurt my son that day, is because my boy yelled at Robert to get off of me."

The sheriff's brows furrowed as he said. "I've heard enough. Take him away."

Robert struggled vigorously as the deputies hauled him away.

Robert hollered out in anguish. "I'll get you for this Mathew! As God is my witness I'll get you!"

Once Robert was out of view, Sheriff Briggs turned to Mathew and said. "Since slaves are not considered people by the constitution the most I can charge Robert with is trespassing on private property for each of the counts of rape. I can charge him with poaching and destruction of private property for each of the counts of murder."

Mathew replied in disbelief. "Poaching! As in the unlawful hunting or killing of animals! Robert murdered numerous people!"

Sheriff Briggs replied. "Slaves are not considered human beings, and you'll need more evidence then a bolt from a carriage to prove he murdered Katherine McKinley. Her own father is convinced she ran away. Katherine left a note in her own handwriting telling him so."

Mathew asked in frustration. "How much time will he get?"

The sheriff answered. "That depends on how long he takes to pay your family the amount in damages owed."

Frank walked over to the sheriff to plead on behalf of his son. "I'll mortgage my home in the city and work for the Colburns for free. Please don't send my boy to prison. I'll send Robert far away from here; to New Orleans with my wife's family."

Sheriff Briggs looked at Frank Welch with remorse and said. "Fine, but your son is hereby banished from the state of Missouri. If I ever see that sick son-of-a-bitch set foot on Missouri soil again, I will personally throw away the key to his prison cell."

As the sheriff walked away Mathew thought. *I can't believe they're just going to let Robert go. What if he returns to hurt someone? What if he returns to hurt Sarah?*

Chapter 24

September 12, 1836

Five months passed on the Colburn Plantation. Mathew, with the help of a few others, rebuilt the new infirmary over the entrance to the tunnel. He added a trap door in the floor. This made it easier for Sarah and him to slip away to White Water Brook. Mathew placed Sarah's spear and a framed drawing he'd done of Aunt Lizzie over the doorway of the infirmary.

Sarah examined her sister Marlette, who was now five months pregnant.

Sarah's face grew heavy with worry as she told her sister. "There is a complication with your pregnancy. If you don't take it easy you could lose the baby."

Marlette spoke with aggravation. "You should try telling the Master and Mistress that." Then she went on to say, "Sarah, thank you for not telling Momma and Poppa."

Sarah laughed and replied. "You kept me and Mathew's marriage under wraps. I can certainly do the same for you. Considering the father of the child I don't blame you for keeping it a secret."

Marlette smiled and returned to the linen room to make repairs to the slaves' tattered clothing and do the Colburns' laundry.

Mathew walked through the door as Marlette was leaving. He surprised Sarah with a new book and a colorful assortment of wild flowers. Sarah kissed him and received the gifts.

Mathew sat down on one of the beds and said. "I have to leave town for a few days."

"I knew these gifts were a bribe. I barely see you anymore." Sarah said as she placed the flowers in a vase half filled with water.

Sarah sat down and stroked the ruby necklace he'd given her, with a distant look in her eyes. She kept the ruby necklace wrapped around her wrist and worn as a bracelet. It went undetected by Mathew's parents.

Mathew kissed her on the cheek and said. "Don't be sad. If I land this design project, I can make enough money for us to leave this place."

Sarah smiled and replied with excitement. "You mean this is the one."

Mathew nodded his head yes, and Sarah hugged him.

Then he passed her a roll of bills and said. "Put this with the rest."

Sarah hid the money with the rest of the cash Mathew had been saving from his jobs.

He rose from his seat and assured her. "I'll only be gone a few days."

Mathew kissed Sarah's not yet showing belly and said. "Take care of my son in my absence."

Sarah laughed and asked. "What makes you so sure we're having a boy? We could be having a girl."

Mathew gave Sarah a big grin as he walked out the door and said. "I just know it's going to be a boy."

Francesca balled up the letter from her parents and threw it on the floor.

"I can't believe they're not coming to get me until spring!" She shouted in anguish.

She turned to her new lady's maid and said. "I am aggravated, and incredibly frustrated. I need to go for a ride. Have Aaron ready the carriage."

"Yes Miss Francesca." the girl replied and left the room.

Francesca's new lady's maid was Aaron's 13-year-old half sister, Cassie. She was a stunning light skinned beauty with chestnut hair and dark blue eyes. She'd been handpicked by Francesca herself to come in from the field and replace Sarah.

Francesca walked down stairs to the horse drawn carriage that awaited her. Cassie had already climbed aboard.

As Francesca climbed in the stagecoach Aaron asked. "Miss, is there any way I can take you for a ride later? Master Mathew has to be at the train station in a couple of hours."

"Don't worry. We're not going far." Francesca snapped and slammed the door.

Aaron climbed up in the driver's seat and led the carriage away.

They were 5 miles down the road when Francesca gave a knock on the window. Aaron brought the stagecoach to a stop and climbed down.

He opened the door closes to Francesca and asked. "Is there a problem, Miss?"

Francesca climbed out and said. "We're going for a walk in the woods."

As Cassie moved to climb out, Francesca added. "Alone."

Cassie sat back down and Francesca closed the carriage door.

Francesca led Aaron away and said. "We need to talk."

They walked through the trees and shrubs and Aaron replied. "Thank you for bringing my sister in from the field. You won't regret your decision. Cassie will work very hard for you."

Francesca stopped walking with the stagecoach still insight. She turned to Aaron and said. "I want you to please me."

Aaron's brows furrowed with confusion as he asked. "What more could I do to satisfy you, Miss?"

Francesca unlatched one of his shirt buttons and lightly touched his chest.

Aaron pushed her away and said. "No! I could be castrated or even hanged for lying with you."

Francesca smirked and replied. "It wasn't a request Aaron. I can make you."

Aaron shot back. "Do to me what you will but the answer is no. I'll take 15 lashes for insubordination over a hanging any day."

Francesca stood close to Aaron and whispered in his ear. "I figured you'd say that, but what of your sister? I could accuse her of stealing. Have her whipped and banished to the fields from which she came. You see Aaron, I think you are a beautiful man; strong, exotic. I've had my eye on you for months. Did you think it was a coincidence that I specifically chose your sister as my lady's maid?"

Aaron glanced over at the carriage and saw his sister looking at him through the back window. He waived and gave Cassie a phony smile.

Cassie smiled back and Aaron said. "Francesca, you're a beautiful woman. There are plenty of rich white men who would be happy to oblige you. You don't have to put my life at risk or hurt my sister. My father is dead, and my mother was sold off long ago. Cassie's all I have in the world."

Francesca replied. "Rich white men would be inclined to tell others that they've had me. My reputation and prospects would be ruined. You have a much greater incentive to keep our relationship a secret. If you don't lay with me, I will hurt your sister. If you tell anyone you've slept with me, you'll be hanged, and I will hurt your sister. I like Cassie. She's a sweet girl. Don't make me hurt her, Aaron."

Aaron breathed heavily with frustration and said. "What makes you think I won't snap your skinny little neck and make a run for it with Cassie? The stagecoach is right over there."

Francesca scoffed and replied. "I am born of noble blood. In the event that I disappear, the president's own army will hunt you down. I'm sure you don't want to see your sister beheaded as an accomplice to murder. I've played this game with you for long enough. You are my subordinate, and you will please me now."

Aaron spoke vehemently. "You are an evil witch, Francesca! How do I know you won't hurt Cassie regardless?"

Francesca smiled and replied. "As long as you do as I say no harm will come to Cassie. I promise to treat your sister with the utmost respect and dignity."

Aaron walked briskly back over to the stagecoach.

He opened the door and Cassie asked. "Is everything alright? Did I do something to displease Miss Francesca?"

Aaron assured his sister. "Everything is fine, okay. Miss Francesca was telling me how much she likes you, and how glad she is to have brought you in from the field." Cassie smiled and Aaron continued. "Now, Miss Francesca wants me to take her for a walk in the woods. Stay in the stagecoach until we get back."

Cassie grinned and nodded.

Once they were out of site. Aaron snatched Francesca by the arm and led her deep into the woods. He pushed her back against a tree, pulled up her dress and ravaged her body angrily. He took her roughly without an ounce of concern for her comfort or wellbeing.

Francesca whispered in his ear as he devastated her delicate frame. "Oh Aaron, oh Aaron you're incredible."

He yelled at her as he continued to pound away. "Shut up! I can do without hearing your voice."

Aaron pushed even harder inside of Francesca. He gripped her body tight, and groaned passionately as he finished.

He shoved her aside and spoke through labored breaths. "I hate you, you horrible bitch."

Francesca stood for a few moments breathing heavily and at last replied. "You're wonderful when you're angry."

Aaron and Francesca straightened themselves up and walked back to the stagecoach. Francesca climbed in and put her arm around Cassie's shoulders.

Cassie asked cheerfully. "How was your walk Miss Francesca?"

Francesca gave Aaron a sly glance and then said to Cassie. "I enjoyed every minute of it. We really must get you out of those bleak rags. I have a beautiful green gown you can have."

Aaron closed the door and climbed back in the driver's seat. He brought the horses to a gallop and thought. *At least Francesca will keep her word and treat my sister well. I'm sickened at the realization that some part of me actually enjoyed what I did. Oh God.*

They pulled up in front of the mansion and Mathew and Mistress Colburn were standing on the porch.

Mathew called out cheerfully to Aaron as he approached the stagecoach. "I was beginning to think you wouldn't make it back in time."

Aaron scowled and didn't respond. Mathew opened the carriage door and Francesca and Cassie climbed out. Mathew stepped in and closed the door behind him. He gave a knock on the window and Aaron led the carriage away.

As Francesca and Cassie stepped onto the porch the Mistress asked. "Is everything alright Francesca? You seemed upset when you left."

Francesca smiled and thoughtfully replied. "I went for a walk to relieve my tension. I assure you, Dear Aunt, I'm feeling much better now."

Marlette beat on the infirmary door early the following morning before sunrise.

Sarah ran to open the door and Marlette said. "Sarah! I've been having labor pains most of the night."

Sarah helped Marlette onto one of the beds. Then she grabbed a pail of water and some fresh towels.

Sarah propped a couple pillows under Marlette's back and then began dabbing her sister's head with a moist cloth. Sarah walked over to the cabinets and skimmed over the shelf of anesthetics. She gave Marlette a pain remedy she had learned to mix from the medical books Mathew gave her. After administering the pain reliever she turned and saw Cassie standing in the doorway.

Sarah asked Cassie. "Are you having an emergency?"

Cassie replied. "No Miss Francesca has a bruise on her back. I think she must've fallen in the woods today. She wants you to look at it."

Sarah thought to herself. *Francesca actually wants me to examine a bruise at 4:00 in the morning. That bitch is unbelievable.*

Sarah glanced over at Cassie and instructed. "This is very important. I need you to ask Master Colburn to send for the doctor. Marlette's baby is trying to arrive four months early."

Cassie's dark blue eyes widened with surprise as she took off out the door. She ran as fast as her feet would carry her to the Master's bedroom.

Cassie pushed open the door and shouted. "Master Colburn, you have to send for Dr. McKinley!"

He groggily asked. "What the hell is your problem Cassie?"

Cassie explained. "Marlette's in labor. The baby's coming too early."

Mr. Colburn yawned and rolled over, then grumbled. "Go wake up Sarah. I'm sure she can handle it."

Cassie could hear Master Colburn snoring and felt it would serve no purpose to argue the point any further. She ran down the hall to persuade Mistress Colburn next.

The mistress asked in a sleepy voice. "Cassie, what brings you to my bedroom at this hour?"

Cassie explained for a second time. "Marlette's child is coming far too early! Master Colburn won't send the carriage for Dr. McKinley. You have to do something."

Mistress Colburn sat up in her bed then replied. "The master is right. If we called on the doctor every time one of these girls got pregnant we'd go broke. Now go wake Sarah."

Cassie returned to the infirmary and Sarah could tell by the look on her face that it wasn't good news.

For fear of her sister's life Sarah said. "Cassie, tell the Colburn's I'll pay for it."

Marlette shook her head no and shouted. "I won't let you do it! That money is to pay for your freedom!"

Sarah shot back. "We don't have a choice! If you don't see a doctor, you may lose the baby and your life. I won't allow it!"

Marlette hollered out in agony and grabbed Sarah's arm. "Send for Phillip Arrington!"

By the time Aaron returned with Phillip and Dr. McKinley the sun was up and Sarah had already gotten the situation under control. When Phillip entered the infirmary Sarah was still taking care of Marlette. Samson and Violet were standing in the room with disgruntled expressions. Violet and Samson pushed passed Phillip without saying a word and stormed outside. Samson walked over to the pond, and Violet tracked back to the nursery.

Phillip sat on the bed next to Marlette and asked. "How are you my love? I wish I could've been here sooner."

Marlette replied with exhaustion. "I'll live."

Sarah walked over to Phillip and informed. "I managed to stop the bleeding this time, but Marlette needs to be on bed rest until she gives birth. She needs round the clock care; an on call nurse or doctor. The Colburns aren't going to give her that. They will continue to work Marlette until she and your child are dead."

Phillip kissed Marlette and said. "I'll be back in a moment. I need to speak with your father and the Colburns."

Phillip walked up to Samson and said. "I know I should've done this a long time ago. For that I sincerely apologize. I'm in love with your daughter and I want to marry her."

Samson didn't even look at Phillip.

He stared out on the water and replied in an angry frustrated tone. "No one even knew she was pregnant! She could've died today!"

Phillip explained. "You have every right to be angry with me, but I only wanted to finish building our home in England first. My mother would've never allowed Marlette to live at the Arrington Manor here. I didn't want to ask you for your daughter's hand without having so much as a home for her to stay in."

Samson looked at Phillip with respect for the first time and replied. "It's a damn shame a man has to purchase his wife and child isn't it?"

Phillip let out a sigh of relief and said. "Yes Sir it truly is."

Master Colburn was conducting a meeting with Emanuel and four of the overseers when Phillip entered the office. The overseers parted way as Phillip approached the desk Master Colburn sat behind.

Phillip cleared his throat and spoke. "I wish to discuss the purchase of four of your servants."

Master Colburn questioned. "Which four servants do you speak of?"

Phillip answered, "Marlette, Sarah, Samson, and Violet."

Master Colburn sat back in his large arm chair with a ponderous look then replied. "Sarah's not for sale. She's my money maker. Slave owners from all across these parts bring their servants here to be treated. It's cheaper for owners to bring their servants here then for them to have a white doctor manage their care. Sarah's fetched me a pretty penny. Samson's my best overseer. I can't let him go either. I may be able to part with Violet and Marlette if the price is right."

Emanuel fumed with aggravation as he fumbled through the file cabinet. He thought to himself. *This isn't right. I informed Master Colburn that Samson was to be set free years ago. Master Colburn is being offered payment for Samson and he still won't let the man go. Take it easy Emanuel. Don't do anything stupid. To hell with this, I have to say something.*

Emanuel retrieved the file for Samson's family and interrupted the negotiation. "Pardon my interruption, but I must interject. Samson and Violet were inherited slaves. As such they came with a clause in their contracts."

Emanuel threw open the file on Master Colburn's desk.

He pointed to a line on one of the pages then continued. "As this article clearly states, both Samson and Violet were to be set free at the age of 35. As of present they are both 38 years of age."

Master Colburn's face went flush as Phillip said. "If what this man says is true I will have the best lawyers in the country here within the week to comb through all of your files. I'm certain the county magistrate will have copies of all your documents"

Master Colburn replied in a calm manner. "Lord Arrington I can assure you that won't be necessary. I have over 100 slaves on this plantation. It's impossible for me to keep up with all of their documentation. That's why I have Emanuel here. Now that I'm aware of the situation, Violet and Samson are free to go."

Phillip tossed Master Colburn an envelope and said. "This is for the freedom of Marlette. I'm certain you'll find the payment generous. Notify me if you decide to sell Sarah. Have a nice day Mr. Colburn."

Phillip turned and walked out of the office. Master Colburn sprung up from his seat and stomped over to Emanuel. He gripped Emanuel's throat and slammed him against the wall. Emanuel's face turned dark red as he gasped for air.

Master Colburn pinned him there and yelled. "If you weren't my brother's bastard I would cut your throat for this betrayal!"

Master Colburn released him and Emanuel fell to his knees coughing and choking.

The overseers seized Emanuel and asked. "Should we give him the usual 15 lashes for insubordination, Sir?"

Master Colburn snapped. "Did you idiots not just hear me say this man is my nephew?"

The overseers dropped Emanuel immediately and said, "Our apologies Sir."

Emanuel straightened his clothes and let out a sigh of relief; then Master Colburn added. "Give him eight lashes instead."

Chapter 25

Emanuel's cabin was small and unremarkable like the others. It was dimly lit and held only a few pieces of raggedy furniture. Several framed photographs decorated the walls. Emanuel lay in agony on the bed in his cabin. His back was brutally sliced open by a whip only moments ago. Sarah sat on the bed next to him. She dipped a towel into a bucket of water and wrung it out. Then she gingerly cleansed Emanuel's wounds. He groaned and flinched in pain every time she touched him.

Sarah stopped and told him. "Some of these wounds are so deep they'll need suturing. I can sedate you, if you'd like."

Emanuel responded. "I never got comfortable with the concept of losing consciousness as the result of some chemical. It's embarrassing to admit but, I always feared I wouldn't wake back up. I can handle the pain just distract me."

Sarah threaded the needle and applied a local anesthetic, then said. "I will never be able to repay you for your actions. What you did was beyond brave. Thank you for freeing my parents."

As Sarah began to close the bloody trenches in Emanuel's back he gripped the sides of his bed. His muscles tensed and his skin grew heavy with perspiration.

He modestly replied. "I only did what I thought to be right."

Sarah asked. "Did you know you were the master's nephew?"

Emanuel answered. "No but it explains a lot."

In order to take Emanuel's mind off the pain she asked. "If you could do anything in the world, what would you do?"

Sarah continued sewing and Emanuel replied. "I can't tell you. You'll laugh."

Sarah urged. "Come on, I promise not to make fun."

Emanuel's mood lightened, as if he were no longer lying in bed with his flesh torn open.

He smiled and replied. "The first thing I would do is elope with Marie. Then I'd move to France and become a big time chef. I would open my own restaurant and serve everyone; from the lowliest of commoners to the royalty of Europe."

Sarah smiled and set down the needle. She wandered over to the wall and glanced over the pictures. She came across a picture of a beautiful white girl, with light colored hair and dark eyes."

Sarah turned to Emanuel and asked. "Is this your Marie?"

Emanuel replied. "You'll have to bring the photo closer. I can't see that far without my glasses."

Sarah walked over with the picture and Emanuel answered. "Yes that's her."

Sarah began stitching again and replied. "She's beautiful."

Emanuel said. "Sometimes I feel I should just give up. I'll never have her."

Sarah looked appalled, and vehemently told him. "If you truly love her you should never give up! I have faith that things will change one day. The moment they do you should take her for your own. Promise me."

Emanuel smiled and replied. "I promise not to give up until I take Marie to be my wife."

Master Colburn's conscience had gotten the better of him. He paced in the rain for ten minutes in front of Emanuel's cabin. He gathered his nerve and finally let himself in. Emanuel was still lying on his stomach while Sarah bandaged his wounds.

Master Colburn looked down at Emanuel and stammered. "I...I'm not one to apologize, but I..."

Emanuel glanced up at him and said. "I know."

Master Colburn added nervously. "Would you like to know which one of my brothers you belong to?"

Emanuel replied. "What for, whoever it is obviously didn't want me."

Master Colburn turned and walked toward the door. As he gripped the knob he told Emanuel. "For what it's worth, I wanted you."

Sarah received a knock at the infirmary door late that night. She glanced through the window to find a rain drenched Frank Welch.

As she opened the door she asked. "What brings you in Ole Frank?"

"I've been having this problem with my feet." Frank answered as he limped through the door.

Sarah instructed him. "Just hop on the bed and remove your shoes. I'll take a look at them."

Sarah pulled up a chair and sat down in front of Frank. She carefully examined each foot and came to a conclusion. "You have a mild case of jungle rot. I see it all the time. Usually this happens to the slaves that work in the cotton and sugar cane fields. The servants are often forced to trudge around in the rain soaked fields. This results in large blisters on the feet which sometimes become infected."

Frank gave Sarah a look of bewilderment. "Wow. You sure do know your stuff little lady. I want you to know I had no part in what happened to Emanuel today."

Sarah nodded and replied. "I know."

Sarah walked over to the large medicine cabinets and said. "Give me just a moment and I'll fetch you something for it."

She began sorting through the many containers and announced. "Ah. I've finally found it. This will fix you up in no time Ole Frank."

Sarah turned around to find Frank naked from the waist down. A sinister expression swept across his face as he lunged in her direction.

Chapter 26

Present

Krista sat the book aside when she heard her cell phone ringing. She glanced at the screen but didn't recognize the number.

"Hello" She spoke into the receiver.

"Hi, I was trying to reach Krista." The voice at the other end called back.

As soon as she heard the British accent she already knew who it was. She pulled the phone away, took a deep breath, and brooded over what to say.

From a distance she heard the voice calling out. "Hello? Hello?"

She placed the phone back on her ear immediately. "Ox? Hey what's up?" She stated, giving her best effort to be nonchalant.

He then replied. "I was wondering if you wanted to hang out today?"

The door bell rang around 3:00pm and she still wasn't quite finished curling her hair. *Oh well, this will have to do.* She thought as she stood in front of the full length mirror and judged her reflection. *Blue jean mini skirt, a red spaghetti string top, and red sandals nothing real fancy.* She doused herself with Tommy Girl perfume, applied another coat of Victoria's Secret lotion and sauntered down stairs.

In the few seconds it took Krista to get to Ox, her father had already managed to threaten his life if he even thought about doing anything inappropriate.

Her mother asked. "Will you guys be back in time for dinner? Your dad's barbecuing."

"I don't know yet. We'll see." Krista answered, then took Ox by the hand and dashed out the front door.

She made a clean get away before her mother could go into one of her embarrassing spells.

"It was nice to meet you Mr. and Mrs. Colburn." Ox stated as Krista rushed him down the cement porch steps.

"Have fun pumpkin." Krista's dad called out from the door way as he shot Ox a final mean glare.

The weather was perfect, a 90 degree day with a gentle breeze to balance the heat. The skies were blue with a few scattered clouds. The squirrels and chipmunks were scampering about the emerald lawn, and the air smelled like fresh lilacs and blossoms. Ox drove a glimmering new Jeep Grand Cherokee. It was stealth gray with tinted windows. He was wearing gray cargo shorts and a red and gray designer T-shirt.

Krista explained to Ox as he opened the passenger side door for her. "I'm sorry you had to experience that. My parents are so embarrassing. My dad thinks I'm too young to date a college guy, even though I told him that you're only 19. We're just two years apart."

Ox laughed and assured Krista. "Don't worry about it. My parents are five times worse than yours are."

Krista and Ox had managed to catch a matinee, bowl two games, and still make it back to the mansion by 8:30 pm. They sat parked in the gravel driveway in front of the mansion. *Come on kiss me already.* Krista thought to herself. An awkward silence quickly fell over the vehicle.

"This is a nice pile of bricks you got here. You'll have to give me a tour some time." Ox stated to ease the tension.

Not wanting the night to end so soon Krista suggested, "How about now?"

He agreed and turned off the jeep.

As they entered the mansion Krista's mom said. "I'm glad you two could make it back in time for dinner. It'll be ready in about an hour."

Krista replied. "Alright that should give me just enough time to show Kevin the property?"

They explored the mansion room by room until they reached the second floor.

"This is my bedroom right here." Krista stated, and then opened the door so he could take a look around.

Ox said as he wandered into the bedroom. "It's really nice. My room at the frat house isn't a quarter the size of this thing."

He walked straight to the set of double glass doors at the far wall and pulled them open. Outside sat a spacious balcony made of granite and marble. Krista followed close behind him, setting foot on the elegant balcony for the first time in many years.

"This is some view you have here." Ox stated as he put an arm around Krista, and kissed her on the cheek.

His lips feel soft and warm against my face, and he smells of expensive cologne. For God sake kiss me already. She thought.

From her bedroom balcony they could see, the garden, the orchard, the slave quarters and even the pond. Acres and acres of the estate had become visible and they could even catch a glimpse of a perfect mountain sunset. Krista glanced out at the magnificent display and was instantly reminded of why she had always chosen that bedroom.

Krista pulled Ox by the hand and said. "Come with me. I want to show you my favorite room on the third floor; the master's chambers."

As Ox entered the room he studied the wall length maps and shelves of antique books.

Krista asked. "So do you have any brothers and sisters?"

He blew the dust off one of the books, began thumbing through the pages, and then replied. "Yes I have a half brother and half sister from my mother's previous marriage. They're in their late thirties and I don't see them often. They were both grown and on their own by the time I came along. How about you?"

Krista answered. "I'm an only child." Then she went on to ask. "Do your parents live in Missouri, or did you come here by yourself for school?"

Ox stated jokingly. "My mother and father were never married. I was an oops. My mother lives in London, and my dead beat father is from Poplar Bluff. He convinced me to transfer here so we could get to know each other. I could probably count on one hand the number of times I'd seen my father before I moved here. What brought you to Missouri?" He asked.

Krista walked over to the window, pulled it open and took in a deep breath. The air was finally beginning to cool off a bit, and she could smell the mouth watering aroma of her dad's hickory smoked ribs all the way up on the third floor.

Ox joined her by the window, and she began to explain things to him. "My grandfather passed away recently. He had three sons. Uncle Mark is the oldest. My dad, Brian, is the middle child and Uncle Vince is the youngest. My grandpa left my Uncle Vince the beach front property in Miami, Florida, and my father the Colburn estate here."

Ox gave Krista a bewildered look then asked, "But what about your uncle Mark? Didn't you say he was the oldest son? I would've figured that he would inherit the Colburn estate."

Krista sat on the large wooden desk and began to give further explanation. "My uncle Mark is a con artist, thief, and a career criminal. From what my father told me he was a normal guy twenty years ago. He was going to art school in England when he got mixed up with the wrong crowd. He became addicted to gambling and he owed the wrong people money. My grandparents spent the next two decades paying off his debts. They also shelled out for multiple lawyer fees. They were constantly bailing him out of jail. Uncle Mark showed his appreciation by conning, and stealing from my grandparents every opportunity he got. Right before Grandpa passed he told Uncle Mark that he wouldn't inherit the property. Instead Grandpa left a large sum of money and split it between my dad and Uncle Vince to ration out to Uncle Mark. This way he wouldn't gamble away his entire inheritance at once, and end up homeless and begging on the streets again. My grandpa explained this to him and he got angry and left town. He didn't even stick around for the funeral. Now he's serving ten years in a Dallas prison for armed robbery. It was his third strike and the judge showed no leniency."

All conversation ceased when Krista saw that Ox had wandered over to the fireplace and picked up the book she'd been reading. *I was so excited about our date that I just ran off to get ready. I had completely forgotten to hide the book first.* She thought.

"This one looks interesting: White Water Brook." Kevin commented as he read the cover and started flipping through the pages.

Krista relieved him of the book and said. "This one is off limits."

Ox asked, "Why? Is that your diary or something?"

"No not exactly." Krista replied.

"Now I'm really intrigued. What's this story about?" Ox asked grinning trying to get the book back from her.

Krista sighed and said. "You wouldn't believe me if I told you."

Ox gave her a comforting embrace and replied. "Try me."

Krista stood wrapped in his arms thinking. *For some reason I feel unusually comfortable with Ox. Almost as if we share a kinship or a special bond. It feels like we've known each other forever. I haven't even told Stacy and Angela about my uncle Mark, but I had no problem telling Ox. Now I'm about to tell him about White Water Brook.*

After giving him a brief summary of all she'd read so far, Krista was glad to see that he took a genuine interest. *He actually believed me.*

Kevin asked, still astounded by the whole story. "Have you visited any of the places described in the book yet?"

Krista answered. "From what I can tell, I believe I'm staying in Francesca's old room. I'm certain that the office we're standing in now was my great, great, great, great, great grandfather's chambers. Other than these two rooms I haven't gone in search of anything else."

Just then her mother entered the room and said. "Dinner's ready."

They walked outside, and she could still hear the freshly seasoned meat searing on the grill. Krista and her mother lit torches and citronella candles so everyone wouldn't be eaten alive by mosquitoes. Krista helped prepare the picnic table. She was glad to see her father warming up to Ox a little.

"How would you like your burgers?" Krista's dad asked from in front of the grill.

Ox and Krista replied simultaneously. "Medium well, no onions, and no barbeque sauce."

They looked at one another in disbelief and quickly brushed off the coincidence.

After dinner Krista walked Ox back to his jeep. She found herself waiting once again for their first real kiss. *Ahhh, he's a gentleman. He's not gonna go for it on the first night. I admire that.* Krista thought and gave Ox a hug and a peck on the cheek as a consolation.

Ox said as he climbed into his vehicle. "If you'd like, I can come back tomorrow to help you search for some of the places described in the book."

Krista smiled and replied. "I'd like that."

Ox started up the SUV and drove away. Krista watched as his jeep kicked up dust and disappeared down the gravel path. Then she returned to the house.

Krista picked up a bottle of Windex and two squares of paper towel. She grabbed her robe and walked to a bathroom upstairs. *I can do without anymore creepy messages from my cousin Alex.* She thought as she sprayed the mirror with a blue mist, and wiped it with paper towel.

Krista took a brief shower. She was stunned and horrified once again when she climbed out and saw another message written in the steam. **W. S. C. 1929**

Chapter 27

Krista strolled down stairs the next day to find her parents in another meeting with Mr. Cambridge and Dr. Veronica Clark. Mr. Cambridge was a pudgy, balding man, who was usually seen looking over his glasses instead of through them. He wore a white button down shirt, under a gray suit, with a tie. Dr. Clark was a tall slender woman in her late 30's. Her black hair was kept short and professional. She was friendly, polite, and spoke with an accent of the deepest south. Krista walked past the room without bothering to interrupt the conference.

She heard Ox's vehicle pull up shortly before the meeting ended. She briefly gathered the book, a blanket, and a picnic basket then met him outside in front of the house.

Ox stepped out of his jeep and noticed the two extra cars. He turned to Krista and offered. "I can come back tomorrow if this is a bad time."

Krista assured him. "No it's cool. They're probably just here to discuss my grandpa's insurance policy."

"In that case, what's on the agenda?" Ox asked.

He gave Krista a peck on the forehead, and relieved her of the hefty basket of treats she was holding. Krista took him by the hand and they strolled in the direction of the pond at the far end of the slaves' quarters.

It was a scorcher, 94 degrees and not a cloud in the sky. They hadn't walked a quarter mile yet and they were both beginning to perspire.

Ox asked as they passed several abandoned cabins. "Are we stopping to look in any of these?"

"Not today." Krista answered, and then went on to say. "I've had one place on my mind since I opened this journal, that's the hidden brook. I need to know if there's any truth to this story."

Ox gave her a half smirk then said. "I find it remarkable that you've spent almost every summer here since you were born and you've never seen it. How do you suppose we'll find it today?"

Krista went on to explain. "Well first we'll have to find the entrance to the tunnel that leads to White Water Brook, which is right over there."

She pointed to the largest cabin in the slaves' quarters. It was built only a few feet off the pond under an enormous weeping willow. She glanced back and forth collating the sketch in the book to the structure in front of her.

"This has to be it." Krista declared as she brushed the hanging branches aside, and led the way into the old infirmary.

Her heart grew heavy as she thought to herself. *Part of me still isn't ready to find out if what I've read is true.* She gathered her nerve and pulled aside the ratty old floor mat. *Well there it is: a 3ft X 3ft trapdoor.*

Ox flung open the trapdoor and said. "I'll go first to make sure it's safe."

Krista grabbed a flashlight from the basket and climbed in after him. The tunnel was extremely dark, and at least twenty degrees cooler than outside. It looked approximately 7ft high and nine 9ft wide, with an arched ceiling. There were small tree roots and plants growing up between the bricks that composed it. The stone walls were lined with torches that hadn't been lit in over 150 years. Krista stopped mid stride just to take it all in. *I had always been told that my family acquired this property from others who previously owned slaves. I was convinced that we never dealt in such a cruel, inhumane, and immoral practice ourselves.*

Ox asked with compassion in his voice. "Are you alright?"

Krista faked a smile and assured him that she was. She pulled a lighter from her pocket and began igniting the torches; which made the tunnel glow.

Krista and Ox continued following the tunnel. They eventually began to hear the faint sound of rushing water. They stumbled into a large cavern, and the flow of water grew even louder. Sunlight flooded in through the opening at the far wall, and she blinked several times to give her pupils a moment to adjust. Krista and Ox weaved through the colossal stalagmites and stalactites that constituted the ceiling and floor of the cave.

Ox reached the opening and said. "Krista you've got to see this."

He climbed out of the cavern first and reached for her hand. What lie outside could only be describe as something out of a dream. They found themselves at a bowl shaped body of water beneath a waterfall. A utopia of lilies, daisies, violets, and lilacs flourished in bloom. A rainbow of shrubbery, moss, and vines lie strewn about an emerald green lawn.

Krista made a pallet near the edge of the water next to a red maple tree. A curious salamander scampered onto their blanket then retreated once it was spotted.

Krista joked as she unloaded the picnic basket. "I guess my mom packed the entire refrigerator."

Ox tossed a grape in the air and caught it in his mouth, then replied. "I'm not complaining."

He sat back against the trunk of the tree and Krista leaned against him. They opened the book to the page she'd marked and took turns reading.

Chapter 28

Sarah dropped the glass bottle and ran toward the door. She struggled with the knob but Frank had locked it when she wasn't looking. Frank bolted over and grabbed Sarah from behind with one arm around her waist, and the other hand placed firmly over her mouth to muffle her screams. She swung her fists and feet violently, clawing hitting and even biting her attacker in a ferocious attempt to free herself. Frank pushed Sarah down on the floor. He forced himself on top of her and began to pull up her dress.

He struck her hard and growled. "Stop struggling girl and give yourself to me!"

Sarah could feel her attacker's sweaty swollen flesh pressed tightly against her. She could smell the sour odor of whiskey on his musty breath. Sarah mustered up all the strength in her body and grabbed a piece of the broken medicine vile. She swung the large shard of glass blindly, slicing Frank clear across the left side of his face. Frank bellowed in agony and immediately withdrew. Sarah climbed to her feet and backed against the wall.

Frank gripped his badly bleeding jaw and yelled. "I'll get you, you little harlot!"

He walked slowly toward her, and she grabbed a black serpent from its aquarium.

Frank laughed scornfully and said. "Is that the best you can do, a gardener snake?"

The serpent lunged and snapped at Frank as Sarah threatened him. "This is a black mamba, one of the few animals that escaped the fire. One venomous bite, if left untreated, will kill you within hours. Two bites will end your life in minutes. This snake was smuggled in from Africa. I have the only one of its kind, and therefore the only anti venom. If you take one more step toward me, I will allow you to die an excruciating horrible death."

Frank threw on his pants and darted back to his cabin in the pouring down rain. His shoes were still in his grasp as he ran. Once Frank was out of view, Sarah returned the mamba to its home on the shelf of poisonous reptiles and insects. *I've worked with these venomous animals for so long and I've been bitten so many times, I've developed immunity to most of them.*

Sarah took off to Aaron's cabin and pounded on the door as hard as she could.

Aaron answered the door still in his sleep attire. "Sarah come in, you're soaked. What the hell's going on?" he demanded, noticing the frantic state she was in.

Sarah's entire body quivered. She was crying hysterically.

She finally collected herself and announced, "Frank Welch attacked me!"

Aaron wrapped a dry blanket around Sarah and assured her. "I'll sleep in the infirmary with you until Mathew returns."

The next day Aaron left the infirmary to pick up Mathew from the train station. There were no patients at the moment. Sarah spent half the time studying her medical books, and the other half, trying to repair her ruby necklace. The clasp had been broken the night before in the terrifying scuffle with Frank Welch. Sarah briskly abandoned the effort and closed the necklace in her book when she noticed Francesca standing in the doorway.

Sarah asked in a startled voice. "Miss Francesca! What brings you out here?"

Francesca gave Sarah a suspicious glare and replied. "I originally came out here because you never examined the bruise on my back. Now my only concern is what in God's name you're doing with my Aunt Arial's necklace!"

Chapter 29

Before Sarah could choke out a response Francesca snatched the book containing the necklace and slapped her across the face.

Francesca screamed, "You little thief! Are you aware of the penalty for stealing?!"

Sarah explained stumbling over her words. "Miss Francesca, I can assure you that's not the mistress' necklace!"

Francesca's face turned beet red with anger as she replied. "Well I see thievery isn't your only talent. You're also a gifted liar! My uncle Mathew Sr. had this necklace special made. It has the Colburn family crest on the back of it. If this isn't my Aunt Arial's necklace than whose is it! And why is it in your possession!"

Sarah broke down and told Francesca. "Mathew gave it to me. He'll be here soon. If you don't believe me, please wait and ask him yourself. He'll explain everything."

Francesca ignored Sarah's pleads and marched out to the cotton field in search of an overseer to carryout Sarah's punishment. The penalty for stealing was fifteen lashes.

Francesca called up to a wiry red haired man on a horse. "I've caught a thief and I need you to discipline her."

The man called down. "The master and mistress are at a town meeting. Master Mathew isn't back yet either. I don't feel comfortable enforcing such a punishment without prior authorization from one of them."

Francesca heard a voice call from behind her. "I'll do it!"

She glanced back to find Frank Welch, who was more than delighted to crack the whip in Sarah's direction.

Sarah was dragged kicking and screaming to the whipping post. She heard the muffled conversations of over a hundred slaves. The servants formed an enormous circle around the grassless plot of land where the whippings took place. Any time a slave was being punished all the servants were required to attend. This practice was enforced to make an example of the person being chastised, and to intimidate the watchers. She was stripped naked to the waist and tightly bound to a tall round wooden post. Moments before the punishment took place Sarah caught a glimpse of Frank. The scar on his face looked horrific. *He almost appears to be smiling.*

Frank swung the whip forcefully through the air. Sarah could hear a faint whistling sound just before it made contact with her back. She screamed in anguish as it split the flesh right open. Tears rolled down her cheeks and blood began to trickle out of the wound when she felt the second vicious blow. Within sixty seconds Frank managed to deliver at least three more violet strikes. As Frank reared back to whop Sarah a sixth time Mathew caught his arm.

Mathew grabbed Frank by the collar and punched him in the face repeatedly. Frank fell to the ground with blood running from his nose and mouth.

Mathew untied Sarah from the whipping post, and she collapsed in his arms.

As Mathew carried her off, Frank called out in his delirium. "I was only following orders!"

Mathew yelled back. "Aaron told me what you did! You were not ordered to come into the infirmary and attack her!"

Frank climbed to his feet and spat out a bloody tooth. He replied. "I was ordered to whip her!"

"By who!" Mathew demanded.

Frank answered. "Your cousin Francesca ordered the whipping."

After taking Sarah to the infirmary to be cared for, Mathew stormed to the big house still covered in her blood. He forcefully entered Francesca's room, and snatched her up from the cherry wood vanity by both arms. Cassie dropped Francesca's dress and bolted from the room.

Francesca screamed and struggled to free herself. "Mathew let go! You're hurting me!"

Mathew yelled at her. "You've pulled some underhanded stunts but this is by far the worst! I gave Sarah that necklace. She's my wife and the mother of my unborn child."

Francesca looked up at Mathew shocked and repulsed by his statement and said. "I guess the little whore wasn't lying. She told me you gave her the necklace, but I thought even a pathetic hillbilly such as you would have more class than to wed a Negro wench. You disgust me!"

Mathew glared down at Francesca with pure hate in his eyes. It took all the strength in his body to restrain from striking her.

He shook her and yelled. "Francesca don't you realize what you've done! You had the woman I love beaten and humiliated for no reason at all!"

An uncaring expression swept across Francesca's face. She nonchalantly shrugged her shoulders without showing the least bit of remorse for her actions.

He argued with himself. *Don't do it Mathew. You can't just hit your cousin as if she were a man.*

At last he pushed her down on her bed and yelled out in anguish. "You're lucky you're not a man!"

Mathew stormed out of the room to his father's chambers convinced that Francesca possessed neither a soul nor a conscious.

Mathew burst into the office and said. "Father, please send Francesca back to France before I kill her with my own two hands! And we must have Frank arrested!"

Mr. Colburn replied. "None of this would've happened if you hadn't been so bold about the affair."

Mathew lashed back at his father. "You told me that I could give the necklace to the woman I love and intend to marry! Whether you like it or not that woman is Sarah!"

Mr. Colburn tried his best to calm Mathew and explain things. "Son I understand you may think you like or even love this girl but you can't legally marry her. I know Sarah's a beautiful girl, I may be old but I'm not blind. However, for you to give our family crest to a Negro wench would shame not just you but all of us. What in the world were you thinking?"

And under what charges should I have Frank arrested? We're a little short handed on overseers right now since Samson left and Charles started a plantation of his own. Besides, from what I hear, it was all a big misunderstanding. Frank told me he came to the infirmary late that night because he had an infection in a very private area. He went to show Sarah and she mistook his actions for an advance."

Mathew asked in frustration. "If that's what really happened then how did he get that huge cut and all those scratches!"

Master Colburn answered. "I was told that his mare got spooked by a snake and threw him into a thorn bush."

Mathew shot back. "That little pudgy bastard is lying through his teeth! Are you too blind to see what's happened here? Frank was the one killing those women all along! He allowed his son to take the fall. Frank was the first one in the office when that ear came up missing. The deputies found those body parts in a cabin he and Robert shared. He's been stalking Sarah all this time. He torched the infirmary to keep her here!"

Master Colburn asked. "If Frank's been stalking Sarah all this time, why didn't he try something a long time ago?"

Mathew answered. "Her entire family left for England and I was out of town. This was the first opportunity he had."

Mathew awakened late the next morning in the infirmary. He'd spent the night out there to keep a careful watch on Sarah.

She was sleeping on her stomach. Tiny spots of blood seeped through her bandages. He kissed her forehead and slipped out without waking her.

The beautiful Missouri weather made a wicked turn for the worse. It was late in the morning but the sky was almost black. Mathew walked to the tobacco field under a blanket of gray clouds and heavy rain. *In the heartland of America weather like this only means one thing: a tornado is brewing. I need to round up the field slaves in order to ensure their safety.*

Mathew signaled to Frank Welch, who was mounted high on his horse, to bring in the servants. A stampede of slaves came roaring in. Lightening cracked and lit up the sky for long enough for Mathew to spot Saphirra in the rolling green sea of tobacco.

As she walked passed with her child Mathew pulled her aside. He spoke as calmly as he could to prevent scaring her. "Saphirra, I need you to tell me the truth. I promise you won't be in trouble. Did Robert Welch ever rape you?"

Saphirra replied. "No, Robert never showed an interest in me or any of the women here, but the man was an abusive tyrant who broke my son's leg. I'm not sorry for what I did."

Mathew assured her. "I understand."

Saphirra picked up her son and ran to her cabin.

Mathew stood in the pouring rain and glared over at Frank Welch thinking. *It's been you killing these people all this time. If I don't stop you no one will.* Mathew gripped the sharpened eight inch screw and pulled it from his pocket. *I can't allow you to hurt anyone else. I won't allow you to harm Sarah again.* Mathew raised the weapon and honed in on Frank.

Chapter 30

Mathew snatched Frank Welch off of his steed. Frank fell flat on his back in the mud. Frank threw up his arms to shield himself as Mathew brought his arm down swiftly with the blade. Seth appeared expeditiously and tackled Mathew to the ground. Frank ran for his life and disappeared into the storm.

Seth subdued Mathew and shouted over the violent winds. "He's not worth going to prison over! Think of Sarah! Think of your child!"

Mathew climbed to his feet and yelled. "I was thinking of my family! I was thinking of all the families! Frank Welch is a plague upon this earth!"

Seth pulled Mathew toward the mansion and replied. "I know how you feel. If someone hurt Leah I would try to kill him, but I know you would be there to stop me. Frank messed up when he killed Katherine McKinley. That's one murder he will spend the rest of his life in prison for. We've just got to prove it."

Mathew reached the big house and walked straight to his room. He peeled off his wet muddy clothing and threw on a dry set. As Mathew buttoned his shirt he heard rapping on the door.

"Come In!" Mathew shouted in reply to the knocking.

Master Colburn entered the bedroom in an unusually good mood, which confused the hell out of Mathew. His father almost appeared to be smiling. Mathew gave his dad a suspicious glare and thought. *That man never smiles unless he's done something to make my life a living hell. Dear God in heaven, what has he done now?*

Mathew snapped at him. "Please state your business. I have work to do."

Master Colburn replied. "I just wanted to inform you that Francesca has just agreed to marry you."

Mathew shot back. "I don't recall asking that wicked wretch for her claw in marriage!"

Master Colburn began to explain the arrangement. "Your mother and Aunt A`lice arranged the wedding many years ago. Why else do you think Francesca's been coming here every summer to get better acquainted with you? Your mother and I thought you would've asked her yourself by now. We were concerned for a moment that the youngest Arrington was going to steal her out from under you, but she came around."

Mathew pushed passed his father and stormed out of the room.

He walked up to Francesca and said. "My parents have been asking you for years to marry me! You've never loved me or anyone but yourself for that matter. What has suddenly changed your mind?"

Francesca grinned at Mathew and arrogantly replied. "You carrying on with this Sarah girl would have brought us all disgrace and public humiliation. I'm just doing what's best for everyone especially you."

Mathew replied bitterly. "What's best for me is for you to find the highest cliff in Missouri and leap off of it."

Francesca reached for Mathew's hand and said. "You should be thanking me that you'll be a count one day. Can't you see this heathen girl has bewitched you? I'm trying to save you cousin. I'm simply doing what needs to be done."

Mathew jerked his hand away from Francesca and growled. "Keep your talons to yourself, you damned witch."

Francesca stormed away from Mathew toward the front entrance of the mansion. Aaron and Cassie were standing in the anteroom. Cassie was dressed in an elegant blue gown and fine jewelry supplied by Francesca.

Francesca snapped at them both. "Come now, make haste."

Aaron walked up to Francesca and said. "Do you not realize this is twister weather?"

Francesca replied. "Stop whining its just a little rain. This trip can't wait. I need to go to the Cathedral and prepare my soul for marriage."

Aaron replied angrily. "You don't have a soul! If god wiped out all of existence, the desolate black abyss of turmoil and despair that remained would be your soul, Francesca." Francesca rolled her eyes and Aaron continued, "If you want to kill yourself then fine! But you're not taking my sister with you." Aaron turned to Cassie and ordered. "Go to Miss Francesca's room and wait out the storm."

Cassie could tell her brother meant business. She took off up the stairs immediately. Francesca was appalled by Aaron's actions.

She scowled at him and said. "How dare you give orders to my servant! A proper lady is never to travel alone."

Aaron scoffed and replied. "I'll inform you when I see a lady."

Francesca slapped him and scolded. "I'll see you whipped for your insolence. Now prepare the stagecoach."

The rain continued to plummet as Aaron pulled the carriage up in front of the mansion. As the driver, Aaron was left outside in the pouring precipitation with the vicious gusts of wind. Francesca would be able to ride inside the carriage well protected from the elements.

Francesca walked outside with an open umbrella. She closed it with one swift motion and climbed into her seat. The horses began to trot as Aaron led the stagecoach away. Francesca cast aside her soggy umbrella and pulled out a book to read.

Bolts of lightening flashed, and thunder rolled with the force of the gods. The storm shook the stagecoach as it ventured forward. She turned the page and continued to read. The storm grew worse, and it began to rain tree branches. Aaron and Francesca were two miles from the church when the tornado came through.

Aaron woke up in excruciating pain. He was no doctor, but could tell his ribs were broken. A stabbing sensation shot across his chest every time he breathed. He found himself doubled over a tree branch several feet in the air. It was dark outside, and the rain was still falling heavily. The crumpled up stagecoach lay a few yards from him. Scraped and bruised, he climbed to the ground and hobbled around in search of Francesca. He spotted her trapped, from the waist down, between two fallen trees. The side of her dress was covered in blood.

Aaron called out to her. "Francesca! Hang in there I'm coming to help you!"

She moaned in pain and moved about sluggishly. Aaron grabbed a fallen limb and wedged it between the trees that snared Francesca. He pushed with all his might against the limb in order to force the smaller tree to roll free. This action intensified his pain so much he bellowed in agony.

Aaron paused as he noticed a constant screeching noise. He looked up and discovered an enormous branch swinging back and forth over them. It was dangling by a thread, threatening to fall at any moment.

Aaron shouted and pulled even harder on the makeshift pry bar. "Francesca you have to help me or you'll be crushed!"

Francesca snapped her head up and caught sight of the dangling branch. She desperately pushed on the smaller tree with both hands but it didn't budge. Her eyes filled with tears and sorrow as she realized she was doomed.

Francesca shouted to Aaron. "You have to get out of here! If you don't leave you'll die too!"

Aaron climbed on top of the larger tree and wrapped his arms around her torso.

In spite of his pain, he pulled on her as hard as he could and yelled. "I'm not leaving! I can pull you out!"

Francesca pulled Aaron down to her eye level, and pressed her trembling lips against his.

She put a hand on his cheek and sadly replied. "You can't free me. You'll only get yourself killed trying. For the love of god, please just leave."

Aaron's face grew distraught, and a hush fell over him. He shook his head in disbelief.

"Go!!!" Francesca shouted, and shoved him away from her.

Tears cascaded down Francesca's face as Aaron disappeared into the darkness. She trembled in horror, sobbing uncontrollably. She placed her hands over her ears to deafen the eerie creek of the giant tree limb swinging over head. Then she closed her eyes firmly; anticipating the moment she'd be crushed to death.

The giant tree limb came tumbling from the sky. It eviscerated everything in its path and killed Francesca instantly. She stood outside of her former body. She panicked at the sight of just her bloody arm sticking out from underneath the giant piece of wood. The forest around her became engulfed in flames. Francesca did not find herself in front of a divine glow at the end of a majestic corridor. She was in a place of mayhem and destruction. Innumerable tortured souls cried out as they were ripped apart by three headed beasts and flying demons. The fire began to singe her flesh as she realized. *I'm in hell!*

Chapter 31

At last a winged demon had spotted Francesca. It swooped down from the sky and landed ten feet in front of her. The creature was as red as the fire that scorched Francesca's flesh. It possessed long black talons and razor sharp teeth. The monster had no eyes, only two desolate black pits where eyes should be. Francesca screamed in horror as the demon lunged toward her.

She began to repent for her sins and recite the *23rd Psalm of David.* "The lord is my shepherd I shall not want. He maketh me to lie down in green pastures: he leadeth me beside the still waters. He restoreth my soul: he leadeth me in the path of righteousness for his name's sake. Yea, though I walk through the valley of the shadow of death I will fear no evil: for though art with me....."

Francesca was seized from her prayer as Aaron limped back to her. She opened her eyes and the vision of hell vanished. She glanced up to discover the limb had not yet fallen.

Francesca shouted through her tears, relieved to see Aaron. "I told you to leave!"

Aaron shouted back as he climbed atop the large tree. "And I told you I wasn't leaving! I only ran to the carriage in search of my knife. Be very still. I'm going to cut you out of your dress."

Aaron shoved the knife in Francesca's sleeve and sliced the material up to the collar. He repeated the action on the other side. He cut the ribbons to her corset, snatched it off, and threw it on the ground. Then he gripped her upper body once more and pulled hard. Francesca wiggled and squirmed as the dangling branch snapped. It came hurdling from the sky, decimating everything in its path. The ground rumbled and a deafening blast echoed through the forest as the massive limb came crashing down.

Once the earth settled Aaron called out. "We made it Francesca!"

He climbed to his feet and extended a hand to her.

Francesca looked up at Aaron in a daze and stammered "You... You... came back."

She passed out seconds later. Aaron wailed in pain as he lifted Francesca's unconscious body onto his shoulder. He limped into the darkness in search of refuge.

Francesca regained consciousness hours later. She was lying on the floor, in front of a cozy fireplace. She shed the quilt she was wrapped in and groggily rose to her feet. Francesca promptly retrieved the cover once she realized she was only wearing her silk lingerie. Aaron walked in from the kitchen with two dry logs of wood for the fire.

"Where are we?" Francesca asked.

Aaron arranged the logs on the fire and answered with irritation. "We're at the Thompson's summer villa. It's fall so they're at their home in New York right now. We're the only people here."

Francesca dropped the blanket and walked over to him.

She looked into his dark mysterious eyes and said. "You risked your life to save me: a terrible person who threatened your sister and forced you to do things against your will."

Francesca leaned forward to kiss Aaron, and he brushed a soft blonde curl away from her face.

He leaned close to her and whispered. "Is this the part where you *make* me do something for you? For Christ sake you're engaged to my best friend, Francesca. Have you no conscience what so ever?"

Aaron walked away in aggravation.

Francesca sadly replied. "I'll never make you do anything ever again. I know it means nothing to you coming from me, but I truly am sorry."

At that moment Aaron heard the sound of trotting horses drawing closer. He took a lantern outside and ran to the end of the gravel path. He flailed his arms wildly, and flagged down the passing carriage.

As the stagecoach came to a halt, Aaron was relieved to see Mathew and Seth behind the reigns.

"Thank God we've found you!" Seth called down.

Mathew added. "When I saw the carriage obliterated on the side of the road, I feared you might be dead."

Francesca walked up barefoot with a quilt wrapped around her.

As she climbed in the stagecoach Mathew called out angrily. "You're an idiot, Francesca!"

"Go to hell!" She responded.

Seth looked at Aaron and asked. "Where are her clothes?"

As Aaron boarded the carriage he replied, "Long story."

Dr. McKinley finished examining Francesca and left the room. She lay awake in bed running her finger tips over her bandages. Both of her thighs were ridden with contusions and she had a small cut on her left side. Her thoughts grew heavy as she struggled to rest. *Why must I be threatened with eternal damnation in order to realize right from wrong? I'm going back to that horrible place of fire and death, if something doesn't change. I can't believe I told Aaron to leave me. I really must care for him. Not that it matters; he hates me, and for good reason.* Francesca grabbed a tissue from her night stand as she began to sob.

She heard a tap on her balcony window. She opened the sliding glass doors to find Aaron standing there. He was shirtless but nearly his entire torso was wrapped in bandages.

He scowled and asked. "Where is my sister?"

Francesca answered. "She's sleeping over there on the lounge."

Francesca pulled the wooden divider that cut the room in half. Cassie continued resting on the other side.

Aaron walked into the bedroom and spoke with irritation. "I have something to say." Francesca moved to apologize and Aaron snapped. "Don't interrupt me until I'm finished. I've earned that much. I hate you for hurting my friend Sarah! I hate you for threatening my sister! And for nearly getting me killed! But what I hate you for most of all, is in spite of how much I try to convince myself that I hate you, I turn right around and make a two story climb in the middle of the night, with three broken ribs, just to make sure you're alright! Are you alright?!'"

Francesca jumped with fear and nodded her head yes. She briefly replied. "Just a few bumps and bruises. I'll be fine."

Aaron nodded and continued. "I hate the fact that I enjoy our little walks in the woods! I hate the fact that even though you *never* have anything nice to say, I still look forward to hearing your voice. I wouldn't have been able to sleep tonight unless I was certain you'd be fine." Francesca smiled through her tears and Aaron yelled. "I hate you for that! I hate that against all logic, reasoning, rational thought, and a general sense of self-preservation, I love you."

Tears fell from Francesca's eyes as she whispered. "I love you too."

Aaron gently embraced Francesca, and gave her a long tender kiss.

The following day Till entered the cooking quarters of Arrington manor. The kitchen was vast with stark white walls. Shining copper and silver colored pots hung from several racks. Mabel stood in front of the stove slicing vegetables into a large pot of boiling broth.

Till walked in carrying two large containers of milk and asked. "Where should I put these?"

Mabel called out from in front of the stove. "I want you to divide that milk among those nine small containers on the table."

Till snapped. "I don't have time for this Mabel! I have to get to the Colburn Plantation."

Mabel replied sarcastically. "I thought you only delivered to them on Mondays."

Till spoke with angst as her eyes filled with tears. "If you must know, I'm not going there for a delivery. My husband has passed. I'm going to see if the Colburns ever found Anna and Mali. I hope the girls got away for good, but if they didn't they will at least be able to attend their father's funeral tomorrow."

Mabel dried her hands on her apron and walked over to Till. She smacked her lips and said. "You must not have heard."

"Heard what?!" Till demanded with a concerned look.

Mabel glanced up at Till and smugly announced. "Frank's boy Robert killed them and a bunch of other people."

Till slapped Mabel across the face and shouted. "Take it back you evil old hag!"

Mabel rubbed her jaw and replied. "All they found of Anna was an ear, with a black arrowhead earring."

Till shuddered and shook her head in disbelief.

Mabel added. "Ahhh you know the jewelry I speak of. Let's see if you can recognize another piece. All they found of Mali was a finger with a silver and onyx ring on it."

Till's face went flush as she became light headed. The room began to spin and she collapsed on the floor.

Chapter 32

Till's master, Lincoln Miles, took a seat at the end of the dinner table. He read a newspaper while waiting for his family to join him for dinner. Miles was in his forties with thick brown hair sprinkled with gray. He was a wiry man with a full beard and mustache.

Atop the dinner table sat five large silver platters, covered by dome lids. Till walked in from the kitchen with a sixth platter. It had been a trying day for her, and she was still forced to serve as if nothing had happened.

Lincoln Miles commented as she sat the platter before him. "I'm starving I may have to start without them."

"Well you're the boss, Sir." Till replied as she forced a smile for him.

Till lifted the lid off the platter and a black snake shot out. It struck Lincoln Miles on the throat; sinking its' poisonous fangs deep into his flesh. In a matter of seconds the snake bit him twice more on the face.

As he cried out in agony Till announced vehemently. "You have ten minutes to live; so you listen and you listen well! You took my daughters from me! You put them in harms way! You promised my husband that if he made you enough money you'd get them back. In spite of his heart condition, my husband worked himself into the grave for you!"

Lincoln Miles' face began to swell with venom and bruise.

He writhed in pain and called out. "It isn't my fault Till! Robert Welch killed your girls not me! Please call a doctor for Christ sake."

Till replied with a deranged look in her eyes. "You had twice the amount of money you'd need a month before Anna and Mali disappeared. My husband made certain of that. Every week you had another excuse why you wouldn't go get my daughters, and every week my husband worked harder for you. Now he's dead and so are they."

Lincoln Miles pleaded as his face grew more swollen and distorted. "I'm sorry Till. I was never in debt. I was trying to bait your husband into raising profits. I didn't know anyone would get hurt!"

Till gave a sinister smile and said. "Don't be sorry for my daughters. They have their father to look after them now. Before you leave this earth, I just want you to know that your family did join you for dinner tonight."

Lincoln Miles screamed out in horror as Till walked around the table flinging off the lids of the five other platters. The grotesque severed heads of his three sons, his daughter and his wife stared back at him.

As poison coursed through the veins of Lincoln Miles he called out. "You'll never get away with this!"

Till shot back, "I never planned to get away."

Lincoln Miles fell over on the table and foam spewed from his mouth. As he gagged jerked and took his last breath, Till finally found peace.

She left the house and went to her cabin. She smashed two kerosene lanterns on the floor and watched as the tiny wooden shack ignited. Till laid down next to the body of her deceased husband and downed a vile of poison. The cabin was in flames in no time.

She rested her head on his chest and said. "My dear James, I'll be with you soon."

Chapter 33

On the other side of town a multitude of guests gathered for Mathew and Francesca's engagement dinner. The feast was served in the grand dinning hall. Two massive tables sat forty guests each; including Seth, Emanuel, Dr. McKinley and Lady Arrington. Mathew sat at the end of one of the tables, with Francesca to the right of him.

The eighty guests went silent as Mathew stood to make a toast. "First I'd like to thank all of you for coming here in spite of yesterday's twister."

Mathew held up his glass of white wine and spoke poetically. "I would like to propose a toast to my fiancée, the beautiful Viscountess Francesca Demoniet." Applause roared from the many guests as Mathew took Francesca by the hand. She rose graciously from her seat and Mathew went on to say. "Francesca reminds me of Greek mythology."

The women at the tables called out in awe. "Does she remind you of Helen, the face who launched a thousand ships? Or does she remind you of Aphrodite, goddess of love and beauty?"

Mathew smiled and answered. "If Hates, lord of the underworld, were to impregnate his three headed hell beast the offspring would be Francesca." The visitors gasped and an awkward silence fell over the room as Mathew continued. "Francesca Demoniet is a vile plague upon humanity, who only revels in the suffering of others. I am most willing to endure a thousand agonizing deaths, before spending the rest of my life bound to this wicked crone. So please enjoy the food and drinks set before you, but as I have previously stated to my parents, there will be no wedding."

The volume rose abruptly as the visitors gossiped to one another. Francesca's face turned crimson with humiliation. She bolted from the grand dining hall in anguish and disbelief.

Mathew downed his glass of wine and casually sauntered out of the dining area. *Man that felt good.*

Master and Mistress Colburn marched out after Mathew, and snatched him into a private room.

Mistress Colburn slapped her son and began to yell. "Do you realize you've just publically humiliated your cousin?! And not only that, you've shamed your father and me! Why are you so against this union?"

Mathew shot back. "How many times must I tell you? I'm already married! Sarah is pregnant with my child for Christ sake!"

Master Colburn asked casually. "Is that all? If you're that attached to this girl then marry Francesca and keep Sarah as a mistress. Take Sarah and your little bastard to France with you. Give them the best of treatment but never claim them as your own. Why the hell do you think we've always been so good to Seth?"

Mathew narrowed his eyes at his father and spoke. "Seth is your son! You damn hypocrite!"

Master Colburn shot back. "Seth is your mother's son!"

Mathew shook his head in disbelief. He looked at his mother and said. "None of this is true! You were sent here twenty years ago to marry Father!"

Mathew's mother confessed with teary eyes. "I was sent to Missouri twenty years ago to conceal the pregnancy of a bastard black child. I fell in love with your father and decided to stay."

As Mathew stormed out of the room Master Colburn said to his wife. "We've played this game with Mathew long enough. He won't listen to reason. Our family would gain control over Francesca's fortune if they were to marry. It's time to do what we talked about."

Mistress Colburn reluctantly agreed.

Sarah stood in the infirmary packing her things when she noticed the black mamba was missing from its aquarium. She was in the middle of searching for it when Francesca walked in from the party.

Francesca sat on a stool and said. "We need to talk."

Sarah shot Francesca an evil look and thought. *It's your fault Mathew and I have to runaway tonight. If it weren't for you, his parents would've never found out we were married. They would've forked me over, no problem. Because of you, Miss Demoniet, I was stripped and beaten and the Colburns have refused to allow Mathew to buy my freedom.* Sarah took a deep breath and scolded herself. *Don't hit her Sarah. You're better than that. Who am I kidding? No I'm not.*

Sarah balled up her fist and sent a brutal blow to Francesca's face. The force of the punch sent Francesca flying backward from her seat, feet over head. There was a loud smack as she collided with the floor, landing flat on her back.

Francesca covered her hemorrhaging nose with a handkerchief and yelled. "Christ! Is it abuse Francesca night!"

Sarah yelled down to her. "You have some nerve to show your face here! You're already stealing my husband! What more could you possibly want from me!"

Francesca climbed to her feet and told Sarah. "I know you are running away with my cousin tonight. I only came out here to apologize and give you this." Francesca handed Sarah an envelope full of money and continued. "It's my weekly allowance. I won't gain control of my inheritance until I'm married or my parents have passed away. It's not much, but I hope it helps you."

Sarah stood speechless for a few moments before finally accepting the gift.

Sarah glanced at Francesca with guilt and said. "I should probably take a look at your nose."

Francesca lay back on the bed while Sarah examined her.

Sarah palpated Francesca's nose and said. "It doesn't look as if I broke it. Keep it covered. It should stop bleeding soon." Sarah glanced down at Francesca and added. "I have to know. What made you hate me so much? Cassie is your lady's maid now, and you don't treat her in the foul manner you treated me."

Francesca admitted. "I've grown accustomed to being the center of attention. When I came here you were all my cousins could talk about: Sarah's so smart. Sarah's so pretty and nice, Sarah loves kittens. Blah Blah etc.... You always seemed to upstage me. You always out shined me. Even though it was trivial and ridiculous, I hated you for that."

Francesca sat up and handed Sarah the ruby necklace then said. "I believe this belongs to you. Good luck to you both."

"Thank you." Sarah replied as Francesca left the infirmary.

Mathew walked in a few minutes later with a bag on his shoulder.

He hugged Sarah and said. "It's time. Seth is taking us to the train station."

At that moment a gang of overseers kicked in the door. Four of the men grabbed Mathew and slapped shackles on his wrists and ankles. The other three grabbed Sarah and administered the heavy chains to her body as well. They were both drug outside on the lawn in opposite directions. Mathew caught a final glimpse of Sarah as she was forced into a stagecoach and hauled away.

Chapter 34

Frank Welch stood in the master's chambers at dusk awaiting further orders. Master Colburn took a puff from his cigar and let out a cloud of white smoke.

He flicked off the excess ash into a glass tray and spoke with mild irritation. "Is the cellar the best you could come up with, Frank?"

Frank answered. "We have Mathew bolted to the wall. I can assure you, Sir, he won't escape."

Master Colburn took another hit from his cigar and released a mist of acrid smoke. He put out the cigar with a twisting motion and laid it against the side of the ash tray.

Master Colburn rose from his seat, and yelled at Frank. "Do not underestimate the brilliance of my son! Mathew was a child prodigy. His former teacher use to tell me he'd never seen any student like Mathew. He's a genius when it comes to the structure and composition of things. I need to keep him prisoner for at least a few weeks in order to break him. If you don't move him to a more secure destination, I guarantee you, he will break out!"

Frank Welch replied as he left the room, "As you wish, Sir. I'll bring Mathew food and drink for now, and move him tomorrow evening."

The wine cellar, which served as Mathew's prison for the past two days, shut out all light and sound. He sat against the wall with heavy iron cuffs around his wrists. The wrist cuffs were attached to long chains; which were bolted to the brick wall behind him. He scratched the tip of the eight inch screw against the cold cement floor. He thought to himself. *How ironic is it for me to be trapped in this place without Sarah; the very place I asked her to marry me. If anything's happened to Sarah my father will rue the day he laid a hand on her.* He pushed the bad thoughts aside and lectured himself. *I can't think that way. Sarah's fine. She has to be ok.* Mathew gave the large bolt a half turn and continued to scrape it over the cement. *If I can file this bolt down to just the right size, I may be able to use it as a screwdriver.* Mathew placed the makeshift screwdriver against the groove of a bolt on the wall. *It almost fits, just a little more to go.*

Mathew quickly placed the tool back in his pocket when he heard the loud clink of the cellar doors. They swung open and allowed in what little sunlight was left. He shielded his eyes and bellowed for help. The doors flew shut at once. He heard footsteps in the darkness followed by the strike of a match. The cellar began to glow as a torch on the wall was lit. Mathew could now see it was Frank Welch, who had been sent with food and water.

Mathew called out to him. "I should've pierced your black heart when I had the chance!"

Frank kicked the plate over to Mathew without a response. Frank walked back up the stairs and flung open the doors once more. This time Mathew heard the faint sound of a familiar song. The slaves were in the cemetery singing.

Swing low sweet chariot coming for to carry me home.
Swing low sweet chariot coming for to carry me home.
I looked over Jordan and what did I see?
Coming for to carry me home.
A band of angels coming after me.
Coming for to carry me home.
Swing Low … …

Mathew sprung to his feet. The chains rattled and clinked, as he yanked vigorously against them.

He called up to Frank. "Whose funeral is it?!"

Frank Welch looked back over his shoulder and gave a sinister smirk.

Mathew shouted once more. "Who died, Frank?!"

Frank walked out and slammed the doors shut.

Mathew scolded himself. *I can't think negatively. Sarah's not dead. She can't be dead.* Mathew slumped back onto the floor and retrieved his eight inch bolt. He started the filing process again. *Sarah's alive. I know she's alive. And I'm going to get out of here and rescue her.*

Mathew tried, once more, to gauge the screwdriver he'd made. *Thank God it finally fits.* He struggled to force a screw to turn, and at last it shifted with a squeak. He quickly unscrewed the first one and went on to the next. *One down seven to go.*

In a matter of minutes Mathew took all eight of the screws out. He rose to his feet in triumph as the chains came unbolted from the walls. The long chains remained cuffed to Mathew's wrists, but at least now he could move about the cellar. He walked over to the crates of wine dragging the heavy shackles behind him. The chains created a trail of sparks as they swept over the floor. He busted open a crate and removed a bottle of wine. Then grabbed the bottle by the neck and smashed it against the wall. *This should serve as a weapon the next time Father sends one of his faithful lackeys. I can wait until someone brings food tomorrow, and break out of here then. But Sarah may not have until tomorrow. I need to figure out a way to get the cellar doors open. They're locked from the outside, but I may be able to maneuver the hinges.* Mathew felt along the hinges of the cellar doors and smiled. *This won't prove difficult at all.*

He hid in the shadows of the cellar as the sound of footsteps drew closer. The doors flew open and two intruders descended the stairs. Mathew leapt out of the darkness and took the first intruder hostage.

Mathew held the broken bottle against the man's throat and threatened the other. "Free me now, or I'll kill him!"

"It's us, Mathew! Let go of Seth!" Aaron called out.

"I'm so sorry." Mathew announced as he released Seth.

"How did you manage to find me?" Mathew choked out; relieved to see Aaron and Seth had come to his aide.

Aaron answered as he unlocked Mathew's wrist shackles. "I noticed Frank acting strange. I followed him and stole his skeleton key when he wasn't looking. I figured he might be after another girl, but low and behold."

Seth added. "I was supposed to take you and Sarah to the train station after the engagement party. When you never showed up, I knew something was terribly wrong."

The three of them emerged from the cellar at night. They brought Mathew to the busted up infirmary to mend his scrapes and bruises.

The bag he'd packed had been ripped open, and the contents strewn about the infirmary. All the money he saved to run away had been stolen. Mathew looked around the place and spotted Sarah's Ruby necklace lying on the floor.

Mathew grew hysterical at the sight of it and frantically asked. "Do either one of you know where Sarah is? Is she safe? We've got to find her."

Seth and Aaron bowed their heads and the infirmary became silent.

Mathew yelled as he grew impatient and even more concerned. "You have to tell me where she is!"

Seth finally broke the silence. "I'm so sorry. She's dead Sir. Your father had her burned at the stake for witch craft. The charge was harboring abortifacient remedies."

The words pierced Mathew's chest like a razor sharp dagger. It physically felt as if he'd been stabbed in the heart. He grew sick, confused and unable to breath. Mathew fell to his knees and gripped her ruby necklace. Tears filled his eyes as he looked up at Seth and Aaron.

Mathew stammered in a shallow voice. "That… funeral I heard today… was for Sarah. Wasn't it?"

Seth and Aaron regretfully nodded yes.

Chapter 35

Mathew kneeled in front of the mound of unsettled earth where Sarah had been buried. A small wooden cross stuck out of the ground to mark her grave. He pulled the rosary from his pocket and hung it on the cross.

Mathew turned to Aaron and Seth and asked. "Would you mind preparing the carriage? I need a few moments alone. I'll meet you both up front."

They nodded and left him to his thoughts. The moment they were no longer in sight Mathew dashed out of the cemetery. He grabbed a pile of rope and headed for the mansion. He checked his pocket for the bottle of ether he took from the infirmary. He gripped the bottle in anguish thinking. *Abortifacients, my father killed Sarah for harboring abortifacients. I overheard that hypocrite explain to my Catholic mother, that long before I was born many women were raped on this plantation. These women refused to bear the children of their attackers. Many committed suicide. Numerous others died in attempts to self abort. For these reasons, Father was the one who put the abortifacients in the infirmary. He was losing too much money on the deaths of the rape victims. There have been abortifacients in the infirmary for the past two decades; long before Sarah began working there, years before she was even born.*

Mathew stealthily crept into his bedroom window, then up the stairs to his father's quarters. Master Colburn continued to sleep soundly as Mathew appeared in the doorway. Mathew gave his father a wrathful glare, and poured the ether onto a piece of cloth.

Mathew quietly entered the room and pressed the cloth firmly over his father's mouth and nose. Master Colburn's eyes went wild. He fought and struggled with all his might but Mathew overpowered him. Within seconds his eyelids grew heavy and fell once more.

Master Colburn regained consciousness minutes later. He was hanging by his feet from his bedroom balcony. One end of the rope was tied securely around his ankles. The other end was tied to his bedpost. He stared down at the ground from a distance and began to panic. He was terrified of heights; a fact only known by his closest relatives.

"Help!!" He called out again and again.

Mathew peered down at him from the balcony and yelled. "The only crime Sarah was guilty of, was loving me!"

Master Colburn pleaded. "Pull me up son. Please! Let's talk about this!"

Seth, Aaron, Francesca, and Mistress Colburn ran to Master Colburn's bedroom they each struggled to open the locked door.

Seth bellowed from the other side of the door. "Mathew, stop! You can't kill your own father!"

Mathew anchored himself and untied the rope from the bedpost. Master Colburn let out a terrified wail as he slipped several feet, before Mathew got a good grip on the rope. Aaron kicked in the door and he and Seth ran in.

Francesca and Mistress Colburn appeared behind them, pleading with tear soaked faces. "Please don't do this! He's your Father!"

Mathew gripped the rope tightly and yelled. "If anyone comes any closer I'll drop him!"

Everyone froze mid step as Mathew went onto say. "This man murdered my wife! I may have very well been next, had I not been discovered!"

Master Colburn called up. "Mathew! I never meant to hurt you! My intentions, however vile you believe they were, were in the best interest of my only son! That girl had you under her spell! I'm sorry, but Sarah had bewitched you! Would you kill your own father?"

Mathew growled with anger as he released the rope. "You are not my father."

The onlookers gasped and screamed as Master Colburn went hurdling to the ground.

They bolted down stairs to find Master Colburn lying on the lawn in a pool of blood. He hollered in agony and writhed in pain as they ran to his aide. His arm was severely broken. The bones pierced through the skin.

Mathew trotted up on a black steed and called down to his father. "I knew the fall wouldn't kill you, you heartless son-of-a-bitch. I had already done the math in my head. Killing you isn't what Sarah would've wanted, and it sure as hell won't bring her back."

Master Colburn moaned with an outstretched hand. "Son… Please… I'm sorry."

Mathew peered down from his horse and spoke vehemently. "You stopped being my father the day you killed my wife. From this moment forward you're dead to me. If you come near me again, you'll be dead to the world."

The stallion neighed with intensity as Mathew galloped away into the night.

Chapter 36

December 21, 1836

Four months had gone by since the tragic death of Sarah. The weather had grown cold and bitter. The trees bid farewell to their leaves and the ground lay covered in a light snow. Aaron pulled the carriage up in front of Seth and Leah's house. It was a massive two story home with elegant pillars. Mathew had designed and built it himself. Francesca climbed out of the stagecoach and walked up to the house with Aaron. Leah answered the door holding her four month old daughter, Athena.

"It's so nice to see you." Leah said as she smiled at Aaron and gave him a one armed hug.

Leah shot Francesca a dirty look and led them both to the parlor where Mathew and Seth were sitting. With no money and nowhere else to go Mathew went to stay with Seth and Leah.

As they walked in the room Seth kissed Leah and relieved her of the baby.

Seth greeted Aaron and Francesca. "Please come in, stay awhile."

Francesca looked at Leah and Seth and said. "I only have a short while. My aunt and uncle don't know I'm here. I came to tell you that I overheard Uncle Mathew saying he would repossess your property if you don't tell him where Mathew is."

Francesca turned to Mathew and said. "My parents will be coming to take me back to France soon. Marry me cousin. It will be in name only. We'll gain access to my inheritance. You can leave this place. Rid yourself of your parents for good."

Aaron sighed and added. "I think you should do it Mathew. Either way I'm going to lose Francesca. If her parents take her back to France unmarried I may never see her again. If she marries you, we may have a chance."

As they turned to leave, Francesca told Mathew. "Just give it some thought."

Mathew nodded and Francesca and Aaron walked out.

Leah walked over to Mathew and said. "Am I the only one who remembers that woman is the anti-Christ? Don't marry Francesca, Mathew."

Seth added. "Leah's right. I just don't trust Francesca."

Mathew replied. "You both have shown me more then enough kindness by taking me in when I had nowhere else to go. I won't put you in a position to lose everything you own."

Leah replied. "That was an empty threat. Your father adores Seth."

Mathew turned to Seth and said. "My father killed Sarah. I wouldn't put anything past him. You have to think of your family. You and Leah have a daughter now. You have another child on the way."

Leah glanced at Mathew appalled and snapped. "I do not have a child on the way."

The uh oh expression spread across Mathew's face as he confessed. "The men on my father's side have a strange gift. I don't know where it came from or why, but we have the ability to tell when women are pregnant."

Leah and Seth laughed and Mathew continued. "I'm serious. I knew Sarah was pregnant before she did. If I touched your stomach I could even tell you the sex of the child."

Leah stopped laughing once she realized Mathew was serious.

Mathew touched her belly and said. "You're having a son."

Seth laughed as Leah walked over to the calendar. She flipped the page back and forth counting the days over and over again.

Leah's eyes widened with surprise as she announced. "Oh my god, I'm late. I'm never late."

Mathew took Athena and Seth picked Leah up and swung her around.

Seth kissed Leah then turned to Mathew and asked. "How did you do that?"

Mathew smiled and replied. "I don't know how the men on my father's side do this. As long as we're related to the child, we can tell the woman is pregnant as well as if the baby is a boy or girl."

The smile faded from Seth's face as he asked. "Mathew, how are you related to my child? Please don't make me kill you."

Mathew stammered, "No…No it isn't like that. I would never touch your wife."

Leah playfully shoved Seth for being paranoid.

Seth glared suspiciously at Mathew and repeated the question slowly. "How are you a blood relative of my child?"

Mathew broke down and confessed. "I probably should have told you this a long time ago but I didn't know how. Seth, we have the same mother. That's where you get your gray eyes from. That's how I knew Leah was pregnant. We're brothers Seth. Your child is my nephew."

Seth shook his head in disbelief and snapped. "My mother's name was Lillian! I remember her. She died of yellow fever."

Leah rubbed Seth's back to comfort him and Mathew said. "No Seth, Lillian was the woman who adopted you. The reason you've always gotten such preferential treatment is not just because my mother was friends with your mother. You were treated well because my mother is your mother."

Seth rubbed his head and left the room with a distraught look on his face. Athena began to cry and Leah relieved Mathew of the baby.

Leah assured Mathew. "He'll be fine, just give him some time."

January 9, 1837

Five months after the death of his beloved Sarah Mathew sat alone in a room at the Catholic Church. Down on his luck and out of options he had reluctantly agreed to wed Francesca. It was just moments before his wedding was to begin and all he could think of was Sarah. *Sarah had asked me to run away with her so many times. I always rejected the idea of running away because of the horrific things that would be done to her if we were caught. I only wished for everything to be legal when we left and started a family of our own. Now I wish more than anything we would've just taken our chances with running. So now I'm here marrying my cousin. Why am I the only one on this god forsaken planet who finds the idea of wedding a relative repulsive; especially one who looks just like my sister? It's disgusting.*

Mathew's racing thoughts were interrupted by Seth knocking on the door.

"Mathew, it's time." Seth called from the doorway.

As Mathew approached the sanctuary he noticed his mother and father were sitting amongst the many guests. He obverted his eyes and refused to acknowledge either of them. He walked to the front of the cathedral and stood next to Seth. The organ began to play and Mathew waited for Francesca to saunter down the aisle.

The guests rose and faced the back of the church as Francesca appeared. She didn't look the least bit happy. The abundance of tears cascading down her face, were not tears of joy. They were tears of extreme emotional distress. She eventually made it down the isle and stood in front of Mathew. The music ceased and the guests sat back on the pews. Francesca couldn't even hear the priest talk for sake of her own thoughts. *Mathew and I have finally become friends and I know he's not up to this. He's still in love with Sarah, and in some small way I feel as if I'm betraying them both. I love Aaron more than life itself. He should be the one I marry today, not a grieving cousin who's still broken hearted over the death of his wife.*

When Father Murphy asked Mathew if he would take Francesca to be his bride, he took her by the hands and leaned close to her.

Mathew spoke to her in a voice nearly a whisper. "I am truly sorry, but I will never be able to see a cousin as more than a cousin."

Francesca hugged Mathew and smiled for the first time at her wedding. The guests gasped and rose from their seats as Mathew and Francesca left the sanctuary.

Francesca's parents were outraged. Mathew watched as they ranted in French for about ten minutes then climbed into a stagecoach. Francesca scribbled on a piece of paper and handed it to Mathew.

She whispered to her cousin. "Now that the wedding plans have fallen through, my parents have no further reason to leave me in Missouri. They're so angry that we're boarding a ship for France this afternoon. I know you said that you would never return to the home of your parents, but please give this letter to Aaron. You're the only one I can trust."

Mathew received the letter and asked. "Don't you still need to return to pack your things?"

Francesca shook her head no and explained. "They're having my belongings mailed."

Mathew walked Francesca to the snow covered stagecoach where her parents waited. He hugged her and opened the door. The count and countess both gave him bitter scowls.

Francesca climbed in and Mathew said. "I really am sorry."

Francesca smiled and replied. "You have nothing to apologize for. It took me a while, but I finally understand how you felt about her."

Francesca's father slammed the carriage door shut, and Mathew watched as it pulled away.

It had been five months since Mathew had set foot at the Colburn plantation. He stood outside in the cold and knocked on Aaron's door.

When Aaron answered Mathew said. "I missed you at the wedding."

They took a seat at a small table and Aaron replied. "I'm sorry. I couldn't bring myself to watch."

Mathew pulled the letter from his pocket and said. "Francesca asked me to give you this. We didn't go through with the wedding, and she had to leave in a hurry."

Aaron passed the note back to Mathew and said. "I can't read it, Sir."

Mathew opened the letter and began reading it to Aaron.

Dear Aaron,

We always knew it was bound to end at some point, but that doesn't make writing this letter any easier. With the wedding not taking place my parents have decided to take me home to France. I would love nothing more than to spend an eternity in your loving embrace; however, we both know this is impossible for I too am a slave. I am a slave to my title and family name, and must also do as I am so commanded. Even though this is goodbye I want you to know that I am a better human being having known you. I hope you are blessed to find true love again someday. Until then please keep the promise that you will think of me whenever the stars gleam brightly in the mid night sky and every time the sun sets just perfectly behind the far off hills. For at those very moments I shall surely be thinking of you.

With all the love that I posses,
Viscountess Francesca Demoniet

Mathew folded the letter and passed it back to Aaron.

Emanuel barged into the cabin and spoke to Mathew. "I apologize for interrupting, but I heard you were back on the property. I need to talk to you right now."

Mathew glared at Emanuel wondering what could possibly have him so worked up. *Emanuel's always been such a level headed fellow. This type of behavior is outside of his character.*

Emanuel explained. "I've been meaning to tell you, but no one has known where you were for the past five months."

Mathew asked with anticipation, "Tell me what?" Emanuel took a deep breath and rattled out. "Your beloved Sarah is alive."

Chapter 37

Present

Ox protested as Krista closed the book. "You can't just stop reading there. We don't know what actually happened to Sarah."

Krista laughed and replied, "This story really draws you in, doesn't it? I have to get back. I promised my parents I would help them decorate the house for their big anniversary dinner."

Krista folded up the blanket and Ox grabbed the picnic basket. They weaved back through the cave then journeyed into the tunnel. The brick tunnel was still glowing from the torches they had lit.

Krista marveled at the structure and told Ox, "I can't believe this was all constructed by a 16-year-old boy genius."

Ox replied, "16 years of age was not considered a boy at the time. Things were a lot different than they are now. People younger than we are had full time jobs and families."

Krista and Ox climbed the ladder and came up through the trapdoor in the infirmary.

As they headed back toward the mansion Krista said. "I can't figure out for the life of me what any of this has to do with the death of a British writer a century later."

Ox questioned, "What British writer?"

Krista answered, "Oh did I leave that out? I'm also being stalked by a dead man, the very guy who wrote this book."

Ox laughed and replied, "Krista, come on."

She snapped, "I'm serious he invades my thoughts and dreams. He writes things on the bathroom mirror. His name is Alexander Monroe."

Ox stopped laughing when he realized she was really upset.

He turned to her and said, "I'm sorry. That must've been terrifying for you."

Krista replied. "I was horrified at first but now I'm not. I don't think Alex wants to hurt me. I just think he wants my help."

They reached the door of the mansion and Ox asked, "How do you know, Krista?"

She looked him in the eyes and replied, "Because he told me. Why did he even choose me to contact? I wasn't bitten by a radioactive spider or sent to earth from Krypton as an infant. I'm just a girl from the suburbs. My dad's an accountant. My mom's a school teacher. I'm nobody."

Ox stopped and assured her, "Alex spoke to you for the same reason I did. You're special. That's something even a dead man can see. We'll figure this thing out."

They walked into the parlor on the first floor to find Krista's mom sitting with Stacy and Angela.

Angela and Stacy ran over to hug Krista and shouted. "Surprise!! Your mom and dad said you were home sick so we drove down here to visit."

Angela was average height with voluptuous curves, mystic black hair, full lips and silver eyes. She was dressed in fitting, dark colored blue jeans and a red and white Von Dutch top. She had an excellent since of style, not that it really mattered. She was one of those girls who could walk out of the house in a garbage bag and still capture the admiration of the entire male population.

Stacy could be most vividly described as having the face of a male model and the body of a Greek god. He was around 5'10" with messy light brown hair and a frame so perfectly toned that God himself must've chiseled it from marble. He had blazing blue eyes that gleamed like two sparkling sapphires, over a flawless nose, and impeccable lips. He wore long cargo shorts and a black t-shirt displaying the logo of an old band, Led Zeppelin. No one knew why his parents named him Stacy. It's not as if any good came of them giving him a girl's name. It didn't make him the least bit sensitive or caring. He was still the biggest man whore at South Lyon High School.

Krista made a brief introduction and the four of them walked down the hall to the game room. The game room was an in house arcade. Among the many games were darts, pinball, table hockey, and a couple billiard tables. Krista racked the billiard balls and everyone picked out a pool stick.

Angela called out, "Guys against girls."

The guys agreed and Stacy made the break.

Krista's turn came around and she rubbed the tiny blue cube over the tip of her pool stick.

She aimed to take her shot and called out, "3 ball in the corner pocket."

She made the shot and Angela gave her a victory high-five. Krista's pocket began to vibrate. She walked away from the table and asked, "Angela, would you take my next shot so I can answer this?"

"Hello" Krista spoke into the phone.

The voice called back, "Hey, it's La`Kiesha from the university."

Krista replied, "Hey, how's it going?"

La`Kiesha answered, "I'm out with Rachel and your cousin Jessy. We were wondering if you want to go to the club tonight."

Krista replied, "I left my fake ID back in Michigan."

La`Kiesha went on to say, "Don't worry about it. One of the perks of having a famous rapper for a brother is being able to get yourself and your friends into bars. Shit, I'm not old enough either. I won't be 21 for another four months."

Krista laughed and asked, "A few of my friends came down to visit. Can you get them in too?"

La`Kiesha answered, "Yeah, no problem."

Krista called over to the pool table, "Hey, you guys wanna go out tonight?"

They all shrugged yeah and Krista told La`Kiesha, "We're in."

She hung up the phone and grabbed Angela by the wrist.

Krista told Ox and Stacy, "We'll be back in just a minute."

The guys continued to play pool and Krista and Angela walked outside to the garage. As usual Krista found her father underneath the hood of the 1966 Charger. She gazed at the jet black beauty thinking. *I'm going to get this car for graduation but I can't help wanting to drive it now. I've always loved this car, even though it seems like my dad and grandpa spent more time fixing it then driving it. I remember helping them a few times before I evolved into a girl.*

Krista walked up and asked, "Dad, do you mind if I take the Charger for a spin?"

Her father wiped the dirt and oil from his hands with a red shop rag.

He turned to her and said, "I would feel a lot better if you took the Durango we rented because….."

Krista's father began to ramble off a long complicated guy explanation, for what was wrong with the Charger. Krista stopped listening a third of the way through. Her eyes glazed over and she began to hear the tune from Jeopardy.

By 10:30pm the Charisma night club was packed with people. The club was located in a larger city outside of Poplar Bluff called St. Louis. Krista sat with her friends at the bar sipping a fruity umbrella drink. La`Kiesha had no problem getting everyone in. The music was great and the atmosphere was easy going.

La`Kiesha sat down next to Krista and called the bartender/owner, "Hey Dan, can you grab us another round?"

Dan was a short muscular bald guy, in his late twenties. He leaned over the bar and shouted to La`Kiesha, "I'm not serving another drink for you or your friends, unless you agree to perform tonight."

La`Kiesha laughed and said, "Fine."

Krista turned to La`Kiesha and said, "Rachel's shit-faced. She didn't strike me as the type to drink."

The smile left La`Kiesha's face as she replied, "Rachel's not the type to drink. She's usually the designated driver. She received some really bad news today. I took her out to cheer her up."

Krista inquired, "What happened earlier?"

La`Kiesha went on to explain. "She got an acceptance letter in the mail from law school."

Krista sat down her empty glass and said, "I don't understand. Wouldn't that be good news?"

La`Kiesha added, "At the bottom of the letter it said she was denied for the loan to go. What good is an acceptance letter with no money to pay the tuition? What most people don't know is the government is only required to fund your education up to the first bachelor degree. After that they can tell you to fuck off. Any graduate degree program such as law school or medical school requires loans based on credit. Most college students are first generation broke. This is where you have no money yet, but your parents are doing alright for themselves. Your mom and dad can do useful things like cosign for a loan for law school. But when you're 4-5th generation broke like Rachel, you have no one to fall back on. I know this because before my brother's career took off I was in the same predicament as Rachel."

The drinks arrived and Stacy, Angela, Rachel, La`Kiesha, Jessy, Ox and Krista, all raised their glasses high and toasted. After downing the drink La`Kiesha climbed on top of the bar.

The DJ silenced the music and announced, "Give it up for La`Kiesha Blaze!"

The crowd cheered and surrounded the bar as La`Kiesha played *The Devil Went Down to Georgia* on her fiddle.

At the end of the song La`Kiesha's boyfriend Corey arrived to take everyone to Redwood Cliff. Corey was a university basketball player. He was tall, dark skinned and very clean cut. He was dressed in loose fitting designer jeans, an expensive red and white button down shirt, and a crisp white pair of Nike Air Force Ones. He was very good looking and athletic, but not the brightest bulb on the Christmas tree. If it weren't for sports Corey's only hope would be finding a job breaking large rocks into smaller ones.

The eight of them packed into the black Cadillac Escalade. As they drove past the homeless people, drug addicts, and prostitutes Krista thought to herself. *This must be the bad part of St. Louis. It reminds me of inner city Detroit, MI.*

Rachel smiled and drunkenly announced, "I really appreciate everyone for coming out to cheer me up. I love you guys."

La'Kiesha teased, "Why is it that drunken people only feel two emotions? They either love you or they hate you. Any feeling that falls in between is far too complex to decipher after four drinks."

Everyone laughed and Stacy yelled out the window at one of the prostitutes, "How much!"

Corey's eyes narrowed on the hooker, then he asked, "Rachel, isn't that your mother?"

Rachel's smile was quickly replaced by shock and humiliation. She spotted her mother flashing cars as they drove by.

Chapter 38

The vehicle went silent.

La`Kiesha elbowed her boyfriend Corey and said. "What the hell!"

Corey gave a dumbfounded shrug and Rachel yelled. "Pull over right now!"

Corey pulled the Escalade into the next parking lot, and Stacy called out. "I'm sorry Rachel. I didn't know."

Rachel jumped out of the SUV and stormed across the street to confront her mother.

Her heart filled with sorrow as she thought. *I barely recognize the smelly, emaciated, crack whore standing before me. My mother's taken such a long fall from grace.*

Rachel began to yell, "You've been clean for six months huh! You promised me you quit for good this time!"

Rachel's mother hesitated a moment then said, "I'm sorry I lied to you Rachel."

Tears streamed down Rachel's face as she replied, "No you're not, or you wouldn't do it so often. I don't think you can breathe without lying! I'm trying my best to do something with my life and you have been no help what so ever. I would be going to law school next year if I had a responsible parent who could cosign for a fucking loan! All my friends saw you tonight. It's so damn humiliating. Will you ever get your shit together?!"

Her mother's eyes filled with tears as she replied, "Rachel, you don't understand. I really did try this time."

Rachel felt her heart break as she noticed the ring missing from her mother's finger.

She took a deep breath and asked, "Where the hell is the ring I gave you?"

La`Kiesha pulled Rachel away.

Her mother cried out, "Wait I can explain!"

Rachel yelled back, "I wish you had died instead of Dad!"

They crossed the street and climbed back in the vehicle. The ride was silent all the way to Redwood Cliff.

On the way there Krista sent her dad a text message:

Do you mind if a few friends spend the night? They all agreed to help us get the house together for the anniversary party.

Krista's phone vibrated and the screen lit up. She checked her inbox for her father's reply.

His message read:

I could use a few extra hands, but first I have to set some rules. The boys sleep on the first floor. The girls sleep on the third. Your mother and I will be patrolling on the second floor. You have to arrive by midnight; no later, no excuses. Lights out at 2am.

Krista's phone lost its signal as they drove up the side of the mountain. They reached Redwood cliff and parked. It was a beautiful night. The stars were shining and the moon was full. They lined up along the guard rail and gazed out over the cliff. The view was magnificent.

Krista watched as Stacy gave Angela his most irresistible smile, baring the dimple in his left cheek. Then he slipped his arm around her tiny waist. Stacy whispered something in Angela's ear and she laughed out loud and gave him a playful shove. Krista thought to herself. *Let's face it, on a good day Stacy could sweet talk the robes off a Catholic nun. The guy is a wordsmith. I even dated him for six weeks in the seventh grade, before dumping him for being monogamously challenged. I can honestly say that the only girl Stacy's ever had true feelings for is Angela. Wait for it. Wait for it. Here it comes. Denied!* Krista laughed as Angela brushed Stacy off for the 100th time. *He's always doing stupid things to impress her and she won't give him the time of day. Angela only dates college guys. I feel bad that some part of me finds it amusing to see Stacy get shot down again and again. He's broken so many hearts and karma is a bitch.*

Ox walked up behind Krista and wrapped his arms around her.

He pointed and said, "Look you can see the Colburn Estate from here."

Krista laughed and replied, "You're right. This place is close to the house. No wonder I'm getting such crappy service."

Ox pointed and replied, "That's why the city installed the emergency phone over there."

Krista glanced at the beat up old phone and said, "It probably doesn't even work."

Krista turned to face Ox and put her back against the rail. She looked up at him and thought. *Would you please kiss me?* Once again it didn't happen.

Ox whispered to her, "Can I talk to you alone?"

Krista nodded her head yes and they climbed into the back seat of Corey's Escalade.

Ox looked at Krista and said, "If I tell you this, it doesn't leave the vehicle."

Krista glanced over at him and replied. "I promise. You can tell me anything."

Ox took a deep breath and began to confess, "I know you're probably wondering why I haven't made a move yet. When you live in a frat house with a bunch of other guys they expect things from you. They expect you to sleep with hot women and share the gory details afterward. But…"

Krista interrupted in shock, "Oh my God, you're gay. You're dating me so your fraternity brothers won't find out you like guys."

Ox laughed and replied, "Calm down Krista. I'm not gay."

Krista asked, "Then what is it? What's wrong with me?"

Ox went on to explain, "There's nothing wrong with you. You're hot, really hot. But I'm a virgin. I just didn't want to start something and have you expecting to get the experience in bed a seasoned veteran would provide. I wanted to warn you first, that I'm an amateur."

Krista laughed and replied, "So am I. Don't worry, your secret's safe with me. I can see why you, as a guy, wouldn't want people to know you're a virgin."

The next morning Krista was startled from her sleep. She sat straight up in bed sweating and breathing heavily. She'd had the same recurring nightmare. Alex Monroe had been shot to death almost every night since she came to Missouri. She threw off the covers and dressed thinking. *I saw the killer's face this time. I'll never forget that sinister smile and those cold black eyes.* Krista walked past the other guest rooms on the way down stairs. They were all empty. She was the last one up.

She entered the small dining room. A bunch of serving dishes and used plates cluttered the table. Everyone else had already eaten. Krista grabbed a cinnamon bun and a glass of milk and cut through the main living room. She gasped in utter shock at one of the paintings, and dropped her milk. The glass shattered spilling the contents all over the marble floor.

Krista's mother ran in and asked, "Krista, are you alright?"

Krista grabbed a broom and dust pan to clean up the mess.

She swept the shards of glass, and glared at the painting of the black haired man smoking the pipe. *Why did you kill him? Why did you kill Alex?*

Krista asked her mother, "Who is that man in the painting? Are his initials W. S. C.?"

Her mother replied, "No, It's your great grandfather, Thomas Colburn."

At that moment they received a loud knock on the front door. Krista and her mother sat the task aside and went to answer it. They opened the door to find a plain clothed detective. The man was around 25-years-old, African-American, well dressed, nice looking.

He flashed his badge and said, "Detective James Edwards of the Poplar Bluff Police Department. Is Rachel Wilcox here?"

Krista's mother replied with a concerned expression. "Rachel's decorating the grand ballroom with the rest of Krista's friends."

Detective Edwards asked, "Is there somewhere I can speak with her in private?"

Krista's mother instructed, "Krista, take Detective Edwards to one of the parlor rooms. I'll go get Rachel."

Krista led the detective to an elegant parlor and asked. "Would you like anything to drink?"

Detective Edwards replied, "No thank you. I'm alright."

Rachel walked into the room and hugged the cop, then said. "James, how long has it been? How's your mother?"

Detective Edwards answered, "My mother's doing fine. Thank you for asking." He turned to Krista and asked, "Would you mind excusing us?"

The smile faded from Rachel's face as she asked him. "This isn't a friendly visit from an old friend is it? You're here on business."

Detective Edwards replied, "Rachel you should sit down."

Rachel slowly lowered to her seat. Her brows furrowed with concern as she enquired, "Is my mother in jail again? How much will it cost to post her bail this time?"

Detective Edwards took a deep breath and said, "Rachel I'm sorry, your mother's been murdered. I need you to come to the city morgue and identify the body."

Chapter 39

Krista sat at the rear of the tiny, white, shack of a church. The funeral for Rachel's mother, Lela A`Rue-Wilcox, was held way out in the country. The small Baptist church was a rickety structure with no central air, and one raggedy ceiling fan. It was sweltering hot and the place was packed with mourners. An usher passed Krista a hand held fan. It was made from, what looked like, a piece of thin cardboard stapled to a tongue depressor. She stared at it a few seconds before using it to cool herself. She fanned until her wrist was tired, and then switched hands.

Krista sat on the very back pew between her cousin Jessy and Rachel. La`Kiesha played the piano and sang *Yesterday, By Mary Mary,* as the visitors walked around to view the body.

I've had enough heart ache. And enough headache.
I've had so many ups and downs.
I don't know how much more I can take.
That's why I've decided that I cried my last tear yesterday.
Either I'll trust you. Or I may as well walk away.
Stressing don't make it better. Won't make it better no way.
That's why I've decided that I cried my last tear yesterday...

Rachel whispered to Krista and Jessy as people continued to walk passed the coffin. "Thank you for coming to support me."

Jessy replied. "I would've understood if you chose to sit on the front pew with your family."

Rachel spoke with a bitter scowl on her face. "These phony people you see crying and falling all over the casket never gave a damn about my mother or me. I spent the rest of my childhood in foster care. I don't have a single living relative on my dad's side, and no one from my mother's side cared enough to take me in. I've been on my own since I was seventeen without a helping hand from any of them. My dorm room burned to the ground and I didn't receive so much as a phone call from these people."

Krista's eyes filled with worry as she asked, "Rachel, are you sure you're alright? I haven't seen you shed one tear since you received news of your mother's death."

Rachel explained, "My mother died ten years ago when she first picked up a crack pipe. I suppose my anger just won't allow me to mourn the death of a stranger."

The funeral commenced and Rachel, Krista, La`Kiesha, and Jessy stood outside in front of the church. Detective Edwards walked up in a suit and sunglasses.

He removed his shades and hugged Rachel, then said, "I'm doing everything I can to find your mother's killer, but the St. Louis police aren't being very cooperative. They don't like answering questions from small town detectives like me. Your mother was found with several pieces of jewelry I'm not sure belonged to her."

Rachel nodded and said, "I'll see if I recognize any of it."

Detective Edwards pulled an envelope from his pocket. He began removing the jewelry from the envelope. Each piece was packaged in a small zip lock bag.

Rachel looked at the first piece and said, "This bracelet belongs to my friend La`Kiesha. My mother must have stolen it the last time she came to visit us." Rachel examined a pair of diamond earrings and said, "I don't recognize these at all. She must have stolen them from someone. My mother's ears were never pierced. She was terrified of needles."

Detective Edwards pulled out a third bag. It contained a thin silver necklace with a mothers ring on it.

He said to Rachel, "This was found around her neck. She must've stolen this too. There's no way your mother could have fit this ring. It's far too big for her."

Rachel covered her mouth with a trembling hand as tears streamed down her face.

She cried out through choked sobs, "That ring belonged to my mother. I gave it to her years ago for Mother's Day. She lost so much weight because of her addiction that it just didn't fit her finger anymore. That's probably why she was wearing it on a necklace."

La`Kiesha hugged Rachel and Detective Edwards asked, "The man I believe killed your mother has a string of murders under his belt. He takes a trophy from each of his victims. Is there anything missing?"

Rachel wiped her eyes with a tissue and answered, "A gold toe ring; my mother's family was upper-middle class, and my father's family was dirt poor. My mother's parents disapproved of their relationship, so when my father proposed he gave my mother a toe ring instead of the usual rock."

Rachel smiled through her tears at the happy memory of her parents' forbidden love.

Detective Edwards gave Rachel a supportive hand on the shoulder and vowed, "We're going to get the son-of-a-bitch who did this."

An hour after the funeral Krista drug herself up the front steps of the mansion. She bent down to pick up the news paper. This time the headline read: *St. Louis Slaughterer Takes a Fourth Victim*. Next to the article was a younger picture of Rachel's mother. Krista dropped the newspaper when she was pegged in the back of the head by Jessy's little brother, Alex.

Alex loaded his sling shot with another marble and Krista yelled, "I'm not in the mood to deal with you, you little shit!"

Alex pulled back on the sling shot and pegged her again. Krista chased her cousin around the yard for several minutes. She finally caught up with him and wrestled him to the ground. She relieved him of his sling shot and the small sack of marbles he used for ammunition. She stormed up stairs to her room thinking. *I pray my cousins, Alex and Chase, are only back to attend the Anniversary Dinner. Please, God don't let camp be over for them this soon. I don't think I can take an entire summer of them. I would lose my sanity.* Krista kicked off her shoes and fell back on her bed. *Stacy finally convinced Angela to go on a date with him. They probably won't be back until just before the party. The guests won't be arriving for another five hours or so. I suppose that gives me plenty of time to read.* Krista pulled the book from the drawer of her bedside table and began to read.

Chapter 40

Mathew shook his head in disbelief and exclaimed, "Is this some sort of sick joke?! Her body lies in the slave cemetery as we speak!"

Emanuel assured, "I would never play such a cruel prank. I usually handle all the paper work here, including the mail. Your father had not anticipated that Sarah would know how to read and write. I was sorting the mail as usual when your father walked into my office. He looked down at the pile of letters and abruptly snatched them all. All I saw was the name Sarah in the return address."

Mathew replied, "As much as I want to believe she's alive, Sarah is a very common name. How are you sure it was my wife?"

Emanuel added, "Your father frantically shuffled through the letters. He immediately tossed that particular one into the fireplace. Why would he burn a letter without even opening it? From that day forward he insisted on handling all the mail himself."

Mathew inquired, "Did you notice a return address?"

Emanuel answered, "I'm sorry. All I saw was the name Sarah and the abbreviation for Louisiana. There is no body in that coffin. There can't be."

Mathew was unable to believe what he was hearing without adequate proof. He grabbed Aaron and Seth and walked out into a blizzard. The three of them proceeded to the cemetery to exhume Sarah's coffin. As they approached the graveyard Mathew realized. *This is going to be an extremely difficult task. It's the middle of January and the ground is frozen solid. The snowstorm is growing worse by the minute.*

The snow was flying wildly, and the wind felt so cold it burned the flesh. In spite of the unforgiving weather conditions Mathew took the first stab at the icy soil. Seth and Aaron followed his lead. The men chipped away at the frigid mound of earth with picks and shovels. A trench began to form and they shoveled even more vigorously.

At last Mathew struck the pine casket with his shovel. They swept the dirt off, and started prying out the nails that held the top closed. Mathew climbed even further down into the gaping hole with the coffin. His entire body froze with fear. His muscles tensed up and he grew sick to his stomach. *Do I really want to see what's in this coffin?* Mathew asked himself.

Aaron and Seth could see the state of shock he was in and climbed deeper into the burial plot with him.

Seth gave Mathew a reassuring hand on the shoulder and said, "You don't have to do this."

Mathew replied, "I'll never have a moment's peace unless I do. I have to know for certain what happened, even if I never find her."

Mathew gathered his nerve and took a deep breath. They lifted the heavy wooden lid. He gasped in horror at the unsightly, foul smelling remains. Her body had been burned beyond recognition. All that remained was a chard black corpse. Mathew's heart sank and a single tear rolled down his cheek. He replaced the lid and climbed out of the grave.

"At least now I know." Mathew said with a somber tone.

Aaron flung the lid back open.

"Wait! I don't believe this is Sarah." He said glancing over the body. Aaron studied the corpse a bit longer then explained, "I dug graves with my father for two years. When a person is burned to death they are wearing wrist and ankle restraints. For this reason the wrists and ankles are the only parts of the body left unburned. Do you see Sir?" Aaron stated, pointing to the wrists of the corpse. "The wrists on this body are burned to a crisp. This person wasn't burned at the stake. In fact the only part of this corpse left unburned is the right ankle. And that is not an Akashi tribal tattoo. These markings are that of the Mahili tribe. The only two slaves I've ever met from that tribe were Anna and Mali. This is probably their mother, Till."

Seth added, "As a matter of fact Till always wore a brace on her right ankle. That may be why that's the only part that didn't burn. It was all over the papers. Till went insane. She killed the entire family who owned her, and burned herself up inside of her cabin. They hanged Mabel for inciting the mass murder."

Mathew called out, entirely overwhelmed, "She's alive. I can't believe Sarah's alive."

Chapter 41

Mathew knew that if he interrogated his father Emanuel would be severely punished. At dusk he went to question the only other man that would have the slightest clue about where to find Sarah; his father's partner in crime Frank.

Mathew raced on the back of his stallion to the cottage of Frank Welch. He climbed down from his steed and pounded loudly on the door. Frank opened the door a crack and tried to slam it closed immediately when he saw Mathew standing there.

Mathew yelled as he barged into the house, "Frank we can do this the easy way or the hard way! Tell me what happened to Sarah!"

Frank grinned and shouted, "We tied that little witch to a wooden post and burned her like the heathen she was!"

Mathew punched Frank in the face causing him to topple onto his kitchen table. Then grabbed him around the collar and hemmed him up against the wall.

Mathew shouted at Frank, "Let's try this again! What really happened to Sarah?"

Frank lay firmly pressed against the wall struggling to breath. His feet were dangling in the air.

Frank finally choked out, "Ok. Ok. I'll tell you everything."

Mathew released Frank and he collapsed to the floor gasping for air.

After Frank caught his breath he stood up and began confessing to Mathew, "Your father had her kidnapped the night of you and Francesca's engagement party. I held her prisoner until I could take her to New Orleans. I sold her to my late wife's family. Till is the one who is actually buried in Sarah's grave"

Mathew asked impatiently,

"Where is Sarah now?"

Frank passed Mathew a piece of paper with a trembling hand and said, "This is the sales receipt. It will have the address on it."

"Why do you have it?" Mathew demanded.

Frank confessed, "I kept it to blackmail your father with. I told him that if he didn't pay me a lot of money I would give it to you."

Mathew stuffed the receipt in his pocket and grabbed Frank around the throat.

He spoke to Frank in a menacing tone, "As much as I'd love to squeeze the very life out of you, I won't. I prayed to God every day I was locked in that cellar that if he would spare Sarah's life I would live to serve only him. So I can't kill you." Mathew released Frank and said, "You're a pathetic excuse for a human being, and you'll reap what you sew one day."

Mathew walked toward the door and Frank pointed a revolver at his back.

Frank drew back the hammer of the gun and said, "You're a meddler, you know that boy. You couldn't just leave well enough alone could you? I'm sorry but you left me no choice. Right now I got your father's money and dozens of young girls at my disposal. All that will end if you go digging that Sarah girl up from the dead. Your parents will know I said something, and my employment at the Colburn plantation will end."

Frank grabbed a heavy iron skillet and struck Mathew on the head, rendering him unconscious.

Chapter 42

Mathew woke up freezing cold with a splitting headache. It was the middle of the night. He could see the stars stretched out overhead. He lay in a fishing boat with his wrists and ankles tightly bound with rope.

Frank boasted as he rowed the boat out on the partially frozen lake. "I'm truly going to enjoy this. It's been a long time coming. You had my son banished! I'm going to drown you and make it look like a fishing accident!"

Mathew began struggling vigorously against his restraints at the sound of Frank's cold heartless words. He caught glimpse of a small fishing knife, but couldn't quite get to it. Frank grabbed him by the legs and started pushing him over the side of the boat. Mathew wiggled his left foot loose and gave Frank a powerful kick to the chest. Frank flew backward causing the tiny vessel to flip right over. Mathew's body nearly went into shock when he went under the icy frigid water. He kicked his feet rapidly until he reached the surface. Mathew managed to capture just one chest full of air before Frank grabbed his head and forced him back under. Mathew fought for his life beneath the surface of the freezing cold water. He felt his body growing weaker and weaker as he began losing consciousness. He took a final swing and felt his exhausted arm graze the small fishing knife. Mathew grabbed the blade and shoved it into Frank's thigh. Frank let out a blood curdling wail and released him right away. Mathew sprung out of the water breathing heavily, and threw his still bound arms around Frank's neck. Frank desperately kicked and splashed around in the lake as Mathew pulled the rope tighter and tighter around his throat. Frank pried at Mathew's arms as he struggled to breath. Mathew squeezed even tighter. Franks eyes bulged and his body went limp.

Mathew released Frank's lifeless corpse into the lake. It bobbed along the surface of the water face down.

Mathew snatched the remaining rope off of his wrists. He used what little strength he had left to swim to shore.

He climbed into the driver's seat of Frank's carriage, unable to feel any of his appendages. He cracked the whip and brought the horses to a gallop. He rode to the nearest house he could think of.

Mathew reached Seth and Leah's estate and fell down from the carriage. He crawled up the snow covered steps and collapsed on the porch.

"Dear God!" Seth cried as he opened the door.

All the color was drained from Mathew's skin. His lips had taken a blue coloration and his black hair lay covered in ice crystals. *His body is frozen stiff. I can't tell if Mathew's dead or alive.*

Chapter 43

Mathew regained consciousness the next afternoon in one of Seth's guest rooms. Leah was looking after him.

She sat a tray of hot soup on his lap and said, "You're lucky to be alive, Mathew. Dr. McKinley informed us that your temperature dropped so low your system went into shock. He could barely detect a pulse."

Mathew stammered, "Frank, he tried to kill me."

Leah replied, "I know you had to kill him in self defense. You told us all about it in your delirium. Everyone in town believes Frank went fishing on his day off, and drowned after his boat tipped over."

Seth walked into the room holding up a train ticket.

He walked over to Mathew grinning and said, "One first class ticket for New Orleans, Louisiana."

Mathew sprung to life and set the soup aside.

He reached for the ticket and Seth said, "First you have to promise me that the next time you go to confront a homicidal maniac you'll take Aaron and me with you."

"I swear." Mathew called out and grabbed the ticket.

Leah scolded, "Seth, what the hell! Mathew nearly died yesterday. He needs time to recuperate, regain his strength."

Mathew assured her, "I'm fine. I promise, Leah."

Seth added, "He'll have plenty of time to rest up on the train."

Chapter 44

January 20, 1837

It was the middle of winter and Sarah hadn't seen a single snow flake yet. The weather in New Orleans was similar to an autumn day back in Missouri. It was chilly but nowhere near freezing. The roosters crowed as the sun began to rise. Sarah joined several other servants in the barn. Some were feeding the chickens and collecting the eggs. Others were tending to the horses. Sarah sat on a stool in front of a dairy cow. She placed a metal pail underneath it's utters, and began to milk the cow. *Of all the people to be sold off to, why did it have to be the grandparents of Robert Welch? This is the very place Robert was banished to. It's the largest plantation I've ever seen, and Robert was out on business the week I arrived. So I managed to avoid attracting his attention so far, but I won't be able to elude him forever. Where are you Mathew? Why haven't you come for me?*

Robert Welch prowled slowly through the barn. Sarah put her head down and continued to work diligently. The 10-year-old girl collecting the eggs trembled with fear at the sight of Robert. Sarah let out a terrified gasp as the child accidentally dropped one of the eggs.

Robert Welch snatched the basket the child was holding and yelled, "We don't have money to waist on your incompetence!"

Sarah watched him slap the girl to the ground and thought. *Oh no, Robert's going to hurt that poor child if I don't do something.* She kicked over the bucket of milk to create a diversion. To Sarah's misfortune it worked. Robert abruptly turned his attention from the child and stormed in Sarah's direction.

He snatched her up by the arm and bellowed, "You just wasted an entire gallon of milk!"

Robert paused and looked Sarah over for a moment. A cold chill ran down her back. She cringed with fear.

He grinned and said, "You're a long way from home Sweet Heart. I remember you. Your father attacked me."

Sarah grew sick to her stomach as Robert pushed her against the wall and felt her up.

He whispered in a menacing tone, "You're not my type, but this time I'll make an exception. I'll be seeing you tonight."

Sarah replied breathing heavily, "I'll be hanged for cutting your throat before I ever allow you to have me."

Robert brushed off Sarah's threat and said, "I hope you bring all that fight to the bedroom this evening."

He groped her backside and walked out of the barn.

At nightfall Sarah cradled her knees and rocked back and forth on her bed. She shuddered in fear. Her eyes lay fixed on the door of her cabin. She clenched a knife in her fist and anticipated the arrival of Robert Welch. Tears formed in her eyes as she remembered the time she was brutally ambushed by Robert's father, Frank. *When he comes through the door I'll go straight for the jugular. I'll kill him and run as far as I can from this place.* Her heart raced as the door knob turned. The door began to open and Sarah gripped the knife even tighter.

Chapter 45

Sarah sprung from her bunk and dropped the knife as she realized the intruder was Mathew. She cried tears of joy and relief, as Mathew wrapped her in a long awaited embrace.

Sarah cried out, "I was beginning to think I'd never see you again."

Mathew replied, "I thought you were dead. My father intercepted your letters."

Mathew looked at Sarah's once again flat stomach and enquired, "You're not due for another two months. What happened?"

Sarah explained in a solemn tone, "As it turns out I was right. Laboring twelve hours a day in a field is an excellent way to lose a child. He came too early. I'm sorry Mathew."

Mathew gave her a comforting hug and said, "Let's get you out of here."

Sarah inquired, "How much did Robert's Grandparents want for my freedom?"

Mathew replied, "The night you were kidnapped someone stole all the money we'd saved. I'm an architect. There isn't much work for me during the winter months. I'm going to have to steal you."

Sarah informed him as she gathered her meager belongings, "Robert Welch and three other overseers are standing watch tonight."

Mathew smiled and commented, "I slipped them all sedatives. They're not watching anything but the back of their eyelids."

This was the first time Sarah had ever left the plantation since she arrived in New Orleans. It was just after midnight and she was surprised to see the city still so alive. Everywhere she turned there were bright lights and music. People were drinking wine and dancing in the streets. The scent of exotic spices consumed the air almost thick enough to taste. It was as if the city never slept.

Mathew brought Sarah back to the casino he'd been staying in. Sarah approached the white two story building and read the sign above the entrance: *Madam Lafayette's House of Cards.* Mathew wrapped on the door with the iron knocker. The bouncers, Ashton and Devin, opened the door for them. The bouncers were large imposing men; dressed in vests, button down shirts, black pants, and bow ties. Ashton was dark and Devon was of Creole decent.

Sarah looked around the noisy packed room. The entire first floor was consumed with blackjack, poker, and roulette tables along with darts, craps, and many other games used for the purpose of gambling. There was a bar at the far west wall, and a stage and piano at the far east. The House of Cards smelled like an agreeable mixture of multiple perfumes, colognes, fine cigars, and pipe tobacco. Eighty percent of the customers were male but there were a few ladies willing to try their luck at the roulette tables.

It wasn't long before Mathew was bombarded by a stampede of attractive, scantily clad women. Most of the girls were waitresses and a few were stage performers. The women were clothed in lacy satin and ruffled dresses that came just above mid thigh. The tops were very low cut and the dresses came in an assortment of red, purple, blue, black, and emerald green.

"How may we be of service to you Monsieur?" The ladies asked flirtatiously.

Mathew replied with a well accustomed but apologetic grin, "As lovely as you all are, I merely require a room with which to spend the night with my wife."

A pretty brunette in a blue dress spoke with disappointment, "Right this way, Sir."

She led Sarah and Mathew upstairs to a small guest room.

The waitress asked from the doorway, "Is there anything I can get for you?"

Mathew replied, "Just food and wine for me and my wife. We'll have whatever tonight's special is."

The waitress sprung to life and asked, "Is this the elusive Sarah?"

Mathew grinned and nodded yes.

The waitress smiled with excitement and shook Sarah's hand. "Hi I'm Elizabeth. I've heard so much about you. I'm charmed to finally make your acquaintance."

Sarah smiled and replied, "It's nice to meet you too."

Elizabeth walked out and said, "I'll be right back with your dinner."

Sarah looked at Mathew and asked. "What all did you tell these people about me?"

Mathew answered, "Enough to get them to help me; as it turns out this place serves as a refuge for runaway slaves. It's part of the underground railroad."

Sarah inquired, "Are they going to help us get to Canada?"

Mathew pulled out two tickets and said, "Even better, we're going to France. New Orleans is a French port. It would be much easier to board a ship to France tomorrow, then risk running all the way to Canada."

Madam Lafayette walked in with a platter of food and drinks. She was a short, voluptuous, brunette with dark brown eyes. She was in her late 40's with a presence that demanded the attention of any room she entered.

She took the bowls, plates and glasses off the platter and set them on a small table by the window.

Mathew put a generous sum of money on the tray and said, "I do not wish to be served by the lady of the house."

Madam Lafayette replied, "Under normal circumstances you wouldn't be. I came up here to inform you that there's been a set back. I was told by one of the customers that blacks are no longer allowed to board a ship without proper documentation. If she stows away on the ship they may take her prisoner or throw her overboard.

Chapter 46

Robert Welch aroused from his snooze at one am. He glanced around the poker table. The other overseers were still out cold.

He shook each one of them and shouted, "Wake the hell up!"

Each one of the drowsy men yawned stretched and rubbed his exhausted eyes. Poker chips and playing cards fell on the ground as they climbed to their feet.

Robert pointed at a short pudgy overseer and said, "You're no longer in charge of buying the booze for our poker games. I've never had two shots of moonshine knock me on my ass before. Watch my post I have business to tend to."

The overseers scurried back to work and Robert headed toward Sarah's cabin. *I'll teach that little wench a lesson or two.* He opened the door and walked in. The cabin was dark.

Robert unbuckled his belt and said, "Wake up Sarah. I got something for you, darling."

Robert unzipped his pants and loomed over the bed. He snatched the covers off to find a couple pillows in the place of Sarah's body.

He punched the wall and screamed, "Son-of-a-bitch!"

Robert quickly fastened his clothes and ran into the court yard. He sounded the alarm bell. Within minutes the overseers were scouring the property with rifles and hound dogs.

Robert pointed and shouted an order, "You two, prepare the carriage and come with me! We're going to the House of Cards."

Robert boarded the stagecoach with two overseers and a ferocious pack of dogs.

Robert vowed to the other overseers, "I'll be damned if I let that Lafayette bitch help another one of my slaves escape!"

Robert's stagecoach pulled up in front of the House of Cards at 2am. The place was still packed. He could hear the stage performers singing all the way outside. Robert and his lieges burst through the door.

The angelic voices of the stage performers were interrupted by the blast of gunfire and the barking and snarling of loud ferocious dogs. The crowd broke into a screaming frenzy.

Elizabeth ran into Mathew and Sarah's room and warned them, "You have to hide! There are men here looking for Sarah!"

Chapter 47

Mathew sprinted toward the door and asked. "I heard a gun go off. Is anyone hurt?"

Elizabeth cut him off mid way to the entrance and answered, "No one is hurt. They only shot in the air to get everyone's attention. You must stay in here or you'll lead them straight to Sarah."

Mathew obeyed the warning.

Elizabeth tossed a fat envelope to Mathew and said, "This letter from your cousin came in the mail today."

Elizabeth crept back down stairs and watched from the stairwell. Robert was pointing a small silver hand gun at Madam Lafayette. He was accompanied by two other men. The man to his left stood holding the chains attached to the vicious pack of canines. The dogs were still barking and growling hysterically. The man to his right stood grasping a pile of cast iron shackles.

A hush came over the crowd of screaming on-lookers as Robert shot in the air once more and began to speak, "Are you still harboring fugitive slaves, Ms. Lafayette?"

Madam Lafayette spoke in an unusually calm manner for a person with a gun pointed in her direction, "Are you still cheating at poker, Mr. Welch? How's your lying thief of an uncle been doing since I fired him? As you already know, I'm running a business here. You'll need to tie your animals up outside."

Robert brushed off her insults and said, "You know that housing runaways is a crime Ms. Lafayette."

Madam Lafayette announced, "I can assure you there is no crime being committed here, but there will be if you don't pack up your thugs and your beasts and hit the road. You have no warrant from the magistrate to search my place of business. I'll only ask you once more to be on your way!"

Robert snapped, "We'll leave once we've found what we came for!"

At that instant Devon, the bouncer, broke a bottle across Robert's face. Shards of glass flew in all directions. Robert's hands shot straight to his face causing him to drop the revolver. Ashton, the other bouncer, grabbed the gun as it slid across the floor. Ashton pointed it at the man with the dogs.

The man bellowed, "Boy don't you know these animals will rip you limb from limb!"

Ashton replied, "That may be true but not before I put a bullet in your brain. Sir, I'm certain you're not willing to die just to prove how tuff your dogs are. I'd suggest you take your animals and get going."

The man ran outside and jumped in the carriage with his dogs. Robert threw his hands up in the air when Madam Lafayette pulled the double barrel shot gun from behind the bar. She cycled it and aimed it at his chest.

She boasted with a smile, "Looks like mine is bigger than yours Robert." Then she looked over at Ashton and Devon and said. "Do what you do best."

The two of them grinned at each other like two children who had just received a shiny new toy. The bouncers threw Robert and the other man outside on the ground. The customers came pouring out on the porch to have a good laugh. Robert stood up sweeping himself off. He spat the dirt out of his mouth.

Devon looked over at Ashton and boasted, "I got at least ten feet on that throw. Pay up."

Ashton handed over a fist full of bills and said, "Excellent form Devon. Bouncing truly is an art."

As Robert climbed in the carriage and disappeared with his goons, Madam Lafayette scolded the bouncers, "Did you two seriously make a sport out of how far you can toss people?"

Ashton answered in a jovial manner, "Yeah, you should try it sometime. It's a lot of fun."

Devon added. "It makes me feel all warm and tingly inside, like Christmas."

The guests went back to gambling and drinking as if nothing had happened. Mathew and Sarah walked downstairs and helped sit the toppled chairs up right.

Sarah swept the broken glass as Mathew said, "Thank you all for protecting us. We're very sorry to have brought this problem to your home. We'll pay for any damage this may have caused."

Madam Lafayette replied, "I'm an abolitionist. It comes with the territory. We've got to put our heads together and come up with a way to get Sarah aboard that ship tomorrow. Robert may be a scoundrel but he's no simpleton. It's only a matter of time before he's back with that warrant."

Mathew ripped open the letter from Francesca and smiled at the contents.

He picked up the heavy iron shackles one of the overseers left behind and said, "I just may have a plan."

Chapter 48

Robert waited impatiently outside the office of the magistrate.

He glanced at his watch every few minutes and questioned the court attendant, "Would you mind seeing if the magistrate will meet with me now?"

The court attendant walked into the office and returned a few moments later to say, "The magistrate is in a meeting with Commodore Wales. Is there anything I can assist you with, Sir?"

Robert snapped, "No you idiot! Now fetch the magistrate. This is an urgent matter."

The court attendant sneered and replied, "In that case he'll be with you shortly."

Robert shouted, "That's what you said nearly an hour ago!" Then he pushed the attendant aside and interrupted the meeting.

Both men turned and faced the door abruptly as Robert barged through it. The magistrate was in his late fifties, slightly over weight, and wore black court robes. The commodore was in his early thirties and sat dressed in a gray and blue captain's uniform. Both men wore stylish, white wigs.

The magistrate bellowed, "I beg your pardon, Sir!"

Robert walked over and said, "Please forgive my intrusion, but time is of the essence. I'm requesting a warrant to search the House of Cards in pursuit of a runaway slave."

The magistrate snapped, "Well are you going to give me a name Robert?"

Robert informed him, "The girl's name is Sarah Colburn, most recently owned by my grandparents, the Parkers."

The magistrate removed his spectacles from a small black case, and searched his cabinet of files. "Let's see, Omar, Pain, here it is Parker." He pulled the file and scanned the list of names. "Are you sure that's the right name?" The Magistrate asked.

Robert suggested, "If you can't find her under Colburn try Parker. My grandparents may have renamed her when they took ownership."

The Magistrate went over the list once more and said, "Looks like I found your girl."

Robert let out a sigh of relief.

The magistrate continued, "There's a note here. It looks as though your grandfather recently removed her from his list of taxable assets. See it says right here, sold to a slave hunter named Mathew Colburn Jr."

Robert exclaimed, "What!! That was no slave hunter! It was her lover! That slave fornicator thinks he'll get away with this."

Robert snatched the file and read it himself, "Brought into custody and sold on January 21, 1837! That was just this morning. You're this town's magistrate. How is it possible that you didn't know?"

The magistrate straightened his robes and replied with a hint of irritation in his voice, "I'm a very busy man. My assistant handles all slave transactions. Now if you'll excuse us we were in the middle of a meeting."

Robert approached the court attendant with a much better attitude this time.

He gave his best attempt to be polite and asked, "You authorized the sale of a slave named Sarah Parker. What direction did she go in?"

A snide grin appeared over the attendants face as he replied, "First you insult me, and now you want my help? You can no longer take her into custody. Mr. Colburn is her legal owner now. What could you possibly still want with her?"

Robert answered, "It's personal. Me, Colburn, and that little wench of his go way back. I have a vendetta to settle."

The attendant asked, "Why should I help you?"

Robert poured out a small sack of silver coins on the counter.

The court attendant quickly pocketed the bribe and said, "Colburn requested paper work to board the Clara Marie. Departure time is 2:00pm."

Robert glanced at his watch, 1:47.

He sprinted down the courthouse stairs and shoved an adolescent boy off of his horse. Robert leaped onto the boy's steed and bolted down the street. The citizens of the busy town leaped in all directions from his path as he raced to the harbor.

Robert reached the docks and climbed down from his horse. He pushed, shoved and waded through the crowd of sailors, travelers, and fisherman. He spotted Sarah and Mathew in line to board the enormous Clara Marie. He removed his gun from its holster and charged in their direction. He ran up behind them and pelted Mathew three times with the pistol. Mathew dropped liked an anchor faced down on the dock. Sarah screamed for help in French and kneeled to his aid.

Frantic onlookers scattered in all directions as Robert shouted, "Roll over and face me you coward!!"

Mathew didn't respond. He was obviously unconscious. He didn't even appear to be breathing. Robert took the heel of his boot and forced Mathew onto his back.

"GOD DAMN IT!" He screamed as he realized he'd assaulted the wrong man. The girl he mistook for Sarah held her poor assaulted fellow in her arms and cursed Robert repeatedly in French.

He scanned the crowd thinking. *Finding Sarah and Mathew will be a more complex task then I previously assumed. The races mix freely in New Orleans. The harbor is crawling with interracial couples.* He took one last glance over the crowd and noticed Madam Lafayette and the entire gang from the house of cards waiving up at the ship. He traced an exact line in the direction they were waiving at, and spotted Sarah onboard waiving down at them.

Robert shouted as the first mate prepared to set sail, "Hey! Hey! I have to board this ship!"

The sailor explained, "I'm sorry but you're too late. This ship is scheduled to leave the New Orleans' port at 2:00pm. You'll have to catch the next one."

Robert argued and tried to push passed him. "But I'm sure I saw a fugitive aboard this vessel!"

The sailor shoved him back and shouted, "I don't care if you think you saw Jesus! You're not boarding my ship late."

Robert walked away and desperately searched the hull of the ship for another way in. He spotted an opportunity on the loading dock. He snuck onboard through the cargo area and made his way up on deck. He shoved passed the numerous passengers until he spotted Sarah.

Robert pointed the gun at Sarah and hollered, "I demand that you tell me where your lover is, heathen!"

"I boarded alone!" Sarah answered.

Robert hurled her onto the floor and began to shout again. "Girl don't you realized you have no rights here! I could put a bullet in your heart right now and all I'd have to do is reimburse your boyfriend the amount he paid for you! Now you've got three seconds to tell me where he is! One! Two!"

Sarah's body began to tremble when she heard the unmistakable clink of Robert drawing back the hammer of his firearm. Her thoughts raced. She could barely breathe, but she still refused to give up Mathew. Her heart pounded forcefully in her chest and she shut her eyes tight as she anticipated the number three: the dreadful number certain to be accompanied by the bullet that would end her life.

"THREE!"

Chapter 49

Mathew appeared expeditiously and grabbed the arm aiming the gun. A loud blast pierced the air as the bullet grazed Sarah's shoulder. The two men wrestled and fought over the pistol and it went off again. The second bullet ricocheted off the railing and embedded its self in the hull of the ship. Mathew gripped Robert's wrist and slammed his hand against the guard rail until he released the weapon. The gun fell over the side of the railing and was lost to the sea. Robert and Mathew tussled about the ship pelting one another with forceful punches.

Robert swung a bottle of wine at Mathew and missed. Mathew came up and clobbered Robert with one forceful blow after another. Robert stumbled backward holding his arms up over his face. This was a big mistake. It only left his torso unprotected. Mathew landed a brutal punch to Robert's left kidney and he dropped like an anchor. Robert lay curled up panting heavily. He was exhausted, bloody and bruised.

Mathew demanded, "Stand up and fight me like a man!!"

The captain shouted firing once in the air, "That's enough!!"

Robert climbed to his feet, relieved to see the captain.

He pointed a finger at Sarah, and choked out through heavy breaths, "This woman is a fugitive."

The captain looked at Mathew and asked, "May I see your ticket stubs and the paperwork for your servant?"

Mathew complied, and the captain browsed through the wad of papers and stated, "Looks authentic to me."

The captain then turned to Robert and asked, "May I see your ticket stub, Sir?"

Robert fumbled, "Well Sir you see uh… I only ran onboard to pursue this man. He fraudulently persuaded my grandparents to sell him their runaway slave. That's the only reason he has those papers."

The captain unsheathed his sword and stomped in Sarah's direction. Mathew jumped in between them and prepared to defend her. The captain raised his sword high and it flew through the air with a swish. Then he picked up the piece of table cloth he'd sliced off.

The captain passed Mathew the piece of cloth and instructed, "Tie this around her shoulder to stop the bleeding. It seems the bullet only grazed her. She should be fine."

Mathew nodded and took the cloth.

The captain then turned to Robert and spoke, "If you're trying to tell me that you boarded my ship without a ticket, the only fugitive standing here is you. Would you mind reading rule number four of the Clara Marie?"

Robert glanced over at the gigantic slate of rules. *#4 All stowaways are to be thrown overboard.*

The captain looked back at Mathew and said, "Would you mind enforcing rule four for me?"

Mathew seized Robert by the vest and launched him over the railing. Robert screamed the whole way down and hit the water with a huge splash.

Ashton watched from the dock and commented to Devon, "That had to be at least fifty feet. It seems we have a new record to beat."

Devon added, "Mathew's technique was flawless."

Madam Lafayette smirked and shook her head disapprovingly at both of them.

The crew from the house of cards called up as the Clara Marie sailed away, "Bon voyage!"

The ship plowed through the sparkling ocean water like tilled soil. Sarah stood at the front of the enormous vessel and peered out on the horizon. She basked in the sensations of the wind in her hair and the spray of the sea on her face.

Mathew said as he embraced her from behind. "I bet you figured Francesca would be the last person on earth who would buy your freedom."

Sarah admitted. "It did come as a shock to me."

Mathew added. "Her parents married her off as soon as they returned to France; granting her full access to her inheritance. Once I had the money all I had to do was slap you in shackles and pretend to be a slave tracker."

Mathew pulled Sarah's engagement gift from his pocket and fastened it around her neck. Sarah stared out on the dazzling sea and felt the beautiful ruby necklace with her finger tips.

She smiled and said to Mathew. "It feels wonderful to finally wear my necklace the way it was meant to be worn. I don't have to hide it anymore."

Mathew gave his wife a long awaited kiss and told her. "Sarah, we're going to France. We never have to hide anything again."

Chapter 50

July 11, 1841

Mathew and Sarah spent four years in France. Sarah studied medicine, in spite of the prejudices of her male counterparts. Through perseverance she won them over, and was eventually granted the title of doctor. Mathew had built one of Europe's most successful architectural engineering firms. He was twenty years old, and the founder and CEO of *Colburn Designs Inc (CDI)*.

Things had been going well until Mathew received a letter requesting that he come home, because his mother was dying of liver cancer. Mathew corresponded refusing to come home unless his parents freed all the slaves they owned. The mistress grew more ill and even more desperate to see her child. Master and Mistress Colburn emancipated all their slaves in a final effort to make peace with their son.

Mathew and Sarah had taken a ship to America and now sat on a train destined for their home town. The train rumbled down the tracks. Sarah gazed out the window at a lovely summer day. A blue sky with puffy white clouds stretched over head. The locomotive came to a screeching stop at a crowded station. Sarah and Mathew stepped off the train delighted to see that Aaron had come to pick them up. Sarah put down her luggage and ran over to hug Aaron.

Mathew called out to him, "I thought you might have fled north with the others."

Aaron commented as he and Mathew loaded the suitcases onto the stagecoach. "I'm one of the few who stayed to work for a small salary. My sister Cassie lives with Seth and Leah now. She took a position as their nanny."

Sarah took a seat inside the carriage and Mathew climbed up onto the driving bench with Aaron.

Aaron brought the horses to a trot and Mathew asked, "Which of my relatives have shown up so far?"

Aaron replied, "Your sister Lillian was the first here. The Count and Countess Demoniet came earlier this week. And Francesca arrived with her husband, the Marquis Adrion La`Cour, yesterday."

As the stagecoach ventured forward Aaron turned to Mathew and grumbled, "I just don't like that La`Cour fellow."

Mathew laughed and commented, "Your dislike may be stemming from the fact that he's sleeping with the ex love of your life."

Aaron stated in his own defense, "It's nothing like that. Francesca and I had a stupid affair when we were kids. I've moved on with my life and so has she."

Mathew teased, "Of course you're over her. That's why you hate a good man for no reason at all. I've been in France with Francesca and the Marquis La`Cour for four years. If you give him a chance you'll find out he's a really nice person. The people of France love him."

Aaron scowled and replied, "Well I hate him."

As Aaron pulled the stagecoach in front of the mansion Mathew said, "Sarah's parents returned to the Island of Samson's origin. When we leave here we're going to visit them. You should come with us."

Aaron nodded in agreement. Then he climbed down and began to unload the luggage.

Mathew stood at the entrance wondering what to expect. *I haven't been home in four years. And I didn't leave on the best of terms. My father kidnapped my wife and led me to believe she was dead. I threw my father off of a balcony. I'm a slave owner's son with a black brother and a black wife. My family isn't exactly normal.*

Mathew was shocked to see Master Colburn answer his own front door. All the servants really were gone. Master Colburn's reaction was so strange it nearly startled Sarah. He hugged both Sarah and Mathew so tight they could barely breathe. Mathew thought to himself. *What the hell! My father has never hugged me before today. Father always believed that showing affection to a male child would only make the boy weak. He wouldn't even allow my mother to hug me.*

Mathew snapped out of his thoughts as Master Colburn said, "I always knew you two had a thing for each other."

Sarah asked with a look of bewilderment, "You really knew all along?"

Master Colburn laughed and replied, "Of course I knew. You'd have to be an idiot not to know. Why didn't you bring the grandchildren? They could've played with Seth's kids, Athena and Seth Jr."

Mathew stood in stone silence with a confused expression on his face.

Sarah stepped forward and confessed, "We haven't had any luck in that department. I lost a child four years ago and haven't been pregnant since."

Master Colburn gave a disappointed look and led them into the mansion.

Mathew whispered to his wife, "Who is this man, and what has he done with the overbearing tyrant formally known as my father?"

Sarah smirked and shrugged her shoulders.

A couple of hours after Sarah and Mathew settled into their rooms they met the rest of the family in the small dining hall for lunch. Seth and Leah took a seat, overjoyed to find out Leah was pregnant with kid number three. The Count and Countess Demoniet sat at the table in their usual smug demeanor. Francesca sat across from them with her husband, the Marquis Adrion La`Cour; who was tall with light blonde hair and cerulean eyes. He was handsome, strong, regal, and filthy rich. There was no wonder Aaron hated him.

Lillian walked in and took a seat at the table. She was now seventeen and had bloomed into a lovely young woman. There was barely a trace of the tomboy she use to be. She now dressed in extravagant gowns. She wore her lustrous black hair in elegant buns adorned with jewels and feathers.

Master and Mistress Colburn sat at the head of the table. The Mistress had lost a great deal of weight. Her lovely fair skin had transformed to a strange yellow. She was jaundiced, due to her liver failing. She appeared weak and spoke in a frail voice almost a whisper.

Coping with his wife's illness had streaked Master Colburn's black hair with gray. The stress had put creases on his forehead and lines in his handsome face. He sat at the table with one of Seth's kids perched on each knee.

Master Colburn fed each of the children an appetizer and asked, "Will someone see what's taking Emanuel so long? My grand kids are hungry."

Sarah excused herself from the dining room thinking. *I've served breakfast countless times on this table and I still don't quite feel welcome sitting at it.* Sarah walked into the kitchen surprised to see Emanuel cooking.

She hugged him and asked, "Is there anything you don't do around here?"

Emanuel went back to slicing the fresh vegetables and said, "I'm leaving to Europe soon to open my own restaurant. I always wanted to be a world class chef. The law changed in this county. It now states that one must be at least 1/8 African to be considered black. I'm only 1/16. By the new statute, I've been free for the past six months."

Sarah asked ecstatically, "Does this mean you can marry Marie now?"

Emanuel smiled and nodded yes. He scraped the vegetables off the cutting board into a large salad bowl.

244 | W W B :   C a b i n   o f   W h i s p e r s

As he tossed the mixed greens he said, "Marie's coming to dinner tonight, if you still want to meet her."

Sarah replied, "Of course I still want to meet her. Is there anything I can help you with?"

Emanuel passed Sarah a porcelain casserole dish and said, "Would you mind carrying this one? It's filled with cream of mushroom soup. It's the only thing the Mistress will eat lately."

Sarah removed the lid from the dish and took a whiff.

She smiled and commented, "It smells delicious. You're going to be one hell of a chef. Promise me that when you're a big shot and you own an entire chain of restaurants, you won't forget to save me and Mathew a table."

Emanuel laughed and assured her, "You guys will get the best table in the house."

Emanuel and Sarah brought the serving dishes to the small dining hall and set them on the table. Sarah took a seat next to Mathew while Emanuel served everyone.

The mistress noticed the grim look on her daughter's face and asked, "Is everything alright?"

Lillian answered, "I'm supposed to have tea with Maxwell and Lady Arrington shortly."

Mistress Colburn replied, "I don't see why that's a bad thing."

Lillian sighed and explained, "The woman hates me. I overheard her calling me a boorish, distasteful, country girl. I'm not charming like you, Mother."

Mistress Colburn assured, "Yes you are. The Lillian Lady Arrington met was a 13-year-old gamine. Let her get to know the lovely young lady you've become. She's certain to love you. As you already know Maxwell will be gone for two months on an African safari. Use that time to get better acquainted with Lady Arrington."

The Countess Demoniet added, "Your boyish ways may have captured Maxwell's attention, but that sort of behavior will not be enough to capture his heart. I've been around enough royalty to know that when it comes to getting married Maxwell will take the bride of his mother's choosing. You must listen to your mother. Impress Lady Arrington at all costs."

Mathew excused himself thinking. *I'm so tired of hearing my mother and aunt brainwash Lillian. She's just fine the way she is.* He returned to his old bedroom on the first floor and pushed open the door. He froze in shock at the site of his bed. There was a letter stabbed into one of the pillows by a small fishing knife. The color drained from Mathew's face as he recognized the tool. *Christ, it's the same knife I shoved into Frank Welch's thigh in order to stop him from drowning me.* Mathew peered down at the note. A cold chill came over him as he read it:

I know you murdered my father! I'm coming for you!

Chapter 51

Mathew and Lillian stood watch as the sheriff's deputies searched his room for vital clues.

Sheriff Briggs approached Mathew and said, "Robert Welch was exiled from the state of Missouri. He was warned that in the event of his return he'd spend the rest of his life in prison. I assure you that when we catch Robert that's exactly what he's going to do. I'll leave two of my best deputies on patrol just outside of the mansion."

Sheriff Briggs tipped his hat to Mathew and Lillian and left the room. The deputies filed out after him.

Mathew turned to Lillian and said, "You should get going if you want to make it to the tea on time."

Lillian looked at her brother with concern and said, "Are you sure you'll be alright."

Mathew scoffed and replied, "If that coward wants to come after me let him come."

Lillian pleaded with her brother, "Mathew, promise me that if Robert shows up you won't try to be a hero. Let the deputies take care of him. And you should go check on Sarah. She's a little shook up."

Lillian walked outside and Mathew went to check on his wife.

Sarah's room was set up like a laboratory. She brought with her a microscope, several magnifying glasses, and numerous medical books. She was frantically flipping through the pages of one of her medical books when Mathew walked in.

Sarah walked over to him speaking in a hurried, panicked voice, "I can't help but wonder how Robert even knew we would be here. What if he did something to your mother to lure you back here?"

Mathew assured her, "Sarah, my mother is dying from liver cancer. Robert Welch didn't do that to her. She did it to herself. Decades of partying and drinking men twice her size under the table have finally caught up with her."

Sarah continued to speak in a frazzled manner; flailing her arms like a crazy person, "If I can just figure out what Robert's done to your mother I may be able to save her."

Mathew embraced his wife and urged her to calm down.

He held her close and said, "My mother has cancer. There's nothing you can do for her. She's in God's hands now."

Lillian arrived at Arrington manor and Maxwell escorted her into the enormous court yard. Maxwell was now nineteen. He had grown taller and even more handsome in her absence. Lillian now had womanly curves to fill out her elegant blue gown.

Lady Arrington sat under a large oak tree with two of her sisters having tea.

Lillian whispered to Maxwell, "I hadn't prepared to deal with three of them. I feel as if I'm walking into a lion's den."

Maxwell kissed Lillian on the cheek and said, "You don't have to do this. I don't care what they think."

Lillian assured him, "I'll be fine."

As they approached Lillian overheard Lady Arrington and her sisters debating over a painting in the anteroom. Lady Arrington and her sisters stopped debating over the author of the painting as Lillian stepped forward.

Lady Arrington took a sip from her tea cup and commented in her British accent, "I see much has changed in the last four years, Miss Lillian. You're actually wearing clean clothes. I half expected you to show up in dirty trousers with a hunting rifle."

Lady Arrington's sisters laughed, and whispered to one another.

Maxwell took Lillian by the hand and said, "Let's go Lillian. You don't have to take this from them."

Lady Arrington and her wicked sisters went back to sipping tea and debating over the painting.

Lillian retreated with Maxwell and paused after a few steps. Her mother and aunts words were all she could think of. *I must impress the mother at all costs.*

Lillian turned to face Lady Arrington and boldly announced, "Actually you're all incorrect. The painting which hangs in your anteroom is a 17th century portrait of Gerard de Lairesse, painted by artist Rembrandt van Rijn."

Maxwell's mother and aunts were rendered speechless. They all gave Lillian impressed nods.

Lillian went on to say, "You were right about one thing Lady Arrington. Much has changed in the past four years. I've become well versed in literature, music, European history, and the arts. I speak three languages and play several instruments. I assure you that I'm no longer the 'boorish, distasteful, country girl' I once was."

Lady Arrington rose from her seat.

She smiled at Lillian and asked, "Would you like me to give you a tour of the palace?"

Maxwell cast a confused glare as Lillian replied, "I would love to be shown around the palace."

After a tour of Arrington Palace, Lillian stood on the front porch with Lady Arrington and Maxwell's Aunts.

Maxwell walked up with a large elongated box topped with a big red bow.

He smiled and questioned, "Why are you leaving so soon?"

Lillian replied, "I have to go home and get ready for your going away party tonight."

Maxwell replied, "Well I wanted to give you this before all the guests arrive."

Maxwell held the box as Lillian removed the lid. There was a shiny new rifle inside. Lillian nervously glanced over at Maxwell's mother and aunts. They were all shaking their heads disapprovingly.

Maxwell went on to explain, "I postponed the safari for weeks in hopes that you would come with me. You said you dreamt of hunting the largest most dangerous game on every continent. Why not start with Africa?"

Lillian glanced back and forth between Maxwell and the wicked trio.

At last she told Maxwell, "Ladies of class don't hunt."

Lady Arrington gave an approving smile.

Maxwell replied with an appalled look on his face, "You're Lillian Colburn. The girl who took down the biggest buck I've ever seen. You're the girl, who desired a life of adventure; who wanted to travel and see the world. Are you the girl I've been writing all these years or not?"

Lillian stood in silence thinking. *I don't want to be the girl Maxwell toys with while he's young only to be cast aside for a proper girl later. I must impress the mother at all costs.*

Lillian took a deep breath and answered, "I'm sorry but I'm not that girl anymore."

Maxwell replied with agitation, "Well I'm disappointed. I really loved that girl, but the Count and Countess obviously took that girl to France and killed her. It's over Lillian."

Tears formed in Lillian's eyes as Maxwell stormed away with the box containing the rifle.

Night fell and Aaron scaled the tree by Francesca's bedroom. He climbed onto the balcony and Francesca leaped up from her vanity. She threw open the glass double doors and charged out on the balcony. She stood in front of him shivering; her arms crossed over her chest for warmth. It was a windy night and her curls danced wildly in the breeze.

Francesca scolded trying to scream and whisper at the same time, "Jesus Christ Aaron! What are you doing?!"

Aaron replied, "I just wanted to talk to you."

Francesca shot back, "The middle of the night is hardly an appropriate time for a chat."

Aaron placed his hands on the small of Francesca's back and pulled her close to him. He tenderly grazed his lips along her neck. All the chemistry she felt with him years ago consumed her once more. She resisted her desires and walked away to clear her head.

Francesca turned to Aaron and explained, "Things are different now. I'm a married woman. I can't just abandon my title and responsibilities and gallivant off to Canada with you. I'm born of noble blood. I have to do what makes my country's men happy."

Aaron took her by the hand and said, "And what about what makes you happy? If you can look me in the eyes and tell me that you love your husband and you are truly happy, I'll be able to let you go."

Francesca looked down at the floor and stammered, "Well... You see... there are many types of love."

Aaron smirked and replied, "If you can't bring yourself to say that you love your husband. At least gain the courage to tell me you don't love me anymore."

Francesca walked into her room and sat on the bed. Aaron followed her and sat next to her. He lifted her chin and looked into her eyes.

Then he asked, "Have you stopped loving me?"

Francesca's eyes filled with tears as she explained, "My husband is a really nice man and..."

Aaron interrupted, "That's not what I asked you. As much as I hate to admit it, I already know your husband is a good man."

Francesca broke down and confessed, "No Aaron! I never stopped loving you, even for a second. In four years, you never once left my thoughts."

Aaron wrapped his arms around Francesca and kissed her long and deep. Her husband, Adrion La`Cour, watched in stunned silence from the doorway.

Aaron jumped as he caught a glimpse of Francesca's husband. His heart pounded in his chest as he realized. *I'm going to be killed.*

Chapter 52

As her husband walked into the room, Francesca called out. "Adrion, I'm so sorry."

Adrion La`Cour took a deep breath and spoke to his wife. "Dinner is almost ready. Please go down stairs. I need to talk to Aaron, man to man."

Francesca nodded and left the room. Her husband closed the door and walked over to Aaron.

Aaron swallowed hard and asked, "Are you going to have me castrated, shot or hanged?"

Adrion looked Aaron over and replied, "If I was going to do any of those things I would've already given the orders. I love my wife. We've been best friends since the age of six. When we turned fourteen I revealed a terrible secret to her. I confided in Francesca that I have desires not of the usual persuasion."

Aaron gave Adrion a discombobulated glare, and Adrion went on to explain, "I'm a homosexual. Out of fear that I would be persecuted, Francesca and I made love. We were under the naive assumption that it would fix me. It didn't. To this day that is the only time I've ever been with my wife. Upon Francesca's return to France we married. The marriage allowed her to gain access to her inheritance. The union also got my parents off my back about settling down with a proper girl."

Aaron sat speechless as Adrion continued, "You can love Francesca in a way that I can't. When you leave to go to that island take her with you."

Aaron breathed a sigh of relief.

Adrion threatened him without losing his regal composure, "Francesca is my best friend and I care about her wellbeing. If I hear that you've made her the least bit unhappy, I'll have you castrated, shot, and then hanged."

Adrion gave Aaron a slap on the shoulder and casually walked out of the room.

Mathew walked down the hall and stopped as he heard crying coming from Lillian's room. He let himself in to find Lillian lying on her side with a soggy ball of tissue in her fist.

Mathew sat next to Lillian and questioned, "What are you doing here? You're supposed to be at Maxwell's going away party. He's leaving tonight."

Lillian sobbingly replied, "It's over." She wiped her tears with the tissue and asked her brother. "Have you ever felt trapped between the person you are and the person you should be?"

Mathew replied, "Have you ever considered the possibility that the person you should be is who you already are?"

Mathew rose from the bed and announced with irritation, "What have the Count and Countess done to you Lillian? No sister of mine would ever lay here and just allow this to happen."

Lillian sat up and explained, "I just didn't want to be cast aside one day for a proper girl."

Mathew replied in a frustrated tone, "You've got to stop listening to our mother and aunt! Sarah is my wife and I might have written her five notes in the entirety of our relationship. Men don't like to write! And this man has been writing you for four years. How could you ever get the impression he wasn't serious about you!"

Lillian smiled through her tears as Mathew stormed over to her closet.

He grabbed an arm full of Lillian's expensive dresses and hurled them over the balcony.

Mathew turned to Lillian and scolded, "Stop pretending to be someone you're not!"

Lillian grabbed two handfuls of expensive trinkets from her jewelry box. She threw the dazzling jewels over the balcony without a second thought.

Lillian smiled at her brother and said, "Wow. That did feel good."

Mathew grinned and instructed, "Now let's get you to that party."

Lillian gave her older brother a big hug.

Mathew walked toward the door and Lillian asked sarcastically, "Hey genius, what am I supposed to wear now that we've thrown out all my nice dresses and jewelry?"

Mathew laughed and replied, "I'm sure you'll think of something."

Aaron pulled the stagecoach up in front of Arrington palace. Lillian climbed out and took her brother by the arm. Mathew escorted Lillian up the steps to the ballroom.

A servant at the entrance gave them a funny look and asked, "May I see your invitations?"

Lillian complied, and the servant reluctantly allowed them to pass. They walked through the luxurious anteroom, and Lillian smiled at the Rembrandt painting. Two armed guards thrust open the double doors to the grand ballroom. The smile faded from Lillian's face as she caught site of the numerous guests; dressed in extravagant evening gowns and expensive tuxedos. She spotted Maxwell across the room surrounded by women.

It wasn't long before everyone turned to look at Lillian. She had entered the majestic grand ballroom wearing her safari uniform. Aghast expressions covered the faces of the guests.

Lillian whispered to her brother, "I don't know if I can do this, Mathew."

Mathew whispered back, "To hell with these people, Maxwell's over there. Go get him."

Lillian grinned and released her brother's arm. She confidently marched into the party. Over a hundred pairs of condescending eyes were fixed on her. As she made her way across the palace ballroom, even the musicians ceased to play their instruments. An awkward silence fell over the party. The only sound was that of the colliding of Lillian's hunting boots against the marble floor.

As Lillian ventured forward the pompous men and women gossiped to one another, "I can't believe she's wearing pants."

"What sort of unruly woman wears trousers?"

"What do you expect from a Colburn? I heard her brother actually married a slave girl."

Maxwell fished through his retinue of admirers and met Lillian half way. All eyes were on them.

He smiled at her and commented in his British accent, "You make quite an entrance."

Lillian replied in a jovial manner, "My brother threw away all my evening gowns."

Maxwell took her by the hands and assured, "You never needed them. You look absolutely beautiful. Like the day we met."

Lillian took a deep breath and said, "I'm still the girl you fell in love with that day. If the offer still stands, I want to leave with you tonight."

Maxwell wrapped his arms around Lillian and kissed her passionately.

He released her and whispered, "Let's get out of here."

Lillian and Maxwell walked out of the ballroom hand in hand. Maxwell stopped in the anteroom to shake Mathew's hand, and Lillian gave her brother a hug goodbye. The three of them exited the palace and jogged down the steps. Mathew smiled at his sister and boarded the stagecoach Aaron was driving.

As Lillian walked away Aaron called down to her, "Be sure to watch out for the recoil, Miss Lillian!"

Lillian looked back over her shoulder and called out, "Sure thing!"

Two of Maxwell's guards finished strapping the safari equipment to the carriage. Both guards were very large and intimidating. One had black hair and blue eyes, the other had blonde hair and green eyes. They boarded the stagecoach behind Maxwell and Lillian.

Maxwell put an arm around Lillian's shoulders and said, "I'd like to introduce you to the crew. These are my guards, Bortus and Oliver."

Lillian gave a smile and a wave at the guards as the horses broke into a trot.

As the stagecoach ventured forward, Maxwell went onto say, "Bortus, Oliver this is the woman I've been telling you about."

Oliver, the guard with the blonde hair, gave Maxwell an approving nod and said, "I'm charmed to make your acquaintance, Miss Lillian."

Bortus, the dark haired guard, smiled and said, "It truly is a pleasure to finally meet you, My Lady."

As they traveled out onto the road Mathew's stagecoach caught up with theirs. Lillian flashed her brother a big grin and flexed her bicep in the window. Mathew replied with a flex of his arm as his carriage rolled passed.

Once her brother was out of site Lillian picked up the gift box Maxwell had given her earlier.

She removed the hunting rifle and commented, "It truly is a magnificent firearm."

Lillian's eyebrows furrowed with confusion as she pulled a rolled up piece of paper from the barrel of the gun.

It read:

Will you marry me?

Lillian glanced up; shocked to find Maxwell holding a ring with a humongous diamond.

Lillian hugged him and replied, "Of course I'll marry you."

Maxwell placed the ring on Lillian's finger and kissed her.

Lillian glanced at the enormous rock and said. "You didn't have to buy such an extravagant ring. I was happy with the hunting rifle."

Maxwell laughed and replied, "Four years ago I lost a wager to a lovely young woman for two week's allowance. It was the least I could do."

Lillian gasped and questioned, "This gigantic diamond cost just two weeks of your allowance? Who are you people?"

Maxwell laughed once more and replied, "Lillian, your engagement ring was only one week's allowance."

Back at the mansion, Sarah flipped through another medical book on poisoning. She scanned the page until a passage jumped out at her. *This fungus may cause jaundicing of the skin, liver failure and ultimately death. The biological name: Amanita phalloides. Commonly referred to as the Death Cap; the world's most deadly mushroom.* Sarah sprung to her feet and raced down the hall. She collided with Emanuel in the hallway and almost knocked him over.

Sarah rambled frantically, "The cream of mushroom soup is poisoned! The only reason Master Colburn isn't sick is because he doesn't eat mushrooms."

Emanuel looked horrified as he replied, "I imported most of the vegetables, spices, and herbs from Europe. Robert Welch must have intercepted one of my shipments, My God, what have I done?"

Sarah assured him, "It's not your fault. The very lethal amanita mushroom looks very similar to the straw mushroom, which is commonly used for cooking. Poisonous mushrooms are even known to have a pleasant taste."

Emanuel instructed, "Sarah, go inform the deputies of what's happened! I'll run downstairs to make sure no one eats the food!"

Sarah took off down the stairs and sped up the corridor. She ran outside and spotted one of the deputies. He was posted at the rear entrance under a large tree. The officer was dressed in a law enforcement uniform with a wide brim hat. As Sarah walked over to him, drops of water fell from the tree branches.

She called out to the deputy, "Mistress Colburn has been poisoned!"

The deputy smiled and said, "Mushrooms right?"

Sarah looked up and asked, "But how did you know…"

The deputy pointed a revolver at Sarah and threatened, "If you scream I'll kill you."

As the man stepped out of the shadows she could see he was no officer. *Christ, It's Robert Welch.*

Sarah froze with terror as another drop of water hit her. She glanced down to see it wasn't water dripping from the tree at all. Her dress was splattered with blood. The real deputy was lying on a tree limb above her. His brown eyes were wide open, and flies were buzzing in and out of his mouth. Blood trickled from a deep wound in the man's throat. *Oh my God he's dead.*

Robert struck Sarah with the butt of his gun and knocked her out cold.

Chapter 53

When Sarah opened her eyes she was tied to a bed in the cellar. Each of her limbs was bound to a bedpost. The torches on the walls were lit and she could see Robert Welch looming over her.

Robert slapped Sarah hard and bellowed, "Do you know where I've been the last four years?!" Sarah shook her head no, and Robert vehemently announced, "I've been in prison serving a sentence for manslaughter! I assaulted the wrong man in pursuit of you and Mathew! I'm going to thoroughly enjoy watching you die."

Sarah pleaded with him, "You don't have to hurt me. My husband has money. He'll pay you whatever you want."

Robert flashed her a sinister smile and replied, "Your husband and his entire family will be dead soon. Besides, I'm already being paid."

The cellar doors clanged and Robert announced, "Here comes the money now."

"Who would pay you to hurt me, Robert?" Sarah demanded.

Robert's only reply was a vile burst of laughter. The heavy iron doors opened and Sarah heard footsteps approaching. At last the villain emerged from the darkness.

Sarah called out in shock and confusion, "Emanuel how could you!"

Robert casually asked, "Do you have the rest of my money, Emanuel?"

Emanuel reached inside his medical bag and replied, "Yes, it's right here."

Robert walked over and Emanuel pulled a gun out of the sack. He'd stuffed a potato on the end of the pistol to muffle the blast.

Robert raised his hands and pleaded, "No! Please! No!"

Sarah screamed in horror as Emanuel shot Robert in the head. Robert's body slid down the cellar wall, leaving a lumpy red mess on the bricks. A pool of bright red blood grew around him. Emanuel kneeled next to Robert's corpse and put the revolver in his lifeless hand.

Sarah trembled in fear as Emanuel walked toward her. She was unable to believe her eyes. She became nauseous and her stomach quivered.

He sat on the bed next to her and said, "I promised you would meet Marie tonight, and here she is."

Emanuel pulled a mirror from the sack and held it up in front of Sarah.

Sarah stared in bewilderment at her own reflection and questioned, "What the hell is going on? Why do you want to kill me?"

Emanuel pulled a document out of the bag with Sarah's full legal name printed on it.

He pointed to her middle name and confessed, "I have no intention of killing you. I could never bring myself to harm you. It's you I've been in love with all these years, Sarah *Marie* Colburn. Do you remember that day, four years ago, when Master Colburn informed you of my proposal? That was entirely my idea. I really wanted you to marry me. I assumed you'd come to me in time, but my patients have worn thin over the years. Now I'm willing to take you anyway I can."

Sarah shook her head in disbelief and said, "No, there was a picture of a girl in your cabin. I saw it the night I mended your wounds."

Emanuel smiled and replied, "That was an old picture of my mother. I'm in love with you Sarah. Why else would I take eight lashes to free your parents?"

Sarah called out in utter shock, "You gave me away at my wedding for Christ sake!"

Emanuel brushed a lock of hair from Sarah's face and said, "I have to admit. That was difficult to endure, but it was the only way to keep you from running away out of fear of marrying Abraham. I knew you'd stay for Mathew. Your husband's original plan was to elope with you. I was the one who tricked him into staying. The night of Seth's wedding I told Mathew how dangerous it would be to run away with you. I killed the plantation nurse to keep you here."

Sarah's eyes filled with tears as she replied, "No. Aunt Lizzie died in a fire."

Emanuel shook his head no and said, "I'll let you in on a little secret. I didn't get out of the field of medicine because I was squeamish or I hated it. I avoided that occupation because the dissecting of human flesh invoked a lust in me that frightened me at first. I fought to control the monster within, but in time I grew to embrace it."

Tears streamed from Sarah's eyes as she announced, "I knew that Anna's ear had been surgically removed. You were the first one I showed it to. You stole that ear, to cover your ass! You raped and murdered all those women, you sick bastard!"

Sarah struggled and screamed as Emanuel ran his hand up her thigh.

He whispered in her ear, "You're not jealous are you Sarah? I imagined myself making love to you every time I took one of them. You said yourself that the killer knows this plantation well. Who knows this estate better than me? I told Mathew you were alive because he's a brilliant man. I knew he would find you. Then all I'd have to do is find him. I poisoned his mother in order to lure you here. It worked like a charm."

Emanuel removed a scalpel from a black case and began cutting the laces to Sarah's bodice.

Sarah begged him through heavy tears and labored breaths, "Please… Please don't do this."

As Emanuel sliced the ribbons he said, "Mathew is a smart fellow. He almost caught me years ago. It's a good thing Robert Welch makes an excellent fall guy. Mathew was hot on my trail. So I planted evidence in Robert's cabin. Truth be told, Robert didn't even like women. He was into little boys."

Sarah suddenly remembered a comment Robert made to her. *You're not my type, but this time I'll make an exception.*

Emanuel went on to say, "Robert was a pervert, but no killer. Saphira confided in me that he tried to rape her son one day. He broke the kid's leg in the process. A woman will do most anything to protect her child. When I proposed a plan to get rid of Robert Welch, Saphira lied for me without a second thought. She made it easy to implicate Robert. Frank Welch had issues with lust as well, but he never killed anyone either."

Sarah pleaded with Emanuel, "Your issue is with me. I swear I'll leave with you willingly if you don't kill anyone else. If you have even a modicum of love for me, please don't hurt Mathew."

Emanuel ripped the front of Sarah's dress and said, "I can't promise you that I won't end his life, because there's no way around it. But I can promise you that Mathew won't feel any pain. Don't you see, My Love? I've been skimming money from Master Colburn for years. I always knew I was a relative of the masters. I used that money to bribe the magistrate into changing the law, which made me a white citizen. After tonight I'll be the closest surviving male heir. I'll inherit everything, and I plan to share it all with you. The sheriff will believe Robert killed everyone and then shot himself. The entire town knows Robert Welch was a severely unhinged individual with a vendetta against the Colburns."

Sarah protested, "You'll never get away with this! Master Colburn still has a living brother, Pete."

Emanuel laughed and replied, "You have been gone a long time. Pete Colburn died six months ago. You would be amazed how much a syringe full of air to the jugular resembles a heart attack. Son-of-a-bitch never treated me like a son anyway."

Sarah screamed and struggled vigorously as Emanuel pulled off his shirt. He unbuckled his pants and placed himself on top of her. Sarah's thoughts began to race. *What terrifies me most about Emanuel is that he isn't violently assaulting me. He's so gentle it's almost sickening. He really does love me in some sick twisted way. In his mind he's not raping me. I have to imagine I'm somewhere else; pray it's all over soon.*

Emanuel kissed Sarah's neck and whispered affectionately in her ear, "I've waited so very long for this moment. If you stop fighting, I promise you'll enjoy it."

Chapter 54

Sarah cried out as Emanuel fondled her breast, "So that's it then. You're just going to rape me? How can you vow to love me and then ravish me against my will?"

Emanuel looked down at Sarah compassionately and said, "Sarah, please stop crying. We're going to make love, that's all. I've anticipated this night my entire life. I know you want this as much as I do. You're just scared, and I can understand that. I promise I'll be gentle."

Sarah stopped struggling as a disturbing idea came to mind. *I'm going to have to sacrifice myself to save Mathew. As long as Emanuel's out here on top of me. He's not in the house killing anyone. Maybe I'll break a sweat and slip out of my restraints. If I can manage to escape I may be able to stop him. I have to block out the image of Robert's lifeless corpse lying just twenty feet away, and get on with this horrible deed. I'm so sorry Mathew. Please forgive me for what I'm about to do.*

Sarah looked into Emanuel's pale blue eyes and whispered, "I love you too."

She kissed him long and deep.

Emanuel smiled and asked, "Are you ready?"

Sarah thought to herself. *I can't just allow my husband to die for sake of my own pride. I have to endure this violation and buy myself time to escape. I must stall Emanuel at all costs. I love you Mathew. I'm sorry.*

Tears streamed down Sarah's face as she reluctantly nodded her head yes. Emanuel removed his pants and ripped off Sarah's panties.

She grew sick to her stomach as Emanuel smelled the panties and played with them.

Sarah pulled herself together and lied convincingly, "I wish I could hold you. Come on Emanuel. It's not as if I can over power you."

Emanuel pondered over it for a moment or two then cast the panties aside. As he cut Sarah's arm restraints she thought. *It worked like a charm. My arms are free now. As soon as he's finished with me I'll untie my legs. Mathew told me how he was planning to unhinge the cellar doors to free himself. I'll break out of here in the same manner, as soon as Emanuel is gone.* A waive of nausea washed over Sarah as he climbed back on top of her. She and Mathew had never been with anyone but each other. She coached herself. *I can do this. I have to do this or Mathew will die.*

As Emanuel took Sarah by the waist a disgusted look swept over his face. He jumped away from her in shock and sprung off the bed.

Emanuel shook his head in disbelief and shouted, "I won't allow you to have another man's child!"

At that moment Sarah realized what had happened. *Emanuel is related to Master Colburn. He has the same gift as Mathew and the other male Colburns. What a hell of a time to find out I'm pregnant.*

Emanuel threw on his clothes and yelled in anger, "I was going to allow your husband to die without pain! I put powerful sedatives in everyone's dinner, so that I may burn down the house while they slept. Mathew would've died peacefully in his sleep of smoke inhalation."

Emanuel grabbed a fist full of smelling salts from his medical bag and said, "Now I'm going to revive your husband and stab him at least fifty times! As he bleeds out, I'll ravish you in front of his dying eyes!"

Chapter 55

Emanuel gave Sarah a cold glare and said, "Once I've killed all the Colburns I'm going to mix you up an abortifacient. And you are going to drink every last drop of it. After you've miscarried Mathew's child I'll plant a seed of my own. You were meant to have my children! Not his!"

Sarah screamed in anger as Emanuel picked up his case of razor sharp scalpels, "You're a monster! It's inhuman to be so cold! You promised me you wouldn't cause Mathew pain! How could you claim to care for me and then murder my husband before my eyes?!"

Emanuel reluctantly set aside his surgical blades and looked down at Sarah with pity.

He threw the smelling salts on the ground and growled with frustration, "Mathew is lucky I can't bring myself to break a promise to you. He'll die without pain as I agreed."

Emanuel stepped over the body of Robert Welch and ascended the steps. He exited and pad locked the cellar doors behind him.

Sarah quickly untied the restraints from her ankles. She stepped off the bed into a puddle of Robert's blood. As she tiptoed around the corpse she grew extremely ill. *As a doctor I've seen several people die in front of me, but I've never witnessed anyone murdered. Emanuel just shot Robert without remorse or sympathy.* She caught a glimpse of the gaping hole in Roberts face. His cold blue eyes stared up at Sarah. Her stomach rolled and quivered. She doubled over and lost her lunch. *I have to be strong.*

Sarah wiped her mouth then examined the hinges on the door. *They have half pins like Mathew said.* She searched the cellar for a tool. She found a spoon covered in dust and cobwebs. *Frank Welch brought Mathew food when he was being held hostage. That must be where this spoon came from. I'll use the handle to push the holding pins out of the hinges.*

The first pin came out easily. The second pin proved difficult. Sarah was forced to hold the heavy iron door up with one hand and work the pin loose with the other. She cried out in triumph as the pin finally came out. Then grabbed the door and eased it aside.

Sarah gathered the few smelling salts that didn't land in Robert's blood and exited the cellar. She stealthily crept back to the mansion. She could see through the windows, a fire was started in Master Colburn's office and bedroom. Flames flickered in two other chambers as well. The mansion was filling rapidly with smoke. Sarah was able to see Mathew lying lifeless on his bed. She pushed open the pane of glass and climbed into the room coughing. The smoked burned her eyes as she closed and locked Mathew's bedroom door. She opened the windows wide for ventilation then walked over to Mathew. *Please still be alive. I pray you haven't already inhaled too much smoke.*

Chapter 56

Sarah sat next to her husband on the bed and shook him. Tears filled her eyes when he didn't respond. She quickly checked his vitals. *He isn't breathing and his pulse is shallow and weak. He's turning blue from lack of oxygen. Honey, please wake up.*

Sarah broke the smelling salt and waved it under Mathew's nose. *For the love of God, come back to me. Mathew, please come back to me!* His nostrils and lungs filled with ammonia and he sprung to life. He sat up in bed coughing violently. Sarah cried tears of relief and embraced him.

Mathew glanced back and forth disoriented, and Sarah said, "The house is on fire. We have to get you out."

She pulled him off the bed and helped him outside on the lawn. The color gradually returned to Mathew's face and he rose to his feet.

He looked over at Sarah and said, "I have to go back in. There are still four other people in the house."

Sarah blocked his path and warned, "You should at least go to the hunting lodge and grab a rifle first. Emanuel's gone mad! He's trying to kill everyone and take the property. He was going to rape me until he figured out I was pregnant. He's the one who committed all those atrocities."

Mathew replied in disbelief of Emanuel's act of betrayal, "By the time I get to the hunting lodge and back Francesca, Adrion, and my parents will already be dead. The house is full of smoke. They may only have minutes to live. My father keeps a gun in his room. I'll be fine."

Sarah handed Mathew a few smelling salts and instructed, "Break these and waive them underneath your parents' noses. Aaron use to scale a tree to sneak into Francesca's room. I'll climb onto her balcony and pull her out. Adrion's room is across the hall. I'll wake him too."

Mathew protested and Sarah said, "You won't be able to get to everyone in time. I promise I'll be careful."

Mathew hugged her and she took off across the lawn. Sarah scaled the tree with very little effort. *Damn that's a long way down.* She thought as she leaped onto the balcony. The room was so black with smoke she couldn't see through the glass doors. She pushed open the doors and the smoke came barreling out. Sarah crawled into the room and the first person she noticed was Adrion lying on the couch. *Thank god they slept in the same room tonight.* She pulled him onto the floor, and dragged his unconscious body out onto the balcony. She put her cheek to his mouth and smiled when she felt warm breath on her face. *Amen he's still breathing.* Sarah carefully administered the ammonia tablet. *Come on Adrion, you're a big strong man Wake up for me.* His eyes flashed open at once.

Adrion asked through heavy coughs, "Is... Francesca... alright?"

Sarah assured, "I'm going back for her right now."

Adrion rose groggily to his feet and said, "No, you stay here where it's safe. I'll run in and get her."

Sarah watched anxiously from the balcony as Adrion disappeared into the abyss of black smoke. She picked up the smelling salt she used to revive Adrion thinking. *I pray there's enough chemical left in this tablet to wake Francesca. It was the last one I had.* Adrion burst onto the balcony with Francesca in his arms. He quickly laid her on the marble before Sarah.

Sarah told Adrion, "Francesca's completely cyanotic and she's not breathing. I feel a pulse but it's very shallow."

Sarah waived what was left of the smelling salt under Francesca's nostrils. She didn't respond. Adrion's face filled with worry.

Sarah stood up and said, "I have to get to my room. There are more smelling salts in my medical bag."

Adrion protested, "It's far too dangerous. You could get yourself killed. I'll go in and retrieve the bag for you."

Sarah explained, "You won't be able to find my medical bag in all this. I know exactly where it is. I'll be back shortly."

Sarah took a deep breath of fresh air, and then battled through the smoldering room. She entered the hallway and it was blistering hot. The corridor was red with flames. She quickly became light headed from the heavy smoke. The hall began to spin and she grew dizzy. *Damn I'm losing my balance.*

Sarah scorched her hand on the fiery wall as she braced herself from falling. She cried out in agony as she choked on the ash. *My room's just a few doors down. I can make it.* She soldiered on, until she reached her destination. Then grabbed her supplies and made an about face.

Sarah battled back through the hall of flames, with the medical bag clutched within her arms. *It feels as if my nose and throat are on fire. There's Francesca's door; just a few... more... steps...* Sarah ventured forward and collapsed in the doorway of Francesca's bedroom. She lay on the floor in a semiconscious state, unable to move or call for help.

Chapter 57

Sarah lay helplessly in the smoke filled mansion yelping in vain, "Adrion... Please... help me..."

Her calls went unanswered. Lucky for Sarah, the air closest to the floor was cooler and easier to breathe. She regained an ounce of strength and crawled a few more feet.

As Sarah collapsed once more she called out, "Adrion! Please get me out of here!"

Adrion La'Cour finally heard Sarah's pleas for help. He dashed into the room and quickly pulled her outside.

Adrion carefully laid Sarah next to Francesca and questioned. "Are you alright?"

"I'll be fine." Sarah assured as she dumped out the contents of her medical bag on the balcony.

She groggily waived the tablet beneath Francesca's nose to revive her. Francesca opened her eyes and began to cough and gag.

Sarah instructed, "We'll be safe on the balcony for now. Once we're all capable, we can climb down the tree to safety."

When Mathew's mother fell ill she was in need of consolation. His father now slept in the bedroom with her every night to comfort her. Mathew stood a ladder against the house and climbed up onto his parents' balcony. He opened the double glass doors wide to let much of the smoke escape. Then he ventured in. The tapestries and paintings were engulfed in flames.

My chest and eyes still burn like hell, but at least I can see where my parents are. He found his father lying in bed with his arms wrapped around the mistress. Mathew pulled his mom from his Father's embrace and laid her outside on the balcony. Tears filled his eyes as he checked the pulse in his mother's wrist. *Not only is there no pulse, my mother is as rigid as a board. Rigor mortis has already set in. She probably died hours ago from the poison, before the fire ever started.* His heart pounded hard in his chest and he began to hyperventilate. *I've got to pull myself together. Father may still be alive. I must keep my wits for long enough to save him.* He climbed back into the room after his father. He put an ear against Master Colburn's chest. *Thank god there's still a heartbeat. He's still breathing, but barely.* Mathew pulled Master Colburn outside and administered a smelling salt. His mind grew heavy with dread as his father neglected to blink, cough, or move the slightest bit.

Mathew desperately shook Master Colburn and shouted, "Wake the hell up! I beg you! Please don't die! I can't lose both parents in one night!"

Mathew frantically administered a second smelling salt that was meant for his mother. He felt relived as Master Colburn's eyes shot open for a brief moment. But they closed again almost immediately. Mathew looked on, in heart wrenching desperation, as his father took his final breath.

Emanuel jogged out the back door of the flaming mansion. He had a hefty sack of money and expensive jewelry hanging from his shoulder. He kneeled on the cool wet grass and pulled out a small gardening shovel. He contemplated as he picked at the earth. *I'll retrieve the last of my fortune from this hole in the ground and rightfully claim the estate tomorrow. Lillian and Seth escaped my grasp but they're inconsequential anyway. The property won't go to Seth because he's black; which makes him illegitimate. The inheritance won't pass to Lillian because she's a woman. Once I've convinced Sarah to love me and forgive me, I'll have everything.*

Emanuel jumped to his feet as he noticed Mathew's bedroom window was open. He ran to the gaping window, and peered through the smoke at an empty bed.

"Son of a bitch!" Emanuel yelled and dashed back to his belongings.

He glanced into the distance and saw a ladder leading up to Mathew's parents' room. Emanuel smiled bitterly. *Mathew you're so predictable. You would be foolish enough to go in after your parents, instead of just get the hell out of here.*

Emanuel pulled a razor sharp machete from his bag and vowed scornfully, "When I'm finished with you, cousin, you'll wish you died in that fire!"

Chapter 58

Mathew climbed to his feet, overcome by irrepressible rage. He reentered the fiery chamber and rifled through his father's dresser. *Father always slept with a pistol.*

"Where is it!" Mathew called out in anger.

He flung entire drawers full of clothes on the floor. The clothing ignited and burst into flames within seconds. He turned over the bedside table and searched the contents. Then he hurled the pillows and mattress off the bed. *What did Father do with his gun!*

Emanuel ran into the blazing room and lunged at Mathew with the machete. Mathew jumped back and dodged the first few swings but the fourth one sliced him clear across the abdomen.

As Mathew clutched his bleeding stomach Emanuel yelled, "You're a dead man Colburn!"

Mathew yelled back, "Is this little scratch the best you can do, you damned traitor!"

Emanuel sliced forcefully through the air with the enormous blade. Mathew ducked and the machete embedded itself in the dresser. As Emanuel tried to yank it out Mathew sent a brutal punch to his face.

Mathew shouted as he followed up with another blow to Emanuel's head and a sock to the stomach. "You're not so tough now are you?! What can I expect from a pathetic scoundrel who attacks defenseless women!"

Emanuel struck Mathew with a porcelain jewelry box and tackled him to the ground.

Emanuel squeezed Mathew's throat and growled scornfully, "After I choke the life out of you, cousin, the first thing I'll do is fuck that pretty little wife of yours and piss on your corpse."

Mathew clobbered Emanuel with a board from a broken drawer and Emanuel fell back. Red hot flames danced all around them as they tussled about the burning bedroom. Fiery planks of wood and ash rained from the ceiling, as they continued to trade violent punches. Emanuel hollered out in pain when his sleeve caught fire. As Emanuel frantically waved his arm to put out the flames, Mathew removed the machete from the dresser.

Emanuel pointed a revolver at him and shouted, "Drop the blade Mathew!"

Mathew cast the weapon aside and spoke with fury, "Before you kill me you could at least be a man and admit what this is all about!"

Emanuel replied, "You already know why I'm doing this. Sarah and I were meant to be together."

Mathew stood undaunted, and spoke with unwavering fortitude, "You and I both know this isn't really about her. You're obsessed with me. You've been competing with me since we were children. Your pathetic father raped your mother and nine months later there you were. Your mother chose to kill herself rather then look at you. Your disgusting father never stepped forward to raise you. You've envied me your entire life because I had a family and you didn't! You don't just want my wife. You want my inheritance, my birth right, all that I possess."

Emanuel bitterly confessed, "I always hated you! I tried for years to steal your father's affection. That's why I strived to be his right hand man. Medical classes were the only thing you were bad at. So I chose to study medicine. I vowed to show you up, make you look bad. I made it a point to screw every girl who ever liked you; as well as anyone you showed the slightest bit of interest in. If you could have her, I *had* to have her. I raped and murdered Anna and Mali because both of those whores use to throw themselves at you. How dare they choose you over me! I killed Katherine and Sally because I followed you to Blue Valley and saw them flirting with you. In fact you had your tongue down Katherine's throat. She really had to go!"

Mathew remained intrepid and boldly spoke without fear. "I didn't really care for any of those girls, which made them expendable to you. The only reason you didn't kill Sarah is because I love her, which means you're in love with her. My father said something interesting the other day. He said you would have to be an idiot not to have known Sarah and I liked each other, and you're no idiot. You knew I was in love with Sarah. That's the reason you proposed to her in the first place. All these years I assumed Sarah was the one being stalked. When in all actuality it was me. So go ahead and shoot, you damned coward! You'll spend the rest of your life trying to be me! But all you'll ever amount to is a pussy with a gun in his hand!"

Emanuel's eyes grew red with hate. His nostrils flared and his brows furrowed with anger.

He drew back on the hammer of his firearm, and spoke with pure contempt and bitterness, "I've lived in your shadow for long enough. Goodbye Mathew."

Chapter 59

The blast of gunfire was all but deafening. Mathew glanced up in shock to find his father alive. Master Colburn was standing in the balcony doorway with a smoking pistol in his grip.

Emanuel dropped his gun as he realized he'd been shot by Master Colburn. He clutched the gaping wound in his gut, in utter disbelief. A look of sheer terror covered his face, as dark red blood ran between his fingers. He cringed in agony and collapsed.

Master Colburn gripped his chest, and plummeted to the balcony floor. Mathew retrieved Emanuel's gun, and then ran to his father's aid.

Mathew kneeled beside his father and said, "I thought you were dead."

Master Colburn jokingly replied in a voice nearly a whisper, "Of course you did, son. You were always terrible at your medical studies. You know the last time we were on this balcony together you were throwing me off of it."

Mathew laughed a little and said, "I should've known that fire was no match for you. You're the strongest man I know."

Master Colburn's expression grew serious as he replied, "I need you to listen and listen well. I may not have much time."

Mathew shook his head and protested, "Father, don't talk like that. You're going to be fine."

Master Colburn replied, "I don't have your lungs, son. I've smoked for over two decades. In case I don't leave this balcony there are some things you need to know. Don't be like me. Tell your wife you love her every day, even if you're angry with her. And support your children in whatever path they choose, even if you may not agree with them. I'm leaving the estate to you. I trust you'll look out for your sister. I promised your mother I would take care of Seth." Master Colburn handed Mathew a folded up piece of paper and instructed. "Give this to your brother. I love you son."

Mathew unfolded the note. It read:

To my oldest son Seth:
Your inheritance lays eight
paces beneath the stars.
Your Father,

Mathew Sr.

Mathew tucked the note away and asked, "Father, what does this mean?"

Master Colburn didn't respond. His dark brown eyes stared blankly into the night.

"Father!" Mathew called vehemently, again no response.

He listened to his father's chest in despair and anguish. *His heart has ceased to beat. Not a single rhythmic thump to bring me piece of mind.* Mathew gently closed his father's eyes. His heart grew heavy with grief. Consumed by sorrow, he rose to his feet.

He cast a final mournful glare on his deceased parents and prayed, "Dieu vous garde (God keep you) until we meet again."

Mathew reached for the ladder to climb down, and Sarah screamed from Francesca's balcony, "Mathew!! Look out behind you!!"

Mathew made an about face in time to catch a scalpel to the chest. Mathew staggered back and grasped his wound. Blood streamed down the front of him.

Emanuel gripped his stomach wound and whispered to Mathew, "The bullet I took was a clean shot. I'll survive, but you won't. Any last requests, cousin?"

Mathew choked out in agony, "Would you please... tell... Lucifer who sent you."

Emanuel looked up with surprise as Mathew stabbed the eight inch bolt into his heart.

Emanuel stared at Mathew and stammered, "You… carried it all these… years?"

Mathew whispered to Emanuel, "Goodbye, cousin," Then shoved him off the balcony.

Emanuel plummeted two stories and collided with the ground. Sarah walked around his disfigured corpse and scaled the ladder to get to Mathew. She climbed onto the balcony and Mathew collapsed in her arms.

He looked up at Sarah and said, "Looks like I'll be meeting my parents sooner than I thought."

Tears cascaded from Sarah's eyes. She put pressure on the wound and lied to him, "You're going to be alright. Don't say such things."

Sarah kissed her dying husband and said, "I love you."

Mathew passed Sarah a bloody slip of paper and instructed, "Please give this to my brother Seth." She sadly nodded yes and Mathew continued, "And Sarah?"

"Yes Mathew." She answered mournfully.'

He touched her cheek and whispered, "I love you."

He coughed up blood and his body became still. Sarah held Mathew close until his eyes fell shut.

Chapter 60

August 22, 1841

The island of Samson's origin was astonishing. It was a tropical paradise of dormant volcanoes, palm trees, and dazzling waterfalls. Waves crashed on the sandy shore as Sarah walked along the beach. Her heart ached as she glanced at all the happy couples. Aaron and Francesca were peacefully sleeping together in a hammock. Seth and Leah were taking a late afternoon stroll on the beach. And Marlette and Phillip stood watching the sunset over the vast sparkling ocean.

Sarah watched the beautiful sunset alone in deep contemplation. *Who would've known my father was prince of his tribe before he was captured and taken into slavery. Now he's king and my mother is his queen. Marlette and I are to be crowned in this evening's ceremony. It hardly seems fair, that after all Mathew and I have been through together, he won't be by my side on this night.* Her eyes filled with tears of sorrow.

Seth walked over and spoke to Sarah, "Are you ready? It's almost time, Princess."

Sarah solemnly replied, "Seth thank you for offering to escort me to the ceremony. But I'll understand if you would like to take your wife instead."

Leah walked up and said, "That's nonsense Sarah. I don't mind if Seth goes with you. This is your night. You shouldn't be alone."

Sarah gave an appreciative nod and took Seth's arm. She could already hear the beating of the drums in the distance.

Sarah asked Seth, "Did you ever figure out the riddle on that slip of paper?"

Seth smiled and answered, "Eight feet from the back door of the mansion I found a hole where Emanuel had been digging. Inside laid a chest containing a substantial amount of cash."

Sarah paused, mid-step as Mathew approached her. He was shirtless with half of his chest and stomach wrapped in bandages.

Mathew called to the others, "Carry on without us. Sarah and I will catch up."

The rest of the couples continued on to the celebration, leaving Sarah and Mathew alone on the beautiful beach. The sunset painted the sky and sea in a breath-taking array of colors. They strolled along the cool wet sand and waves washed over their bare feet.

Sarah smiled at her husband and scolded, "Mathew! You took a stab wound to the chest less then a month ago. I had to surgically remove 50% of your left lung in order to save your life. What are you doing out of bed! You should be resting."

Mathew let out a painful laugh and told her, "I've been resting for almost a month. Besides I wouldn't miss this night for anything in the world."

Sarah's eyes filled with concern as she said, "As your doctor, I recommend you return to bed this instant. If that blade had entered one centimeter higher, it would've pierced your heart."

She laughed as Mathew replied, "You're fired Sarah. You're no longer my doctor. Tonight you're simply my wife."

Mathew wrapped Sarah in a loving embrace and looked deep into her eyes.

While they stood in each other's arms he whispered, "Sarah, you never had anything to worry about. The only one who's ever been capable of piercing my heart is you."

As Mathew and Sarah kissed passionately on the beach of the Island, they knew they would be together for all eternity, in this life and the next.

Chapter 61

Present

Krista smiled as she finished the book. *It was one incredible story, but I still don't understand what it has to do with some really hot dead guy from the 1920's. Why did my great grandfather murder Alex Monroe? And who the hell is W. S. C.?* She placed the book aside as she noticed music playing downstairs. *Crap I'm late for the party.* She quickly brushed her hair and slipped on a floor length formal gown. The elegant dress was cranberry red. She added red clips to her hair to match. She spritzed herself with perfume and dashed down the hall to her late grandmother's room. Krista searched through the trinkets in her grandma's jewelry box. *There has to be something in here that matches my dress. Ah, perfect.*

Krista pulled out a beautiful ruby necklace and noticed Ox standing in the doorway. He was all spruced up in a black tuxedo with a red vest and tie.

He walked in and said, "You look phenomenal."

Krista grinned and replied, "You don't look so bad yourself." She passed him the necklace and asked, "Would you mind?"

Ox clasped the ruby necklace for Krista and escorted her downstairs.

There were already over fifty guests in the grand ballroom, all dressed in formal evening wear. Waiters circled the party with silver trays of hors d'oeuvres and champagne. Angela and Stacy were sneaking into the wine. Krista's parents were on the floor dancing.

Jessy set a present on the gift table and walked over to Krista joking, "You're the only one I know who can live at a party and still be late for it."

Krista laughed and replied, "I was doing some research and lost track of time."

Ox told Krista, "I'm going to the men's room I'll be right back."

After he left Jessy asked, "What were you doing research on? Perhaps I can help."

Krista replied, "I appreciate it, Jessy. If anyone can help me figure all this out it's you."

Jessy smiled at her cousin's compliment, and Krista thought to herself. *Jessy's a computer whiz she might be able to find out more about this Alex fellow. If I can figure out what he wants I may be able to help him. Then perhaps he'll stop haunting me.*

Jessy turned to Krista and said, "Right this way."

Krista followed Jessy down the hall to an empty room. Jessy pulled her laptop from underneath a couch and set it up on a coffee table.

Krista asked in astonishment, "Do you take that computer everywhere you go?"

"Just about." Jessy answered as she took a seat, and logged on with her password.

Krista instructed, "I need you to look up a guy with the initials W. S. C. He may have either been born or died in 1929. The **C** most likely stands for Colburn."

Jessy typed in the keywords and performed a search. As information popped up on the screen she announced, "The first thing I can tell you is that W. S. C. is not the name of a person. It's an event; the **W**all **S**treet **C**rash of 1929 to be exact."

Krista threw up her hands and said, "Now I'm really confused."

Jessy questioned, "What's going on?"

Krista replied, "I'll explain everything after the party. For now would you mind finding any information on Alexander Monroe, Thomas Colburn, and the Wall Street Crash of 1929?"

Jessy nodded and continued to type.

Krista darted back to the ballroom in search of Ox. She glanced over the room but couldn't find him anywhere. The guests came to attention as Krista's mother and father clinked their champagne glasses.

Her father spoke into a microphone. "I have an announcement to make. Dr. Veronica Clark is buying the family house."

Krista let out a horrified gasp as the guests cheered triumphantly.

Krista stormed up to her parents and shouted, "What do you mean you're selling the house?! This property has been in our family over seven generations. We built it from the ground up."

Her father pulled her aside and replied in shock, "Krista my parents bought this property in the 1950's. Besides, it was you who begged us to sell the mansion. You called it a worthless pile of termites remember."

Krista looked up at her father and said, "Grandma and Grandpa lied to you out of shame and embarrassment of our family's history. You're making a huge mistake by selling this place!"

Krista stormed across the ballroom floor, and ran outside for some fresh air.

As the party continued Ox pulled Angela into one of the slave cabins.

He questioned vehemently, "Why did you come here with Stacy? You know you don't like him!"

Angela explained, "It would look suspicious if I showed up without a date tonight. And to be perfectly honest, I wanted to see if it would make you jealous! Nothing happened!"

Ox answered with irritation, "Of course I was jealous! I'm not just fucking you, Angela! I care about you."

Angela questioned, "Have you told Krista yet?"

Ox looked down at the floor and answered, "I wanted you to be there when I told her the truth about everything. She's going to be crushed. She'll never forgive me. Sometimes I wonder if it's too late to make things right."

Angela held his hand and stated, "It's never too late to do the right thing. I vandalized someone's truck the end of this school year. But I'm going to pay for my mistakes and apologize to him because it's the right thing to do. If you tell Krista the truth, she'll forgive you."

Ox wrapped his arms around Angela and said, "Let's go tell Krista everything right now. I'll try my best to fix this whole mess."

Angela smiled and replied, "Now that's the spirit."

He kissed her deeply one last forbidden time.

As Ox released Angela he said, "Time to do the right thing."

They both froze when they saw Krista standing outside the window with tears in her eyes. Krista shook her head with disappointment. Her heart broke as she witnessed the betrayal. She took off without saying a word.

Ox exited the cabin and hollered after her, "Krista I'm so sorry! Please wait! I can explain."

Krista ran to the garage, and Ox and Angela sped after her. Krista jumped into the black 66 Charger and pulled the keys from the visor. She started the car, threw it in gear, and squalled tires out of there. Ox ran after the car until it disappeared. Angela ran up to him crying.

She announced through heaving sobs, "Ox, you have to stop Krista! Her father said that car isn't safe to drive!"

Ox shouted back, "What's wrong with the car?!"

Angela replied, "I don't know. He said something about replacing the lines and drums."

Ox yelled in frustration, "Shit! The car has no brakes!"

Krista flew down the deserted dirt road in the classic car. Her hair flailed in the breeze, and she felt as if she were flying. *Behind the wheel of the charger I feel free. All the bad things that happened tonight don't hurt so much anymore.* Krista's phone lit up and vibrated. She pushed the ignore button and tossed it on the passenger seat. *Ox has some nerve to be calling me.*

Ox sped up in his jeep alongside her and yelled, "Krista! It's important that you listen to me!"

Krista screamed back, "Go to hell Kevin Oxley!"

She rolled up her window and punched the gas. She quickly left him in the dust and yelled out in anguish, "The nerve of that asshole!"

Ox stepped on the gas and caught up with Krista. He yelled out the window to warn her, "The brakes on the Charger are worn down! You have to pat the brakes to come to a complete stop!"

Krista couldn't hear him because her windows were rolled up. Ox gasped in horror at the approaching intersection. He knew there was nothing he could do to overt the catastrophe. The screen on Krista's cell phone lit up once more with a text message. A cold chill rolled down Krista's spine as she read it.

NO BRAKES ON THE CHARGER!!!! - Angela

Krista panicked and stomped the brake pedal to the floor. The car didn't slow down at all. She flew into the intersection at over fifty miles per hour. She screamed in terror as she saw the head lights of the truck barreling down on her.

Ox watched helplessly as the semi-truck crashed into the side of Krista's vehicle. The car flipped five times before landing on its roof. Bystanders were screaming and dialing 911 on their cell phones. Ox jumped out of his jeep and ran to the scene of the accident. There were shards of metal and broken glass all over the street. The semi-truck crushed Krista's Charger like a Coke can. Ox climbed through the window and pulled Krista's body from the car. She was unresponsive and covered in blood.

Ox held her in his arms and cried out, "Krista I'm sorry! This is all my fault."

Chapter 62

The ghost of Krista snapped out of her contemplation as she noticed a handsome black man staring at her.

She rose from her seat in the hospital corridor and asked, "Excuse me Sir, can you see me?" The man nodded and Krista went on to say, "You're the first one who's been able to see me and..." She stopped mid sentence as she noticed the man's old fashioned clothes. *He looks so familiar.*

The man stepped forward and spoke in a British accent, "Hello Krista, I'm Alex Monroe."

Krista gathered her nerve and said, "I'm obviously dead if you're here. Have you come to take me to heaven?"

Alex shook his head no. Krista announced in a panic, "You haven't come to take me to hell have you!"

Alex laughed and replied, "I haven't come to take you anywhere. I only ask for your help. Would you mind taking a walk with me?"

Krista accompanied him on a stroll through the hospital, and commented, "I don't know how much use I can be to you now that I'm a poltergeist."

Alex smiled at her and explained, "You're not dead Krista. You're just in an unresponsive state. Time is relative. Have you ever noticed that when you're doing something you love, time flies? But when you're doing something you don't enjoy, like walking around a hospital in spirit form, time has the tendency to drag. In all actuality your heart has only ceased to beat for two minutes."

Krista breathed a sigh of relief, and followed Alex into an empty lecture hall. The room was made like a movie theatre with a large projector screen covering the front wall. Alex and Krista flipped down their chairs and took a seat.

Krista turned to Alex and said, "I need you to tell me what that journal had to do with your death. Maybe if I gain a greater understanding, I can seek justice for you. And you can finally rest in peace."

Alex solemnly replied, "I'm not trapped between worlds because I seek justice for myself. I'm trapped here for the same reason I came to Missouri. I promised a dying girl I would never rest until I found justice for her family."

Krista watched as Alex turned on the projector. Moving pictures began to display on the screen.

Alex turned to Krista and said, "This will explain everything."

Krista gazed in awe at the scenes which displayed before her.

Chapter 63

April 13, 1933

18-year-old Aurora Colburn sat at the desk of her family's two bedroom shack. She glanced over her shoulder to make sure the coast was clear, and then continued to write her letter.

Dear Mr. Alexander Monroe,

Upon return from an Island near Africa my ancestors Seth and Mathew Colburn invested together. They built an architecture/construction business. The two brothers were very successful, and for many generations the white and black Colburns lived in harmony and prospered.

Six years ago my great uncle, Thomas Colburn, invested his entire fortune in the stock market. Thomas lost everything in the Wall Street Crash of 1929. At the time he was engaged to a girl from a wealthy prominent family. His fiancée's parents would've called off the wedding had they found out he was penniless. Though Uncle Tom is the descendant of a slave woman by the name of Sarah Colburn, he passes himself off as white. His ability to pass for a white man put the law on his side. He used the legal system to rob us, the black relatives, of our inheritance. Seth's descendant's, including myself, are now destitute. We are forced to live in the old slave cabins and work on Thomas Colburn's property for meager earnings. He denies all blood relations to us for appearances sake. Please help us to regain what is rightfully ours.

Your Greatest Admirer,

Aurora Colburn

Aurora hid the letter as her mother, Bridget and 7-year-old sister, Lucinda entered the room. Aurora's mother was a stout built light skinned woman with a no nonsense mentality. Lucinda was a small pesky child. She wore pig tails and a powder blue dress.

Bridget snapped, "That better had been homework you were working on."

"She's probably writing him again. This is the fourth letter she's written him." Lucinda commented as she pointed to a wall decorated with Alex Monroe's newspaper articles.

"Shut up Lucinda!" Aurora shouted at her little sister.

Lucinda puckered her lips and made kissing noises. She pointed at Aurora and teased, "You love Alex. You love Alex."

Bridget scolded, "Knock it off Lucinda."

A girl and boy the same age as Lucinda appeared in the doorway with their mother.

Bridget passed the mother an overnight sack and said, "Thank you for keeping Lucinda tonight. I have to drive one of my white relatives to college today. I won't be back until morning and Aurora has to work this evening."

The woman assured, "It's no problem at all."

"Come on Jonathan and Katy, I have something to show you." Lucinda said as she dashed out the door with the children.

Once Lucinda was gone Aurora's mother turned to her and said, "You can't just live in a fantasy world, waiting for this Monroe fellow to ride in like some British knight and save the day."

Aurora shot back, "We didn't always live this way. It isn't fair what Uncle Tom has done to us. We should fight for what's rightfully ours."

Bridget solemnly replied, "Your father and I, God rest his soul, fought in court for over a year. The lawyer fees and court costs only placed us further into debt. Now I'm working for the very bastard who stole all our money."

Bridget tossed Aurora a white paper bag. Aurora took a pill from the sack and chased it with a glass of water.

Her mother went on to say, "Right now Thomas Colburn is still charitable enough to pay for your medication. I beg you Aurora. Don't cause any trouble."

Bridget grabbed a sandwich, and returned to her job as Thomas Colburn's driver.

Aurora thought sadly to herself. *Maybe I am only dreaming.* She sighed and pulled a book off the shelf. She owned every one of Alexander Monroe's novels. She set the book aside when she heard a knock at the door. She walked over to answer it and stood in the doorway speechless.

"Alexander Monroe at your service," Called the handsome stranger in the doorway.

Alex was 28-years-old and clean cut. He possessed medium brown skin and dark eyes. Aurora was a short pretty girl with dark brown skin and gray eyes.

"Please… Come in." Aurora stuttered.

Alex Monroe took a seat at the table. He pulled a black leather bound book from his brief case.

Aurora stammered, "Can I get you anything?"

Alex smiled at her and replied, "Maybe later; we have a lot to cover and I prefer we get straight down to business."

Aurora smiled and replied, "As you wish, Sir."

Alex flipped through the pages of his book and said, "Please just call me Alex." Aurora nodded and he went onto say, "I composed this journal from the information in your letters. Please gather any legal documents as proof to back up your claims."

Aurora left the room and came back moments later with a folder full of documents.

She handed it to Alex and explained, "This folder contains slave records, birth certificates, marriage licenses; everything that proves we are the blood relatives of Thomas Colburn. The last judge refused to hear us out or even see the evidence."

Alex assured, "I found a different judge who's willing to listen to your case as long as you can provide these documents."

Aurora sat across the table from Alex overjoyed and said, "Thank you so much for helping our family. I can't believe you're really here."

Alex replied, "What your uncle Thomas did was despicable. The moment I received your letter I vowed to seek justice for you."

Alex pulled out a pen and turned to a blank page in the journal.

He glanced at Aurora and said, "I need to know everything about your family history. Spare me no detail."

Aurora began to unfold the tale of her ancestors, "One day I was cleaning the mansion of, my great uncle, Thomas Colburn. I stumbled across the diary of a slave woman named Sarah Colburn. Before Uncle Tom confiscated the diary and destroyed it, I read the whole thing. This is what it said….."

Alex vigorously jotted down every word in his journal.

As the story came to a close Thomas Colburn burst into the house.

Aurora shouted vehemently, "Have you ever heard of knocking?!"

Thomas grabbed Aurora up by the arm, and waived a document in her face.

Thomas yelled angrily, "This is a subpoena! I've been summoned to appear in court! I know this was your doing Aurora. Your mother's not stupid enough to challenge me again."

Alex rose from his seat and bellowed, "I demand that you let her go at once!"

Thomas gave a nonchalant laugh and replied, "Or you'll do what?"

Alex stared at Thomas and candidly spoke, "As of now Aurora is only suing you for what rightfully belongs to her. If you don't release her, this instant, not only will you be sued, I'll destroy your reputation." Alex slammed the black book down on the table and continued, "I know all about your black slave lineage. I swear, Mr. Colburn, I will publish this journal and ruin you."

Thomas Colburn let go of Aurora's arm at once.

Aurora pointed to the door and said, "I'll see you in court Uncle Tom."

Thomas Colburn stormed out of the house and slammed the door behind him.

Aurora let out a sigh of relief and said, "I should thank my lucky stars that you were here."

Alex glanced up thoughtfully and asked, "What did you just say?"

Aurora answered with a confused expression, "Thank you."

Alex questioned, "No after that?"

Aurora replied, "Lucky stars."

Alex shuffled through the documents in the folder. He pulled out a stained slip of paper that read.

To my oldest son Seth:

> *Your inheritance lays eight paces beneath the stars.*
–Your father, Mathew Sr.

Alex turned to a page near the beginning of the journal. He read a small passage out loud.

> *"Sarah paused for a moment and let out a long sigh. She stared wistfully up at the constellations painted on the master's ceiling."*

Aurora questioned, "Where are you going with this Alex?"

Alex smiled and replied, "You informed me that there was a fire years ago. Several rooms were burned and later refurbished. Is it possible that Master Colburn's office originally had stars painted on the ceiling?"

Aurora smiled and replied, "I suppose that's possible."

Alex looked up at her and said, "Maybe Seth Colburn never found his true inheritance. Maybe all Seth found outside that day was money that Emanuel had been skimming from Master Colburn. What if Seth's true inheritance still lies within the floor boards of Master Colburn's office, eight paces beneath where the stars use to be."

Aurora replied with excitement, "It's certainly worth looking into. Will you excuse me for just a moment?"

Aurora went into her bedroom and came out moments later dressed in a maid's uniform.

She glanced at the clock and took another dose of medication.

Alex questioned, "If you don't mind me asking, what are those pills for?"

Aurora looked down at the floor and explained, "I have a genetic heart condition. But as long as I continue to take my medication I'll be fine. My father died of the same affliction a year ago because he could no longer afford the medication for both of us. My mother promised Uncle Tom that if he continued to pay for my pills she wouldn't raise a stink over our inheritance anymore."

Alex nodded and said, "Now I see what's at stake."

Aurora glanced up at Alex and replied, "I'm on my way to work right now. Tonight I have to cater Uncle Tom's poker game. Maybe we can look around Master Colburn's office, see if we can find Seth's true inheritance."

Alex gathered the folder full of documents and the journal.

He glanced around the tiny shack and said, "We should put these in a safe place."

Aurora removed the ceiling panel and stashed the folder and journal. Then she replaced the panel, and led Alex toward the mansion.

On the way Alex asked, "Mathew Colburn Jr. designed and built a home, as a wedding gift, for his half-brother Seth. Whatever happened to it?"

Aurora angrily answered, "My family and I use to own that house. Thomas manipulated the legal system and seized our property; along with our half of the family business. After the stock market crash he sold everything, without giving us a dime."

Aurora pulled Alex to the side of the mansion and instructed, "Wait here. In ten minutes I'll toss a rope ladder down from Master Colburn's office window."

Alex nodded and Aurora entered the mansion through the back door. He hid for several minutes and at last a rope ladder fell. Aurora gazed out the window and beckoned him up. He stealthily climbed up the side of the house.

Alex whispered as he entered the office, "I estimate this ceiling to be about eight feet high. What do you think?"

Aurora replied in a hushed tone, "I agree, but where should we look?"

Alex dropped to his knees and started rolling back the large rug in the center of the room. Aurora kneeled next to him to assist.

Alex turned to her and whispered, "We should look for any mysterious markings on the floor boards. Maybe Master Colburn left a key of some sort."

They crawled about the floor examining each piece of wood.

"I think I found something." Aurora announced ecstatically.

Alex scurried over to find a tiny star engraved in a plank of wood. The board lifted freely. Aurora glared into the desolate black hole.

She announced with disappointment, "I don't see any money. Someone must have gotten to it already."

"Wait." Alex called out.

He shoved his arm into the hole in the floor and felt around. At last he emerged with a small black velvet sack in his fist. Alex opened the sack and poured the contents into Aurora's hand. She gazed down at the glittering precious stones within her palm.

Her eyes lit up as she said, "Phillip Arrington gave the mistress a similar black bag after a party. These jewels must've served as payment from the royal family, for hosting Phillip's inaugural ball. How much do you think these are worth?"

Alex smiled and replied, "I'm no jeweler but my guess would be, a lot."

Aurora poured the sparkling jewels back into the bag, and pulled the draw string tight.

She passed the bag to him and said, "Leave this place Alex, and send for me later. I want to forget about the lawsuit, and get my mother and sister out of here."

Alex asked as he slipped the sack of jewels in his left boot, "You would trust me to return to England with your family's entire fortune?"

Aurora gently pressed her lips against his and replied, "If it weren't for you I would have never found it?"

A shocked expression covered Alex's face.

Aurora stammered, "I'm sorry. I don't know what came over me. I just kissed you without enquiring whether or not there's a Mrs. Monroe."

Alex solemnly assured, "I was too busy saving the world to save my own marriage. I'm embarrassed to say. I'm now divorced. You're a charming girl, but I'm much too old for you Aurora."

Aurora shook her head no and replied, "Your ex-wife didn't realize what she had, but I do. Age is nothing but a number Alex."

The servant's bell sounded and Aurora said, "I'm being summoned. For now I'll return to work as if nothing happened."

Alex walked back over to the window. He pulled Aurora close, and gave her a kiss that took her very breath away.

He climbed onto the rope ladder and spoke through the opened window, "I'll send for you as soon as I can. After this is all over, I'm going to take you out on a date; where ever you want to go."

She smiled and replied, "I would like that."

As Aurora returned to work she thought. *This is the best day of my life.* She entered the smoke filled parlor and saw her uncle Thomas and four of his drunken friends. His poker buddies included: his lawyer, the judge from the previous hearings, and two local police officers. They were engaged in a game of five-card-draw, sucking on expensive pipes and fine cigars. Aurora glared at the company her great uncle kept, thinking. *My parents never stood a chance. All these men were taking bribes from Thomas.*

Thomas held up an empty glass and ordered, "I'll have another scotch."

"Gin and tonic for me." The judge barked.

Smug bastards. Aurora said under her breath as she walked behind the bar. She fixed up the drinks and returned to the table.

She passed them the glasses and asked, "Is there anything else I can get for you?"

Thomas took a sip of his scotch and asked, "What would it take to make that journal and those documents go away?"

The judge and lawyer turned to him and said, "Tom if you just tell us what she has on you. We may be able to help."

Thomas stuttered. "No, I... I can't tell you."

Aurora grinned as she thought to herself. *Uncle Tom, I can see why you wouldn't want your white elitist friends to find out you're part black. They would put you in the same boat as me. In their eyes you'd be just another nigger.*

Aurora finally replied, "I've decided I want nothing from you. I'll give you the documents. Burn them for all I care."

Thomas rose from his seat, and snatched Aurora up by both arms. He demanded. "That's a mighty charitable act! What brought about this sudden change of heart! I know you want something! Just tell me what it is!"

Aurora's heart began to pound, flutter and skip beats. *I can feel my chest tightening as if the life is being squeezed right out of me.*

She gasped for air and uttered, "I... swear... I don't want... anything from you."

Her uncle taunted, "You don't look so good Aurora. I pray this is the heart attack that kills you."

He flung her to the ground and went back to playing cards. Aurora pulled herself off the floor and journeyed home. As pain shot across her chest and back she thought. *I can't possibly be having a heart attack! I've consistently taken my medication; just as the doctor prescribed.*

Aurora made it home and burst through the door.

She called out through gasping breaths, "Alex... what are you still doing here?"

Alex answered with excitement, "After thinking about it I came to the conclusion that. You should leave with me tonight. We can pick up your sister, and take her with us. We'll send for your mother at a later date."

Aurora was perspiring heavily. She frantically downed two pills and a glass of water.

Alex's face grew heavy with concern as he asked, "Are you alright?"

Aurora fell to her knees gripping her chest.

"Aurora!" Alex shouted as he ran to her aid.

He climbed down on the floor and held her in his arms.

She stared up at him and whispered, "You must take the stones and leave now. My uncle is drunk and extremely angry. I don't know what he's capable of. Run north to the old infirmary. Take the trap door to White Water Brook. Wait there until the coast is clear."

Alex protested, "No! I'm going to pull my car around, and take you to the hospital."

Tears poured from Aurora's eyes as she pleaded, "You'll have to drive three towns away to find a hospital that accepts black patients. I'll never make it. Alex, promise me that when you get out of here you'll take care of my family."

Alex sadly vowed, "I promise I will never rest until I'm certain your family's alright."

Aurora smiled through her tears as she struggled for air.

She whispered faintly, "You have to go now."

Alex kissed her and wrapped his arms around her tight. A battle took place in his head between, raw emotion and logic. *By the time I get Aurora to a hospital she'll already be dead. All common sense is telling me to flee. I'm wasting time by sitting here, yet I can't bring myself to leave her. I'll hold her until she's gone. She doesn't deserve to die alone.*

Emotion had won the fight. Aurora died in his arms four minutes later.

Alex jumped at the boom of the door being kicked in. An inebriated Thomas and his four poker buddies burst into the room.

Thomas pointed a gun at Alex and laughed. He spoke without care or remorse for his own kin, "Placebos don't work nearly as well as the real medicine."

Alex asked in shock, "You've been giving Aurora sugar pills! You cold son-of-a-bitch!"

Thomas replied with angst and irritation, "After I caught Aurora with Sarah Colburn's diary, I knew the cat was out of the bag. I had to get rid of her in order to protect my reputation. I promised Aurora's mother that I'd pay for her medication in order to make sure she never got it. I've been slipping her phony pills for over a year, and she just wouldn't die! Now that this insufferable pain in my ass has finally ceased to breathe. I can move on with my life. I just need you to hand over the journal and the documents."

Alex continued to cradle Aurora's lifeless body. He spoke with great fortitude, "If I give you that journal I'm a dead man!"

Thomas drew back on the hammer of the gun and shouted, "You're a dead man regardless."

Alex boldly replied, "That doesn't give me very much incentive to cooperate then. One day you'll be exposed for who you truly are. May you rot in hell!"

The blast echoed and reechoed as Thomas shot Alex in the heart.

Thomas turned to the others and said, "Search the place."

"What should we do with the bodies?" The lawyer asked.

Thomas replied as he looked for the journal, "We should clean up the blood and bury the man. Leave Aurora's body for her mother to find. Bridget was well aware of her daughter's heart condition. I'll pretend to be shocked when I receive news of her death. Give her mother a little cash and my condolences. The whole thing will blow over."

Once Thomas and his friends had found neither the journal nor the documents, they pulled up the floor boards of the shack. They buried Alex Monroe's body in the ground beneath the Cabin of Whispers. A small treasure still lay within his boot.

Chapter 64

Present

Alex turned off the projector and announced, "I must get you back to your body now."

As they left the lecture hall Krista said, "I'm sorry about what happened, Alex. I'll do what I can to find the rightful heir of those stones."

Alex replied, "The worlds were never meant to communicate. You won't remember ever having this conversation with me. The most I could give you is a dream."

They stopped in the trauma center were Krista's body lay. Dr. Veronica Clark and her team of specialists were still hard at work trying to save Krista. Dr. Clark had come straight from the party. She was still dressed in her silver formal gown.

Alex gave Krista a hand on the shoulder and warned, "The amulet you were wearing belonged to Sarah Colburn. It's the only reason you survived the accident. You must wear it at all times to protect you from harm. I fear you are in danger. When you wake up, leave the hospital at once. Take care of yourself."

Krista nodded and rejoined with her body.

Dr. Veronica Clark announced in anguish and defeat, "Time of death: 10:45pm."

As Dr. Clark turned to leave, one of the nurses announced, "We have a rhythm!"

Hope filled the room as waves bounced across the heart monitor.

Krista regained consciousness around 2:00am. Her friend Stacy was sleeping in a chair next to her bed. His hand was closed around hers.

She gently shook him and asked, "Stacy, where are my parents?"

Stacy sprung to life ecstatic to see Krista awake.

He announced, "Your mom and dad went on a coffee run. I'll go get them right now."

Krista protested, "No don't. Just give me a minute first."

Stacy nodded and Krista asked, "Where's Angela?"

Stacy explained, "Angela was here earlier, but she fled to a hotel in shame. Apparently she had a thing for your boyfriend. She blames herself for the accident."

Krista sighed and replied, "I'm sorry Stacy. I know Angela was the only girl you ever gave a damn about."

Stacy kissed Krista's forehead and said, "Angela's not the only girl I ever gave a damn about."

Krista's face grew distraught as she began to remember a dream and a warning from Alexander Monroe. *I fear you are in danger. When you wake up, leave the hospital at once.*

Stacy asked with concern, "Are you ok? Do you want me to get a nurse?"

Krista replied anxiously, "I really need you to trust me right now. I have to retrieve something very valuable from the property. It can't wait. The keys to the Durango are next to the phone. Pull the truck around. I'll meet you out front."

Stacy replied in a worried tone, "You could've died, Krista. The only thing you should be doing is resting."

Krista pleaded with him, "Please. Staying here only puts me in greater danger. I swear to you. I'm a little sore but I'm fine."

Stacy reluctantly nodded his head yes and grabbed the keys. He briskly left the room and boarded an elevator.

Krista groaned in pain as she climbed out of bed. She limped across the room; pulling her I.V. pole with her. She searched the transparent plastic bag which contained her belongings. *Where in the world is that amulet?* Krista leaped back into bed as she heard a knock on the door.

"Come in!" Krista called out.

Dr. Clark entered the room wearing her usual professional attire. She'd finally gotten the opportunity to change. Her white lab coat swung as she walked.

Dr. Clark examined Krista and spoke in her country accent, "It's truly remarkable. Most people don't walk away from a collision that bad. You didn't get a single broken bone; just a few cuts and bruises."

Krista looked at all the bandages and said, "Somehow the words, thank you, seem too small for saving my life. I'm sorry I overreacted at the party, but the house means a lot to me. Please don't have it turned into a parking ramp."

Dr. Clark passed Krista the ruby necklace and explained, "Theft occurs in hospitals like anywhere else. This jewelry looked expensive so I kept an eye on it for you."

Krista gave an appreciative smile and put the necklace on at once.

Dr. Clark went on to say, "Your parents decided not to sell the property. None of us were aware how attached you were to it."

Krista let out a sigh of relief as Dr. Clark concluded her examination.

Dr. Clark smiled and informed her, "From what I can tell you're going to be fine. I'll just administer this antibiotic and be on my way."

Dr. Clark injected a syringe full of meds into Krista's I.V. Krista became groggy within seconds. Dr. Clark glared down at Krista thinking. *Stupid girl, I just gave you a sedative. You'll be out cold before I withdraw the needle. You and I are going to take a little trip.*

Chapter 65

Krista woke up in a small dark compartment. *It's pitch black in here. There's barely room to move. This place reeks of gasoline and motor oil.* She panicked at the realization. *I'm locked in a trunk!*

"Help! Can anyone hear me?!" She shouted as the vehicle raced down the road.

"Krista?" She heard a voice call in the darkness.

Krista calmed herself and asked, "Stacy is that you? Are you hurt?"

He grabbed hold of her hand. It was both comforting and disturbing to have him next to her.

Stacy replied, "I'm ok. How about you?"

Krista answered, "I'm fine. I'm not hurt."

They tumbled around as the vehicle came to a stop. They heard footsteps just before the trunk lid opened.

Mr. Cambridge, the real-estate agent, beckoned with his gun and ordered, "Let's go."

Krista climbed out of the trunk after Stacy. She was still barefoot dressed in her hospital gown. She looked around to find she was back at the plantation. It was still the middle of the night.

Krista watched in astonishment as Mr. Cambridge threw off his glasses and clawed at his own face. Hunks of latex and phony facial hair fell to the ground. Krista cringed as she recognized the face beneath the disguise. *He looks so much like my father.*

Krista asked in a complete state of confusion, "Uncle Mark?"

Stacy turned to her and questioned, "You know this psycho!"

Krista looked at her uncle and demanded, "Why did you kidnap us? You should be rotting in a prison cell in Texas right now!"

Mark replied with the gun still pointed at Krista, "Dr. Clark ran the prison infirmary in Dallas. After I promised her a fortune, she helped me escape. The only reason we tried to gain control of the property is so we'd have free range to search it. I know about the stones, Krista. You didn't think you were the only one Alex talked to, did you? Once when I was very young he told me that there was a fortune buried on the property. Then all of a sudden he stopped communicating with me. He must've found me untrustworthy. He had to have known I would've taken it all for myself. But you he trusted."

Krista lied, "I don't know what you're talking about."

Mark replied angrily, "Cut the shit Krista! My son told me everything."

Krista replied, "You don't have a son. You don't have any children."

At that moment Ox walked up and said, "I'm sorry Krista."

Krista shouted in utter shock, "What the hell!"

Mark laughed and replied, "I did more than study theatre makeup in England. Ox here is my son."

Krista screamed at Ox, "You knew we were cousins! That's why you never made a move. How stupid of me to believe you were a virgin!"

Stacy interjected, "Krista, no guy on the planet who lives in a frat house is a virgin."

Krista shot back, "It's not the time for sarcasm Stacy."

Mark gripped the gun tight and spoke to his niece, "Tell me where the stones are."

Krista replied undaunted, "I don't know where they are."

Mark turned the gun in Stacy's direction and said, "I don't have all night. I swear I will shoot him in the head if you don't tell me what I need to know."

Tears fell from Krista's eyes as she confessed, "The stones are buried underneath the Cabin of Whispers."

Ox tossed Stacy a shovel and Krista led the way.

They reached the shack and Krista instructed, "Tear up the floor boards. There's a dead man buried underneath. In his left boot lies a sack of precious stones."

Mark kept a gun on Krista as Ox and Stacy busted into the floor. The decaying wood cracked and splintered with ease. It wasn't long before they were digging at the soil beneath. A rotten putrid smell, unlike any other, engulfed the tiny shack.

Mark announced in response to the odor, "We must be getting close. Keep digging."

Within a shallow grave lay the filthy brown skeleton of Alexander Monroe. Shreds of clothing still clung to his rotting corpse. Ox pulled a boot off the decomposing foot and retrieved the sack of stones.

Ox climbed out of the hole with the bag of jewels. Stacy climbed out behind him.

Krista shouted, "You have what you came for, now leave!"

Mark pointed the gun at Stacy and said, "We may just need a hostage. I think I'll shoot him and take you along for the ride, Dear Niece."

Ox struck his father with the shovel. Mark wailed in pain and fell to the ground. Ox grabbed the gun and aimed it at Mark.

He yelled at his father, "You swore no one would get hurt! You're a sick man who forced me to seduce my own cousin in order to get information!"

Mark pleaded with him, "Please son, just listen to me."

Ox protested, "No you listen to me! I told you I didn't want to do this. I told you how twisted it all was. All you had to say was: 'Fuck her if you have to, Son. Just get the location of those stones.'"

Ox turned to Krista and said, "I really liked Angela, so I confessed my sins to her. She told me it was never too late to do the right thing. She convinced me to tell you the truth. I was planning to come clean at the party. I was planning to stop your parents from selling the property. But then you got into that accident, and things just got out of hand."

Ox pulled out his phone to dial 911. **Searching**.... displayed on the screen.

"Damn it!" Ox shouted in frustration.

Mark replied smugly, "What's wrong, Son? No service?"

Ox tossed the bag of jewels to Krista and said, "Run! Get out of here and call the police!"

Krista and Stacy took off while Ox kept the gun pointed at Mark.

Ox announced, "I'm going to hold you here until the police come."

Mark rose to his feet and grinned.

Ox asked, "What the hell are you smiling about? You're going back to prison, Dad."

At that moment Dr. Clark snuck up behind Ox. She stabbed him in the neck with a syringe.

Ox collapsed within seconds and his father yelled, "You didn't have to do that Veronica! I had things under control!"

Dr. Veronica Clark shot back, "Relax, it's just a sedative. It won't hurt him. And from the looks of it you don't have shit under control! Where the hell are the hostages? Where are the stones?"

Mark picked up the gun and stuffed it in the back of his pants.

He walked outside and said, "There's no land line in the mansion and the nearest neighbor is miles away. They're on foot. We'll track them down in no time."

Dr. Clark followed him to the car and commented, "This property is huge. They could be hiding anywhere."

They both climbed in the vehicle and Mark replied, "Yes there are a plethora of places to hide here, but there's only one phone within two miles of this place. I've changed my mind. I think I'll take the boy for a hostage and kill Krista instead."

Chapter 66

Krista and Stacy reached the top of Redwood Cliff exhausted and out of breath.

Krista grasped the busted old phone and exclaimed, "Thank god there's a dial tone!"

She quickly punched the digits 911 on the key pad.

"911 Emergency." The operator called out.

Krista rambled off, "I need police sent to Redwood Cliff and the Colburn plantation!"

The operator urged her to calm down and asked, "What is your name and emergency?"

Krista answered, "My name is Krista Colburn. There's an escaped convict by the name of Mark Colburn! He's trying to kill us!"

The operator assured, "Units are on the way."

Krista dropped the phone at the sound of an approaching vehicle.

She glared over the edge of the cliff and informed Stacy, "We made a mistake by coming here. There's nowhere to run. If my uncle comes for us we're sitting ducks."

Stacy hugged her and assured, "Ox had a gun pointed at your uncle when we left. And the police are on the way."

They squinted at the vision of approaching headlights. Dread and fear washed over them as they recognized the car. Her uncle Mark put the car in park and stepped out with Dr. Clark. He walked toward them aiming his pistol. Krista screamed as Dr. Clark shocked Stacy with a stun gun. Stacy shook violently as the electricity coursed through his body. He collapsed on the ground unconscious. Mark passed Dr. Clark his gun. The doctor kept the pistol pointed at Krista while Mark dragged Stacy to the car. He threw him in the backseat and slammed the door.

Mark walked back over to Dr. Clark and said, "You should get in the car. You're not going to want to see this."

Dr. Clark passed him the pistol and instructed, "Make it quick. The police are probably on the way."

Then she climbed back into the front passenger seat.

Mark spoke to Krista in a cold calculating voice, "If you don't tell me what I want to know I'm going to enjoy killing you."

Mark attached a silencer to his gun and shot Krista in the thigh. She screamed in agony and dropped like an anchor. Blood poured from the wound as she writhed in pain. She could actually feel her flesh burning.

He yelled at her, "Where are the stones?!"

Krista grabbed her wounded thigh and hollered, "How do I know you won't kill us as soon as you have them?!"

Marked put his gun away and announced in a calm manor, "I promise not to shoot you. Just tell me where they are."

"No! I don't believe you!" Krista protested.

She fought with all her might as her uncle wrapped both hands around her throat.

Mark leaned close to Krista and growled bitterly in her ear,

"I swear I will squeeze the life out of you, if you don't give them to me!"

Krista's swings grew sluggish and even less effective as she began to run out of oxygen. Mark retrieved the gun with one hand and continued to grip Krista's throat with the other.

He threatened in a menacing tone, "I will put a bullet in your brain if you don't tell me this instant!"

Krista spoke in a choked whisper, "You'll shoot me no matter what I do."

Mark put the gun so close to Krista's face she could feel the heat wafting off of it. She gasped for air and glared down the barrel of the pistol. *This is it. He's going to kill me.*

Chapter 67

Krista laid on the edge of the cliff in complete horror. Mark's grip grew tighter around her throat. His cold dark eyes stared down at her without an ounce of remorse. His gun sat only inches from her face. *Everywhere I look there's death. He could strangle me, shoot me, or even hurl me off the cliff if it suits him. I'll tell Uncle Mark what he wants to know, and pray he'll keep his word about not killing me.*

At last she coughed out, "Ok, Ok, I'll tell you."

Mark released Krista's throat and she coughed several times. The oxygen rushed back to her brain, causing a temporary sensation of being high.

She confessed through heaving breaths, "I stashed the gems in the old infirmary, on the way here."

Krista breathed a sigh of relief as Mark put away his gun and said, "I promised not to shoot you."

His lips parted in a sinister smile as he went onto say, "I never said I wouldn't push you off the cliff."

Krista screamed and clawed at the ground as Mark shoved her over the cliff. She clung desperately to the ledge; dangling hundreds of feet in the air. He pulled out a lighter and put the flame on her fingers. Krista cried in pain as she continued to clutch the edge for dear life. As she felt her fingers slipping she prayed. *If there is anyone out there who watches over me, I need you more than ever at this moment.*

Krista began to feel a warm tingling sensation on her chest. Mark looked down surprised to find the amulet glowing. A beam of light shot out and singed both his eyes. He jumped to his feet wailing in agony. He staggered blindly about the cliff. He could smell his corneas burning.

Dr. Clark called out the window, "Mark, what's wrong!"

Stacy blinked sluggishly as he regained consciousness in the back seat of the car. He quietly picked up a flashlight off the floor. When Dr. Clark reached for the door handle to get out Stacy struck her on the head. She slumped over in her seat. Stacy looked out through the windshield and couldn't find Krista anywhere. All he could see was Mark. Stacy became distraught at the realization. *That asshole threw Krista off the cliff. She's dead!*

Stacy climbed into the driver seat, overcome by anger and sorrow. His eyes narrowed on Mark. He threw the car in gear and floored the gas pedal. Mark hollered out in excruciating pain as the vehicle collided with him. He could feel the tremendous devastation to his organs and the crunch of his bones breaking. Dr. Clark woke up just in time to find Mark alive, plastered to the hood. His black eyes stared helplessly into hers. Stacy leaped from the car as it demolished the guard rail.

Krista stared up in terror at the under carriage of the vehicle as it roared over head. The car hurdled over Redwood Cliff, transporting Dr. Veronica Clark and Mark Colburn to their deaths.

Stacy crawled to the edge of the cliff as he heard Krista screaming for help. She was still dangling on the ledge. The demolished vehicle lay in flames at the bottom of the valley. He pulled her up and noticed her gown was saturated with blood.

Krista announced, still in a state of shock, "I've been shot!"

"Where?!" Stacy questioned.

"Here on my thigh," Krista answered pulling aside her hospital gown.

Stacy ran a hand over the surface of her thigh and said, "It must've just grazed you. I don't see a wound anywhere."

Krista glanced down shocked to find the hole in her thigh had disappeared. A large contusion had taken its place. She looked at her fingers. *No burns from the lighter.* She snatched off her bandages, which covered the lacerations she attained in the car accident.

She called out in complete disbelief, "All my cuts are gone."

Stacy looked her over and asked, "Are you sure you had cuts? All I see are bruises. Cuts don't just vanish."

Stacy wrapped his arms around Krista and went on to say, "It doesn't matter. We survived, that's all that counts."

"Here comes the cavalry." Krista commented at the sound of approaching sirens.

As police and paramedics swarmed onto the scene Stacy questioned, "So what happens now?"

Krista smiled at Stacy and joked, "I'll find the rightful owner of the stones. Tattoo an **S** on my chest and save the day."

Stacy asked flirtatiously, "An **S** on your chest huh? Can I be present for that tattoo?"

"Stacy! You're such a slut," Krista shouted as she playfully smacked him on the chest.

Stacy replied with a nonchalant shrug of his shoulders, "What? I like boobs."

Krista embraced Stacy and gave him a kiss on the cheek. *Some things never change.*

Epilogue

Two Weeks Later

The weather was sunny and beautiful. The university band marched to the school spirit song as an abundance of students gathered on the front lawn of the Colburn estate. Among the crowd were Ox and Rachael. La`Kiesha was on tour with her brother. The local news crew came out to catch footage of history in the making. A red ribbon stretched across the entrance of the mansion. Krista stood on the porch with her parents and the mayor. Mayor Wilson was an older man with white hair and shoulders that slumped forward. As the mayor shuffled in front of the microphones the band ceased to play. A hush fell over the anticipating crowd.

Mayor Wilson announced to the press and the students of the university, "As we all know, a recent fire left a multitude of students homeless. Many of which had no relatives in the state or even the country. I am pleased to present the Colburn family with this key to the city, for housing our displaced students."

The crowd cheered as the mayor passed Krista's mother a wooden plaque with a large key on it. He passed an enormous pair of scissors to Krista's father.

Krista's father spoke into the microphones, "I'm going to allow my daughter to do the honors. She put this whole thing together, and we're very proud of her."

As he passed the scissors on to her the crowd began to cheer and chant, "Krista! Krista! Krista!"

The press set the microphones in front of her and asked, "Is there anything you'd like to say to the students of the University of Missouri?"

Krista sliced the large red ribbon and shouted, "Welcome Home!"

The band began to play once more as Krista led everyone into the Mansion. Krista's parents gave the students their initial tour. Paintings of their ancestors, black and white, now decorated the walls of Colburn museum. The White Water Brook journal presently sat on display. It was in a case with several other artifacts.

Her father announced, "Colburn Hall is the university's only coed dorm. As you can see, much of the first floor has been transformed into a museum. Students will reside on the second and third floors; ladies in the east wing, gentlemen in the west."

Her mother added, "The grand ballroom will serve as the cafeteria. There will be emergency phones and campus security installed by summer's end, just in time for fall semester."

Krista pulled Ox, and Rachel aside as her parents continued the tour.

Krista hugged Ox and said, "I'm sorry about your father."

He replied in a somber tone, "You shouldn't be sorry. He brought it on himself. Have you heard from Angela?"

Krista nodded and answered, "Angela still wants to be with you. She went back to Michigan with Stacy to complete her community service; not because she was ditching you. She wants you to give her a call."

The news brightened Ox's mood.

Krista went onto say, "You two should come with me."

They followed Krista to a small parlor. Jessy was sitting in front of her laptop. She was accompanied by two men in suits.

As they walked in and took a seat Jessy announced, "The full inheritance of one, Mark Colburn, has been awarded to his only son Kevin Oxley."

Ox glanced at the amount on the documents and said, "Damn that's a lot of zeros."

He thanked both Krista and Jessy and squeezed them so tight they could barely breathe.

Once Jessy caught her breath she went on to say, "In regard to the precious stones, we had them appraised and auctioned off.

After Uncle Sam took his slice of the pie, the amount of 20 million dollars remained. I started with the last known living descendent of Seth Colburn and worked my way forward." A dramatic silence fell over the room as Jessy continued, "That descendents name was Lucinda Colburn. She later married a neighbor by the name of Jonathon Wilcox."

Rachel shook her head in disbelief and murmured, "Grandma Lucy?"

Jessy nodded yes and went onto say, "Since Krista turned down the 10% finder's fee, the entire 20 million goes to Rachel Wilcox, Seth's only living descendent."

The room filled with tears of triumph and hugs of appreciation.

Once the atmosphere calmed, Rachel turned to Krista and asked, "You would give me an entire fortune, why?"

Krista smiled and replied, "Because it's never too late to do the right thing."

Krista did a double take as she noticed a familiar couple walk passed in the hall. *I couldn't have possibly seen who I think I did.*

Krista turned to Jessy and asked, "Would you mind walking Ox and Rachel through the necessary paper work?"

"No problem." Jessy assured.

Krista thought to herself as she trailed the couple. *There's no way they could be Aurora and Alex.*

She looked on in shock as they walked through the wall. *It's definitely Aurora and Alex.*

Krista opened the door and entered the room after them.

As they stood in the empty parlor Krista asked, "How is it possible for me to see you?"

Alex smiled and explained, "Because you're still wearing the amulet. It connects you to generations passed. You've only begun to unlock its capabilities."

Aurora smiled and told Krista, "Somehow the words thank you just don't seem enough."

Krista grinned and asked. "What's next for you guys?"

Aurora replied, "Now that we can finally let this place go, we're free to enter the world to which we belong. People think after you die you live on a mountain of clouds in the sky. But in truth there's a whole other life that awaits you. Alex owes me a date, anywhere I want to go, as I recall."

Alex announced sarcastically, "I said that 80 years ago. Do women forget anything?"

Aurora and Krista both shook their heads no.

A celestial light shined down as Alex said, "So long Krista Colburn. Dieu vous garde."

Krista replied as Aurora and Alex vanished before her eyes, "God keep you both, as well."

Later that evening the stars gleamed brightly over White Water Brook. A campfire illuminated the sky with flickering orange flames. Water rushed over the falls filling the air with the refreshing scent of the beach. Krista popped a bottle of champagne in the company of her three cousins: Ox, Jessy, and Rachel.

Krista filled everyone's glasses and proposed a toast, "To a love that conquered all, undying determination, and most importantly to family."

They clinked glasses and drank triumphantly.

Rachel turned to Krista and asked, "How did you figure it all out?"

Ox questioned, "Who is this mysterious Alex?"

Jessy urged, "Yeah tell us the story."

Krista poured another round of champagne, and announced theatrically, "The legend of the Cabin of Whispers begins with a man named Mathew, his true love Sarah, and the journal of Alexander Monroe."

LaVergne, TN USA
19 April 2010
179843LV00001B/96/P